SCARLET ANGEL

England, 1948. To escape from the shabby confines of Queen Street, with her adored young sister Ginny and their invalid mother, beautiful twenty-year-old Silvie Marsh chooses a desperate path. Four men love Silvie — and two women do not . . . Jack Thorndyke considers himself as the 'sow's ear' and Silvie the 'silk purse'. Mark Pemberton, her young husband, is heir to a business empire. Adam is an older man to whom she makes a shocking promise. The Reverend David Bradley would gladly relinquish his soul to the devil for her love. Dora Glasspool hates her enough to plot murder, and Laura Pemberton has good reason to wish that her son had never set eyes on Silvie Marsh.

Books by Peggy Graham
Published by The House of Ulverscroft:

STONE WALLS

PEGGY GRAHAM

SCARLET ANGEL

Complete and Unabridged

ULVERSCROFT
Leicester

First published in Australia in 2002

First Large Print Edition
published 2003

The moral right of the author has been asserted

British Library CIP Data

Graham, Peggy
   Scarlet angel.—Large print ed.—
   Ulverscroft large print series: general fiction
   1. Large type books
   I. Title
   823.9′14 [F]

   ISBN 0–7089–4770–0

Published by
F. A. Thorpe (Publishing)
Anstey, Leicestershire

Set by Words & Graphics Ltd.
Anstey, Leicestershire
Printed and bound in Great Britain by
T. J. International Ltd., Padstow, Cornwall

This book is printed on acid-free paper

Acknowledgement

With grateful thanks to Christopher Oakeley, BA, MBA
For his invaluable help during the editing and printing
of this book.

1

The black Humber slowed as it left the main road and turned into the first of a maze of small back streets. Each row of tiny houses was identical in size and structure; the narrow doors mere dark green or brown detail in an unframed canvas which depicted a scene of underprivilege. For most of those who lived behind these doors there was no escape route through the maze to the affluent world beyond its perimeter. All the streets bore names of false grandeur, invented by some long past developer to belie the humble architecture, designed with thrift and profit in mind and not the comfort of the dwellers. King Street . . . Prince . . . Queen . . . Earl . . . Lord . . .

In the narrow confines of the streets the children could play freely; the only motor traffic which came through, besides the Humber, was the baker, the milkman and the local dustcart which came on Fridays always on time to the minute. All other callers such as the rent man, the insurance, the gas meter reader and the postman travelled either by bicycle or on foot.

As Jack Thorndyke turned the Humber into Queen Street his accustomed, yet ever-offended, eye glanced at the name plate bolted to the brickwork over the corner shop.

Even as a child he'd been aware that better places to live existed. This he had discovered on his ninth birthday when Granfer Thorndyke had presented him with a second-hand bicycle paid for with money earned by doing repairs and mending punctures on the bicycles brought to his home. Granfer had always been keen on bicycles but owning a cycle repair shop had been an impossible dream, for times were lean back in the depression years. Presenting his only grandson Jack with the handsome present of the old bike had given Granfer, now dead, much pleasure.

On the old bicycle Jack had gone chestnutting and discovered Baron Wood. That day, on the threshold of his tenth year, he had gazed in awe on the grand houses that bordered the wood and had promised himself that he would one day own one of them. Nineteen years later that youthful promise had been fulfilled. For more than a year now Jack had been the proud owner of one of the best houses in Baron Wood Drive. He didn't consider that he'd robbed anyone to do it either.

Long exhausting hours in the munitions factory during the war had earned him promotion to foreman and good wages which he had invested wisely in sound business projects. Many times he had worked two shifts straight off to ensure that he did his bit towards the war effort. He had volunteered to join up in the Armed Forces at the outbreak of war but had been turned down by the medical examiner for a reason which seemed trivial to Jack who looked robustly healthy; he knew some had wondered about that and he had been touchy on the subject, more on account of the rejection itself than the reason.

The war had ended three years ago. Jack was no longer employed at the factory. He was now a successful business man.

He stopped the motion of the Humber while a barefoot toddler waddled duck-like across the street, chuckling delightedly at its sudden freedom. A loud female voice preceded a small plump woman with a tired face who emerged from an open doorway. 'Come back here you little devil.' She ran to swoop and snatch up the laughing child and called a greeting to Jack who wound down the car window to return some jovial remark. Moments later she was swallowed up by the small dark doorway from which she had appeared. Still grinning from the brief exchange Jack moved the Humber on between the two rows of tiny houses which opened straight onto the pavement from the front parlours and admitted no one over the height of six feet two inches without they first duck their head.

With the soft look of love his eyes rested on the closed door of number 24 behind which lived heart-stopping beauty Silvie Marsh. Wistfully his thoughts dwelt for the moment on the countless times he had begged her to marry him. If she would only let him at least take her to see the Baron Wood house she might change her mind. As he'd so often told her it was large enough for herself, Ginny and their mother. He wouldn't expect her to leave them behind — she knew that.

But with her looks she could take her pick of the world. She did not fit into this back-street scene. She came and went from the street with a brief smile and greeting for the neighbours, nothing more. The local boys eyed her with awe and respect. To these she was an impossible dream, unattainable, for she not only had rare beauty but also an inborn class which set her beyond their reach. There was no match for her amongst them, they knew it and accepted it.

Jack had now passed number 24. Many of the front doors stood wide open. Perhaps those within the claustrophobic confines felt some physical need for contact with the space outside.

Further along the street a small group of boys moved aside respectfully to let the Humber pass through, and a football rolled off into the gutter, forgotten briefly, as they each followed the car to its parking place outside number five.

'Hi ya Jack.'

'-lo Jack.'

Each boy greeted him reverently and closed about the car as he got out.

'If any of you little perishers put your dirty maulers on it I'll cut your bloody arses off.'

Amiably they accepted Jack's customary greeting in the form of this unlikely threat. They knew where they stood with him when he acknowledged them in this manner. If ever he forgot they'd worry and know something was amiss, and he might just forget their sweet money when he left his ma's house. 'We won't Jack.' One replied for all as Jack ducked his head and entered the ever open door which was held in place by a giant grey pebble stone.

Then dirt-smudged faces went as close as they dared to the car windows without making actual contact as the boys devoured the plush interior of the shiny black splendour with eager adoring eyes.

'I'll get a car just like this when I'm old enough to work,' vowed one.

'Garn — where ya gonna get the dough,' questioned another contemptuously,

'Black market o'course. In the black market,' came the confident reply.

'Where's the black market then?' piped a younger voice.

'It ain't a place dopey! It's to do wiv the war — I fink. Our Ma says Jack got 'is money in the black market during the war.'

'But there ain't no war on now — so how c . . . '

'There might be by then,' interrupted the young hopeful.

'Careful — don't put yer 'ands on it or you'll leave finger marks and we won't get our tanners off Jack,' warned one.

'I ain't touchin' it,' protested the accused. 'And 'e'll only give us frupence each today. Too many of us for a tanner,' he calculated.

They each took their attention briefly from the car as two more boys joined them. Having seen the Humber pass they had come with expectant palms and hungry eyes; for they all knew of Jacks handouts, and never tired of peering through the car windows to feast their sights on the tan leather luxury within, the walnut dashboard with its fascinating knobs and buttons, and each dream their own childish hopes of unknown riches to come.

But they all knew the rules. Not a finger among them left its mark on the shiny black paintwork.

2

In the front parlour of number 24 Silvie Marsh held a lighted match through the opening of the gas globe above the fireplace. The merest feather-like touch to the fragile gas mantle would bring about its disintegration to a fine white dust. The sudden flood of light lit the astonishing beauty of her upturned face as she adjusted the pressure of the gas jet by turning a small lever on the curved pipe attached to the wall.

In the narrow iron frame bed set against one wall Alice Marsh blinked against the first brightness.

Dusk came early to the small room, for no front door stood open here. Silvie drew the Miss Muffet print curtains. From the street the raised voices of the boys floated in through the open window. A smile touched her lips, erasing briefly the small frown of preoccupation. She had seen the Humber pass and knew that even waiting teas would not lure the boys to their homes until Jack left his mother's house.

A fit of coughing seized Alice Marsh as a down current of smoky air from the chimney was drawn into the room. Silvie closed the window to cut off the cause.

In the gaslight the fire embers paled. She bent to take up a small coal shovel from the hearth. At this familiar sound Ginny Marsh glanced up from her school exercise book. 'I'll fetch the coal Silvie.'

6

Before she had time to put aside her pen she was forestalled.

'No — it's all right Ginny, don't interrupt your homework.' Silvie's face relaxed into a soft smile as her eyes rested briefly on her young sister.

Alice watched Silvie leave the room with the shovel and a coal hod to fill from the cupboard in the back room. Familiarity had not bred a blindness to her eldest daughter's rare beauty. When they were out shopping strangers never passed without a second glance. With characteristic humour Ginny had once remarked, 'It's because they don't believe their eyes first time.'

Almost two years had passed since Alice had been out shopping with them; not since the stroke that had left her partially paralysed. Her gaze now rested on the bright copper-coloured head bent over the school book. It was some consolation that Ginny would be left in reliable hands and loving care when the final stroke came. Since the day of her birth she'd been idolised by Silvie who, as a child, had spent what scant pocket money had come her way on small treats for her baby sister. Alice brought to mind an occasion when the gift had been a green satin bow on a hair slide. She recalled above all eleven year old Silvie's words as she'd fastened the slide to the bright copper curls, 'Only the best for Ginny.'

She had taught them decent speech and manners. From the age of fourteen and until her marriage she had been employed in service to a wealthy upper class family and in consequence she had passed on what she had learned of their social graces to her own girls. It was of some comfort to her that she had prepared them for a higher class background when eventually they were able to leave Queen Street behind them.

Since Alice's stroke Silvie had given up her daytime job in the fashion department of a large store in town and now worked evenings in the cocktail bar of an elite hotel. This change to evening work ensured that Alice was never left alone. Ginny was there in the evenings. At first Alice had protested at the late hours Silvie worked and said she could manage well on her own during the day; that if she ever needed help she had only to knock on the wall and Mrs Barnes next door would come round.

But Silvie had been adamant. She wanted to be there during the daytime when Ginny was at school.

Sometimes Alice wondered just how long she would linger in her semi-paralysed state before the end came. At times she secretly prayed to die in order to relieve the girls of the burden. At the same time she knew they would be horrified if they had known her thoughts, and that neither looked upon her as a liability. The expense of a nurse was out of the question. On her widow's pension and Silvie's wages which made up their present income they barely managed to scrape through. Idly she cast her eyes over the room. The rugs on the lino were threadbare now. Frank had wanted better things for them. Although up until the war the district had not seemed as shabby as it now was. When they had married in 1926 Frank was in no position to improve their lot financially. Opportunities did not exist in the path of the General Strike. And on its heels had come the depression years. Then the war which had claimed him.

How quickly the time had passed since then. Frank had been a good father and the girls had loved him dearly. When the news had come to inform them that he'd been killed in action Silvie had been the one who had eased the grief and pining of Ginny. Often in the night she would read her back to sleep when she woke fretting over the absence of the father whose favourite name for her had been Ambertop.

The sound of the fire being banked up interrupted Alice's reminiscence. Moments later Silvie set the tea things on a small drop-leaf table. One half of this was folded down and the straight edge placed against the wall halfway between the front door and the room at the back. As with all the houses in the area there was no passageway, its tiny front parlour opened straight onto the pavement.

Ginny glanced up and put aside the school book. 'Mmm — those tea cakes look good. I'm positively starving! I'll have to go and wash my hands — pen leaks. Won't be a tick.'

In the back room she collected soap from the dish in a small metal cabinet attached to the wall and from the rail beneath took a handtowel which she flung onto her shoulder before going out through the back door into the yard. Here the only source of household water was from a tap attached to the brick wall of a lean-to scullery. This outer room housed an old stone copper, a black cast-iron gas stove and a large galvanised steel bungalow bath

9

which hung from a giant nail driven into the whitewashed wall.

The tap was outside in the open and placed low on the bricks. Ginny bent over with her feet spread far enough to avoid the splashing stream of cold water as she lathered and rinsed her hands. At the end of the small yard stood the whitewashed brick lavatory, the Siamese twin, back to back, of the one next door. The simple wooden doors were cut along the top in zigzag fashion for ventilation. The toilet receptacle was completely boxed in wall to wall with scrubbed pine boards leaving only the inside of the bowl exposed. Such was the mode of its, now long outdated, construction.

Ginny turned off the tap and straightened up. As she dried her hands she studied her reflection in the six by nine inch strip of mottled mirror fixed to the bricks above the tap. Much of the quicksilver backing had weathered away. It had been there for as long as she could remember and since she'd reached the age of twelve had been just the right height without the need for her to stand on tiptoe. With a critical eye she frowned on the scattering of freckles which marched across the bridge of her small straight nose, petering out to extinction on her ivory-toned skin and emphasising her pale amber eyes and gold-tinged lashes. In disapproval she wrinkled her nose, then eyed the abundance of deep tawny hair, tilting her head to consider her profile, recalling the remarks of Davy Turner on their way home from school that day — 'Y'sister's a smasher Gin, but y'not so dusty y'self. I like the colour of y'hair.' A flicker of amusement touched her lips

10

before she dismissed her reflection and went back into the house, her mind now on tea.

Since Silvie had started working evenings they took their main meal at midday, which left ample time for Ginny to come home from school, ten minutes walk from the house, and return in the allocated break. For this meal they helped Alice up to sit with them.

Ginny seated herself at the table.

'Have you finished your homework Ginny?'

'Almost. Just a bit of revision. Won't take long.'

Satisfied Silvie nodded. She'd left school herself at the age of fourteen. Most had back then. With the war on even a small wage was welcome. In any case nobody had concerned themselves too much with education at that time. Many schools in the area had been requisitioned for various wartime purposes, and makeshift premises had to be utilised as temporary school quarters. No homework was assigned either. Who could have settled to homework anyway when air-raid sirens were likely to sound off at any time after dark. Several bombs had fallen locally, the bombsite gaps were still there to prove it.

But all that was in the past. Things were going to be different from now on. She intended to make certain of this and had already made a big decision to bring the change about. For the past four months now she had contemplated a plan and today she had made up her mind to take the first step of the only path open to her which would bring about a change in their circumstances and ensure a better future for Ginny and a more comfortable life for their mother.

But neither of them would ever know the truth behind their social rise when it came. Many sleepless nights were behind her in the process of making this mammoth decision. She hoped her courage wouldn't fail her when the crucial moment came. To free them from the stifling poverty which exuded from Queen Street and the surrounding area had become of paramount importance to her.

She knew this could be achieved by marriage to Jack Thorndyke. But she had known Jack too long. Besides he would never quite shake off the Queen Street tag.

The path she was about to choose would allow her to keep her independence without too final a commitment. It would enable her to pay the high fees required to send Ginny to MISS MEACHER'S COLLEGE FOR YOUNG LADIES, and to rent a house in a better neighbourhood, also to buy a few luxuries for her mother who had never owned more than the bare necessities of life, at times scarcely those. The means by which she planned to achieve all this appalled her, as did the thought of having to deceive the two people she loved best in the world.

She placed the tea tray bearing a few thinly-cut sandwiches onto the bed. 'Are you warm enough Mum?' She leaned across to adjust the old cardigan which had slipped from the thin shoulders.

'Yes thank you dear.' The stroke-slurred speech had improved. At first they'd had difficulty in making out her words.

'We'll get a proper bed-jacket for you soon. I've seen just the one. I shan't tell you what it's like or it won't be a surprise.' The promise helped boost

Silvie's determination to go ahead with her plan.

Alice Marsh was aware that Silvie got much pleasure in giving small gifts when their meagre finances stretched to this, but she'd rather the money wasn't spent on her. With her health in such a precarious state it seemed hardly worthwhile buying new clothes. Yet she couldn't say so. But she didn't want to appear ungrateful. 'It would be nice dear, but I like this old cardigan, it's comfortable and certainly a nice warm one.'

Silvie went to join Ginny at the table and as casually as she could manage said, 'We'll be able to afford extra things if I take the job.'

'Job?' Surprise showed on Ginny's face. 'What job? You never mentioned . . . '

'No,' Silvie interrupted without looking at the candid eyes, 'I only decided this morning to go for an interview.'

'Interview? When? Where?' Ginny's young voice rose with interest. 'What kind of job? Oh Silv!'

Silvie found she had no appetite and rose from the table. Collecting up her plate she replied, 'I must leave by six so that I'll have time to go on the way to work. If I do take the job it will mean more money. That's if I get it of course.'

'Oh Silv!' Ginny often used this abbreviation of Silvie's name when she was surprised or excited about something. 'Of course you'll get it. You're bound to. They'll snap you up — whoever *they* are.'

Without comment Silvie went through to the back room, glad to escape for a moment of brief reprieve from the questions that would have to be faced sooner or later; away from the trusting amber eyes.

13

She seated herself on a wooden kitchen chair as she heard Ginny asking . . . 'What kind of job Mum?' Then their mother's low muffled tones in reply, 'Dressmaking dear. High class. You know how clever Silvie is with the needle.'

'Funny time for dressmaking-evenings!'

'Apparently they don't mind when the work is done so long as it's done well. Rich clients I daresay.'

'How did she get to hear of it?'

'At the hotel. One of the customers in the cocktail lounge mentioned it. Silvie telephoned when she went to the shops this morning and made an appointment.'

In the back room Silvie listened to the unsuspecting answers of her mother. How very easy it was to deceive those who loved and trusted you. Yet how very hard. Doubts crept back as she questioned her conscience. It was madness to go to such lengths; to overstep the boundary of self esteem and common sense.

Ginny came into the room carrying the tray. 'I hope you're not sickening for a cold Silvie. You didn't eat anything for tea.'

Silvie felt guilty at the unwarranted concern on the young face. 'No — I'm fine. Had rather a big dinner today.' Lies, she thought. There would be many lies from now on. Small ones as well as the one big one. For days she hadn't eaten a proper meal.

'I'll wash the tea things. You go ahead and get ready so you won't be late for the interview.'

Silvie nodded agreement, glad to escape further

14

questions and from the lying answers she'd be bound to give.

Twenty minutes later when she was dressed ready to leave she noticed that Ginny had the sewing basket out and with great concentration was threading navy blue cotton into a needle. Ginny saw her look of inquiry and explained, 'I've torn my skirt again on the desk at school. Nail sticking out. Ages ago I asked Mr Johns to get the caretaker to fix it but he's so absent-minded. I asked the caretaker myself today. He said he'll do it first thing in the morning before school.'

Silvie eyed the rent in the navy serge. 'You need a new skirt. This one's a bit short now anyway. We'll go shopping on Saturday morning and buy one. Mrs Barnes will come in and sit with Mum.'

The young face lit up but only briefly. 'This one will do fine for a while yet — honestly. They're wearing them shorter now anyway. It can wait a bit longer.'

'No it can't. I insist. It's about time you had a new one.' Silvie turned towards the front door. 'Must go now. Bye Ginny — bye Mum.'

'Bye now dear. Take care.' Alice Marsh knew there was something on her eldest daughter's mind. Something which caused that slight frown to come and go. It couldn't be anything to do with the coming interview. It was not in Silvie's nature to be affected by such. She'd always had a natural self-confidence which seemed to be the hallmark of good looks. Don't take the job unless you're absolutely certain you'll like it dear, or if the hours are too late. The money's not that important.'

15

Hand on the door knob Silvie paused to look back at the troubled face and gave a smile of assurance.

Ginny looked up briefly from her sewing to say, 'Bye Silvie. You can tell me all about it in the morning.'

With a nod of agreement Silvie stepped out into the street. They listened to the receding tap of her high heeled shoes against the black brick pavement.

Alice sighed deeply. Ginny returned her attention to the tear in her skirt.

★ ★ ★

The shrill voices of the boys at the end of the street told Silvie without the need to glance back that the Humber was still parked outside number five. She stepped off the kerb to pass some children sprawled across the narrow pavement playing dibs. Further along a tiny girl seated on the edge of the kerb turned a bright smile up to her. Earlier tears had washed pink rivulets down the dirt-smudged cheeks. 'Huwow . . . ' The rich baby tones rose endearingly at the end of the word.

Silvie stopped and bent to the upturned face. 'Hello and what have you been crying about?'

The big blue eyes looked puzzled in the effort to remember. Recollection brought a slight tremor to the rosebud mouth and a small plump knee was held up for inspection. 'I fawed down!'

Silvie transferred a kiss from her finger tips to the grazed skin. 'There — all better now.'

A bright smile of agreement now lit the cherubic

features. Silvie patted the fair curly head and walked on.

She half turned as the long strides of Jack Thorndyke brought him abreast with her. She glanced down at his silent shoes, she had not heard him coming. He stepped off the kerb to leave more room for her on the pavement as he fell into step beside her. He had seen her stop to speak to the child. 'Poor little sods. Not much prospects for them living around here.' His tone became resigned and tinged with regret as he continued, knowing in advance what her reply would be, 'Wish you'd let me give you a lift to work Angel. If you'd marry me you wouldn't have to work at all. You'd be able to take care of your mum full time and Ginny could go to a decent school. She's too good for that mob where she is now. Plenty of room for all of you at my place. I hope you at least give it a bit of thought sometimes. I'll never stop asking and hoping, you know that.'

Despite her present preoccupation she gave a fleeting smile. 'You never give up do you Jack?'

'Not on you Angel. Never give up hope and never say die, that's my motto.'

Disinclined to engage in idle conversation she responded automatically. 'You haven't managed to persuade your mother to move in with you yet then Jack?'

He shook his head. 'I know by now that she'll never leave Queen Street. She's made that quite clear. Lived here since she was first married. Even before then she lived in the next street. Born in these parts and she'll die in these parts. She's been to my place though. I took her there just after I bought the house. She thinks it grand. Big as a palace she said.' He chuckled, 'Well to her it is I suppose. She's happy enough here it seems. I call in every week to make sure she's okay and not in need of anything. I'm just off to the corner shop to buy some ham for her tea. I like to spoil her a bit.'

Silvie liked the mild-mannered little woman who was Jack's mother. He had been her only child and she idolised him. Since the age of twelve he'd been fatherless. One day she'd remarked, 'I don't understand my Jack's business life or how he came to be so well off, but I do know this, he'd only make his profits from those as could afford it. He's got brains and a good business head on him. His father would be proud of him if he was alive today. He's gone and bought himself a bowler hat and one of those gents' umbrellas.' She had paused to chuckle at the idea before adding. 'He says he's joined the bowler brigade. Only wears it when he goes up to London on business. Must admit he does look smart in it though. A proper gent. I wish he'd find a nice girl to settle down with.' And then that wistful smile at the girl whom she wished it could be, before shuffling off in the old carpet slippers which she wore on account of her bunion.

Now, as the tapping high heels and the silent crepe soles covered the short distance along Queen Street Jack was saying, 'Not very romantic having to propose to you in the street, especially one such as this. But it's the only chance I get to see you. Anyway — one of these days I might strike lucky. Think about it sometimes blue Angel.'

She cast a brief glance down at the pale blue suit she was wearing and smiled faintly. Ever since she was a very young child he had always called her his angel. Often the angel would take on the colour of the dress she was wearing at the time. She merely sighed now in response. Any reply would be as repetitive as the question.

As they neared the corner the crepe-soles slowed and willed the high-heels to do likewise. But Silvie did not slow her steps. 'So long Jack.' She half turned as she left him outside the corner shop and with a brief wave walked on.

'So long Angel.' With all his yearning in his eyes Jack stood outside the shop watching her walk away. She had class. Something he'd never have himself and he knew it. She was the proverbial silk purse and he the sow's ear. Beneath his fine clothes and acquired manners his lowly born tag still showed. Even so he knew that he'd never want to lose the common touch altogether. He'd seen what money could do though. Certainly it had changed his life and social standing. It had acquainted him with people who otherwise would not have rubbed shoulders with him; particularly women. Among them some good lookers. But their looks were dimmed measured by the beauty of Silvie Marsh.

She turned the next corner and was out of sight. He sighed and entered the small shop. His presence was announced by the loud jingling of a bell attached to the inside of the door as he stepped into an atmosphere heavy with the mingled smells of cheese, pickles, corned beef and laundry soap.

3

Silvie Marsh stepped off the tramcar one stop before her destination. Eyes followed her from her seat and necks craned at the window for a last glimpse. The conductor groped blindly for the bell signal, and the bone-shaking movement of the transport resumed.

The shops were now closed and very few people about. She paused to look in the window of the small drapery store where the blue bed-jacket was displayed. Thankful that it was still there she stood for the moment admiring the blue angora trimmed with white swansdown. From her bag she took a silk scarf and tied it over her conspicuous long pale hair before walking on. Ten minutes later she drew level with three large white Georgian houses on the opposite side of the street. In the window of one was placed a large notice boldly printed . . . JOSEPH LEVENE BESPOKE TAILOR. On the wall of the next was fixed a large brass plate inscribed . . . O M TANDIE CHARTERED ACCOUNTANT. On the third house her eyes dwelt longest. Its heavy black painted door bore a gold printed announcement on an oak plate. MADAM RACHAEL MOSS DRESSMAKER EXCLUSIVE. A bright red geranium in a pot on a tall wooden stand was visible through the white lace curtains at one of the downstairs bay windows, and presented to the outside world a deceptive aspect of innocent propriety.

She moved on but her attention stayed discreetly on the third house. The black door was suddenly opened and an attractive, expensively dressed girl ran down the five white steps to a waiting taxi which seemed to appear from nowhere suddenly and was as quickly gone.

Further along the street Silvie crossed over and made her way back to the third house. Briefly her steps faltered. She forced herself to think of the blue bed-jacket and above all MISS MEACHER'S COLLEGE FOR YOUNG LADIES. Bracing herself she turned quickly towards the house, ran up the five white steps and pressed the shiny brass bell button at one side of the heavy wide door. This was opened almost before she withdrew her hand. She entered. Only when she'd stepped inside did she see that the person who had admitted her was a young girl of about seventeen.

With a quick glance the girl noted that no parcel of cloth for a sewing order was in the hands of the caller and gave a silent look of inquiry.

Silvie responded instantly, 'I'd like to speak with Madam Moss please.'

Without a word the girl disappeared through a heavy cherry-red velvet drape behind which there apparently was a door.

Silvie glanced about her. The spacious hall was thickly carpeted in cherry-red to match the drape across the door. A brass coat-stand held a solitary bowler hat. On one wall a large ornate gilt-framed mirror reflected back the red and gold tapestry-clad wall opposite and gave the impression of great space as well as rich ostentation. In contrasting relief was a

21

beautifully carved mahogany newel post at the base of a wide red-carpeted staircase up which red tapestry lined the walls. A second matching gilt-framed mirror hung on the facing wall of the first landing. Expensive perfume lingered in the air.

The low murmur of voices floated out from behind the drape through which the girl had gone.

Now having announced the presence of the visitor she reappeared. With a fleeting glance at Silvie she disappeared into a room further along the hall.

The elaborate crimson decor impacted on Silvie's sensibilities, symbolising the gross step which she was about to take. Before she could retreat under the onslaught of late doubt the velvet drape was pulled aside and a large woman appeared. Top heavy in high-heeled shoes, which showed signs of strain from their burden, she came forward. Despite her size her movements did not lack grace and suggested the remnants of an ex-dancer. Her well tailored black silk dress was relieved only by a diamond brooch pinned to the décolleté neckline. Overflowing breasts quivered as she moved and indicated a strong supportive undercarriage.

Barely able to conceal her revulsion at the sight Silvie told herself that she could still change her mind and claim to be there on a dressmaking inquiry. But the woman spoke first.

'Goot evenink. I em Rachael Moss.' She spread her hands, and jewels flashed on many fingers. Her accent was distinctly foreign, 'Vot ken I do for you?'

'May I speak with you in private?'

'Come in heah then my deah.' Rachael Moss pulled aside the velvet drape again revealing a heavy oak-panelled door which she closed behind them as they entered. Her shrewd mind was busy with conjecture as she motioned Silvie to a chair. Except for dressmaking inquiries people called at the house for one reason only.

With well concealed surprise she contemplated the young face before her. It was not one to forget and she'd seen it before. Instantly she recalled where. The cocktail lounge at the Golden Knight, which was just one of the venues where she procured some of her wealthiest clients. Always the very best places where, in accordance with her modus operandi, she would engage in brief conversation with carefully selected men whom she judged might be potential clients at her Georgian House. To these she would discreetly pass her scarlet and gold business cards ... MADAM MOSS DRESSMAKER EXCLUSIVE HIGHEST STANDARD GUARANTEED. On the reverse side in smaller print the address of the Georgian House. They understood perfectly.

If by chance the cards came into the possession of their wives it would result in no more than a brief telephone inquiry regarding a gown or coat, and easily dispensed with.

The rule was that Esse, whose job it was to answer the door, must refer any such inquiries to Sara Hoskins in the small sewing room off the hall. Here Sara could accept or reject the needlework according to her whim. Just lately she was inclined to do the latter. But that was her own affair. Madam Moss had no financial interest in the dressmaking aspect of the house. She merely paid the little seamstress a retaining wage to provide the necessary front to disguise the true function of the premises.

With the same infinite care with which she selected her potential clients she chose her girls. For these not only good looks were the criteria but also their social level and potential. On occasions they might be required to accompany clients to elite social functions, and at times brief trips abroad, all expenses paid.

One of the scarlet and gold cards, left behind in the Golden Knight, had been collected up with various litter by the waiter. Knowledgeably he had made some brief comment on it to Silvie before tossing it in the waste bin.

Curious, she had later recovered it and made a mental note of the address.

Rarely did Rachael Moss disclose her private thoughts to those around her, except perhaps to Sampson. At this moment her pencilled, deeply arched brows resisted the urge to raise further in surprise. From her daytime nook in the white laced bay, where she kept constant vigil, she had seen Silvie pass by on the opposite side of the street, and moments later cross over to double back and run up the steps to the front door.

Already with the few words spoken so far Madam Moss had noted the cultured speech. Now she cast a quick glance at the ringless fingers. The girl could get the catch of the century if she chose. Here she would be worth a fortune.

Despite unaccustomed nervous qualms Silvie could not help but notice the luxurious furnishings of the room. Although she considered the decor too ostentatious for her own taste she appreciated the cost involved. The style was predominantly Louise XIV, upholstered in rich dark-red velvet, with the exception of a small chaise lounge which was covered in exquisite tapestry, and a relief from the dominant red which overflowed into the room from the hall.

Rachael Moss resumed her place in the bay on her elaborately carved wooden throne-like chair with a cherry velvet seat. Here she sat day after day, like some gargantuan goddess, at a vantage point to view the activities of the street. A police raid could not be entirely ruled out, despite the fact that the sergeant in charge of the nearest police headquarters was in her pay and as much in her power now as she in his.

Yet there always remained the possibility that other branches higher up the constabulary ladder might get wind of the Georgian pleasure house. Being no fool she knew that men talked amongst themselves and word got around. An inquisitive wife perhaps might come across one of the scarlet and gold cards and if suspicious could be her worst enemy. A number of dressmaking inquiries had been received on past occasions and easily dispensed with. At times, if the inquirer was persistent, Sara Hoskins, whether inclined to or not, had to get off her lazy backside and run up whatever was required.

Natural reserve came between Silvie Marsh and her present mission. Now, as she regarded the heavy jowls, the folds of chin, the large nose, and garish hennaed hair at war with the sallow complexion powdered shades too light, she began to doubt her own sanity. Again she forced herself to think of the reasons why she was there. Of Queen Street and it's stranglehold, and of the future for her mother and Ginny. Yet still she hesitated to commit herself to the unknown, the unsavoury.

She made a move as if to leave, but the watery-grey eyes which were studying her so intently seemed to immobilise her for the moment.

'Did you come heah to discuss becoming vun of my girls deah?' Rachael Moss spread her hands as though to display the many rings on her fingers.

Silvie nodded.

'Very vell. But you must understend that I vant no tloubel. If you hev any boyfrinds thet — '

'There is no one,' Silvie cut in quickly.

'Thet is good deah. All my cli-inks are from high social posishinks, in commerce, politishinks, high society. They come heah to relex in comfort and releef their stresses. We hev heah only girls from the very best beckgrounds.'

Silvie wondered why they were working for this woman and in such a manner if they already had comfortable homes and lives.

To some extent Rachael Moss could have answered this. At least one of her girls from the upper level of society had left home because of family disagreement. Others for independence: some merely for diversion in their lives. One girl hated her parents and felt a certain satisfaction in flouting their strict religious standards with which they had oppressed her childhood years, although they were unaware of her secret life.

Madam Moss paid them well, even if only a mere

fraction of what she charged the clients. She never skimped on the wines and spirits provided, or the decor for their comfort. The men liked to feel pampered, they were used to good surroundings. Most were middle-aged, but some of the non-regulars were young and merely indulged themselves on money leeched from rich parents.

She could have retired years ago. Only greed postponed this final step.

'The cl-inks remain anonymous,' she continued. 'I gif them names for identification purposes ven they call, and no kveshtinks asked.' She paused briefly before adding. 'I hev seen you verkink in the Goldink Knight.'

To this Silvie made no response since she considered none necessary.

Madam Moss was silent for a moment while she recalled her most recent visit to that night spot. Being observant of such things she had noticed that there hadn't been a man in the room whose eyes hadn't lingered on this girl. She continued now, 'Some of the girls lif in. Ver you thinkink of livink in?'

'No. In fact I'm not free in the daytime.' Silvie had no intentions of giving more information about herself than was necessary.

'Mmm — pity deah. Some of the cli-inks ken only visit durink the day time.' Madam Moss shrugged her massive shoulders and spread her hands as she explained. 'Ven they are supposed to be verkink at the office you understend. If you ken arrange some days it vould be verth your vhile.' She paused speculatively before continuing. 'You hef somevun to look after durink the day maybe?'

'I have daytime commitments yes. I can be free evenings only.'

'Ah vell, you vill be able to afford to get somevun in to help out. I don't know how much pay you get at present for standink on your feet till late et night in thet cocktail bar, but I ken tell you thet you vill earn a lot more on your beck deah.'

Silvie found this natural coarseness distasteful and unnecessary. At twenty she was not yet a woman of the world and had no experience of a sexual nature with men. But she realised only too well that her sensitivity had to be overcome. Assertively now she replied. 'I am not prepared to discuss my family or my private life. I too must remain anonymous.'

Rachael Moss appeared to accept this. 'Thet's all right deah. I don't vont to know anythink except thet nobody vill make tloubel — femily I mean.'

'There is no possibility of that. They are as unaware of my intentions as they are of your existence.'

The big woman rested her heavy-lidded gaze on the beautiful features. There was, she perceived, an impenetrable reserve about the girl. Her shrewd mind considered this aspect. Certainly it could prove an additional attraction. Men might find it titillating. A potential gold mine sat before her.

What Rachael Moss didn't know about men wasn't worth knowing. Already she was calculating the price she could demand for her newest acquisition. Placing her plump palms down on the carved arms of her throne-like chair she assisted her heavy bulk onto her feet. She crossed the room and opened the intricately carved doors of an antique cocktail cabinet and produced a decanter of wine and two glasses which she set down on a side table covered by a cream Nottingham lace cloth. 'I em goink to hef a sherry deah. Vill you join me vhile ve hef a little chet?'

Silvie shook her head. 'No thank you. I don't drink alcohol.'

'Really!' Surprise showed on the flabby face. 'End you verk vith dlink! Or perheps thet is the reasink eh? You hef seen too many people makink fools of themselfs?' Without pausing for response she indicated the glass in her hand by raising it slightly as she returned to her seat in the bay. 'Svedish clystal.'

Silvie cast a brief glance upwards to the chandelier hanging below an elaborate plaster centrepiece in the ceiling.

Rachael Moss noticed. 'It's an eye ketchink piece isn't it deah. Came from Paris. I like a bit of luxury around me. I hef made the whole house qvite luffly. This is my fafourite room though. I started vith nuthink. A Russian refugee. I vos vunce a chorus girl. Filled out a bit since then.' She gave a short harsh laugh and eased herself back into her chair.

Silvie eyed the geranium, its colour harshly emphasised by the white lace curtains in the bay. Then she returned her attention to the painted face and hennaed hair, both in unison with the garish flower. She glanced at her wrist watch. 'I can stay only another fifteen minutes. I have to be at work by seven thirty.'

29

'I see. Vell you ken gif in your notice es soon es you like. I em sure you vill be heppy vith my terms.' Rachael Moss took a long swig of her drink before adding. 'Ven ve hef hed our little chet I vill show you over the house and take you to meet my son Sempson.'

★ ★ ★

'End this is the very best room.' Rachael Moss switched on pink shaded lights as they entered, then spread her ringed hands fanwise like a magician who had just conjured the room from a top hat. 'I call this the Rose Room for obfious reasinks.'

Close behind her Silvie glanced about the room. Luxurious drapes of rose pink velvet reached to the floor at the bay window. A heavy Indian carpet, ivory coloured and deeply inlaid with pink and green floral design almost covered the floor, leaving only a narrow border of dark polished wood visible. A scroll-end chaise longue upholstered in rose silk damask was placed near the window. The large bed was covered with a quilted rose satin spread which matched its headboard. The pink shaded lights gave the room an all over rosy glow.

'Sara Hoskins my resident dressmaker made the kvilt and headboard. She is hendy vith the needle ven she hes to be. You vill hef this room deah.'

Only her top paying clients came to this room. She intended to take full advantage of the fact that she could, and would, ask a very high price for this new addition to her Georgian pleasure house. Even so she did not propose to pay her above the rates of

30

the other girls. Rachael Moss could see that this one was as green as grass and did not know her own worth.

'End now,' she continued as she led the way out of the room, 'you shall meet Sempson.' Leaning heavily on the banister rail she preceded Silvie down the stairs. At the far end of the hall she turned a corner into a narrow passageway which led to the rear of the house. Here the luxurious ostentation came to an abrupt end. 'Sempson is our protecshink. This is his den.' She opened a door and they entered a small room.

A massively built man whose age it was difficult to determine lounged on a wooden chair which was tilted slightly onto its back legs, his feet resting on a low table. He was reading a comic magazine, the kind illustrated in washed-out colours which stamped it American. A pile of the same kind was placed beside his chair and a few others scattered about the floor, each liberally illustrated with little clouds enclosing words such as BIFF — PUNCH — WHAM — and GOTCHA.

Rachael Moss rapped out a few words in a foreign tongue which Silvie thought might be Yiddish. Surprised he turned, and in what seemed a single movement threw aside the comic he'd been reading, straightened up the tilted chair, slid his feet from the table and stood up. There was an unattractive heavy cast to his features. His hair was sandy brown and his mouth slack with a protruding lower lip. The only immediately noticeable resemblance to his mother were his watery-grey colour eyes.

31

'Sempson — this is Evette. She vill alvays be in the rose room.'

Silvie nodded acknowledgment. The name Evette had been decided upon. All the girls used assumed names Madam Moss had told her, sometimes their own choice, sometimes hers. She had decided on Evette. Silvie had no interest in what name was chosen for her so long as her own was concealed.

'This is ver you vill find him most times. Any tloubel end you rink the bell button above the bedhead in the rose room.' Rachael Moss pointed to wiring high up on one wall of the room. 'The buzzer vill sound in heah end Sempson vill come up. But rarely ve get tloubel. Only if a cli-ink hes bin dlinking perheps, end never amonk my best regular ones.'

'If you ring I'll be up like a shot,' Sampson grinned showing neglected teeth. His voice was light in tone and at odds with his huge stature. He had no trace of a foreign accent.

Silvie found her eyes straying to the comic magazines as it occurred to her that the few words he'd spoken had been more in the manner of a schoolboy than of a man.

'Now tidy up this room Sempson. Vot does it look like! A pik sty — thet's vot!'

'Sure Momma.' Silvie heard his reply as she turned to leave. Madam Moss saw her to the front door. 'Ve vill see you next veek then deah.'

Silvie hurried down the white steps, her expression grave but determined. The first move was now behind her on the path to a more prosperous future.

4

On the pink chaise in the Rose Room Silvie Marsh sat, tense, waiting. Barely could she believe and accept the fact that she was about to be initiated into whoredom. All her sensibilities were in revolt against this step into unknown territory. To help quash her inhibitions she again concentrated her whole attention on the reason why she was there.

The white cotton gown she wore was simple and costly, of deliberately demure design buttoned high to the neck, and one of the collection supplied by Madam Moss and kept carefully laundered and in good order by Esse. No skimping here. Standards were high and in accord with clients expectations. And all tastes were catered for at the Georgian house.

The awaited client was a regular. Madam Moss was familiar with the reasons for his visits. Secretly she felt a contempt for his kind. Pathetic she considered them. Granted it was through no fault of their own that they were freaks by accident of birth. He was treated with the same cordiality and attention as all the other clients. He would make no demands; he would merely talk. He came because of some psychological need to give the impression to his colleagues at the Government Ministry where he worked that he was just as much a man of the world as they, some of whom made regular visits to the Georgian House. He took great pains to hide the fact that he was what they would term a 'queer.' He arranged whenever possible for his appointments to coincide with that of one or the other of them as proof of his visits and to convince that he was as normal as they. He purposely spoke of his visits as did they all; some boastfully.

Outside the room now a floor board creaked. Apprehensive Silvie stiffened. With effort she calmed herself. She had been promised that no clients with peculiar tastes would be sent to the rose room. This assurance had been prompted by shrewd common sense, Rachael Moss would not chance risking the loss of her newest and most valuable asset.

A floor board creaked again before the door was opened. The man who entered was squat in build, middle aged, balding, not very attractive, and wore thick lens spectacles. His clothes looked expensive and well tailored. As he approached she tensed, although Madam Moss had told her that he would merely want to talk. 'Wont you sit down,' she said, 'and I'll get you a drink. Then you can tell me about yourself.' She went to a small cabinet which was kept stocked for the clients.

'Thank you. Port and lemon please' he responded as he sat down.

She poured the drink and handed it to him, then re-seated herself on the chaise. 'I'm Evette.'

'How do you do Evette. Rachael phoned me you know. Told me there was a new and very beautiful girl here.'

'Phoned you! But I thought she had no outside contact with the clients.'

'Unlisted number. I live alone. Gets lonely at

times. I just like to talk. I expect Rachael has told you that.'

She nodded and sank back into the chaise, pondering on the high monetary cost the man regularly incurred upon himself to appease some strange psychological need.

He spoke of various things, himself, his hobbies and interests without giving away his true identity. There were no awkward silences.

Half an hour later he stood up to leave. 'Thank you for listening to me. Perhaps next time we can discuss classical music and art; both subjects very close to my heart.

'Yes — yes of course.'

A moment later the door closed behind him.

Such was her initiation and her first encounter in the Georgian house.

All she could feel for the present, apart from relief, was a strange pity for the man who had just left.

5

Esse opened the front door to admit the man known as Rossi who was a regular fortnightly visitor to the Georgian house. Madam Moss appeared from her private room and beckoned him in.

'I hef a surprise waitink for you upstairs. You vil be the first.' She was well aware that the pathetic creature who had left barely an hour before would have left her new acquisition in the physical state in which he'd found her. 'A leetle more expensive perheps — but I know you vill not be disappointed.'

Unimpressed by what he considered was merely a crafty move by the grasping bitch to inflate the already exorbitant fees the man Rossi nodded and without comment left the room and made his way upstairs to the rose room which was always allocated to him for his brief fortnightly calls.

Outside the room he paused to knock, then entered.

The first sight of Silvie seated on the chaise near the bay immobilised him in the doorway.

Dressed now in a white flimsy negligee and matching night dress, supplied by Rachael Moss and made by Sara Hoskins, and her hair loosely flowing across her shoulders, she sat nervously awaiting this second client.

For the moment he was at a loss for words. Then mechanically he entered the room and closed the door behind him without taking his eyes from her.

Truth was that he felt mesmerised by the sight of her.

Tense she waited for him to speak first.

At last he did. 'Hello. I'm known here as Rossi.'

In silence she motioned him to the gentleman's wingback, upholstered in pink and grey regency striped velvet, then forced herself to reply. 'I'm known here as Evette.'

'I'm afraid the name doesn't suit you a bit.' He seated himself facing her. 'You look as if you've just fallen out of the sky. Your name should be Angel.' He had noted the nervous tremor in her voice and for the first time in his adult life he felt unsure of his next move.

She sensed his uncertainty and asked, 'Would you like a drink?'

'Thank you. Brandy and soda please.'

As she rose to pour the drink she thought . . . That word Angel again! Reminding her of Jack Thorndyke and her real life at Queen Street when she least wanted to think of it. This new part of her existence was unreal, merely the means to an end, however distasteful.

'Won't you have a drink too?' he asked.

'Never touch it.' She handed him the brandy and re-seated herself on the chaise.

He sipped from the glass then asked. 'What are you doing in a place like this? You don't belong here.'

'I know that only too well,' she replied simply and gave a brief smile of resignation.

Between sips of his brandy he continued to speak. 'You must be in desperate need of funds.' He paused in brief speculation before adding — 'Look . . . how can I put this . . . Why not let me take you away from this place. I can get you a flat of your own and finance your needs. I'd tell you all about myself and my life first of course. Don't form too bad an opinion of me for visiting this place every couple of weeks or so. My wife has absolutely no interest whatever in me except as head of her business empire. I have a flat in the city, conveniently close to the company offices. My family home is in the country. Much too far for day to day travel, like most city business men. Occasionally I go home for the weekend. Please will you think about it?'

She had sat silently listening. Now she shook her head. 'Thank you for the offer Rossi. It's very kind of you to be concerned. But I do value my independence and really couldn't allow you to take on my responsibilities. I have chosen this way and must go through with it.'

He looked disappointed, but as a man accustomed to getting his way he felt certain that eventually he could persuade her to do as he suggested. She looked so pure and fragile. He couldn't bear to think of other men mauling her. At least, as the first, he would treat her with consideration. Others in his position might not do so.

Such was the first encounter between Silvie Marsh and the man with whom her future was irreversibly linked.

6

On the income she was earning at the Georgian house Silvie Marsh was ready to set about making the changes in their lives which she'd promised herself. Four weeks had passed since that first evening.

It was tea time in the tiny parlour of number 24 Queen Street. Over sandwiches and homemade cup cakes they were discussing the immediate future. 'As soon as we can find a decent house and move away from here we can set about enrolling you at MISS MEACHER'S COLLEGE Ginny. Can't do that from this address. Although Miss Meacher wouldn't know this street she'd have a fair idea of the kind of neighbourhood by the name.'

'I wonder why they're always streets in areas like this? In the better class districts they're always avenues or drives, or at the very least, roads. Not that I'd mind anyone at the college knowing where I lived — really Silvie — it wouldn't bother me in the least.'

'Well it would bother me. So a better house is the first consideration.'

'It would be nice for Mum to have a garden to sit out in on the warm days,' Ginny agreed. 'She's never had a proper garden.'

'I have Ginny dear. Many years ago when I was young,' Alice corrected. 'We had a lovely big apple tree. I used to sit under it in the shade on summer days.'

'Maybe we'll strike lucky and find a house with a decent garden and a tree,' Ginny sounded hopeful.

'We'll be lucky if we find a house at all, with or without a garden. But I've been checking the papers every day.' Silvie had not told them what her actual income was: The amount far exceeded the sum which she could reasonably expect them to believe would be paid for a few hours of sewing, regardless of quality.

'How is it that they can pay you so well for the dressmaking Silvie?' Ginny had asked in the beginning. Avoiding the candid amber eyes Silvie had replied, 'Everything has to be of the highest standard and quality, exclusive and expensive and they're willing to pay well for the right people. Only rich clients.' This at least was true about the Georgian house, and only the nature of the work was a lie.

Content that everything seemed to be going favourably for them Alice Marsh relaxed back into her elevated pillows, but a niggling concern compelled her to say, 'I hope so much sewing in artificial light doesn't start to impair your eyesight though dear. If you notice any strain you must give it up. We'll manage the same as we did before.'

Guilt stabbed at Silvie. But she had severed part of her life from the two people she loved best in the world, the part which was, of necessity, deceit and lies. And until she had provided all the things which she wanted for them it would have to remain that way.

★　★　★

Since the war houses were scarce. The advent of rebuilding would not happen for several more years. People needed rehousing on account of bomb damage. Although Silvie kept constant watch on the local newspaper she held very little hope of finding a house vacant. The few that became available required no press notice. A TO LET sign placed in the window was sufficient. Even this was unnecessary, since house hunters often had advance information that a house was about to be vacated. Only the larger more expensive properties with temporary leases were available.

During midday break from school one day Ginny burst into the house, barely closing the door behind her before she squealed, 'Mum! Silv! There's a TO LET sign in the window of a house in Stanford Road. I saw it as we passed on the way back to the bus stop after rounders on the common. It can only have just been put there. I'm certain it wasn't there earlier when we passed! I'd have noticed it. I made a note of the telephone number to contact.' She extracted a small slip of paper from the pocket of her blouse and handed it to Silvie as she came from the back room carrying a tray.

'Really! Stanford Road?' Silvie set the tray down and took the slip of paper. 'Where is that?'

'Just off the main avenue. Congregational church on the corner.'

'What a piece of luck! We'll have to be quick though. Probably be snapped up before we can get to the phone to arrange to see it.'

'You could go straight after dinner Silv! I can stay with Mum. We've only got domestic science and art

41

this afternoon and I can easily miss those.' Briefly she paused as a thought struck her, then continued dramatically. 'And I got such a whack from a bat during rounders. Look bruises already!'

With concern Silvie studied the darkening patch on the indicated leg. Then noticed Ginny's comically exaggerated expression of pain and her laughing eyes. A flicker of amusement touched her lips. 'All right then. I suppose it's as good an excuse as any to miss domestic science and art. But we'll have to get a move on or someone will be sure to beat us to it. I'll ask Mrs Barnes to come in and sit with Mum and we can both go.' With a brief glance at the injured leg she teased. 'That's if you can manage to walk on that leg.'

Briefly Ginny appeared to consider this, then returned the humour. 'Can't I use the other one too? Otherwise I'll fall flat on my face.'

★ ★ ★

The contact number was that of the house owner who lived only three streets away from Stanford Road and they duly collected the key to inspect the house.

'It's just perfect Silv!' Ginny ran from room to room rapturously praising and flicking on light switches. 'Electric instead of old fashioned gas light! And just look at this marble fire place! It's absolutely beautiful.' In the kitchen she turned on taps. 'Water inside the house — and a sink!' She ran up the stairs.

Equally impressed and hardly able to believe their

luck Silvie followed. Before she was halfway up the stairs Ginny's head appeared over the banister above on the landing. 'Three bedrooms up here, a bathroom, and a separate toilet!' She darted off again. Moments later her footsteps and her voice echoed in each empty room in turn. On the landing Silvie paused briefly while she thought about the changes she could now really begin to make in their lives. The high excited tones of Ginny broke into her thoughts and she moved on towards the bedrooms.

'There's a tiny hand basin in this room. Come and see. Mum could have this one. It overlooks the garden. Oh — and just come and see Silv — there's a tree! Perhaps it's an apple.'

At the window now Silvie looked down over the good sized garden. 'Hard to tell with the branches bare. It could well be an apple. It looks a very old one. It'll be lovely in blossom whatever it is.'

'Mum could sit under it in summer. She'll love this house Silv, particularly the tree.'

'I know she will. Clever girl finding it.' They hugged each other in delight.

'I've never seen such a nice house before. Oh Silv — don't you agree that it's the most beautiful house ever!'

Silvie smiled at the lavish praise before replying. 'It depends really on what yardstick you use to measure its attributes. Compared with Queen Street it undoubtedly is a palace. But judged against a country mansion it's only mediocre.'

Ginny chuckled. 'Well I think this house is a mediocre palace. Will we really be able to afford the rent and the college too Silvie? Just living here would be more than enough because I know how much Mum would love it. She does worry that you may be working too hard. College isn't that important.'

'We can afford it. Amazingly the rent is only a little more than twice what we pay now. Probably because of the government control on rent prices. The landlord won't be able to raise it either. At least not without going to the Rent Tribunal. We'll move in immediately. And we can enrol you at the College now. Come on let's go down and look at the garden.'

Ginny led the way out through the French door of the living room.

Together they stood under the big tree staring up at the bare branches, each visualising it in full bloom. As they spoke their breaths misted on the cold air. Underfoot the lawn was stiff with unthawed frost.

'Secluded too.' Briefly Silvie glanced across at the high wooden fence lined with thick privet hedge. Abruptly she turned, and taking Ginny by the hand hurried back into the house. 'Come on then. No time to waste.'

To the tune of the Wizard of Oz she sang, 'We're off to see the landlord . . . '

As she had hoped and expected this distracted Ginny away from the subject of her job and earnings. Ginny readily joined in. 'We're off to see the landlord . . . '

7

Before the week was out they had made the move to Stanford Road. Its distance from the Georgian house was very little more than it had been from Queen Street and late night taxi fares home were still affordable. It was also conveniently on the bus route for the College, although the journey was a little longer than Silvie would have wished for Ginny to travel every day.

At this moment they were attending the interview for Ginny's enrolment at MISS MEACHERS COLLEGE FOR YOUNG LADIES. Both were relieved to discover the little principal Miss Meacher to be mild-mannered and pleasant. Her mouth was tilted at the corners which gave her a permanently sweet-natured expression. They had each secretly been expecting a granite-faced individual.

'I do not rule the College with a rod of iron,' Miss Meacher was at present informing them. 'I sow kindness and understanding. In return I reap their respect, friendship and trust. I find that the girls observe the rules and give their best because they sincerely want to and not from undue authoritative pressures. I aim for harmony and order and that's exactly what I get. Some of the girls live too far from the College for travel on a daily basis so have to board during term. Occasionally some get invited to the homes of their friends who live closer. In such instances a letter of mutual approval from the respective parents or guardians on both sides is required. While the girls are in my care I take every necessary precaution for their safety and well-being. Rest assured that Virginia will be given every encouragement with her studies. I feel confident that she'll settle in quickly and make many friends here.'

'I'm sure she will,' Silvie agreed as she shook hands with the little woman and thanked her.

Now, seated in the bus, they were anxious to get home where for the first time they had left their mother on her own. No longer having Mrs Barnes to pop in they'd had no option but to leave Alice alone while they visited the College.

'I like Miss Meacher Silvie. She's not the dragon I had imagined she'd be.'

'I thought her very nice too. I'm certain you're going to like it there.'

'I know I shall.'

Silvie was satisfied. Things were working out just as she'd planned. The means to this end was made more endurable.

* * *

They carried the tea things upstairs to Alice's room where they took their meals each day now for convenience on account of the stairs. When they told her about the interview she smiled her lopsided smile and looked pleased. She was proud of the way in which her eldest daughter was managing things and coping so well. At the same time she couldn't help but be a little concerned at so much

46

responsibility on one so young.

'You look a lot better since we've been in this house Mum. You've got some colour in your cheeks.' Silvie placed the tray on a table beside the bed. 'It's probably because we can have the window open more now with no smoke coming in from chimneys.' Alice's bed had been placed close to the window from where she could see down over the garden. She eased herself forward to look out on the big tree which she'd confirmed was an apple. 'I wonder if the blossom will be tinged with pink? So pretty when it is.'

But she did not live to see the answer.

8

During those first weeks at the Georgian house Rossi had called at least a dozen times. Although he paid the high monetary cost which Rachael Moss had set on Silvie he made no excessive demands. Much of the time he sat in the wingback and talked.

'Why do you come so often Rossi? I mean — the cost — not that I know what it is.'

'While I'm here no one else can be,' he replied simply. Each time he came he begged her to let him find an apartment for her and allow him to take care of her finances. Each time she declined the offer.

'I would rather remain independent,' she told him. 'As much as I loathe this place and this life, I have family commitments.'

'I would not attempt to keep you from them. I just want to get you away from here. Please. I would consider it a privilege. I know I'm old enough to be your father — but nevertheless I've fallen in love with you.'

A brief companionable silence fell between them during which Silvie regarded him. Probably late forties, she assessed: Very handsome, his dark hair greying at the temples. Height around five feet ten, broad shoulders and chest, with no excess weight. Always expensively dressed. He had a look of authority about him, and obviously wealthy. True, age-wise, he was old enough to be her father, just as he'd said, yet she did not feel this age gap between them. Certainly she felt comfortable with him and was glad of his presence there in the place where she'd rather not be.

He broke the short silence now. 'I wish you'd let me tell you about my life. Especially about my wife who is not a wife at all. Let me at least — '

She leaned across and put her fingers on his lips to stop his words. 'No Rossi. I don't want to know about your family life. You must tell me nothing.'

He grasped her hand and held it tightly. 'Until I walked in here and saw you sitting there with your flowing hair and your white gown I came mainly out of loneliness and only once a fortnight. I guess it's the same for most of the chaps who visit this place. City's full of business men living alone in apartments all week and only able to get home at weekends. For me rarely then. Little to go home for.' He leaned forward in the chair. 'Please come away from this place with me — now — tonight. Trust me to look after your interests.'

Firmly she shook her head. 'I can't Rossi. I've explained my reason.'

'And I say it's *no* reason.' A brief silence fell between them before he continued. 'In all my life I've never seen anyone half so lovely as you are. I swear I die a little every time I have to leave you behind in this place.' He took a tress of her hair between his fingers — 'White Angel.'

Being again reminded of Jack Thorndyke's angel greetings she gave a wry smile and said, 'More aptly Scarlet Angel.'

'No,' he protested, 'Never that — never that.' Still grasping her hand he tried again. 'Listen — have you any idea how much I pay that gargoyle downstairs every time I visit now?'

At the apt description of Rachael Moss she gave a brief half smile of amusement. 'I have absolutely no idea.'

He named a figure and with satisfaction noted her surprise, hoping he might have influenced her to a change of mind.

'Will you promise to give it some thought,' he pressed.

'Yes. Yes I will do that Rossi.'

He wondered why he hadn't thought to mention the money aspect of his visits before, indelicate though it might seem. But he was desperate and desperate measures were called for. 'Promise,' he insisted.

She nodded. 'I promise I'll give it some serious thought.' She had already half made up her mind. The sum mentioned was higher for one of his visits than she was payed for the whole week. But she would have to be absolutely certain before she made the move. Rachael Moss would not be likely to re-instate her after taking off with one of her top paying clients.

As he was leaving he said, 'Until you agree to let me take you away from here I shall come every evening and also tell her to admit no one else to this room. I'll pay her losses.'

'Oh no!' Silvie protested. 'You must not consider such a thing! Just think of the enormous cost!'

'No,' he responded assertively. 'I want *you* to think of that.' In an optimistic frame of mind he kissed her and left.

9

It came as a shock to Jack Thorndyke when he saw the white circular smudges on the windows of number 24 announcing that the house had been vacated. The fact that Silvie had said nothing about the intended move when he'd last seen her a fortnight ago hurt him deeply. But he consoled himself with the thought that perhaps she hadn't known about the coming event herself at that time. He was well aware that quick action was necessary to snap up a house if one became available. So often she'd mentioned that she'd like to move away from Queen Street.

When he parked the Humber outside number five and got out he did not heed the boys who greeted him in their usual way. Nor did he issue his customary threat in acknowledgment.

Each boy was silently disturbed at this as they watched him enter the house and call before he was through the door, 'When did the Marshs move Ma?' Not even his usual 'Hello Ma — it's me.'

'About a week ago Jack.' Mrs Thorndyke came into view from the back room. 'Nobody knew they were going as far as I know. I haven't seen Mrs Barnes though — not since they went. She'll probably know where they moved to. Call in and ask her when you pass.'

But Jack couldn't wait until then. 'I'll nip down now and ask.' He turned and went out again.

Preoccupied he strode past the boys who, subdued by his snub on arrival, had half-heartedly resumed their ball game. Today they'd not risk getting close to the Humber, much as they longed to, for untouched by hand though they would have left it, they did not know this strange Jack who'd ignored their presence as if they'd not been there at all.

Jack knocked on the door of number 26 then opened it to call in, 'Yoo hoo — anyone at home? Mrs Barnes — it's Jack.'

Mrs Barnes came from the back room drying her hands on her apron. 'Hello Jack.'

'When did the Marsh's move and where did they go?'

'Ah — now you've *asked* me! I don't know the name of the road Jack. Silvie did mention it but I didn't take it in. A road I'd never heard of. They'd have made sure to write it down for me if I'd wanted it. But they know I don't go no further than the corner shop if I can help it. They went suddenly when the chance came up. You know how quick off the mark you have to be. I sat with Alice while they went to see the landlord. More than a week ago now. I shall miss them and my little chats with Alice.' She saw the disappointment on his face. 'I'm sorry I can't be of more help Jack.'

Jack smiled briefly and nodded. 'Okay — thanks Mrs Barnes. If you do hear anything will you let Ma know?'

'I will Jack, but I doubt if I shall now. Silvie might get in touch with you though when she's properly settled in their new place.' Mrs Barnes did not really believe this but she felt sorry for Jack, knowing how fond he'd always been of Silvie Marsh who had never given him any encouragement, and was not likely to do so now. From her doorway she watched him make his way slowly back along the street. She saw him stop to speak to the boys. Then she went inside and closed her door.

The boys shook their heads, desperately wishing that they had some information for their idol now that he acknowledged them with questions. They wanted to restore the lively loud spoken Jack they knew best; the one who remembered to threaten them about his car, because that meant money to spend at the corner shop.

Without hesitation they each answered him in turn. 'Dunno where they went Jack.'

'Didn't see 'em go Jack.'

'I'll run and ast our Ma,' volunteered one, and turned out to be spokesman for them all. In an instant they scattered, willing slaves to their hero with the big posh car and pots of money. As they went their voices floated back to him on the cold smoky air.

'I'll see if me ma knows anyfink.'

'I 'spect me ma'll know.'

Jack went indoors and flopped down on the old black horsehair filled sofa. He didn't expect them to bring back any worthwhile information. Silvie wouldn't have told any of the neighbours her business, except for Mrs Barnes. But the boys had scuttled off before he could stop them.

Almost immediately one reappeared at the open doorway. 'Ma says Norrie Smif did the move and there wasn't much.' Then believing it might help he

53

added a few words of his own for good measure. 'Ma says you could ast 'im — 'e'll tell yer.'

Jack suppressed a smile. He well knew that the kids mother would know better than to suggest that Norrie Smith would give out any information about his customers. Many a rent man had tried him in the past. His brother who helped him in the business was also as discreet a brick wall.

One by one now the boys crowded the small doorway. Each had some negative words from home and, like the first, some additional ones invented by their own childish logic in an attempt to be helpful. What could the little beggars know of Norrie Smith's stubborn pride in business ethics, he thought. They probably overestimated his own powers on account of the Humber. He well knew the way they'd be thinking. He'd been one of them himself once.

He took some coins from his pocket. Always he had some ready when he visited his Ma. 'Here you are then you little buggers.'

Grinning now they trooped forward into the room eagerly. This was the Jack they knew. He hadn't changed after all. They liked it best when he called them names like that. He meant it in a friendly way, not like their Ma's and Dad's.

'Fanks Jack.'

'Ta Jack.'

'If we 'ears anyfink we'll let y' know Jack.'

Then they disappeared as if by magic. Jack smiled despite his downcast mood. He could well visualise what it would have been like the day the Marsh's had moved. The neighbours would have been behind their curtains taking note of what was being transported from the house to the removal van. Such rare occasions were the highlights of their drab existence in a back street such as this.

His mother came from the back room carrying a flat iron which she'd just taken from the hob. By turning her wrist she tilted the iron, raising the base uppermost, and lightly and expertly spat onto it. The spray skimmed off barely touching the surface. Satisfied that the iron was hot enough she said, 'I'll just finish off m' bit of ironing love and then I'll make us a nice pot o' tea.'

'That's a bloody dangerous way to hold that iron to test it Ma! It'll slip sideways one of these days and burn your arm.'

'I've been using this iron for nearly forty years love, and it never has yet.'

'If you'd let me find another house for you with electric I could buy you a modern iron. I can't make you out Ma!'

'You know I wouldn't move from here now Jack, otherwise I'd have come to live at Baron Wood with you when you asked me. I'm quite content here. Besides I'd be too nervous of an electric iron.'

A short silence ensued while she ironed and folded. Then her voice broke into his thoughts. 'I'm sure you'll find out where they've gone Jack. Silvie Marsh could do a lot worse than you. I've as good as told her so a few times — in my own way — you know — hinted like.'

Jack gave a wry smile. He could well imagine her singing his praises to Silvie Marsh.

Suddenly the dark claustrophobic confines of the

tiny room oppressed him. He became sharply aware of the Lilliputian size in comparison to his own home. The atmosphere seemed to stifle him. No wonder the door was ever open, the place was too shut in with it closed. With guilt he realised that the real reason why he'd visited his Ma so often in this dingy rabbit hutch was because he'd see Silvie Marsh. Even the mere knowledge that she'd been close by — a few yards down the street, had been sufficient. He'd always timed his visits to the corner shop in order to see and speak with her when she left the house for work. Always with the irrepressible hope that one day she might take his persistent, although hurried, marriage proposals seriously. The fact that number 24 was two thirds along the street with so little distance to the corner left little time to say much. She had never invited him into her home. Although during earlier years when she was still a child he had called in to present her with various gifts on her birthdays; Ginny's too. Slender though his chances had been he had never relinquished his dream of taking Silvie to Baron Wood as his wife. Now the light had gone from his life. His shining star had disappeared. All about him now — the house — the narrow street — he saw in all its shabby reality. Desolate — empty — without hope.

The boys had returned from the corner shop, mouths ecstatically stuffed curtesy of Jack, and resumed their ball game.

To Jack there seemed a stillness in the air. Their calling voices reminded him of the jeremiad cries of gulls on a deserted shore

10

In the Rose Room Silvie Marsh glanced up from the book on her lap as a familiar sound caught her ears. Puzzled she looked at the time by the crystal clock. No client was due for another fifteen minutes, and the door bell hadn't been rung. Yet the floorboards beneath the carpet right outside the room had creaked under the weight of someone who had paused there. She heard the creak again, She knew it would not be Rachael Moss for she seldom climbed the stairs, and only with very good reason, for she claimed the effort was too much. Her quarters were on the ground floor. It couldn't be Esse or she would have knocked and put her head round the door with any message. Whoever this was appeared to be loitering. She put aside the book and was about to speak when she saw the door knob slowly turning. Speechless she watched as the door was opened a few inches. A hand came into view and rested briefly on the light switch before flicking it upwards, leaving the room in darkness.

Stifling a small scream of surprise she stood up and moved towards the bed to grope for the bell to summon Sampson. Presuming that she had the advantage of knowing the layout of the unlit room she decided against switching on the bedside lamp. When her fingers contacted the bell she pressed down hard. Whoever the intruder was he could not be one of the usual clients; these were all intelligent men. This one must either be a practical joker or unstable, perhaps both. She could feel him getting closer and heard his breathing. Harder she pressed down on the bell button. Where was Sampson? Why was he taking so long! Countless times since that first day he had repeated, 'Any trouble ring the bell and I'll be up like a shot.' Most days now when she arrived he would be hovering about in the downstairs hall, always with the same expression of doglike devotion when he looked at her. Almost as though he were waiting patiently at hand for a time when she would need him to protect her. Why didn't he come now!

Harder she pressed down on the bell. It suddenly occurred to her that he might well have left his room to go to the toilet. She edged her way towards the door as the sound of breathing came closer now, just beside her. The intruder had closed the door on entering and not even a chink of light filtered in from outside the room.

Then she smelt the familiar scent of cloves which struck a chord in her memory. Recollection came. In the downstairs hall — a vase of flowers — just recently carnations. Their perfume always reminded her of cloves. The scent was stronger now and his breath closer. Was he perhaps one of the more peculiar clients come to the wrong room in error? About to make a dash for the door as best she could in the dark she froze as she felt heavy hands placed on her head and then move down to her face, tilting it upwards. Then she felt a moist kiss planted firmly on her forehead. She gasped in surprise and staggered backwards as she was suddenly released.

Before she could regain her balance the door was opened and quickly closed again as the intruder left the room.

The scent of cloves lingered. As she was groping her way towards the bedside lamp the door was flung open wide and the room instantly relit by the switch just inside the door. She noted the hand that had flicked it; it was the same hand that had come into view to switch off the lights only moments ago.

His huge bulk filling the doorway Sampson stood gazing at her with that devoted expression which she began to fear. Swiftly he moved across the room towards her. Before she could dodge away he had enveloped her in a bearlike hug and her face was pressed against his powerful chest as he gently stroked her hair. The strong scent of the carnation in his button hole made her feel suddenly sick. Never again would she smell that scent without remembering these awful moments.

'There now — don't be afraid,' he murmured as she struggled to free herself. 'I told you I'd be up right away if you rang for me. You're safe now.'

Gasping with the effort she broke away from his grasp. Since there might well be clients in some of the other rooms she could not call out for fear of embarrassing the whole house. By now she realised that Sampson was harmless. Like a small boy. Even so she would have to speak to his mother about the incident to prevent any repetition. A mere child at heart he had played some boyish, if bizarre, game in order to appear to come to her rescue, and presumably had expected her not to see through his trick! Perhaps, as a diversion from his uneventful life down in his small den, his underdeveloped mind had thought up a way to play out his dream of protecting her — no doubt impatient for a real opportunity which even *he* must have realised was very unlikely.

11

'Are you all right Mum?' Ginny looked up in concern and as she moved the book from which she'd been reading aloud to her mother slid unheeded from her lap to floor.

Alice Marsh put an agitated hand to her chest and attempted to speak. Then exhausted she lay back on the pillow her body relaxed.

At the bedside Ginny leaned over her mother who now lay motionless, eyes closed. 'Mum!' Her voice rose with alarm when there was no reply. 'Are you all right Mum!' For a few moments she waited for some response. When none came she dashed from the bedroom and downstairs. With trembling fingers she took two small slips of notepaper, one folded inside the other, from under the clock on the mantelpiece in the living room where Silvie had placed them when they'd first moved into the house. As she separated the two sheets one slipped from her hand. By reflex she reached out to retrieve it but there was a fire in the grate and the slip of paper was instantly drawn towards the chimney and sucked upwards, evading her grasp. In panic she looked at the remaining slip on which was written the name and telephone number of Doctor Meredith the local practitioner who had been attending her mother. The note which had been lost bore the telephone number on which Silvie could be contacted in an emergency. Moments later she watched the charred remains of the paper float lightly down into the fire. In any case the doctor must be called first. She dashed from the house and ran to the call box on the corner of the road.

The doctor lived only four streets away and in his car arrived at the house just as she was rushing back up the stairs. But there was nothing he could do. Alice Marsh was dead. 'I'm so very sorry my dear. Even if I'd been at hand when it happened I could not have saved her.'

'Oh Doctor — she can't be dead! I can't believe it!'

The elderly doctor put a comforting arm about her shoulders, aware that in this initial stage of shock her mind was unable to accept the reality. 'Chin up my dear. It may help you to know that she did not suffer.' He had attended Alice during a recent bout of bronchitis and knew about the stroke. 'If you'll let me have the telephone number where I can contact your sister I'll do so immediately. Then I'll come back here and wait with you until she arrives.'

Ginny explained about the lost slip of paper. 'I didn't memorise the number. I've never needed to call her at work. But I can run to the phone box again and look it up in the directory. I can remember the name of the dressmaker who she works for. If you will please stay here with . . . with . . . ' she was too overcome to finish and the doctor responded quickly.

'Of course my dear.' He knew that it was best for her to be occupied on some errand at present rather than be left alone in the house while he made the call.

The sound of her hurrying feet died away on the stairs and he heard the front door close behind her. Sighing he bent to pick up the fallen book which lay on the floor between the chair and the bed. She had explained that she'd been reading aloud to her mother when the attack happened. He went in search of a bookcase. Better it was out of sight for the present, the memory would be painful. In her own good time she would seek it out again.

Thoughts kept repeating themselves over in her distressed mind as she ran back to the telephone box on the corner. I must find Silvie . . . I must find Silvie . . . Mum was all right when Silvie left for work . . . all right when she left. Inside the phone box now her shocked mind went blank. Without the slip of paper she had no idea what number to ring . . . and the name . . . the name of the dressmaker . . . what was it. Only moments ago it had been clear in her mind. What was it! Sounded a bit old fashioned . . . ? Suddenly it came back to her — Hoskins! She repeated it over in her mind as she opened the directory. As she turned the pages she searched her memory for the name that Silvie had told her to ask for if she ever needed to call. In an attempt to collect her wits she thought of the College motto . . . COURAGE IN ADVERSITY. The name came back to her . . . Evette — that was it! For several minutes her trembling fingers scrambled through the pages . . . Hoskins . . . Hoskins . . . S. Hoskins. There were so many Hoskins! But no S and none denoted Dressmaker or

63

Tailoress. Feeling helpless she stood there. Courage — she reminded herself. But it was no use, she just wanted to collapse into a frustrated, sobbing heap. Who could help her? Who would know? Not even the operator if she didn't know herself where the premises were. There was no one she could turn to for help. Silvie never told people her business. Despair swamped her and she turned to leave the booth. Almost through the door she remembered Jack Thorndyke. Was it possible that Silvie might have mentioned her work to him? She had started the new job before they'd left Queen Street. Jack had often been passing the house when she left for work. She remembered joking about how he always managed to be passing at the precise time. Silvie might well have mentioned her work to him. It was worth a try. At least she knew where Jack lived, and he was certain to have a telephone. Turning back into the booth she again consulted the directory. Without difficulty she located his number and put the two pennies in the slot. As she waited she prayed aloud. 'Please God let Jack be in — let him be in — let him know where Silvie is.' She stopped in relief when she heard his voice in her ear.

'Oh Jack! Thank heaven! It's Ginny here. Ginny Marsh.'

'Ginny!' He sounded surprised.

'Jack — Mum's just died and I'm trying to find Silvie.' Her emotion charged voice trembled as she fought back dry sobs of mingled relief and grief. The rest of her words came incoherent to Jack as she tried to explain about the lost slip of paper and the sense of her words became obscure. But the first part had been made clear enough.

'Alice dead! Oh God I am sorry Ginny love. Give me your address and I'll come right over.'

'But Jack — I just want you to find Silvie for me. Tell her to come home.' Once again she attempted to explain why she herself was unable to make the contact.' Jack's voice had a steadying influence and her words became clearer. 'I can only remember the name of the dressmaker she works for — but can't find it in the directory. Sara Hoskins — Wyncham area. Silvie told me that if I ever needed to phone her to ask for Evette. That's the name she's known by at work . . . ' her voice trailed off.

'Evette! Dress making evenings!' Jack was unable to keep the surprise from his voice. But now was not the time for questions. But that name — 'Sara Hoskins? Sara Hoskins?' He repeated the name over a few times. Rang a definite bell. No doubts about it. 'Leave it to me Ginny love. I'll trace her. I can get on to directory inquiries. Where are you at the moment — call box or home?'

'Phone box on the corner.'

'Okay Love — now let me have your address before you hang up because I don't know where you live.'

Automatically she gave it then added, 'And Jack — don't forget to ask for Evette. They have to be known by names like that in high class salons to impress clients — but I don't suppose it's too important in emergencies — they'll know she's Silvie.' Again she became confused with distress.

Nevertheless Jack understood. 'Now you go on home Ginny love. I'll find her.'

Too dazed to thank him she hung up and ran back to the house, completely confident that her sister would be home soon. Jack would not fail her.

*   *   *

In his Baron Wood house Jack Thorndyke replaced the receiver slowly, his brows drawn together in an effort of concentration. That name — Sara Hoskins! It nagged at the back of his mind. Suddenly a chord in his memory responded sharply. But he refused to believe it. 'Impossible,' he murmured, 'not *Silvie Marsh*!'

He dashed upstairs to his bedroom and rummaged quickly through the pockets of his suits. Moments later he drew out a scarlet and gold business card which evoked vivid recollection.

They had been sitting in the lounge bar of the BLUE PARROT night club; Sammy Jones, Eddie Knight and himself, celebrating Sammy's birthday. A big woman — dyed hair — she had come to their table and with a wink had put three cards down, including this one. He recalled her exact words and foreign accent . . . 'You vont a nice evenink boys? Beautiful girls? Rink me ven you do.' Then she'd moved off. Probably had seen them flashing money about on drink.

Later Sammy, three sheets to the wind, as were they all, had suggested they have a bit of a lark and find out what happened when the woman got genuine inquiries for sewing. And that's what they did. How could they have possibly imagined they would appear genuine! It just showed how sloshed they all were at the time. Afterwards he couldn't even remember driving them to the Georgian house let alone finding it in the first place.

Together they'd all trooped up the steps, Sammy stumbling on the way. They'd found it difficult to stay serious as one of them rang the bell — he couldn't recall who — probably Sammy. A young girl had answered the door. And the three of them had practically fallen into the hall. Then Sammy had turned everything into a farce which defeated their original aim, mad though it had been, by pirouetting around the big hallway holding the sides of his pants like an imaginary skirt and singing — 'We're the three ugly sisters and we want some dresses made for the ball.' Or that was as close as Jack could remember of Sammy's words. Then Eddie had spotted a door with a white ceramic name plate attached — and that name — he could see it now — SARA HOSKINS DRESSMAKER EXCLUSIVE.

He himself had opened the door to reveal a small room which housed an old treadle sewing machine a chair and little else. The three of them had jammed into the doorway looking in. Then from the far side of the room another door was suddenly opened and a small woman wearing spectacles appeared, obviously having heard the commotion and sensed trouble.

Then like a gargantuan genie the woman who'd supplied them with the scarlet and gold cards had appeared and ordered them to leave. 'Get out — you are dlunk!'

But Sammy had not finished his larking. 'How

much is Sara Hoskins?' he'd inquired trying to keep a serious face, but not succeeding. It was at that moment a huge chap had appeared from a passageway at the back of the hall. Menacingly he had come towards them and they'd fled. All the way home they'd laughed. But the sight of that bouncer had sobered them up a bit. Any other time the recollection would have amused Jack. But not now — not now. Seated on his bed, with the card held in his palm, he leaned forward shoulders hunched, his face in his hands. Surely there must be some mistake! There had to be! Silvie couldn't be working in a place like that. His head moved slowly in denial.

Then he considered the move which the Marsh's had made. She had barely been able to make ends meet in Queen Street. And that assumed name — Evette! And the fact that Ginny hadn't known exactly where the place was, only a phone number. Well he'd soon find out now. He had to. Ginny had put her faith and trust in his help. With a weight on his shoulders he rose to go down and make the call. While he did this his mind kept hearing Sammy's words, 'How much is Sara Hoskins?'

★   ★   ★

As she'd promised Silvie had given a great deal of thought to Rossi's proposition. Her life at the Georgian house was loathsome to her, at times making her feel physically sick. Only by constantly remembering the chance in life she was giving to Ginny, and the brighter existence and extra comforts for her mother made it possible to continue. The idea of living life indefinitely this way had brought her to a conclusion. Although the clients who came to the Rose room treated her with the respect which her appearance and manner evoked, she felt cheap, knowing that beneath that outward respect they could really only consider her a high class tart, even though no saints themselves. Most were high ranking government officials, politicians, and top business executives. All with these secret episodes in their lives, and paying a high monetary price for the privilege.

Having arrived at the decision she did not go straight to the Georgian house. She first went to call on Rossi at his flat, having stopped on the way to telephone him to ensure he would be at home and expecting her. When she arrived he was outside in the street waiting. There was an air of hopeful expectancy about him as he led her into his flat. The moment they were inside and the door closed he spoke ahead of her. 'You must have decided or you wouldn't be here. Tell me quickly — please,' he begged.

'If you're absolutely certain about it Rossi — I'll leave Madam Moss's immediately.'

He pulled her to him fiercely and hugged her. 'I've never been more certain of anything in my life. Let's celebrate. I'll open a bottle of champagne.'

'Not now please. I must go. I'll have to let her know. I really can't just disappear from the scene without a word.'

'I don't see why not.'

'Well — I have some pay due.'

'Don't go just for that,'

'I really must,' she insisted.

'All right. Who am I to argue with the most beautiful girl in the world.' Obviously elated he crushed her against him again, kissing her eyes her hair, her lips before releasing her. 'I just can't believe my luck. Come on I'll drive you there and wait for you. But stay only long enough to tell her you won't be going back. You don't have to give notice in a place like that.'

'Very well,' she conceded, relieved that a decision had been made and that she had his support.

★ ★ ★

'Tell her and leave instantly. I'll be right here waiting,' he said as he parked his car at a little distance from the Georgian house.

'I shall.'

Now in the sumptuous room she set about making the break in such a way as to be in a position to reinstate herself if necessary. She considered it prudent not to sever ties completely. Rossi had a wife. Situations changed however certain he might feel to the contrary at present. 'I'm going to take a holiday,' she announced to the watery-grey gaze.

Rachael Moss was for once not on her throne in the bay, but seated at her ornately carved desk. 'Holiday!' Fat arms raised slightly and ringed hands spread in response to the news. 'Vot you vont a holiday for already! You hef bin heah only a few veeks!'

Silvie sensed suspicion behind the words and in

the cold eyes. She returned the look with steady calm even though the sight of the fat woman repulsed her. Considering the remarks to be superfluous she remained silent, until Rachael Moss was forced to continue. 'How lonk vill you be gone? Vun veek — two?' By her tone it was clear that she understood a longer break was intended. The question was purely obstructive.

'At this stage I can't tell. But I don't have to account to you for my life away from this house. And I have some pay to come.'

Instantly a placating change came into Rachael Moss's tone, concealing her fury, for she feared the permanent loss of her biggest asset. 'All right then deah. You hef your holiday end come beck.' She was at a disadvantage and didn't like the situation, which if handled unwisely could be even worse if the best looker she'd ever had working for her walked out and never came back. If the girl intended never to return she'd have collected her pay and gone off without a word. But on the other hand, which was very possible, she might be intending to make off with one of the clients. At this thought her anger almost surfaced. It wouldn't be the first time such a case had occurred. Which meant the loss of the client too. This underhand practice was not uncommon in establishments such as hers. In any other instance she would have demanded outright to know the truth of the matter. But this girl was well aware of her own power. Besides, she was too remote and sensitive for such outright talking, and would not tolerate being questioned. There was nothing for it but to wait and hope that the girl's absence was a short one. Afraid to lose touch without trace she said, as she took a sealed envelope from a drawer in her desk and handed it across, 'Leaf me your phone number, or let me know vhere I ken contect you — just in case . . . '

Taking the envelope Silvie cut her short, 'No address and I'm not on the telephone.'

'Come beck es soon es you ken deah. You vill be missed,' her tone was wheedling now.

Silvie made no response to this. As she left the room the telephone rang once before being snatched up by Rachael Moss. 'Vot — who? Evette? Who vonts her? Chinny vonts her to come home? Vait — she is just leafink. I'll call her — wait pliss . . . ' When she went into the hall the front door was closing. Running footsteps outside told her that the gist of the message had been heard and understood When she returned to the telephone the line was dead. Alone now she allowed her annoyance to show. She had hoped to gain some information from the caller. She crossed to stand at the window. As she looked out she heard a car further along the road being driven away. Being at her desk earlier she'd not seen it arrive. Not that she'd recognise any car of visiting clients. Most usually arrived and left by taxi. A few parked their cars further along, never outside the house. Soon enough she'd know if the girl had taken off with a client, he would cease to call. If this were the case she felt pretty certain of the man's identity. Who else but Rossi who had been visiting so often since the girl's arrival.

Fuming she focussed her unseeing eyes on the gaudy flower in the pot beside her and to this she

72

addressed her words. 'I'll cetch up vith them. They von't get avay so easily. I em entitled to sumsink.' She seated herself on her throne in the bay. The drumming of her fingertips on its arms an outward sign of the fury within the mountainous bulk it supported.

★   ★   ★

'Quickly please — take me home. My mother — Stanford Road just off the main avenue.' Silvie was in the car and seated before he could get out and open the passenger door. 'Something's happened. Hurry please.'

Without speaking he switched on the ignition; her urgent tone told him that this was not the time for questions. Common sense suggested that some family message had just been passed to her by Rachael Moss. Until now he'd not known where she lived and still didn't know her real name. Desperately he wanted to be part of her life. Just lately he'd wondered whether she would agree to marry him if he could persuade his wife to divorce him, and he didn't anticipate any resistance to that. He cast a quick sideways glance at her, tense and silent beside him.

Smoothly the car sped along the wide avenue, the speedometer wavering over the limit. He hoped now that he would learn more about her family and her life. Above all he wanted to know the reason why she had chosen to work at the Georgian house when clearly it had been an ordeal for her, he'd seen that from the first evening.

'The next turning please,' she indicated with her hand.

He slowed the car to take the corner and for the first time on the journey he spoke. 'If there is anything at all I can do to help — in any way.' He glanced up at the road name as he turned the car into Stanford Road. At a sign from her he pulled in at the kerb.

'Drop me here please.'

Before he could make the move to open the car door for her she was out. 'Thank you. Please don't wait. I'll phone you just as soon as I can.'

'You may need help. I'll . . . ' His voice trailed off as he watched her hurry along the street, her high heels tapping quickly as she ran the few yards to the house and disappeared inside. Suddenly he felt completely cut off from her, for the moment an outsider. A family crisis had occurred in which he could neither share nor help, yet he was glad to have been of some small practical use. Minutes later he watched the doctor with his Gladstone bag leave the house and drive off.

For a further half hour he sat, but she did not re-appear. He hadn't really expected her to. Several times his eye caught the movement of a curtain at the window of the house outside which he was parked. To linger any longer might harm her reputation since she would have been noticed leaving the car. His hanging about might strike the neighbours as odd. Reluctantly he switched on the ignition, made a U turn, and drove away.

★　★　★

74

The moment she entered the house she knew the worst had happened by the stricken look on Ginny's face and the grave expression on the doctor's. 'Was it her heart, doctor?'

He nodded. 'A sudden thing my dear. It happens that way sometimes.'

As if in answer to her own silent self-reproach she said quietly, 'She seemed quite all right when I left the house earlier.'

'No one can tell when a sudden seizure will happen. You couldn't have known.' With a gesture of sympathy he laid a hand gently on her shoulder. 'Is there anyone you'd like me to call or contact? Someone who could come and stay perhaps for a day or two.'

'No thank you doctor. We'll be all right.' Suddenly her legs felt weak from shock and she seated herself on the stairs, pulling Ginny down with her. Cradling the bright head on her shoulder she rocked her to and fro as if this instinctive and mechanical motion might ease the pressure of grief which had been so suddenly thrust upon them.

For a moment or two the doctor stood looking down on them before saying, 'I'll look in again in the morning to see if I can be of any help. Meanwhile I'm not far away. Call me at any time if you need me.'

'Thank you doctor.'

About to turn to go he paused as if considering, then added, 'Would you like me to ask Maureen Carter to call in? She's a retired nurse, lives locally. A very capable person and always available to assist at such times.'

Silvie nodded agreement.

Quietly he let himself out and closed the front door gently on the two rocking together in silent grief.

★ ★ ★

When Jack Thorndyke gave the message to Rachael Moss he waited just long enough to confirm that there was an Evette in the house then replaced the receiver. By waiting and revealing himself as the caller would have embarrassed Silvie. In addition he'd have had to give the news of her mother's death, which would have been harsh. This way she would be half prepared. For the reason of not wanting to humiliate her he could not offer to collect her in his car. He poured a large measure of whisky, for he too had sustained a shock this evening.

Vainly he tried to tell himself there would be some explanation why Silvie was in that place. The tag of whore could not conceivably be pinned on her. He wanted to cling to the tenuous possibility that Sara Hoskins did actually carry out dressmaking on the premises and that perhaps Silvie did work for her. At the same time he realised that his hope was a feeble one. Otherwise why the acquired name of Evette despite what Ginny had said. That night when he and the boys had looked into the room there had been no evidence of unfinished garments — just the old treadle machine.

Dejected he sat for a long while musing. Then he roused himself and drove to Stanford Road, glad that at least he now knew where to find her. It was, he discovered, a smart middle-class area. He'd half hoped it would not be. Any ordinary part-time job would not cover the price of rents here, in addition to the cost of living for the three of them. The slender hope he'd nursed of retrieving his tarnished angel faded completely.

Near the corner of the road he sat for a long while in his parked car, outside the Congregational Church. Although he longed to go to the house to offer his sympathy and help he was aware that, for the present, he would be imposing on their personal grief. He felt deeply hurt and disappointed that he'd been rejected in favour of the choice she'd made rather than marry him and live in comfort at Baron Wood with her mother and Ginny. Even if she'd accepted his financial help only he'd have been quite happy and expected nothing in return. Just being with her would have been sufficient. He loved her unconditionally, totally, and forever, no matter what. She'd always been reserved. Not one for idle chatter like some girls. Only spoke when she had something to say, even as a child. He knew how she'd always worshipped Ginny and he felt certain that it was for her sake and their mother's that she'd chosen to earn money that way. He could only guess at what cost to her self-esteem.

The evening had turned to deep dusk when he finally turned the car and drove home to Baron Wood

12

Silvie wrote letters to both Mrs Barnes and Mrs Thorndyke to tell them of her mother's death and giving them the time and date of the funeral service, in case they might wish to attend. In order that she might arrange transport she requested a reply.

Having assumed that the telephone call to the Georgian house on the day of Alice's death had been made by Ginny herself, she was as yet unaware that Jack knew about her secret life.

Preoccupied with her grief Ginny had given no more thought to the lost slip of paper or her distracted plea to Jack for help, so had made no mention of it. For the present she could think no further than the empty bed in the silent room upstairs. Never again would she trust God. If there was a God. Certainly she had no intentions ever again of joining in morning assembly prayers at the College. If God existed how could he be considered good! Taking her mother like that — so young. Only greedy, selfish people should die young. Mum had been neither of those things. She had wanted so little. And such simple things too — like seeing the apple tree in blossom. God hadn't even let her do that.

Replies to the letters arrived by the second post next day. Jack too wished to attend and would bring his mother and Mrs Barnes in his car.

Three days after the death of her mother Silvie telephoned the man she still knew only as Rossi. 'My mother has died,' she told him, 'I shan't be able to see you for a while.'

'I'm so sorry to hear that darling. There must be some way I can be of help. May I come to the house?'

'No — please don't call on me. We would rather be alone just for the present. Besides how would I explain you to my sister. Just wait a little while. I'll telephone again soon I promise. Good bye.'

With so much to attend to she had little time to think about him during the days that followed. The death of her mother had brought about changes in the pattern of her daily life.

★ ★ ★

After the funeral Silvie invited Jack, his mother and Mrs Barnes back to the house. Jack had awaited an opportunity to speak with Silvie alone but the chance never arose.

Unaware still that she knew nothing of Ginny's call to him for help he assumed that her present grief kept her incurious as to how he'd managed to trace her. And as the answer to that was not a brief one he hadn't yet decided how he would respond.

Ginny helped Silvie serve sandwiches and tea, during which they made light conversation.

After an hour had passed Mrs Thorndyke rose to leave. 'I think we should be getting back now. We appreciate you writing to us to let us know about Alice and about the funeral service Silvie. It was thoughtful of you considering you were so shocked and upset yourself.'

'Yes thanks for remembering us my dear,' Mrs Barnes said as she too got up from her chair. 'I missed you all when you moved away. I used to look forward to coming in to sit with your mother for a bit of company.'

'Thank you all for coming. It was a comfort to have those who knew Mum around us.' Silvie led the way to the front door.

'Nice house Silvie,' said Mrs Thorndyke. 'I expect you were glad to get away from Queen Street the same as Jack was.'

Silvie nodded. 'Yes it was a lucky find.' She and Ginny saw them out.

'Cheerio Jack.' Ginny reached up and kissed him on the cheek. 'Thanks for coming and bringing your mother and Mrs Barnes. It was so good to see you all again.' She gave both women a warm hug. 'Take care of yourselves.'

Jack touched her lightly under the chin with his fist. 'Chin up soldier.'

Silvie kissed Mrs Barnes and Jack's mother then held her hand out to him. He ached to pull her into his arms and crush her against him. As he stepped aside for the two older women to go through the door he turned back to ask, 'Do you mind if I call again some time? I know how upset you must be and how you'll miss Alice. Sometimes a familiar face helps.'

She saw nothing unusual in his searching gaze.

He'd always looked at her in that way. And although she would have preferred not to give him even the smallest encouragement she could hardly say no without appearing callous and ill-mannered. 'Of course I don't mind Jack. Come to tea one Sunday. I'll telephone you sometime.'

With this he had to be content and hope that she'd remember. With a last lingering look at her face he gave a brief smile and left them at the gate waving as the car moved off.

★　★　★

A week later as she folded the blue angora bed jacket Silvie fluffed reverently at the white swansdown trim and touched its softness against her cheek, regretting the short space of time that her mother had enjoyed its luxury. About to put it away in a drawer she hesitated. How pointless and selfish it would be to keep something so beautiful hidden away to rot unseen, when it could give pleasure to someone else. Remembering the expression on her mother's face and her words on first sight of it — 'It's the most beautiful thing I've ever owned — ' she again knew that the means used to obtain it had been worth the personal cost.

She looked up as Ginny entered the room. 'I've just been thinking that it would be a nice gesture to send the bed jacket to Mrs Barnes. What do you think?'

'Yes I agree, it would be a lovely idea. Mum would approve. I'd like to think of it going to Mrs Barnes. She was always happy to help out and sit with Mum when we needed her. And she's probably never owned anything as pretty in her life.'

'My sentiments exactly. I'll parcel it up and send it to her.'

Ginny had gone to stand at the window and was looking out at the garden. 'The apple tree is in blossom now Silvie.' Her tone was soft and sad. 'Come and see. It's all white. Mum didn't see it after all. It wasn't out in time. She'll never see it now.'

Silvie laid aside the bed jacket and went across to stand beside Ginny at the French window. As she gazed out at the emerging mass of snowy flowers she said, 'She will Ginny. She can see it right now.' And Ginny's brief estrangement from her God ended. Although her stricken heart could doubt a whole world, she never doubted her sister.

13

Late on Sunday night Silvie sat by the dying fire. Ginny had gone to bed two hours before. Now and again she bent to take up the brass-handled poker from the grate and stir life into the pale smokeless embers. The late April day had been cold and windy, like a belated February one arriving out of sequence. She shivered and drew her woollen cardigan closer about her, then again reached for the poker to coax the last remnants of warmth from the collapsed ashes. For two hours she'd been pondering on their altered position. With no reason now to keep her at home during the daytime she could take a job. No longer could she see Rossi in the evenings now that Ginny would be home alone . . . Unless she became a boarder at the College. She considered this aspect. Of course Ginny would first have to be consulted on the matter. Extra money would be required to meet the cost. The fact that the financial support of Rossi would still have to be depended upon had not changed. But she felt greatly relieved that she no longer need sell herself at the Georgian house. With Rossi it was a different matter; like having a lover. Being a man's mistress was infinitely preferable. The fact that she was a little in love with him helped her to accept the situation more easily. The fact that he loved her helped a lot. Even so she would have preferred to call her life her own, to be totally independent. But it was Ginny's life which mattered most of all.

With a last look at the dead ashes she made her way up to bed.

During breakfast next morning she discussed the situation with Ginny. 'I've decided to try Silvester's to see if there's a vacancy now that I can take a daytime job.'

Ginny looked pleased, 'Good. You used to work there — I remember. Seems a long time ago. Nice store.'

'That's right. Family owned. John Silvester manages it. I expect he'll fit me in somewhere.'

'Will it mean that you won't have to work evenings any more at that sewing job.'

To Silvie's relief Ginny didn't pause for an answer to this guilt-evoking question, but continued . . . 'It'd be lovely if you could be at home evenings. Even if a daytime job pays less. I shouldn't mind if I have to leave the College.'

Silvie knew this was untrue. Ginny loved it at Miss Meacher's College and had settled in well, just as the little principal had predicted. 'No need for that Ginny. I've been able to save quite a bit. We'll manage.'

They were silent for a while, then Silvie continued briefly on the subject with a gentle reminder, 'We still have the insurance policy. Mum paid it for years especially for us.' This was an aspect that they'd not, so far, touched upon. Any monetary gain through the death of their mother could not easily be discussed just yet. Which was as well, Silvie thought.

84

The less Ginny knew of the exact modest sum in comparison with their present financial commitments the less she would be likely to question how they'd manage.

14

Wednesday was early closing at Silvester's department store. John Silvester had been only too keen to engage Silvie for the cosmetic department where he considered that she'd be his biggest asset. Even though she had very little need of artificial beauty aids herself he knew that she'd draw attention and encourage sales. As she came out of the staff exit now she saw the waiting Jaguar. Other female assistants watched with a mixture of envy and curiosity as the strikingly handsome middle-aged man go out to open the car door for her.

'Thank you for collecting me. I really could have come to the flat by bus.' She sank back into the soft grey leather comfort and eased off her black patent leather high-heeled court shoes.

'You'll do no such thing.' He switched on the ignition and the car moved smoothly off. 'Would you prefer to have lunch out somewhere or sandwiches at the flat?'

'The flat would be nicest. I feel quite exhausted. Had a busy morning.'

★ ★ ★

When they arrived he said, 'You go and sit down and rest while I fix some lunch.'

'I'd like to freshen up. Rather hot in the store today with the rush on.'

'Go right ahead. Linen cupboard in the hall just outside the bathroom.'

The apartment, in a fashionable block, was luxuriously furnished with quiet good taste. This was her second visit. It occurred to her now that the first time had been on the day of her mother's death.

After she'd changed into clean clothes which she'd especially brought with her, she returned to the deeply carpeted room where he sat waiting on a burgundy moquette chesterfield sofa. Sandwiches and coffee were all ready on an oak side table placed close by. He patted the space next to him.

'Come and tuck in.' He handed a plate to her. 'Today I'm going to tell you about myself and my . . . '

He got no further. In her usual soft tone, which did not detract from the impact of her words, she interrupted him, 'If you so much as begin to tell me anything about your private life I shall walk out, for I'd rather not know.' She paused briefly for her words to sink in then added — 'One thing though, I refuse to go on calling you by that awful tag Rachael Moss labelled you with. Or did you choose it yourself? But no matter now so long as we drop it. No more than your first name please. I meant what I said. Mine is Silvie.'

'Silvie — Silvie — Silver . . . ' He savoured the name. 'It suits you perfectly. Your name couldn't be anything else. I wonder that I didn't know it instinctively.' He smiled and took her free hand to kiss it.

'And that's all I shall tell you about myself.' She

bit into a sandwich. 'This is good! I'm positively starving.'

'A sign of youth. You're very young.'

'And what are you? Old Father Time?'

'Middle-aged.' He smiled ruefully before adding. 'And not starving.'

'A very young middle-age then. Come on — your name please?'

Suddenly she felt lighter at heart than she'd been since the death of her mother. She felt completely comfortable with him now.

'Adam.' He reached for her hand again. 'Let me hear you say it.'

She stopped eating briefly to oblige. 'Adam. I like that. It suits you. Your name couldn't be anything else.'

He laughed aloud. 'Now you're mocking me. I was serious.'

'So am I.'

He rose and went to set the turntable going on the radiogram where a Chopin record was placed ready. He re-seated himself and sat watching her.

'Please eat something to keep me company,' she handed across the plate.

'Very well.' He took a sandwich. For a while they were silent, listening to the music. She had become his whole existence. But he was nothing if not realistic, and knew it was inevitable that someone would come along, soon most likely, and snatch her away. Someone younger than himself, and free. Again and again he'd wondered if she would marry him if he got a divorce. For whatever reason — money — he didn't care. That seemed to be the thing she wanted most at present. He had to know; he couldn't bear not knowing. Yet he didn't want her to think it a condition of their relationship, so best not rush; lead up to the idea gradually. 'Why not give up working and stay at home? Or even here during the daytime. You had decided to spend your evenings here when you severed your ties with the Moss woman.'

'Yes I know that Adam. It was possible then. The situation at home has changed. I have no reason to stay in the house during the day now . . . now that . . . ' What she left unsaid she knew he would understand — the words were still painful. 'I don't think it would be right or fair of me to become totally dependent on you financially — not fair to you I mean.'

'You'd make me very happy if you would. I'm relieved to get you away from that place. It was agony for me every time I had to leave you there.'

She put a finger to his lips 'Don't let's talk about that any more. I want to forget.'

He kissed her finger and grasped her slim wrist to kiss her palm before resting it against his cheek. 'And now I aim to get you away from Silvester's.'

'If I stayed at home each day how would I explain my income?'

'Explain to whom?' he coaxed softly.

With a fragment of laughter she replied, 'You can't catch me out that way.'

'Then tell me just one thing — How many people are dependent on you now?'

'Just one, beside myself.'

'I see,' he gave a short laugh. 'I thought there

must be at least half a dozen!'

He looked serious now and did not release her hand as he asked. 'Do you like me a little Silvie?'

She regarded his handsome features: the dark hair — now touched with grey at the temples and still very thick; dark brows above deep blue eyes, sound even teeth, and dependable shoulders. He was most girls dream at one time or another.

'Of course I do Adam. I should not be here otherwise.'

'Enough to marry me if I get a divorce?'

She shook her head. 'I'm sorry Adam. I would never be party to breaking up your home life.'

'I've already told you Silvie, my wife doesn't give a damn about me other than to run the business.'

'Makes no difference. There must be others in your family to be considered.'

'Then allow me to tell you about them. Please. Then you might change your mind.'

'No Adam. No divorce on my account.' She kissed him on his cheek. 'And it's nice to be calling you by your real name.'

And with that, at least for the time being, he had to be content.

15

Silvie raised her eyes from the book on her lap as she became aware that she'd been turning the pages without taking in a word. Ginny was lying on the rug before the fire gazing into the flames. An open book was on the floor beside her. There was an unusual pallor to her skin these days and dark circles framed her sad amber eyes. The time was mid-afternoon on a wet grey Sunday. For two days the rain had not ceased. The house had lacked her effervescent chatter since the death of their mother. Silvie knew she was nursing her grief inwardly and felt powerless to help. An idea suddenly presented itself.

'Why not invite a friend from the College for a weekend?' she ventured. 'One of the boarders perhaps who might appreciate a couple of days of home-life. There must be somebody who'd like a break and a change of scene.'

With a start Ginny turned. 'Oh — I thought you were reading.' Briefly she considered the idea. 'Yes — would be nice. But surely you'd hate having some stranger about the house just at present?'

'Not at all. I think it would be a good idea. Company is what we both need right now.'

A faint spark of the old Ginny flickered as she warmed to the idea. 'Perhaps I could invite Jojo. Remember? I've mentioned her quite often. My best friend. I know you'd like her.'

'Yes — you've mentioned that name. What's the nick name short for — Josephine?'

'Joanne. But only I and her brother Mark are allowed to call her Jojo. It's always been his pet name for her you see. She adores him. He's quite a bit older — about twenty seven or eight I believe. They live in the country. Much too far for her to go home except for the hols. A place called Kings Meadow. Always talking about it, and her two horses. Oh and her brother of course; not sure which she loves best — him or the horses.' Her voice had become quite animated and she gave a brief laugh. The spark flashed again reflecting her old self. Noting this Silvie felt her own spirits lift. 'Well that's settled then. What about this coming weekend. No time like the present.'

Before Ginny could answer a knock came at the front door. They looked at each other in surprise. They never had visitors and no tradesmen called on Sundays. Silvie tensed. Surely Adam wouldn't call when she'd expressly asked him not to! Ginny jumped up from the hearthrug. 'I'll go.'

Silvie relaxed as she heard Ginny greet the caller. 'Hello Jack! What a surprise. Come on in. Silvie was just saying we could do with some company right now. Let me hang up your coat.'

Moments later Jack Thorndyke followed Ginny into the room. His usual self-possessed manner appeared strained, as though unsure of his reception, since he was not expected.

'Hello Silvie. Just thought I'd pay a visit to see how you both are. Hope you don't mind.'

'Not at all Jack. Nice to see you. Come and sit by the fire.'

Jack seated himself. 'Not very friendly weather today. Throwing buckets down out there.'

'Yes. I'm surprised that you came out in such weather.'

'Well it makes no odds in the car. It's worth coming out to see you both.'

Ginny had resumed her place on the hearth rug. Silvie said, 'I'll go and make some tea.' At the door she turned to add, 'Ginny's right — we do need some company. It really is good to see an old face right now.'

As she was closing the door behind her Jack called, 'Not so much of the old.'

Ginny giggled, and Jack felt more relaxed. Despite the repartee Silvie sensed a slight restraint in his manner; not quite his usual breezy mode. Perhaps because he'd had to visit uninvited after all, having not had the promised telephone call, she thought as she set about making tea and cutting cake.

On her return to the room she paused to rest the tray on the hall table while she opened the door. About to reach for the door knob her hand hovered as she heard Ginny saying — 'By the way Jack I never did get around to thanking you for tracing Sara Hoskins for me the evening when Mum died, and for making that phone call to her. When you were here on the day of the funeral I was too upset to give it any thought. I don't suppose I made much sense to you when I phoned to ask for help. At the time I was so shocked and desperate to get Silvie home. I'd lost the slip of paper with her phone number on — it fell into the fire. It's just as well I remembered the name though. I never gave much thought to it afterwards. I never did tell Silvie. Seemed no point afterwards really. Only reopens old wounds. We still don't talk about it yet you see. Makes us too sad. I think a lot about Mum though. I know Silvie does too.'

Silvie's shocked hand was still poised above the door knob while the full implications of the overheard words sank in. Sara Hoskins was not listed in the directory; the telephone number was under the name of Rachael Moss. The knowledge that Jack must have at some time visited the Georgian house, how else could he have heard of Sara Hoskins, did not concern her. But the fact that he now knew of her own connections there did. She wished that Ginny had told her. Although being pre-warned would not have helped the present situation. Jack could not have been prevented from turning up out of the blue like this. Useless to speculate now on what might or might not have been if Ginny had thought to tell her.

It obviously accounted for the slight difference in Jack's manner. She had been too preoccupied to notice it on the day of the funeral. She took a deep breath to sustain herself — she had to enter the room. As she did so with the laden tray she felt her face burning. She did not look at him, and hoped he wouldn't stay long, and also that Ginny would not speak of it or ask any awkward questions in his presence. Feeling ill at ease she served the tea. Although she did not love Jack Thorndyke she did care about his opinion and respect for her.

Constantly she felt his eyes on her but would not meet them. Once she glanced up briefly to try to gauge his thoughts, but saw only, as always, that his eyes clearly revealed his feelings for her. It seemed that nothing would change those.

Unaware that she'd overheard Ginny's words Jack was thankful that she'd not been told about his part in tracing her that evening. Nothing in the world could ever make him cease to love her. He knew that what she'd done had been for her mother and Ginny with no thought for herself. He still wanted her as much as ever. And would never give up hoping. He was determined to call on her again, invited or not. And next time he would make an opportunity to speak with her alone. If she still refused to marry him he would once more offer both herself and Ginny a home with him, with no strings attached. Now that she no longer had her mother to nurse she might reconsider. He'd ask her again very soon.

He became aware that Ginny was speaking to him 'Sorry Ginny love what were you saying?'

'How are your mother and Mrs Barnes?'

'Mum's well enough considering. Her chest plays up a bit in this weather. Trouble is she will leave that front door open in all weathers! Don't see much of Mrs Barnes though. I don't visit Mum quite so often these days. I'm kept pretty busy with one thing and another. Away a fair bit too.'

A brief silence followed. Silvie had spoken little since bringing in the tea. 'Why don't you both let me take you out for a drive in the country next weekend?'

Before Ginny could accept, as she guessed she might, Silvie replied hastily, 'Sorry Jack but Ginny is inviting a friend from the College to stay. Thanks all the same.'

She was glad of this genuine excuse to decline his offer even though Ginny hadn't actually got as far as agreeing to any definite time: Jack had arrived before the idea had been finalised.

'Some other time then perhaps?' he pressed.

'I'll telephone sometime,' she answered, knowing that she never would.

'Promise?'

'I usually am very busy at weekends Jack, as you'll appreciate, being at work all week. I'm back at Silvester's full time.' This, she thought, would at least tell him that she was no longer associated with the Georgian house. 'I will try to call you one day.' Again the lie. But there seemed no other way to stop him asking without hurting his feelings too much. She hoped with this he'd be satisfied and leave soon.

With this half promise Jack had to be content for the present. It had been a great relief to him to learn that she was no longer connected with the Moss woman. But only a fool would fail to wonder how she was still managing to keep Ginny at the expensive school.

At length, to her great relief, he stood up to leave, 'Mustn't overstay my welcome,' he said smiling.

At the front door he held her hand as he said, 'I'd like to have a talk with you again some time soon Angel. Don't be too long in calling me. I can pick you up at work any Wednesday lunchtime — I know it's early closing day. Or any time at all after you finish work. Just say the word and I'll be there.'

Meeting his eyes now she saw the same unchanging devotion and wished it were not so for his sake. He was wasting his life in vain waiting. 'Goodbye Jack. Thank you for calling in.'

Ginny reached up to kiss his cheek. 'Cheerio Jack. It's been lovely seeing you again. Give our love to your mother and Mrs Barnes.'

'I'll do that Ginny love. Be seeing you.'

From the doorway they waved him off. It was still raining hard. Being unaware that only pure chance memory of a brief and innocent call at the Georgian house accounted for Jack's knowing how and where to contact Sara Hoskins that evening, Silvie quite unnecessarily thanked providence for having spared her the ultimate shame and embarrassment while in the employ of Madam Moss, for Jack could well afford her highest fees.

16

Ginny brought Joanne Pemberton home from College with her on Friday afternoon.

They arrived at the house just ahead of Silvie. True to her style Joanne voiced her thoughts on first sight of Silvie as she came in the front door. Both girls had rushed into the hall to greet her.

'Hello Silvie. I've been simply dying to meet you. Ginny's always going on about how gorgeous you are. And it's true.' She spoke with no trace of self-consciousness as she delivered this verbal appraisal.

'Nice to meet you Joanne. Thank you for the compliment.' Silvie laughed lightly to pass the comment off. 'I'm so glad you could come.'

Silvie took to Joanne Pemberton on sight and thought her just the kind of company Ginny needed, especially at present, and very like Ginny herself. They had the same warm affectionate personality, lively, frank, and self-assured. It was not surprising they got on so well.

Later, as they were eating dinner, Joanne asked, 'Can you both come and stay at Briarwood during the hols Silvie?'

'Briarwood?'

'That's the name of Jojo's house in the country,' Ginny explained.

'We keep horses. Do you ride?' Joanne added, as if this might prove an incentive.

'Afraid not. Never thought much about it, or had the opportunity. Thank you for the invitation, but I have no holiday due except bank Monday.'

Joanne looked disappointed. 'Oh what a pity.'

'But Ginny may come by all means. It would be good for her to have a spell in the country.'

'Oh I couldn't go off and leave you here all by yourself, Silvie,' Ginny protested. 'Otherwise I'd love to come Jojo.'

'I wouldn't have time to be lonely, I'd be much too busy. At work all week and plenty to occupy the evenings and weekends. Besides I have to make a start on our dresses for the garden party. There's really nothing on the racks at Silvester's that I'd wear. So old-fashioned!'

'Then it's settled,' decided Joanne before Ginny could demur further. 'Next term hols it is. I'll write to Mother. But remember Silvie, if you can sneak a weekend some time do please come. I want you to meet my brother Mark. He's twenty-eight, very handsome, and not married. He'll be bowled over when he sees you.' This enthusiastic schoolgirl matchmaking idea was so transparent that Silvie smiled despite her secret thoughts. For now that she was in a position to consider marriage to a man who was free and could support both herself and Ginny she had forfeited the right to do so.

★ ★ ★

They had arranged that Ginny would spend the half-term holiday week at Briarwood, the Pemberton's country home in Kings Meadow. During her

99

stay she wrote home twice. From the contents and tone of the letters Silvie knew that her young sister was on the fast road to recovery from her grief.

The house is fabulous! In lots of acres, she wrote. *I've just asked Jojo how many but she says she can't remember, and is not sure if she ever knew. She's teaching me to ride. We're going to ride into the village to post this letter when it's finished. I've now met her brother Mark. He came home especially for the weekend. He's incredibly good looking! I'm not exaggerating! Nice too. What a combination! He says he's looking forward to meeting you some time and if you're as dazzling as we make out he'll have to wear dark glasses or you'll blind him. Jojo's mother is partially paralysed. Strange that don't you think? I mean the coincidence — like Mum was — only due to different reason. Apparently she was injured in a fall from a horse. Not one of the horses they keep now though. Must be awful for her because she used to ride a lot, bred horses too. I think maybe she still does, not sure about that. Can't ask Jojo, she's just gone out to the stables to saddle our horses. She says her mother hasn't been quite the same since the accident and that she's a bit vague at times. But I suspect that's because her mind is always on the horses. She spends a great deal of her time in the stables even though she can no longer ride. She gets about in a motorised wheelchair. The fall injured her spine. As yet I haven't met*

Jojo's father. He works in the city. Jojo says he'll probably come home before our holiday is over. Dora Glasspool the housekeeper also had some kind of accident, she was kicked in the head by one of the race horses. She used to ride a lot and was employed here to look after the horses. I think it happened in the stables a long time ago when Jojo was very young. Dora has been employed in the house ever since she recovered. She doesn't live in, although sometimes she stays over at weekends. She has a cottage in the village. Apparently the accident affected Dora's mind a bit and Jojo's mother felt responsible and kept her employed at the house. Although never again to help with the horses. I hope you're not too lonely on your own. I expect you've already started on our dresses. Still plenty of time before the garden party though. Mrs Pemberton can't come to that so Jojo's father or Mark will attend instead. They take turns each year apparently. I hope it's Mark's turn this year. I know you'll like him. By the way my horse Midge is very placid and I wear one of Jojo's riding hats so don't worry about me. Mark will be driving us to the station to catch the early train back to college on Monday morning, 5 am! He's dropping us off on his way back to the city where he works. See you on Monday when you get in from work. Jojo's now back from the stables and sends her love. Lots of love from — dere luvly Ginny.

Silvie smiled as she read the deliberate misspelt last words, which were meant as a reminder of an oft recalled little message that four year old Ginny had enclosed with a small Christmas gift to her. The term 'dear lovely Ginny' had been the pet name Silvie had used for her small sister around that time. Still smiling she refolded the letter. Ginny's natural humour had returned. Without doubt she was on the mend.

★ ★ ★

As was the usual practice now Adam collected her from Silvester's and drove her back to his flat in the city. Against her protests he had been over generous when, with quiet insistence, he had put a cheque for a large sum into her handbag. 'I refuse to put a price on loving you. And I don't want you worrying over money matters. If you need more — or anything at all — you must let me know. Promise?'

'Is this to try and tempt me to give up my job?'

'Of course,' he laughed, 'But not a condition. Now about this promise — you haven't answered me yet.'

'Yes — yes of course I promise. But I really shan't be in need of anything at all. You have given me much more than I need.'

Satisfied he smiled, 'And now we are going to Alberto's, my favourite place for lunch. It's just around the corner so we can walk. Then we'll come back here for the rest of the afternoon and listen to the music,' he drew her into his arms to kiss her before adding, 'and make love.'

She put on her shoes which she'd kicked off on entering. She liked to feel the soft thick carpet under her feet. 'All ready.'

As they walked to Alberto's she asked. 'Don't they miss you at the office on Wednesday afternoons?'

'No. I have an excellent second in command. I spend more than enough time there anyway. Even sometimes at weekends when I've nothing better to do. As I've said, I don't get home very often and there's little else to occupy my time when you're not with me.' He drew her arm through his. 'I do wish you'd let me see you sometimes at weekends.'

'I can't Adam. I have commitments at home.'

'Tell me about them?'

'There's so little to tell, except that I'm responsible for the welfare of my younger sister and that I love her very much.'

'Thank you for telling me that. I'm content to know that at least there's no man in your life besides me.' But for how long? he wondered secretly.

⋆   ⋆   ⋆

'How would you like to board at the College during the week? Home every weekend of course. We can afford it now.'

'Really Silv!' Ginny looked surprised. 'But you'd be alone in the evenings. I mean one week's not so bad, like when I stayed at Briarwood, but you'd be lonely on your own every evening with no one to talk to.'

Silvie laughed. 'No one to listen to you mean. Just think of it this way; I have plenty to occupy the time, dinner to prepare, housework, sewing. I wouldn't have time to feel lonely. And it would save you two hours travelling each day. The important consideration is whether or not you like the idea.'

'Of course I do, and Jojo would be ecstatic! But the cost! Are you certain?'

'Absolutely. We can afford it. With the policy and the money I've saved — no problem honestly. So we'll consider it settled. You and Joanne can spend the weekends here, if she'd like to'.

'Oh she would — she would! I know it.'

'I'll write the necessary letters to Miss Meacher then.'

17

Long blood-red fingernails drummed on the arms of the throne-like chair in the bay window. Rachael Moss sat fuming on the fact that she had never been able to discover the real identity of the man whom she'd labelled Rossi. For her own convenience she was obliged to allocate aliases to the clients in order to identify them when they phoned. A business of this nature could not be run with all regular clients named Smith or Jones. Naturally they expected utmost discretion, no names or questions, but as far as she herself was concerned this was a sham. Very few clients had visited the house without some clue to their true identity being in her possession before they left the premises. Downstairs the hall coat-stand invited the removal of topcoats, the pockets of which she searched with swift expertise. A second coat-stand on the upper landing further encouraged the removal of jackets for comfort. It was the pockets of these which disclosed most of the information, such as business cards, club passes, driving licences and the like. It was Sampson who carried out the pocket searches on the upper landing. But never once had the man Rossi trusted his jacket to the discretion of the coat-stand upstairs, and his divested topcoat in the hall downstairs had never revealed more than gloves or a handkerchief.

Much of the acquired information was entered in

a special book which she kept locked in a drawer of her desk. There had been occasions when some piece of information entered had proved useful. If a girl made off with a client, to be set up as his private mistress, she had the means at her disposal to trace them. They were not let off scot-free. A little compensation was in order to offset the loss of both girl and client. After all she had done the touting. Hours she'd spent sitting around in cocktail bars and hotel lounges when she could have been in her own comfortable rooms with all her lovely things around her.

In addition to the fruits disclosed by the pockets she had accumulated a vast wad of press cuttings and photographs from the society pages of both local and national newspapers and magazines. Often she sifted through these to keep in touch with the current social scene of the higher society, with its attendant gossip. Most of her clients were from these circles. High incomes, low morals, and with the need for discretion. It gave her a great sense of power and satisfaction to contemplate on some of the socially prominent personages which her scarlet and gold cards had enticed to the Georgian House. She made it her business, whenever possible, to keep herself informed and up to date on their private lives, which on the whole were often not so private.

On the few occasions over the years when she'd claimed compensation for her losses it had been in a subtle manner. No verbal threat of blackmail, but always a hint in the form of a letter addressed to their real identity and to their place of business or government office, and marked private and confidential. In these contacts she merely stated that a certain figure would be acceptable to compensate for her loss.

Always she'd been lucky and they'd obliged, probably having decided that, all costs considered, they had the best end of the bargain.

All her girls were socially compatible, and hand picked from those who presented themselves to work for her. Most were from higher social level backgrounds, wanting independence, some merely out for kicks or adventure. Some were models or ex beauty queens. Some had, for one reason or another cut themselves off, or been cut off, from their families. After engaging them she never asked their business since her main interest was centred on the clients. But some of the girls liked to talk about themselves and her ears were always receptive.

But she had never known what to make of the girl whom she felt certain had made off with the client Rossi. That cool confident manner, and total lack of coarse fibre which showed in some of the other girls despite their backgrounds. She was like no other girl who'd ever come to work at the house. Always distant and uncommunicative. Barely a word all the while she'd been at the house. Even when she'd collected her pay envelope she'd given only a nod in acknowledgment; always arriving and leaving with quiet dignity, no ribald remarks flung over her shoulder like most of the others on the way out. Madam Moss did not take well to losing a girl like that. Those incredible looks had represented more value than the lost client himself. And he had paid highly to keep her to himself those evenings even though an exorbitant price tag had been attached to her from the start. Compensation would be high indeed if she ever managed to trace him. And if she didn't it wouldn't be for lack of trying.

18

For the girls at MISS MEACHER'S COLLEGE FOR YOUNG LADIES the garden party was the most awaited yearly event, enhanced by the fact that it immediately preceded the long summer holidays. It took place on the last Sunday in July. If this fell on the 31st, which was the official 'breaking up day' as the girls termed it, they were permitted to leave with their parents after the party. When the 31st did not fall on a Sunday, as was the case this year, the boarders were permitted to leave with their parents for convenience, to save these a return journey to the College to collect them just for the sake of a day or so. If the weather was unfavourable the party was held in the Great Hall where the double doors would be thrown open for the occasion, allowing those who would chance wet feet to wander out in the grounds if the rain cleared. The main purpose of these parties was to enable parents and teachers to meet and — Miss Meacher cherished the hope — discuss the progress of their offspring. Most however seemed perfectly content in the belief that the prestige behind the name of the College was sufficient to stand the girls in good stead regardless of their academic progress or ability.

This year the last Sunday turned out to be a warm summer blue one. For the occasion the girls wore silky dresses.

For this special weekend Ginny had stayed over at

the College in order to lend a hand with the party preparations. With her bright hair she was noticeably visible in jade green taffeta.

Dressed in summer blue crepe-de-chine and wearing a picture hat of pale cream lacy straw trimmed with a band of blue ribbon, and wearing cream leather high-heeled sling-backs Silvie entered the grounds. As she came through the big wrought iron gates heads turned and eyes lingered.

Almost instantly she saw Ginny and Joanne hurrying towards her. Between them they appeared to be pulling a tall fair young man by the arms, as if by great restraint they held back from breaking into a run. Running was considered unladylike at Miss Meacher's and strictly against the rules. With typical humour Ginny had once remarked, 'In the case of fire I daresay it would be permissible to run.'

The little principal herself was also making her way towards Silvie. The girls and the young man arrived at her side first. In a glow of excitement the girls each spoke at the same time as with equal pride they made the introductions.

'Silvie meet my brother Mark.'

'Mark this is my sister Silvie.'

Attempting to cover his surprise Mark Pemberton held out his hand and smiled, showing perfect white teeth. 'My pleasure Silvie.'

Silvie shook his hand, 'Nice to meet you Mark.'

As Miss Meacher reached them she spoke and the girls and Silvie turned towards her. The eyes of Mark Pemberton remained on Silvie.

'I'm so glad you could come Miss Marsh. May I say how very nice you look.'

Gracefully Silvie accepted the compliment, 'Thank you.'

'I've already met Mr Pemberton today,' continued Miss Meacher. 'We'll all have a chat later.' She glanced at the two girls who were now holding onto Silvie's arms possessively, and smiled in approval, 'I can see you'll be well attended.' Then she bustled off to greet and mingle.

Incessantly the girls talked for the next few minutes, until Joanne announced — 'Afraid we'll have to leave you two together for a while. It's our turn to serve refreshments for the next fifteen minutes. You'll keep each other company until we get back.'

'That sounds like an order little sister — I hope.' Mark Pemberton gave a light laugh.

'Of course it is, and I second it,' said Ginny as the girls hurried off giggling happily.

'At last! Now I can get a word in edgewise. How those two can chatter! Now firstly I'd like to endorse Miss Meacher's compliment, although an understatement as I'm sure she was well aware. You look much more than just very nice.'

'Thank you.' When he continued to stare at her she added, 'Shall we move on?'

'Oh yes — yes of course.' As they walked he continued, 'Somehow I expected you to have auburn hair like Ginny. But you're the sun and the moon. Yours so light, hers so fiery.'

'We've never been compared to the sun and the moon before. Are you a poet?'

'No indeed. I wish I were. Although I don't believe a poet could do justice to you with mere words.' He smiled down at her.

Suddenly they were surrounded by tray-bearing girls offering sandwiches, cakes and tea or lemonade. For the girls these two were the object of attention for the rest of the afternoon. As they helped themselves from the trays they were each aware of this close scrutiny. They detached themselves eventually and continued walking around the grounds. He was a talkative companion, while she, as usual, spoke little. Although she thought a great deal; mostly about Ginny and how happily she had settled in at the College. As she glanced about her she felt contented. This was what she had wanted for Ginny. Queen Street could only have dragged her down like a millstone. This was the end that justified the means.

Continually they found girls at their side offering refreshments. Every now and then Mark Pemberton would take her by the elbow to try to dodge them, as at this moment. Laughing he steered her forward. 'I see more tray-bearing hostesses making a beeline for us. Let's try to lose them. I really couldn't look at another cake or sandwich right now. Even though I hate to spoil their fun.'

Amused she allowed him to guide her through the crowd. 'I can only agree. They do seem to be over-enthusiastic with the fruits of their labours. I expect seeing a handsome young man in such close proximity in the all girls College grounds has gone to their heads and sent them off balance a bit.'

He laughed again, 'Now you know that's not the reason why we've been singled out for so much attention. You're the attraction.'

'It's probably a combination of both. We're closer to their ages than any of the other visitors here, and that's a novelty for them.' She couldn't recall ever feeling so carefree and happy. It was hard to be otherwise in his company. And the weather was so perfect.

Eventually they were rejoined by Ginny and Joanne. 'Phew! We've been caught up in the rush,' Joanne greeted them. 'Had to go and make more sandwiches. We hope you've been enjoying yourselves.'

'I'm not surprised you had to make more sandwiches. I believe I must have eaten most of the first batch.' Mark Pemberton said.

Ginny said, 'Yes we noticed that you were the star attractions. We'll be the most popular girls in the school for a while.'

Three hours later as they were about to leave Mark Pemberton asked, 'May I drive you home Silvie?'

'It would be terribly out of your way.'

'Excellent. I fancy a nice long drive. Quite apart from which you can't possibly know that it would be out of my way at all.' He smiled, having taken her reply as acceptance in any case.

'Didn't you come here from Kings Meadow?'

'No indeed. I came straight from my flat in the city. And as I don't yet know the area in which you live I can't say how long a drive I can look forward to.'

'And as I don't know where your flat is I can't say either. But my home is not all that far from the city.' Silvie caught sight of Miss Meacher looking their way. 'I think we should go and say goodbye to our hostess before we leave.'

'Yes indeed. I'm very much indebted to her.'

'I trust you've had a pleasant day,' the little principal beamed at them as they approached her. 'And I do hope you didn't find the girls too tiresome pursuing you so much. I couldn't help seeing.'

'I didn't notice,' Mark Pemberton lied with a dazzling smile. 'And I can't remember a day which I've enjoyed more.'

'The same goes for me too Miss Meacher. I've had a very enjoyable afternoon. Thank you so much.'

Miss Meacher watched them walk slowly out of the grounds. A smile lingered on her lips. Didn't need second sight to sense that the seeds of a budding romance had been sown between those two in the garden today.

'Thank you for the offer of a lift.' Silvie settled herself in the soft plush seat. 'I daresay I'd have missed the only bus available around this time of day on Sundays.'

'My pleasure.' he smiled.

'Joanne could have left today with you, considering the distance to Kings Meadow. There are concessions about that at end of term.'

'Yes I know. I could have driven her home to give her an additional day or so but she wasn't bothered this time around. Told me she wanted to stay over because of Ginny. They seem very attached.'

'Yes they do. Ginny usually comes home weekends but stayed this time to help with preparations. Do you go home at weekends as a general rule?'

'Very seldom when Jojo's not there. My flat is not far from the offices. I must admit though it does get rather boring at times on the weekends. During the week I take work home from the office. I read a lot too.'

Like most people in the company of a non-talker he spoke a great deal as they drove. Silvie, as usual, said little, speaking mainly in response to his questions or viewpoints. Small talk had never been a strong point with her, she considered it meaningless idle chatter and wondered why people felt the compulsion to talk. Companionable silences that left a person free to think and made no demands on attention were preferable.

'The countryside is lovely. Quite a picturesque drive.'

'Yes it is rather. I must admit I seldom come this way. Once every two years in fact. Father came last end of term party. We take turns you see. Mother claims that she can't make it. She's confined to a wheelchair. Even if she weren't I doubt that she'd take the trouble to attend. Unless they were putting on a horse show, and even then only thoroughbreds.'

She noted that he laughed a lot and had a great sense of humour. So much like Ginny's. When they arrived at Stanford Road he got out to open the car door for her. Then he stood gazing at the house. 'So this is where my little sister spends her weekends nowadays. She often telephones me at the office. She told me about her visits.'

Not to invite him in after the fairly long journey

would be ill-mannered. Quite apart from the fact that he would naturally like to see the house where his sister stayed as a guest so frequently. 'Would you like to come in for some tea or coffee?'

'Delighted. Thank you.' By his eager response he had obviously hoped to be asked.

While she went to remove her hat he stood at the French window looking out at the garden. A moment later she reappeared, 'Tea or coffee?'

'Tea please if you're not short on rations. About time it came off — dashed war's been over three years.'

'I agree. And no — I'm not short. I drink coffee mostly. Dare I ask — would you like a sandwich or cake?' At his expression she giggled. She could read his thoughts. He wanted to say yes in order to delay his departure and at the same time was wondering if he could really manage more food.

He laughed with her. 'I'd best take things one at a time. Just tea for now.'

She went off to the kitchen. When she returned she found him comfortably seated in an armchair. While she poured tea he watched in silence. When she handed the cup across he asked, 'When have the girls planned Ginny's next stay at Briarwood?'

'Wednesday after bank holiday.'

'Why don't you come with her?'

'Thanks for the invitation but I work and have no time off other than Bank Monday.'

'Pity. Jojo likes me to be home weekends when she's there. Although with Ginny for company now she won't depend on me so much. I have promised to be home on Bank Holiday though. I shall look forward to the peace and quiet. Don't care overmuch for the city.' He sipped his tea before continuing, 'Why not just come for the bank Sunday or Monday then? Still plenty of time to arrange things.'

'It's kind of you to ask, but Ginny and I have already made some arrangements. In any case I'm sure your parents wouldn't appreciate a complete stranger visiting at such short notice.'

'I can assure you that it wouldn't make the slightest difference to them. Perhaps you'll consider some other time then. I hope you'll make it soon though.'

Until this moment she hadn't seen him look so serious, and she felt bound to say, 'I do have to work until five o'clock on Saturdays, so the weekends for me really means only Sundays. I work at Silvester's department store.'

'Then it's time you left Silvester's. You should not be a prisoner for six days a weeks.'

'Only five and a half actually. Early closing Wednesdays.'

'Very well, just Sunday it will have to be then. It doesn't leave much time and we'd have to make a very early start.'

She smiled submission, 'I'll see what can be arranged.'

He looked satisfied at this and sipped his tea again before adding, 'You will allow me to collect Ginny from here and drive her to the station on Wednesday?'

'It would be terribly out of your way. We can so easily get a taxi.'

'Not at all. In fact I insist.'

'Very well. If you insist. It's awfully kind of you.' Why not? she thought, just this once.

He looked pleased. 'And I shall keep you to your promise about a visit to Kings Meadow.'

'Half promise,' she corrected

'Very well — if you must dilute it. A half promise is better than no promise. And please don't say I'm kind. My motives are purely selfish I assure you.' He put down his empty cup.

'Would you like another? Or perhaps you may be ready now for a sandwich.'

'I'd like more tea please and maybe just one sandwich.'

She knew that his ready acceptance was merely to delay departure and not due to recovered appetite. She smiled to herself as she went into the kitchen.

He followed her out to watch and asked, 'Will you come out to dinner with me one evening?'

As she made the sandwich she considered this. With Ginny now boarding at the College her evenings were virtually free. On two of these, in addition to Wednesdays, she saw Adam who was constantly pressing her to see him more often. But one evening out with Mark Pemberton — why not? 'Very well. Thank you.'

He followed her back into the living room where she placed the sandwich and coffee on a side table near his chair 'Will six thirty be all right? Shall we say Tuesday?'

'Tuesday six thirty will be fine.' She did not see Adam on Tuesdays as a rule.

An hour later as he was leaving he held his hand

out to her, 'Thank you for a most enjoyable day. I'm so glad it was my turn this year for the party. Father said it was alive with old dowagers last year. I didn't notice any today. Truth is I didn't notice anyone after you arrived. The grounds might well have been swarming with gorillas for all I know.'

At this idle humour, so like Ginny's, she laughed. 'You do say absurd things.'

He held on to her hand, his face taking on a more serious aspect.

'Thank you for the lift home,' she said quickly, hoping he'd release her hand.

He kissed it first. 'My pleasure I assure you.' Then he stepped aside for her to open the front door.

At the gate he turned for a last lingering look before saying, 'Tuesday six thirty then.' With a brief wave he got into his car and drove away.

She stood at the gate and watched until the car turned the corner. Doubts were already nagging at her, questioning the wisdom of the arrangements she had made for Tuesday, and even more so the half promise to visit his home, which was encouraging something that should have ended at the College gates.

⋆ ⋆ ⋆

On the evenings spent with Adam he always called at the house at around seven o'clock. Most times they went out to dinner. Sometimes a popular restaurant out in the country. At times, less often, they went to see a film or show.

This evening she said, 'I thought it might be nice

to stay home for once. I've managed to get two fillet steaks. I've grilled them ready and they're in the oven keeping hot.'

'Sounds delightful darling.'

She'd been lucky about the steaks. A pretty face worked miracles at the butchers. When dinner was over and the dishes cleared they sat side by side on the settee. He gave a deep sigh, 'Pure domestic bliss!' He turned her face towards him. 'I wish you'd marry me Silvie. I love you so much. I can't bear to be away from you. Life would be nothing without you now. Please Silvie — say you will. I know I could get a divorce easily enough.' He pulled her into his arms and buried his face in her hair. 'Please my darling.'

She steeled herself against his pleas. 'No Adam. I won't change my mind. Divorce takes too long, causes too much scandal, and above all hurts too many people.'

'Oh Silvie — Silvie! I've told you so often — my wife wouldn't give a damn. I could buy a house in the country somewhere, although not so far that I couldn't get home every day. It would be wonderful, and your dependent would have two guardians.'

'I know it all sounds perfect Adam but you have others in your family to consider. Even if they are older their lives still get upset.' As he was about to answer this she stopped him quickly. 'No Adam. Don't tell me. I'd rather not know about your home life. Let's be content as we are.'

He took her by the shoulders. 'Then I insist on telling you this much. My first child — now grown up — was conceived because my wife required an heir to the family business. My second, and last, because I forced my unwanted attentions on her. Believe me it was for the last time. She never did have any interest in me that way, or any other man either for that matter.'

Puzzled she asked, 'Then why . . . ?'

'Why did she marry me — why did I marry her? I worked for her father who owned the business and he lacked a male heir. He considered me a good substitute so long as I married his daughter and became part of the family. Not quite heir though. She is still that. But I own half share in the business. The house is in her name only.'

'I'm sorry that your marriage is an unhappy one Adam. But, for the reasons I've given, I won't marry you. You're generous and considerate and I love you for those things. But I have someone else to consider — someone who always comes first in my life — above all else.' She saw the question in his eyes and added, 'And it's not a man.'

He cupped her face in his hands. 'Oh Silvie — you're my life now. I want to keep you with me forever. My love. My sweet love.'

His lips moved softly across her face and neck as he spoke. But even as he declared his intense feelings he secretly acknowledged the inevitability that she would some day be taken away from him by someone younger — someone free.

★ ★ ★

On Friday the College broke up for the long summer holiday. When Silvie came in from work

121

Ginny was already home and dashed into the hall to greet her.

'Oh Silv! Silv! We know all about you and Mark! Jojo and I just knew he'd drive you home from the garden party. I expect he's in love with you already!'

'Ginny!' Silvie protested, 'We only went out to dinner!' She put down her shopping bag to hang up her coat. 'How do you know about the dinner date anyway?'

'Jojo telephoned Mark at his flat to get the latest news and to ask him to pick her up at the city station. From there he drives home with her. All the girls raved on about you both after the party. Jojo and me were the envy of the College. It's all too incredible!' She clasped her hands together and twirled round on one leg, her voice rising to a squeal of delight. 'When are you seeing him again?'

'Steady on Ginny! Why so much fuss! He was kind enough to drive me home from the College, and we only went out to dinner. All very polite and proper. But he's going to collect you here on Wednesday to drive you to the station. I told him there really was no need. We always get a taxi. But he insisted!'

She eyed the travelling cases on the hall floor. 'I hope you got a taxi from the station.'

'Yes — yes I did.' Ginny showed impatience. 'Don't let's talk of such mundane things. Oh he's so handsome!' She looked ecstatic. 'I think I've fallen in love with him myself.'

Silvie laughed as she picked up the shopping bags and went through to the kitchen. 'I'm sure it'll pass. But meanwhile let's just think about getting dinner.

I expect you're starving as usual.'

Ginny followed her. 'Oh Silv! How can you think of food with this marvellous thing happening!'

'Calm down Ginny. You mustn't get silly ideas.' As she spoke she unwrapped the white paper package of meat. 'Now what about dinner? I've got some rump steak and guess what?' She laughed as their voices chorused. 'The butcher didn't take the coupons.'

Ginny giggled. 'If all our food came from the butcher we wouldn't need our ration books at all — providing you did the shopping of course. Now you go and have your bath while I cook this dinner you keep raving on about.'

On her way up the stairs Silvie smiled to herself. Ginny's bright moods were always infectious. Yet she felt an underlying regret that she'd allowed the acquaintance with Mark Pemberton to develop beyond the College gates. She hated to deflate the obvious happiness and expectations of Ginny whose young mind had already built girlish romantic dreams, not knowing they were on foundations of air which could only blow away to extinction.

★   ★   ★

They waved until Ginny was just a speck at the window as the train made its noisy exit from the station.

'You're very attached to your sister aren't you.' Mark Pemberton said as they walked towards his parked car.

'She is my life.'

123

'Bit like Jojo and me really, except that you are both mother and father to Ginny. Although in a way it's like that with us too. Mother's there of course, but she takes very little interest. Too involved with the horses. I daresay Ginny has already told you that Mother's confined to a wheelchair.'

'Yes she did mention that.' Silvie settled herself in the car as he closed the door.

For a while they drove in silence before he asked, 'How would you fancy a drive to the coast? We could have dinner at one of the hotels along the front.'

She hesitated while considering how to respond. What had she expected but this. Obviously he couldn't just be dismissed like a taxi driver after taking Ginny to the station. Yet it had been on his insistence. If she agreed now it would only encourage him further. At the same time it would seem churlish to refuse, he knew that it was her half-day off from work. And she'd told Adam that she couldn't see him today.

Mark Pemberton was still awaiting an answer. Just this once, she decided, then make no more arrangements. — no matter what. 'Yes, that would be nice. I like the sea.'

He looked pleased, and relieved; she'd been overlong in answering. 'Good. Now sit back and relax. Forget little sister for a while. She's quite safe. There'll be a taxi waiting to collect her at the other end, or Joe in his old Ford. Ginny may have mentioned Joe Tarrant our gardener.'

'Yes she has.' Silvie snuggled back in the soft plush comfort. He was right. Ginny was safe. Ginny

124

was happy. Embrace the day she told herself.

'Did you enjoy bank holiday Monday at home Mark?'

'I did. But it could have been nicer. You weren't there and somehow that made a difference this time.'

'How could that be? I never have been there.'

'But knowing that you could have been and weren't made all the difference. Never felt like that about Briarwood before, as if something was missing. I thought about you all the time, wishing you were there with me.' He cast a sideways glance at her. 'Yes I really missed you. That's never been the case before.'

'How could it? You never knew me before.'

'That's exactly what the difference was.'

'Are you talking in riddles?'

'Not to my ears.'

Not liking the way the conversation was heading she eased it to a change of subject by pointing out some aspect of interest in the scenery. At the same time she resolved to discourage any further romantic advances he might make, yet regretted the fact that she must. In his company she felt lighter hearted, more carefree. The reason was perhaps his quickwitted, yet idle humour, so like Ginny's. Or perhaps because he had no connections with the past she wanted to forget. With him she had the feeling of life beginning on a new footing. The shadows left behind. Even if so briefly.

★ ★ ★

125

Silvie brushed her long flaxen hair and twisted it into a chignon. Dispassionately she regarded her reflection in the mirror. Despite her beauty she had never been vain about it. True it came in useful at times. Yet it could also be a definite handicap. No platonic friendship seemed possible. Firstly Jack. Now Mark Pemberton, whom against better judgement she had dated four times since the day they'd seen Ginny off at the station.

When she opened the door to his knock she greeted him with a subtle coolness; she would not dream of being blatantly hurtful.

'Hello Silvie.' He kissed her cheek as he stepped into the hall. 'Where shall we go this evening?'

He looked so bright and cheerful she hated herself for having to deflate his happiness in a clumsy instant. It would have to be done by degrees during the next few hours. 'I'd rather we stayed at home Mark if you don't mind.'

'Not at all. I'm happy anywhere with you, and especially here.'

As he made a move towards her she stepped back. 'I'll just finish seeing to the dinner, it's almost ready.'

Being distant towards him was not easy. He was always such cheerful company, added to which, at the moment he looked totally contented. I must not weaken, she told herself as she served the food onto warmed plates.

'Can I help?'

She turned to find him standing in the doorway. 'Not necessary thanks. Everything ready.' He took the plates from her and led the way into the dining

126

room. 'Smells delicious. Nice to have some home cooking for a change. I eat out in restaurants far too often.'

'I hope you won't be disappointed then.' She was finding it difficult to keep up the cool attitude. It was hard to know where to draw the line. Should she for instance not laugh at his humour. She needed to prepare him, let him down lightly.

When the evening came to an end she felt relief. It would soon be over.

Ready to leave now he stood in the hall looking down into her eyes as though searching for some silent answer to the question he was afraid, for the present, to ask for fear of rejection. 'Your path must be strewn with rejected lovers.' He gave a wistful smile as he took one of her hands in both of his. Then he kissed her and left without attempting to make further arrangements to call again.

She was thankful she'd been spared from telling him outright that she could not meet him again. For his sake they must end their association.

But he did not accept her silent rejection. Things were not made as simple as that for her.

★   ★   ★

Although he had made no attempt to suggest another meeting that evening, this did not mean that he had taken the subtle brush-off seriously and without a fight. One lesson he'd learned above all in a high seat of the big corporate business world was that it didn't pay to lack persistence and perseverance.

The next day at precisely five o'clock he was waiting for her outside the staff entrance of Silvester's. As he opened the car door for her he said, 'I apologise for not having arranged with you beforehand.' He seated himself beside her and switched on the car ignition. 'But I had the distinct feeling that I'd have been turned down. I didn't want to risk that. I believe in fait accompli. So here I am!'

She remained silent but was thinking . . . It's not going to be easy after all. She was about to tell him it would have been best had he not come, but he spoke first.

'You see I believe I know why you intended not to see me again.'

Before dismay could register on her face he added, 'It's because of Ginny.'

She relaxed. For an awful moment she'd thought that her past had caught up with her. Yet she should have known better. Had it been the case she knew that he would not be there at all. 'Ginny?'

'Yes Ginny. You're determined that she must be solely your responsibility and consequently you're not willing to allow anyone into your life on a permanent basis, romantically speaking that is.' He suddenly laughed aloud. 'Now I sound like the answer to a Dear Mary Smith letter in a woman's magazine.'

'How d'you know, do you read them?' She made this idle remark merely to mask her disconcertment. Only by sheer chance had she not arranged for Adam to collect her from Silvester's today.

'Girls at the office read them during lunch

128

breaks,' he was saying as he brought the car to a halt at traffic lights. He took this opportunity to glance at her. 'Tired?'

'Feet are. Sale on. Quite a madhouse today.'

'Then perhaps you are a teeny bit glad that I came. Save you a walk to the bus stop.' He sensed her coolness below the polite surface and intended to tread carefully. To be persistent was one thing, to be thought a bloody nuisance quite another.

The lights changed and he drove on. They spoke very little on the way to Stanford Road, and only to comment on minor passing interests in the streets. She had time to weigh up the situation as it now was and to decide how best to handle it. Because of his uncharacteristic silence she knew there was something serious on his mind. She wished that he hadn't come to meet her. Only by an outright and hurtful snub could she have refused the ride home. Even when they reached the house she knew that she couldn't dismiss him without inviting him in.

'May I take you out to dinner somewhere?' he asked as he switched off the car engine.

'It's been a very tiring day Mark I'd really rather eat at home.'

He made no attempt to veil his disappointment and she felt obliged to add, 'Stay and have dinner with me if you like.'

'Thank you. Delighted.' He was smiling now as he got out to open the car door for her.

'I'm afraid it's only spam today,' she said as she unlocked the front door.

'My favourite food.' he replied.

'Don't lie to me,' she smiled back at him as they

went inside. His disarming manner made it difficult to be deliberately off-hand with him.

★ ★ ★

They had finished dinner and he had helped her to wash and clear away the dishes.

As he now seated himself on the sofa in the living room he reached for her hand and pulled her down beside him. Then took her by the shoulders and turned her to face him.

'I love you Silvie. Will you marry me?'

Further regretting that he'd come to meet her after she'd thought she'd ended the association, she answered, 'I can't marry you Mark.'

He did not release her. 'Can't? Are you thinking of Ginny?'

'I'm always thinking of Ginny.' At least that's half of the whole truth, she thought. But the half that forced her refusal he could not be told. He must be left to draw his own conclusions, even though they would never be correct.

'But surely you understand that she would become my responsibility too. One big family. I'd not only be brother-in-law to her but in a way father too. Think how the girls would love that.' He paused to smile in amusement. 'You know they've been matchmaking us ever since the garden party,'

'Yes I do know.' She laughed to detract from the awkward moments. 'We certainly can't marry just to satisfy romantic schoolgirl fantasies.' She hoped this might relax his serious attitude. She was more comfortable with his light-hearted moods.

130

'I thought you liked me. I've been too presumptuous.' He looked downcast.

'Of course I like you Mark,' she assured hastily. Then regretted it when he persisted, 'In that case will you think about it? Please at least do that Silvie.'

Dearly she wished that she could. Security for Ginny would be assured, aside from the fact that she'd belong permanently in the house at Kings Meadow that she so obviously loved. So very tempting. But so very deceitful. She could not do that to him. The past for her was tarnished, however brief that episode in her life had been. Added to which she was the mistress of a man old enough to be her father. Mark Pemberton would not want her for his wife if he knew these things. Most men would not. There existed an inequality between the sexes in such matters. Adam was an exception, as was Jack Thorndyke. Both understood and accepted. She was convinced that Mark Pemberton would not. She'd always had the distinct impression that he had never bedded a woman. Always he'd behaved in a perfect gentlemanly way to her, and she was positive that he would not accept her as his potential wife if he knew. Yet due to his persistence the mental image of Ginny came between what she knew to be right and fair to him, and the temptation to grasp this golden opportunity. The pressure of his fingers on her shoulders demanded some response.

'Yes — yes I will think about it Mark.'

He detected the uncertainty in her tone and wanted to eliminate it. 'Promise me that you won't let Ginny be the deciding factor against. Things could only change for the better as far as she is concerned. She would still attend the College with Jojo. I know she'd approve. They get on so well. She'd have two of us instead of one to look after her.'

Yet — it all sounded so rosy, so enticing. 'I will consider it Mark.' she said.

'You still haven't promised what I asked.' He tapped lightly on her cheek with his finger, as if this might help to extract the reply he wanted. 'Go on — say it.'

She smiled in brief amusement at this boyish insistence before obliging. 'I promise I shall not let Ginny be a deciding factor against marrying you Mark.' An easy promise to give, since quite the reverse was the case. Ginny was more likely to be a deciding factor in favour of marriage to him.

Satisfied for the present he relaxed and smiled. 'Can I see you on Saturday?'

'No Mark. I need a few days clear to think, uninfluenced by you.'

'Very well. I accept that. I shall in any case be away for a few days as from Sunday. I have to travel up to Manchester on business. Quite a drag but imperative. I should be back late morning on Wednesday. So when can I see you again? Wednesday afternoon?'

'Ginny is due home on Wednesday around three.'

'Good. We'll collect her from the station together. Will you give me you're answer then?'

I've already given it to you, she thought, why won't you accept it. But she said 'Yes I will Mark. Yet I don't see how it can be otherwise than the one I've already given.'

132

Even so he showed no lack of confidence in his smile as he drew her close and kissed her. When he released her he said, 'How can I possibly live until then!'

'You will,' she replied lightly not knowing how else to respond.

'No.' He shook his head, 'I shall only survive.' He kissed her again, this time more fiercely.

★ ★ ★

All day Saturday she was kept busy at the store, which left no time for clear uninterrupted thought. At the same time underlying preoccupation nagged at her. Since Mark Pemberton had left her last evening she'd been unable to reconcile herself with her decision to refuse him. She could well imagine what Ginny's reaction would be if told. For her, one answer only could possibly exist. Conflicting thoughts which tried to justify that answer kept her awake until the early hours of Sunday morning. Over and over, before falling into an exhausted sleep, she had thought about what marriage to him would mean. Had she met him before the Georgian house chapter of her life, and her association with Adam, she would not have hesitated. But this was the order of things and it could not have been otherwise. Ginny could not have gone to the College without money to pay the fees, and only her being there had led to the meeting with Mark Pemberton.

She had attempted to gauge what the risk was of his discovering about her recent past. This was not inconceivable; mere chance could bring it about, since it was from his social and financial level that Rachael Moss drew her clients. As Adam had once pointed out the city was full of business men living in apartments to avoid long daily travel; husbands who were tempted to escape boredom for an hour or so in such establishments as the Georgian house. Amongst these could well have been some of his business colleagues. Therein lay the possible chance of exposure. Yet — surely it was within her own power to avoid any such social contacts. No need to ever go near his offices. Excuses could always be found for not attending social functions or meetings connected with the business and he had once mentioned that since his mother's accident few visitors came to Briarwood apart from her long-standing bridge partners who were local Kings Meadow people.

Now, after slipping a Max Factor lipstick into a small paper bag for her last customer of the day, her mind refocussed logically on this aspect. If I choose, she thought as she left the store, I need never leave the Briarwood estate at all. Yet that would be a paranoiac attitude. Only *social* contact need be avoided.

Adam would be hurt badly. But then — he was not a free man. There could be no future with him, no permanency. Living outside marriage with a man was not the done thing and would not give the security which marriage to Mark would bring.

When Ginny's summer holiday from College had begun he had stopped calling at the house. Silvie had arranged to telephone as soon as she was free again to see him. This she did when Ginny had gone on her visit to Briarwood. Most of her evenings had been spent between the two men. This evening and tomorrow she'd arranged to spend with Adam.

★   ★   ★

'Little sister still away visiting?' he greeted her as he entered the house. This much he'd been told by way of explanation, but nothing more. Not even Ginny's name.

Silvie was determined that there would be no personal connecting link between her sister and this secret side of her own life. 'Yes still away.'

'How do you fancy dinner at the Foresters Inn?' he asked after kissing her. 'We can come back here afterwards darling.'

'Yes I'd like that. It's a lovely evening for a drive through the forest,' she agreed.

'Tomorrow we'll take a trip down to the coast. Fine weather's forecast,' he said.

★   ★   ★

True to the weather report the day was sunny and hot.

They lay side by side on the sand in their bathing suits. He looked so happy and contented. She felt guilt ridden. Little could he suspect that this might well be the last day they would spend together. By now her mind was almost settled on accepting marriage to Mark Pemberton.

She did all in her power to make the day perfect for him. At the same time she attempted to drive the last remnants of doubt from her mind by constantly reminding herself that Ginny mattered most in her life.

Adam turned onto his side and raised himself on his elbow to look down at her. His eyes swept over her slim but shapely form in a white two piece bathing suit. 'I must be in heaven. Or perhaps I'm dreaming. In which case I hope I never wake up.'

When they eventually returned to Stanford Road he made passionate and desperate love to her. It seemed, she thought, as if he sensed or feared that it might be for the last time.

★ ★ ★

During the next day the last tenuous doubts were nudged away by the image of Ginny as a small girl with the green satin bow nestled in the bright copper curls, when she herself at eleven years old had uttered the long remembered words, 'Only the best for Ginny.' The best was in her power to give now. Symbolically a much larger green satin bow. And what Mark Pemberton didn't know couldn't hurt him.

19

Although Silvie had made no arrangements to see Adam on Monday evening she stopped at the telephone booth on the corner of Stanford Road to call him.

'Will you come over this evening Adam? There's something I must tell you.'

His voice caressed her ear. 'I'll be at the house in an hour my darling.' He asked no questions before ringing off, but she knew he would already be wondering.

At six thirty he arrived. She had especially left the front door off the catch in case he arrived while she was upstairs. When she came down he was standing at the French window looking out at the garden. He turned to face her as she entered the room. Unsmiling, and without his usual demonstrative greeting, he waited silently for her to speak.

She sensed his tenseness and guessed that her call had to some extent prepared him. His feelings for her still showed in his eyes. For a moment or two her voice was incapable of releasing the words which she knew would crush him. If only she could make him understand that she did not do it lightly.

As gently as she could she told him. 'Adam — I've had a proposal of marriage and after a great deal of thought I've decided to accept.'

For what seemed like an endless time he stood looking at her before speaking. When he at last did

137

his tone was subdued and tinged with reproach. 'You told me there was no other man in your life Silvie.'

'There wasn't then Adam. I met him only three weeks ago. I know it's a very short time to decide on . . . '

With a brief wry smile he cut her words short, 'Three minutes is all it takes for a man to fall in love with you Silvie. Do you love him?'

'Not exactly. I like him very much. He's a good person. Anyway what I feel is not important. You've been wonderful to me and I love you for that, but I need more permanent security. There could be no future for us Adam, we both knew that.'

'Only *you* thought that Silvie. I always said it was possible for us to marry.'

'Yes — yes I know you did, but my mind remains the same about that.'

She crossed the room to stand beside him near the window. Slowly he pulled her into his arms and rested his cheek against her hair. 'Does he know about me?'

'No Adam. He doesn't know about me either.'

His fingers caressed the silky tresses which hung down her back. 'Why didn't you tell me yesterday?'

By his tone she knew there was pain in his eyes.

'I didn't want to spoil the day for you — for both of us. Also I didn't come to a final decision until after I'd left you.'

He loosened his hold on her and took her face between his hands, exploring the lovely contours with his eyes as if this was to be his last sight of her. 'I have no claim on you. My misfortune. I suppose I

138

always knew it couldn't last forever.'

She heard the hurt in his voice. 'Silvie . . . Silvie . . . Silvie. There'll never be another woman in my life now. Not even casual as there was before we met. There's no substitute for you in the whole world. There never could be. I know that nothing I can say or do will change your mind. You've made your choice.'

'I'm so sorry it had to be this way Adam. Please believe that. I'm not doing this for myself. You must believe that too.'

He put a silky tress of her hair to his lips and turned to leave.

'Stay — just for a while Adam.'

He shook his head. She sensed the infinite restraint in his taut body as he kissed her lightly on the forehead. 'Goodbye lovely angel. I hope you'll find happiness.'

As he let himself out she made no move to follow. Only when the sound of his car engine died away did she stir from the place where she stood. She opened the French door and went out into the garden. Perfume from the night-scented stocks hung on the early evening air which was still warm from the heat of the hot August day. Engrossed in thoughts of Adam she seated herself on the grass beneath the apple tree. Belatedly she wished now that she'd not been so adamant in not allowing him to speak about his private life, or even his work. He had wanted to tell her. She had sent him out of her life as much a stranger as when he'd first entered it.

The clicking of the latch on the side entrance gate disturbed her thoughts and she wondered if Adam had returned to stay a while after all. Expectantly she waited for the footfalls to carry the caller into view.

★ ★ ★

Patiently Jack Thorndyke had waited for the telephone call that never came. Three months had passed since that rainy Sunday when he'd called at the house. There was, he'd told himself, just a flimsy chance that she'd tried to contact him during the couple of weeks which he'd been obliged to spend in Ostend on business. On this he pinned his hopes. At least a half dozen times he'd driven to the street intending to call on her. Each time there had been a car parked outside the house. Two different models in fact. One of which was the Jaguar he'd recognised being driven off only moments ago. On each of the occasions he'd parked the Humber on the corner outside the church while waiting for her visitor to leave. Each time he'd driven away disappointed. Twice he'd waited outside Silvester's on early closing day and had seen her get into the same Jaguar car. The man, he'd noted, looked old enough to be her father.

Today Jack had arrived at the corner of Stanford Road just as the Jaguar was pulling up outside the house. Sick with disappointment yet again he'd parked in the same spot outside the church, not knowing why he bothered, since it all seemed so futile now. On the point of driving away he'd seen the man leave only minutes after arriving and drive off. Surprised he'd sat a while longer wondering

140

what to make of it. No doubt the man was the source of finance which enabled her to send Ginny to that posh school. But why had he not stayed this time. Jack had decided to call at the house. After knocking twice he began to wonder if she was out after all, which would account for the man leaving so soon after arrival. To make certain he made his way round to the side of the house and through the tall wooden latch gate that led into the garden.

'Hello Angel.' The name came automatically to his lips still. 'Sorry if I alarmed you coming round the back way. I did knock a couple of times.'

She recovered quickly from her surprise. 'Hello Jack. How are you?'

'Oh — not so dusty considering.' He feasted his eyes on her. 'Long time no see.'

'Yes I suppose it is.' She patted the grass beside her. 'Come and sit down.' She saw the same old devotion in his look. Would he never give up, she wondered. Yet she was glad in a way that he'd called. When he heard her news perhaps he would stop wasting his life in futile hopes. Then marry and settle down happily with a family as he deserved.

Readily he sat down beside her, and glanced up at the tree. 'Pearmains?'

'I believe so Jack. Not quite ripe yet. Lovely tree.'

'Sure is.' He leaned back against the trunk and stretched out his legs. 'Ah this is the life. Gorgeous weather. It was raining torrents when I was last here, remember?'

'Yes,' she did remember well. There had been days since then when her thankfulness that he'd been able to trace her on the day of her mother's death had outweighed her shame as to how. 'I'll go and fetch some cool drinks, I'm sure you could do with one. It's still very warm.'

As she walked away his eyes followed her. He had always felt a vague sense of ownership towards her on account of having known her since she was born; vague yet none the less possessive. A kind of territorial-like claim, physically felt, yet all in his mind. When she reached the French door she turned to ask, 'Unless you'd prefer tea?'

'No. Cool please.' Abruptly he lowered his eyes for fear of exposing his heart. Minutes later she returned with a tray and two glasses of orange juice which she set down on the grass beside them. It occurred to him suddenly that he'd never before been alone with her, except during those brief snatched minutes as they'd walked together along Queen Street over the years. Yet this present physical closeness seemed almost painful on account of the vast unphysical distance which seemed to exist between them. It almost killed him to think of a complete stranger taking her out of his life forever.

'I hope this weather lasts a while longer Jack.'

'Can't expect miracles Angel, this is Merry England.' To try to cover an unaccustomed tremor in his voice he picked up his glass and sipped the cool drink before speaking again 'Where's Ginny?'

'Staying in the country with a school friend for a few days.' She wanted to tell him her news and get it over with. That look in his eyes made it very hard.

Jack at this point was deciding to ask her again if she would marry him. He knew that he had to try once more. Perhaps a losing battle — but he'd go down fighting. But before he could speak he heard her saying.

'Jack — I'm going to be married.' She spoke the words gently and quickly. Then saw the dark shadow cross his face. A few moments of stunned silence passed before he could respond. He looked, she thought, as if he'd been winded.

At last he spoke, and all life it seemed had gone from his voice. 'I see.' Then in a forced lighter tone he asked, 'Is he rich?'

Beneath the frivolous inquiry she recognised a serious question. 'Yes I believe he is.'

'Young?'

'About your age — perhaps a year or so younger.'

This at least told him that it could not be the chap who'd just called at the house. 'Well Angel — so much for my motto as far as my chances are concerned now, or ever were really. You'll always be the silk purse; and I'm still the sow's ear.' He gave a brief cynical smile before adding, 'I'll decline an invitation to the wedding. You'll make a lovely white Angel bride.'

At the note of underlying sadness in his voice she felt tears prick her eyes.

For a long while they sat in silence sipping their drinks. Jack breathed the scented air of the warm summer evening and wondered if the chap she was about to marry knew of her brief stint at the Georgian house. There was, after all, a limit — even for such a knockout beauty as Silvie Marsh. Most blokes did not marry whores, even past ones. Although he himself would never, could never, bear to think of her in such a term. But it was different for him. He knew her so well and knew her reasons. Also he would have accepted the fact that Ginny did and always would come first in her life. He had watched her grow up and had loved her as a woman, with an unchanging intensity, since she was fourteen years old when the nine years age difference had ceased to count.

For a long while they sat beneath the tree, talking a little between long silences. He saw the setting sun spin gold dust in her hair. He held fast to every second knowing that this would be the last meeting with her and most probably the last time he would ever see her again.

At the same time he wondered why he stayed, prolonging the agony which he was hiding so well.

20

It was Wednesday afternoon. Ginny was due back from Kings Meadow and Mark Pemberton from Manchester. Silvie expected him to arrive at Stanford Road at three o'clock when he would drive her to the station to meet Ginny's train. The day was another warm one. She slipped into the summer blue crepe which she'd worn to the garden party, swept her hair up into a chignon, put on some rose pink lipstick and a dusting of pale pink rouge which was the only cosmetic she used on her flawless ivory skin. Then she went to collect her handbag and lacy summer gloves.

Mark Pemberton had arrived back from his trip a little ahead of schedule. He went first to his offices where he stayed only fifteen minutes discussing his reports with Peter Dunning who deputised for him during his absences. From there he drove to his flat to bathe and change before presenting himself at Stanford Road. Keyed up and impatient now to know her decision he arrived at four minutes to three. She had left the door on the latch. He knocked and walked straight in. She was on her way down the stairs as he entered. He closed the door behind him and leaned his back against it, his eyes on her expectantly, his ears eager, and his breath on hold. On the bottom stair she paused, smiled, and nodded her head.

Releasing his breath he gave a sigh of relief. Then

he moved swiftly to where she stood and lifted her from the stair, swung her round and set her down. 'Now,' he said softly, 'let me hear you say it.'

'Yes I will marry you Mark.'

'I want to kiss you on the lips but you've just painted them to go out.' He gave a delighted chuckle, hugged her close, then kissed her on both cheeks. 'That's just on account. Come on let's get down to the station. I can't wait to tell little sister-in-law to be the news.'

'Mark — if you don't mind I'd rather wait and tell her myself after you've gone.'

'As you like my darling. How can I possibly mind anything any more.'

There are things you'd mind very much, she thought, recalling her earlier doubts as she collected the front door key from the hall table and led the way out.

★ ★ ★

The train was not yet in when they first arrived. Five minutes later she watched it approach with the bright head of Ginny all ready at an open window on the look out for them. Silvie waved to attract her attention and she waved wildly back before disappearing from view to collect her luggage. Before the train had squealed properly to a halt they had reached her door ready to help with her cases, the number of which, Silvie noted, had increased for the return journey.

Ginny shouted to be heard above the noise of the hiss of steam. 'Hello Silvie, hello Mark.' She passed the cases into Mark's waiting hands and hugged her sister.

A moment later she was caught up in a bear hug by Mark who lifted her off her feet and swung her round, before planting a kiss firmly on her cheek.

Enthusiastically she returned his hug, laughing delightedly. 'Now that's what I call a welcome home!'

Looking at their radiant faces eased Silvie's conscience about deceiving him. Surely it can't be too wrong if it makes two people so happy, she thought as they walked to the car.

★ ★ ★

'Steak and kidney,' Silvie said as she served the pie. 'Made it this morning when I got home from work. I left early. Told John Silvester I had to meet the train.'

'Looks delicious, Not only is the lady beautiful but she can also cook.' Mark Pemberton winked at Ginny, who giggled happily.

'Reserve judgement. The proof of the pudding is in the eating, as they say.' Silvie responded catching their gay mood.

During the meal they listened as Ginny talked happily about the days spent at Briarwood. Watching her bright face Silvie could see that all traces of grief had now been expelled. Their mother would not have wanted her to go on grieving.

Mark Pemberton stayed until quite late. As soon as he'd left Silvie gave Ginny the news. 'Something to tell you. Mark has asked me to marry him and I've said I will.'

'Oh! Oh! Oh!' For the moment Ginny seemed incapable of saying more.

Silvie laughed. 'What's that? Some kind of new language? Sounds like Japanese to me.'

'Oh Silv! Silv! It's too fantastic for words. I can hardly believe it's true!' She twirled round several times on one foot, then stopped abruptly. 'Oh can't I indeed! I certainly can. I knew the minute he set eyes on you he'd propose. We both did — Jojo and me — or should it be Jojo and I? It was obvious from the start.' She twirled again in delight before adding. 'No wonder he looked so happy at the station And I thought it was on account of seeing me.' She giggled. 'Why didn't you tell me when he was here?'

'I wanted to wait until we were alone. I wanted to be the one to tell you. Something I didn't want to share.'

'Oh Silv. Silv.' Ginny gave her a quick hug. 'Just wait until Jojo hears! I expect Mark will telephone her.'

'Yes I'm sure he will.'

Voice high with expectancy now Ginny asked, 'Where will we live?'

'Kings Meadow — Briarwood of course — where else?' She felt as if she'd just handed the moon to Ginny. And Ginny looked as though she had.

'I must be dreaming! This can't be really happening. I'll pinch myself to see if I'm awake.' This she promptly did and squealed in delight. 'Are you sure that's where we'll live Silv?'

'Positive. Mark and I discussed it in the car on the way to the station.'

'Oh Silv — Silv — just wait until you see Briarwood and the estate! You'll love it — I know. Just think — you won't have to work again! All that on top of having Mark for a husband! You'll be able to go out riding every day if you want to.'

Silvie laughed at this. 'I can't imagine it. You know I've never been close to a horse before. Unless we can count the huge Shire horse that used to pull the milkman's cart. We used to give it a carrot sometimes — remember? You were only about four at the time.'

'Oh yes — yes I do remember. Monster size!' She shrieked with laughter. 'I can't imagine trying to ride one like that! Clopping across the estate! Oh Silv it's so funny to imagine!'

Silvie saw the funny side too and laughed before saying, 'Yes, it was rather big.'

Momentarily Ginny looked serious, her tone regretful. 'Jojo and I won't be able to get home to see you on weekends. Have to wait until half-term hols. It'll seem endless.' She brightened. 'Still you'll see Mark every weekend and you shouldn't be too lonely during the week.' Her expression changed and she frowned. 'Yes — you might though. Mrs Pemberton won't be much company for you — she hardly ever talks, and she's always out at the stables with the horses.' Her face resumed its normal brightness. 'Never mind you can go for long country walks.'

'Well if you've quite finished arguing with yourself I'll tell you what the arrangements are. We'll be going to Kings Meadow for the weekend so that I can meet his parents.'

'Wonderful!' Ginny clapped her hands. 'I didn't see Jojo's father this time. But I have seen him once before. I like the look of him. I didn't see him for very long so didn't get chance to really speak to him apart from saying hello. He was just going off for a ride with Major Ashdown who lives on the next estate. He left for work early on Monday morning before we were up. He's not at home during the week.'

'Well we'd best start sorting out the luggage you brought back. There must be some washing to do. Then we'll pack a few things we'll need for the visit.'

'When will the wedding be? Jojo and I'll be bridesmaids of course.'

'We can't make plans until I've met his parents. It's just not done. Although Mark wants it to be as soon as can be arranged.'

'Just think — we'll live in that lovely old house forever and ever. I'll never want to leave it. I'll live there until the day I die.'

Unaccountably Silvie gave a slight shudder at the words. It was as if the icy fingers of death touched her lightly.

21

A few of the locals were about in the village at Kings Meadow. Recognising the distinctive car they waved and Mark Pemberton waved back. As he slowed to take the corner Ginny pointed to a little old stone church. 'You must get married there Silvie. The villagers will expect it. Mark's family have lived here for generations. They're practically royalty.' She leaned forward from her back seat, putting her face between their two shoulders. 'Isn't that so Mark?'

In the quiet lane now he turned slightly to tweak her nose. 'I think that's a bit of an exaggeration — the bit about royalty I mean. As for the church, well — yes it is a lovely old place. Would be nice to have the wedding there, with or without local attention.'

'Yes definitely,' Silvie agreed. 'Lovely countryside. Certainly quiet and out of the way. I'd never heard of Kings Meadow until Ginny told me about it.'

'It is rather off the beaten track. Good to come home to after a spell in the city. Can unwind here. When you're part of it it'll be a seventh heaven.' He reached for her hand and gave it a brief squeeze before turning the car in through high, wide wrought iron gates, already open.

The house was not immediately visible. The spreading branches of magnificent horse chestnut trees which lined the long curving driveway formed a shady guard of honour.

On first sight of Briarwood Silvie caught her breath. It was more than a mere house. 'It's huge!'

'Great great grandfather built it. Never been filled with the large families which he must have had in mind for it.

'Yes I'm sure he must have. It's beautiful!'

'I knew you'd love it on sight,' Ginny said as the car swept from the main driveway onto a curving paved path which ran between the lawns and flower beds and continued on out of sight round the side of the house to the garages. 'I expect Jojo hasn't slept a wink, just like me, since she heard the news!'

Mark Pemberton stopped the car outside the front of the house. 'I'm afraid you tend to exaggerate little sister-in-law to be.' He tousled her hair. 'You don't look as if you've lain awake for three whole nights.'

Six white semi-circular steps led up to the heavy oak double doors which were sheltered by a white four-columned portico. The house was built of stone and much of the front aspect was covered by Virginia creeper.

As Mark Pemberton handed Silvie from the car she noticed the front doors were opening. She caught a glimpse of a woman turning away and walking off towards the far interior of the hall. At this same instant another appeared just inside the entrance. Tall, slender and dressed in unrelieved black. Her high-cheek-boned angular features might have in earlier years been considered handsome for they were of a masculine cast. Except in height she bore no physical resemblance to her son.

Ginny, now out of the car, greeted the woman

first by calling, 'Hello Mrs Pemberton,' at the same time taking Silvie possessively by an arm. Mark took the other and between them they escorted her up the steps to the front door and into the hall.

A look of surprise lit the woman's unsmiling face briefly on sight of Silvie. Then her eyes moved to her son who bent only slightly to kiss her cheek. 'Hello Mother.' He smiled broadly as he drew Silvie forward. 'Meet Silvie my future wife. Silvie — my Mother.'

As the woman extended a hand to her Silvie noticed that she supported herself on an ebony walking cane topped with a silver knob. Their first words of greeting were drowned by high excited squeals as Joanne Pemberton swooped up the front steps. 'I knew it! I just knew it!' She stepped into the hall and hugged her brother and reached up to kiss his cheek. Then she turned to Silvie with the same greeting. 'Oh it's too marvellous for words.'

'Well you don't seem to be having any difficulty, even if they're a bit repetitive,' her brother said laughing.

'Do you realise that you'll be my sister Ginny! Or near enough.' Joanne Pemberton hugged Ginny then pulled her by the hand back to the front door. 'I can't come into the house with my muddy riding boots on. Come back to the stables with me for a minute before I change for tea.' As they ran off down the steps she called back, 'We won't be a jiff.'

'I'm afraid Joanne can be a bit overwhelming at times.' The woman leaned heavily on the walking cane as she stepped back further into the hall towards a wheelchair placed close at hand.

Mark Pemberton made no move to assist her, and Silvie recalled something he'd told her . . . 'Mother isn't the helpless feminine kind. She likes to feel independent. Hates anyone to fuss over her, or even offer help. She can cope very well and doesn't like to be regarded as handicapped or an invalid.'

He closed the front doors and when he turned again to his mother she was already guiding the chair smoothly across the marble floor of the vast hallway and saying, 'Your father hasn't arrived yet but he shouldn't be long. He telephoned a while back to say he was on his way. We'll await tea until he gets here.' She led the way into the drawing room.

As they followed, the grandfather clock in the hall chimed the half hour and drew Silvie's attention to its exquisitely carved case. The wheelchair moved less smoothly now as it crossed a Persian carpet before coming to a halt beside an upright wooden armchair with a padded leather seat. Into this, with very little effort, Laura Pemberton transferred herself, and as she did so she spoke. 'Let me get out of this damned chair. Makes me feel too much like an invalid.' For the benefit of Silvie she added. 'I can get about reasonably well without it if absolutely necessary. But too much effort involved and irritatingly slow.'

'It's her speed machine.' Mark Pemberton chuckled.

His mother now settled looked fully at Silvie, but her expression gave nothing of her secret thoughts away. Even her daughter's description had not prepared her for such a face. So this was why her son had acted like a lightning bolt out of the blue. He'd literally sprung the news of his intentions. And not even an engagement — a testing time! Men were such fools — setting too much store by looks. 'So — has a date been settled on?'

'Not yet.' Silvie seated herself on a midnight blue velvet chesterfield.

Mark sat down beside her. 'As soon as possible as far as I'm concerned.'

'I suppose you'll want all the pomp and ceremony?' his mother continued. 'I'll put an announcement in the press next week. Unfortunately we'll have the news hounds around.' She addressed Silvie now, 'As you may know our name is well known in the business world and consequently in the social one too, although we don't participate nowadays. Useless to try and convince news press editors that people aren't interested in us. The unfortunate truth is some of them are.' A cynical note suggested that she despised social circles and traditions. 'Newspaper editors think they have some obligation to keep the general public informed about our private lives from time to time. And a wedding! Well they'll pounce on us.' She turned her attention to her son and remarked pointedly with a wry smile, 'Press photographers will have a field day. Granted it'll be free publicity, but we don't particularly need that right now. Still it never goes amiss in business.'

Silvie had paid no heed to the tail-end of these remarks. After press photographers were mentioned she'd stopped listening. This was an aspect which she hadn't considered, having had no notion that the Pemberton's would attract interest. Here in this quiet countryside she'd expected anonymity, and to be safe from possible recognition providing she avoided contact with their business associates. Even though she'd worked at the Georgian house for such a short time the chance would be always there that she might come across one of the clients — few though they had been because of Adam's expensive arrangement with Rachael Moss. On the other hand, she thought, more logically, the city was saturated with business men and their offices. Chances that any from the Pemberton suite might be visitors to the Georgian house seemed remote even if it could not be ruled out completely.

Smothering her qualms she replied to the earlier question. 'I should much prefer the wedding to be quiet and private — no fuss please. If you're agreeable.' She felt relief at the response.

'Perfectly. I never was one for putting on a show.'

'Unless a horse show,' her son smiled and added, 'I'm more than happy to go along with whatever Silvie wishes. I'm certain Father won't mind if we don't invite all and sundry. I shall of course have Peter as best man. Other than that I couldn't care less if no one other than family attends.'

'Well there are a few whom we're obliged to invite nevertheless. Major Ashdown and the Jackson-Browns. If Silvia will let me have a list of names of everyone whom she wishes to attend I'll send out formal invitations.' She turned her full attention on Silvie now. 'I understand from Mark that you are an orphan.'

Before Silvie could make any response Mark

156

Pemberton corrected his mother. 'It's Silvie — not Silvia.'

His mother raised her eyebrows and looked faintly amused, 'What's the difference?'

'I was christened Silvie. Mother liked the name Silvia but apparently thought Silvie had a warmer ring to it. But if you'd prefer to call me Silvia I shan't mind at all. Teachers at school always did for some reason.'

'Is that a fact?' Mark Pemberton spoke the name several times both ways as if testing. 'Your mother was right. Stuffy old teachers must have thought Silvie sounded too familiar.'

Silvie sensed that his mother too was of the same mind. And never once during her life at Briarwood, even after marriage, did Laura Pemberton call her by her correct name.

At this point a woman entered the room carrying a silver tray bearing a large jug of orange juice and glasses.

'Hello Dora,' Mark Pemberton greeted her, but left the introductions to his mother who with a wave of her hand to indicate the woman said, 'Dora Glasspool keeps house for us. Dora meet Marks intended wife Silvia.'

Dora Glasspool set down the tray, straightened up and nodded.

'Hello Dora,' Silvie said warmly, remembering what Ginny had said about the woman.

After a hard stare and a nod Dora Glasspool looked away and began to pour drinks.

Mark rose and offered, 'I'll serve if you like Dora.'

Dora smiled briefly in acknowledgment of the

offer and left the room. Silvie thought she could detect a slight vagueness about the woman's eyes. But wasn't sure if she was imagining it on account of what Ginny had said in her letters about the accident.

While they were drinking his mother resumed the subject of wedding guests. 'Now as I was saying Silvia — I understand that you're an orphan.'

'That's correct. I have no relatives — so shan't be inviting any guests at all.'

'I see. So I presume that Mark's father will be the one to give you away in the church ceremony. Is that all right with you?'

'Yes perfectly thank you.'

'You'll both need to go along to the Rectory to discuss procedure with the minister. He'll require notice of course.'

'We'll go tomorrow morning. He's fairly new isn't he? Can you remember his name?'

'Reverend Bradley. Yes he's new. You weren't here when he called to introduce himself. I daresay the former one told him he'd never get to see us unless he came to the house.'

'I've put in an appearance occasionally for morning service!' Mark protested mildly. 'Being one of the oldest established families in the parish we're supposed to set an example. As I recall this new chap was quite young. Didn't look much like a clergyman. More like an actor.'

'Isn't that what they all are anyway?'

He smiled. 'Silvie will think you're a heathen Mother.'

'Perhaps she'd be right.'

He took the empty glass from Silvie, then drew her to her feet. 'Come on darling. I'll conduct you on a grand tour of the old place? Should just have time. Excuse us Mother. If Father arrives before we're back ask Dora to sound the gong.'

As Silvie left the room with him she threw a brief smile at his mother to excuse her exit and noted a shrewd expression in the cold eyes. 'No doubt thinks I'm only after her son's money,' she thought. Well in all fairness it must be admitted that she was three quarters correct. His looks and good manners accounted for the rest.

Wealth was evident at every turn as he proceeded to conduct her over the house. Rich Turkish carpet covered the wide staircase which rose from the centre of the hall and was flanked both sides by craftsman-turned mahogany balustrades, hand rails, and heavily-carved newel posts supporting it at top and bottom. The stair carpet was met by matching runners branching off in three directions in the upstairs gallery. Along the widest corridor hung huge family portraits from the past. These captured her attention and she paused beneath one inquiringly, 'Your father?'

'No. That's great great Grandfather who founded the business.' He pointed to another portrait further along on the dark wood panelling, 'That's great Grandfather. Both on Mother's side.'

She studied the faces and observed, 'They both look proud and very commanding.'

He looked amused at the apt description. 'Yes. And Mother's a chip off the old block. Even though she takes no active role in its running she has an intense pride in its success. Father and I report on progress regularly and she's quite satisfied with that. So long as it keeps going the way it does is all she cares about in life besides the horses.'

Beneath the portrait a Chippendale chair was placed, and a marble pedestal on which rested a telephone. With his arm about her waist he led her into one of the first rooms they came to. 'This is the master bedroom. Mother stopped using it after her accident. She now has her sleeping quarters and private rooms downstairs for convenience. Although I believe she can manage the stairs with a bit of effort. Seems no reason for her to though. There's a bathroom suite downstairs in addition to the cloakroom.' He crossed to a large bay window and pulled a silken cord with tasselled ends to part the heavy drapes. The sunlight revealed a large room, the commanding focal point of which was a magnificent four-poster bed with heavily-carved head, base and posts of rich polished mahogany, and its drapes were of ivory silk. 'This will be your room — our room. Until its ours — its yours.'

'It's a beautiful room. Are you sure your mother won't mind my taking it over?'

'Of course not, why should she! Make any changes you wish darling. Order new drapes. Mother hasn't feminine taste, and it's probably about time they were changed. I expect you'll choose pink satin.'

This remark reminded her sharply of the rose room at the Georgian house, and she quickly banished the thought from her mind. One thing was sure — she would not choose pink for the room if she changed it at all.

'There's a nice view over the garden from here — come and see.'

She felt the soft luxury of Aubusson carpet beneath her feet as she crossed to the window and looked out over the well-tended grounds. 'Yes — it's lovely.'

They turned their attention back to the room. 'Throw anything out you don't like.' He indicated a collection of crystal trinket boxes and powder bowls on a carved oak dressing table. 'I doubt very much if Mother has ever used any of these things. Not her taste at all. Unwanted gifts from the past I shouldn't wonder.'

Absently she touched a small jade tiger resting on a crystal tray. As her fingers traced the lines of its back he lifted her face towards him. 'Do you know something — that tiger is the same colour as your eyes.'

She smiled in response and her fingers left the tiger as she glanced across to a door at the far side of the room. 'Where does that lead?'

'Father's dressing room, it separates his bedroom from this one.' He walked across and tried the handle. 'There — it's locked and the key this side.' He held up a large old-fashioned key as he spoke. 'They haven't modernised the locks in this house yet.' He replaced the key in the lock then pointed to another door leading off the bedroom. 'Your private bathroom.'

She glanced in at the gleaming white and gold fittings. The gold dolphin taps caught her attention. Ginny, in one of her letters, had mentioned gold dolphin taps in thc bathrooms.

He took her by the hand and led her from the room. 'We'd best get a move on if I'm to show you the rest before Father gets here.'

'What a pity that your mother has to sleep downstairs instead of in that lovely room. You say she can manage the stairs?'

'With some effort if absolutely necessary. But don't waste pity on Mother. I'm certain she prefers to sleep downstairs. Nearer the stables. She can see the horses from the window of the suite where she sleeps now. Horses have figured most in her life. Even more than Jojo and me.'

'Surely not!'

'Quite true, I assure you. They still do. She used to breed racehorses in a big way before her accident. She was hardly ever in the house. Always out either hunting or some such thing connected with horses and riding. She was an excellent horsewoman. As a matter of fact up until the time of the accident I don't believe I ever saw her wearing a dress except at dinner. Always in riding gear. She must miss it all dreadfully.'

Silvie felt a genuine sympathy for his mother and wondered if the consequences of the accident accounted for what seemed a coldness in her demeanour.

By the time he'd conducted her over the rest of the upstairs she'd lost count of the rooms, besides which there were four on the attic floor. As they passed an oak bookcase in the main upper corridor he said, 'Those are handy for insomniacs. Mostly boring enough to send anyone off to sleep. Mother used to entertain guests a lot, hunting parties and the like. Always horsy people. Most of those books are about horses.'

'Do any of those friends visit her?'

'They did at first, after the accident. But she didn't welcome them. Said they made her feel her handicap worse seeing them all so hail and hearty; which always seems to be the way with horsy people. She'd only have to pick up the phone and any one of them would be more than happy to call on her.'

'Is there no one else besides your mother and Dora in this big house when the rest of the family are away?'

'Domestic help on some days. Dora doesn't actually live in here. As a general rule she goes home at the end of each day, but stays over at times if she feels like it. Lives in the village so not far to come. She rides here on her bicycle.' He hugged her to his side and they went downstairs. 'Maybe you and I will fill this old house yet — just as great great grandfather hoped it would be.'

'Lucky children,' she said smiling.

'I'll show you over the grounds after we've had tea. We can go for a long stroll. The rest of the estate you'll have to see from horseback.'

Before she could reply to this they re-entered the drawing room. His mother was still as they'd left her but was now reading a magazine called Horse Trials. As Silvie seated herself on the chesterfield with Mark beside her the sound of a car door closing could be heard. The room overlooked the grounds at the back of the house so the vehicle could not be seen from the windows. 'That'll be Father now.' Mark got to his feet expectantly.

As a matter of courtesy Silvie also stood ready to meet his father.

The high excited voices of the girls sounded close and as they came nearer their words more distinct. 'I can't come into the drawing room with my boots on Daddy. I'll go round to the side door and change for tea. Won't be a jiff. Come with me Ginny?'

As their voices died away a figure appeared in the open French windows.

Silvie smothered a gasp and for a moment the room seemed to spin round her then right itself. An eternity passed, it seemed, while she stood motionless and ashen-faced, staring at the man who stood silhouetted in the doorway aeons too long before stepping into the room.

Through the fine denier of her nylon stockings she felt the plush of the chesterfield as her legs pressed hard against it for support. This for some strange reason had a sobering effect and returned the nightmare moment to its stark reality.

Shock flashed across the face of Adam Pemberton the moment he saw her. By some miracle reflex he recovered his wits outwardly and responded woodenly as his son spoke.

'Hello Father. Come and meet your future daughter-in-law Silvie.' With concealed amusement he'd seen the expression on his father's face and interpreted it as natural male reaction to her.

Adam Pemberton stepped forward into the room and made a show of acknowledgment his hand outstretched to take hers in a trembling clasp.

Suppressed shock vibrated in his tone despite his efforts to control it as he said hoarsely, 'Hello Silvie.'

Unable to utter a word at present she forced a stiff smile. She felt the room had turned stiflingly hot. Her legs suddenly felt unequal to support her and with physical relief she sat down heavily.

His movements automatic he crossed the room to his wife and placed a dutiful peck on her unyielding cheek. 'Hello Laura.' He avoided looking at Silvie as he continued, 'Sorry if I've kept everyone waiting for tea. Please excuse me while I go and change.'

The eyes of his wife followed him as he left the room. She had seen the expression on his face at first sight of the girl but had attributed no such misconstruction as her son had done. Adam was a seasoned business man, cool-headed, confident and self-possessed, adept at suppressing outward signs of personal feelings when the occasion demanded. Also, she had not missed the effect that his sudden appearance had had on the girl, or that fleeting sign of recognition on her face. She returned her gaze to Silvie who saw the suspicion in the cold eyes and felt her own usual self-command slipping away.

With a sinking sensation she wondered if the shrewd contemplation had seen too much, and what answer to make if questioned. What did Adam intend to say. Surely not the truth! No doubt he needed time to think and recover from the shock. Spontaneous caution had stopped him from admitting to even the slightest acquaintance. It was imperative to speak with him alone to discuss this chance in a million quirk of fate that had led her to the brink of marriage to the son of a man who had been her lover and financial support. She felt stunned almost senseless by it. For the moment all she could feel was a deep regret that she had been so adamant in not wanting to know about his family background; and merely for the reason that she felt more comfortable *not* knowing. She'd not even allowed him to tell her his surname. It had seemed the right thing to her at the time, yet almost frivolous now in its consequence. She became aware that the room had suddenly come to life again as the girls bustled in looking clean and fresh in cotton dresses. They seated themselves beside her on the chesterfield.

Adam had returned, now dressed in an open-necked shirt and light linen jacket. Even at this crucial time she found herself thinking how handsome he looked, how youthful, much younger than his forty-nine years.

Dora Glasspool had also entered the room wheeling a three-tiered rosewood trolley laden with tea things. Silvie fancied that she threw a strange glance in her direction.

During tea of sandwiches and home-made sponge cake Adam avoided looking at her. The pretence of being a stranger to someone who had been her lover for the past six months was absurd and awkward. Yet the embarrassment and the difficult moments had to be borne and survived. In any event it could only be a matter of time. When would he choose to tell his son? Which moment? She wondered. Perhaps he might just allow her to slip away, out of their lives, with some concocted excuse for calling off the marriage. This way would spare them both the humiliation that the truth would bring. Desperately she wished to speak with him alone. How was this possible? Mark was not likely to leave her side for more than a few minutes, and with everyone else present, the chances were nil.

The tense atmosphere between herself and Adam was eased a little by the sustained chatter of the girls as they voiced untroubled views and ideas about the wedding, oblivious to the threat of sudden retraction of a promised happy future which they undoubtedly saw as endless bliss. She risked another glance at Adam. His eyes were downcast and a small frown furrowed his brow above the bridge of his nose. What was he thinking at this moment she wondered. Then noticed the eyes of his wife were on them both by turns. She seemed constantly watchful. Ginny's voice broke into her thoughts.

'Jojo has given Midgie to me as a welcome to the family present Silvie! He's to be my very own horse!'

Silvie nodded dumbly, then forced some vocal response as was expected. 'How generous of Joanne.' She looked away from the amber eyes alight with love for her friend, for the horse, for *life* itself. Both her heart and conscience were deeply crushed as she was drawn into the untroubled world of the two girls as they discussed their choice of colour for the bridesmaids dresses, and of the special time off from the College which would be necessary unless the wedding could take place while they were still on holiday They were even planning ahead for Christmas. All this was interlaced with banter from Mark. They were all victims, including Adam, of her own stupidity and mistake. Sick with regret she wondered how the news would be broken to them. Above all — how to tell Ginny that there was to be no future for her at Briarwood after all. How to take back the moon!

★ ★ ★

Afternoon tea was at last over. During a brief lull in the girlish chatter Adam seized the opportunity to suggest, 'Why don't we all go outside to take advantage of the weather?'

Everyone, with the exception of his wife, rose to their feet instantly in agreement. All eyes turned on her. 'A good idea,' she responded. 'You all go along. I'll be out directly.'

'I vote Mark gives us a push on the swing,' shouted his sister as the girls hurried out through the open French window. The instant he stepped out onto the lawn he was seized by his arms. Protesting mildly he laughingly allowed himself to be pulled across the garden to an old double swing at the far side.

Once outside Adam Pemberton lost no time. To Silvie's relief he called across to his son, 'I'll show Silvie around the grounds Mark if I may.'

'Righto Father,' the words travelled back as the distance between them widened. 'As you see I've been taken captive!'

Silvie cast a quick glance behind and saw Laura Pemberton steering the wheelchair down a ramp which was placed permanently just outside the French window.

168

In low urgent tones Adam Pemberton spoke now as he led the way as casually as he could manage in the opposite direction from the others. 'We must talk Silvie!'

'Yes — yes of course Adam. We must.'

The wheels of the chair rolled smoothly down the ramp and came to rest on the lawn. Its occupant watched the two figures walking across the grass in the direction of the tennis courts at the far side of the garden. Her eyes followed the graceful movements of the girl's hips despite the high heels which sank into the lawn with each step. 'Silly impractical shoes for the country,' she mused absently beneath a more serious contemplation. She had not missed that look of mutual recognition, fleeting though it had been; or that initial startled expression in the girl's eyes. 'The onlooker sees all,' she murmured to herself, 'And there's a lot more to see yet, I'll wager.'

The high voices of the girls penetrated her thoughts and she glanced across at the old swing. Ginny's voice was raised to be heard above its noisy squeak and the words floated across. 'It's not really fair of us to commandeer Mark. We know he'd rather be with Silvie.'

Mark Pemberton's eyes followed Silvie and his father until they were obscured from his view by trees and high shrubs. Laughing now he resigned himself to the pleasure of the two girls. 'It's quite all right you slave drivers. I suppose I do owe you something. If it weren't for you two I'd not have met her in the first place.'

Idly Laura Pemberton watched the trio at the

swing. Her son, tall and fair, not a bit like herself or Adam in looks. The thought that she'd produced both he and Joanne often amazed her for she'd never been the mothering kind, nor had she been interested in their father as a lover. It was just something to be got through in order to produce an heir as far as the first was concerned. The second, Joanne, was the result of his unwanted attentions. It had not been from choice that she'd married. Her father had persuaded her into it. In Adam he had recognised the qualities that would make the ideal business partner who could continue as head of the firm. As the son of an old public school friend, he was well-educated, intelligent, with proven ability, even at that early age, to negotiate big deals and transactions; and a character that consisted of the right ingredients which the position demanded: Assertiveness, confidence, decisiveness and capable of a hard-hitting approach when necessary. Lacking a male heir he'd considered that a son-in-law was the next best thing. *He* had needed an heir. *She* had not needed, or wanted, a husband. But above all else the old-established family business had to be considered. It had suited her in that she had no wish to play any physical part in the running of the company. She hated city life in any case. The idea of being cooped up in an office would not have suited her at all. Adam had been barely twenty at the time. Yet even at so young an age her father had spotted his potential.

The breeze, affected by the motion of the swing, tugged at the dresses of the girls and ravaged the painstakingly curled hair that Joanne had kept in pins for a whole day and night, and fanned Ginny's into long flames of fire ignited by the rays of the sun.

She returned her attention to the two figures now on the path bordering the lawns. She watched them pass on by the rose garden without glancing in its direction. Yet it was a special feature, sunken, with a large sun dial at its centre. No visitor ever passed it without stopping, even if only to consult the dial. It had always been Adam's favourite spot. The fact that he ignored it now proved to her that he was not showing the girl around the grounds at all. Other things were obviously foremost in his mind.

Motivated by deep curiosity she turned the chair and followed them.

The moment they reached the tennis courts, which were screened by a high-boxed privet hedge, Adam Pemberton stopped and spoke the words bottled up since his arrival. 'Good God Silvie! How could such a freakish thing happen!'

'I don't know,' she replied miserably.

'I just couldn't believe it when I walked in and saw you there. How the devil did you come to meet Mark?'

'College garden party,' she explained dully. 'Ginny is the friend that Joanne stays with at weekends. I had absolutely no idea! How could I? I'm completely stunned with shock myself.'

He took a few paces away from her, running his hands through his thick hair. She saw there were beads of perspiration on his brow. He returned to her side, 'Good God Silvie! What a position to be in! It could never have come about if you had let me talk about my family.'

'I'm fully aware of that now Adam! But it *has* happened! What are we to do about it?'

For a moment or two he paced again, agitation in his movements. Never before had he come up against anything as difficult to handle. He stopped pacing and stood directly before her. 'Of course I can't allow you to marry him Silvie.'

'Because I worked for Madam Moss?'

'Partly. And also because you have been my mistress. But more — *much* more than that — because *I* love you Silvie.'

The high voices drifted across the garden to them, mingling with the heavy scent of roses. He glanced round briefly to ensure they were still alone, but failed to see the silent presence now on the other side of the hedge. 'How can I possibly let you marry him? The whole situation is bizarre.' He grasped her by the shoulders 'As it is I don't know how I've lived through these last few days since you left me. I believed that I'd never see you again. Then I walked in and found you in my home! I'm not over the shock yet.'

'It's as much a shock for me too Adam.'

'Yes — yes of course, I know that. If Mark had only mentioned your name when he telephoned on Wednesday to tell me he was getting married and to ask if I'd come home for the weekend to meet you — I might have had some inkling. But he didn't.'

'Well the big question now Adam is — are you going to tell him about me — about us?'

'Not if you give him up. You must call off the

wedding. We have to face facts and do what is right Silvie.'

'And if I don't Adam? What then?' The thought of the crushing disappointment and shock that she would be forced to thrust upon Ginny prompted her to cling to the faint hope that if he cared enough for her he would not oppose what she so badly wanted.

His anguish was betrayed in his tone. 'Don't make things harder than they are for me Silvie. Don't do this to Mark. Let's go on as we were. You know that I'd do anything in the world for you darling — but not this — *not this.*'

'But what would we tell him? We can't hurt him like that Adam. We simply can't!'

'He need never know the truth Silvie. We — '

Before he could finish Mark called across the garden to them. 'How about a game of tennis against the girls Silvie?'

They left the shelter of the hedge and saw him striding towards them, unfastening his tie as he walked. 'The girls have gone in to fetch the racquets.' He pointed to Silvie's shoes and smiled. 'Can't play in those darling. Have to change. Did you bring tennis shoes?'

'No. Afraid not. I'll just watch. Your — your father might like to play.' She had found it hard to reconcile herself to the knowledge that they were father and son. Even harder to voice the fact.

'Righto. We'll make it a quick game then now that I've promised the girls.' He looked questioningly at his father who nodded in silent assent.

'Mother will keep Silvie company while we play. She's about here somewhere. I saw her only a moment ago by the hedge there. I thought she was trying to catch up with you.'

Spontaneously they both turned to look in the direction he was pointing and saw the wheelchair moving away from the hedge. Their eyes exchanged a silent message as each tried to gauge how much she had seen or heard. Adam threw a brief glance at his wife's face. But as always her expression told nothing. We'll soon find out, he thought. She wasn't the kind to keep silent if she had something to say.

'Since it's to be a quick game I shan't bother to change,' he said as he removed his jacket and placed it on a garden seat, relieved to see the girls running towards them carrying a collection of tennis racquets and balls. At least Laura could say nothing in their presence. Meanwhile he'd have time to think how to react if she confronted Silvie and himself later.

'Oh Silvie — aren't you playing?' Joanne asked.

'Father is playing instead,' Mark replied.

Recovering from her brief disappointment she brightened instantly and predicted gaily, 'Oh we'll easily beat Daddy Ginny.'

Mark escorted Silvie to one of the wrought iron framed seats placed between the hedge and the court for the benefit of watchers and resting players. Then, despite protests from his mother he assisted her to line the wheelchair alongside.

'How the devil do you think I manage when you're not around!'

He laughed off her irritation. 'You don't watch tennis when I'm not here because there's no one to play. And you're not much interested in it anyway.

Although I daresay you would be if it could be played from horseback.'

As she watched the four at play Silvie tried to calculate the hearing distance between the spot where she and Adam had been standing and that where they'd seen the wheelchair. Neither of them had spoken in particularly lowered tones since they'd seen no reason to do so. Nor had they expected her to follow them. Even if she hadn't overheard them speaking she might well have seen them when passing the gap in the hedge which marked the entrance to the courts. The hedge was otherwise too high to see over from the wheelchair level. She cast a discreet glance at Laura Pemberton beside her and sensed that she was paying no heed to the game or the players. But perhaps this lack of interest was understandable since, from what Mark had said, she had little interest in the game. By now, if she *had* seen them and was suspicious, she surely would have spoken out. The others were more than enough distance away not to hear above the sounds of their game.

She concentrated on the two men on the court and wondered again at the weird twist of fate that had set her down between father and son without leave now to choose either.

Suddenly the voice at her side cut across her thoughts, startling her and taking her completely off guard.

'How long have you known my husband? And how well?' Laura Pemberton's tone was pitched low and she did not shift her gaze from the players.

Outwardly Silvie reasserted her composure. If all

175

between herself and Adam had been overheard or seen the questions would have been unnecessary. Yet suspicion had obviously been aroused and had to be allayed until he could be consulted. Useless to deny outright. She kept her reply as noncommittal as she could. 'Not very long. I met him before through a mutual acquaintance.' She hoped this would suffice.

But Laura Pemberton turned her eyes now full on Silvie and in the same level tone persisted, '*How well?*'

'Not well enough to know, until today, that he's Mark's father.' And that's all I'm saying, she decided. Any further questions she would treat as impertinent and leave unanswered. She would not be intimidated by this hard-faced woman.

No more questions however were asked during the rest of the game. Although Silvie felt certain that Laura Pemberton was not completely satisfied with the answer she'd been given. To her relief and surprise no reference was made to anything that may have been heard or witnessed earlier. Well so what if they had been seen. No harm in Mark being told that she and his father had met at sometime in the past. A lot depended though on just how much his mother had seen or overheard from that spot by the hedge.

* * *

Dinner, which had seemed endless, was now over and the girls were helping Dora to clear away the dishes. Longing for a brief escape Silvie offered to help, but Mark waved the idea away.

When Dora had finished her work for the day Adam drove her home to her cottage in the village. This was the time that Dora loved best and looked forward to most. In the car beside him she could imagine that she was his woman.

As a general rule she rode to Briarwood and home each day on her bicycle. But on the infrequent weekends when he came home she made a point to either walk, or get a lift in with Joe in his old Ford. When she had no bicycle with her Adam always offered to drive her home at the end of the day.

Snug and happy in the seat beside him she cast a sideways glance at his face. Not like him — that preoccupied look and slight frown. Had it something to do with Mark getting married she wondered. 'What do you think of her?' she asked.

Immersed in his own thoughts he did not hear her until she repeated the question.

'What do you think of Mark's fiancé Adam?'

He half turned to her briefly as though he had forgotten her existence for the moment.

'What do I think of Silvie? She's very beautiful.'

Dora Glasspool felt a pang of envy. She had noticed the soft tone his voice had taken on. Of course he'd think the girl beautiful. No one had the right to be that lovely! It wasn't fair! 'She looks very young. No more than seventeen.'

'Yes that's true.'

'Is she that young?' She persisted for a definite answer on this.

'No a bit older.'

Dora fell silent while she thought back to the time when she'd first come to Briarwood house to help with the horses. Twenty-four she'd been then and quite pretty herself. Adam was at that time twenty-nine, a year older than his son's age now. Although Mark was handsome too he did not have the devastating good looks of his father at that age. Adam's hair was dark. A man had to be dark to be truly handsome. He still was. To her eyes he had changed very little over the years. He used to come home more often in those days. But not to see his wife. Dora knew how things were in that department. Laura's indifference to him always mystified her. Back in those days he used to join in the hunting parties which always included herself, for she too had been an accomplished rider. And from first sight she had fallen in love with his Robert Taylor looks. Often he used to ask her to accompany him on a ride — just the two of them. Laura, he claimed, was too mad-brained on horseback. He liked to ride at a steadier pace.

Sometimes, when staying over for the night at the house nowadays Dora would lie awake in her bedroom and fantasise that he was in love with her. She would imagine him stealing to her room in the middle of the night to make love to her.

During week nights, at her cottage, she would at times be plagued with wild imaginings of what he might be doing in the city — a place about which she knew very little with regards to the night life. She could not banish her images of him in glamorous nightspots with stylishly dressed women. And since she had no notion of city nightlife, having been born and bred in the village, she pictured it was all lights and glitter, with hotels and ballrooms and theatres to tempt him away from his quiet lonely flat. So well she remembered those tortured hours. During his wartime spell away in the army she had written many letters to him. At that time her constant hope, apart from his safety, was that he wouldn't 'get sweet' on some ATS girl. Agonies she'd suffered then, with more wild imaginings, sure that every girl who laid eyes on him would set out to seduce him. In wartime these things happened more than at any other time. Even now, she still suffered agonies when he was not at home.

But she had never succeeded in making him fall in love with her. He had shown great concern for her after the accident and had visited her regularly in hospital, and at her cottage when she was at last able to return home.

After that they hadn't allowed her to take charge of the horses as she'd done before. She couldn't remember the actual accident. Only that everything seemed different afterwards. She had lost interest in the horses and hadn't wanted to go near the racehorses again. But towards Adam she had never changed. She still harboured secret thoughts and desires to have him as her lover — her real lover — not the fantasy one which he was.

She sighed when all too quickly they reached her cottage. He got out to open the car door for her. She revelled in these courtesies, luxuriated in the brief moments of his attention. She felt important, as if special in his eyes. 'Thank you Adam. See you tomorrow. Good night.'

'Good night Dora.'

She would have liked to invite him into the

cottage for a nightcap, just to keep him with her a little longer, but from long experience knew it would be futile. So many times she'd asked and he'd always declined. She watched him get back into the car and drive off with a brief wave.

Alone now he sighed deeply. He needed escape to think. All during dinner he had been aware that his wife was keeping a watchful eye on him. He too had tried to assess how much, if anything, she had seen or heard during that brief time he was with Silvie at the tennis courts. In the presence of the girls he had not expected her to show her hand. But she would later, if she'd anything to show. In any event the wedding must be called off. He would have preferred discretion with regards to the real reason. He feared that she might broach the matter after the girls had gone to bed and as a precaution drove straight back to the house, even though he'd have preferred to stay out alone to think a while.

He garaged the car and went straight into the drawing room. As expected his wife was in her wooden armchair. Silvie was again seated on the chesterfield with Mark. The girls were playing a record on the radiogram.

'My new Frank Sinatra record Daddy,' Joanne greeted him as he entered, 'Time After Time.'

'And she's been playing it time after time,' her brother said with a laugh.

'Well you'll probably be singing it to Silvie very soon now. You just listen to the words.'

'I've been doing nothing else for the last hour,' he said joining in the final words as they were sung. 'And time after time I'll tell myself that I'm — so lucky to be loving you.'

'It's wonderful! I'll never get tired of it. Will you Ginny?'

'Never,' was the reply, followed by a yawn.

'Well it must be practically worn out already. You've played it at least a dozen times straight off this evening,' Mark teased.

'Oh all right,' Joanne responded good-naturedly. 'We're off to bed anyway. Want to be up early to go for a ride. We'll be back in time for breakfast though.' As she spoke she closed the lid of the radiogram. 'Come on Ginny.'

With kisses all round the girls said their good nights. Ginny's approach to Laura Pemberton was a little more restrained as she gave a quick peck on the unyielding cheek. She had noticed that affection was not invited from this quarter, yet knew it would be ill-mannered to bypass her. To Adam she said as she kissed his cheek, 'Now that I'm practically Jojo's sister I can't go on calling you Mr Pemberton can I. So may I call you Uncle Adam?'

He smiled and the tense lines of his face relaxed momentarily. What could he say right now except — 'Why not.'

When they'd left the room Mark Pemberton rose and drew Silvie to her feet. 'Come on darling let's take a stroll around the garden. Excuse us.' His glance flicked from his mother to his father.

In courtesy to Silvie, Adam stood up as they left the room. His eyes followed her as she went. Then he became aware of his wife watching him. He did not resume his seat. Instead he said, 'I'll get a book

181

from the library and have an early night. Goodnight Laura.'

He thought, if she has something to say now is the time she'll choose. She'd not be likely to let him walk away scot free. To give her ample opportunity he paused at a drinks cabinet and poured himself a brandy to take with him, even though there were several bottles kept in the library. To his surprise she did not speak, or even acknowledge his goodnight.

She watched him leave the room. Questions would be futile. With accuracy she could forecast his response. 'You're imagining things again Laura.' So easy for him to use that old dodge since her accident — all on the strength of a few earlier spells of vagueness, which he would remind her of to suit his own convenience. Those strange turns had been due to paralysis of her left side and the shock discovery that she would never again be able to ride. Psychologically she was now fully recovered, having come to terms with it as best she could.

Imagination had *never* been a failing of hers and it *wasn't* now. She had seen what she had seen. Neither of them had noticed her as she'd passed the gap in the hedge at the entrance to the courts. His back had been towards her, his broad shoulders obscuring the girl from view. That semi-embrace attitude as he'd held her by her arms, his head bent too close, pointed to something more than just mere or casual acquaintance. Yet neither of them had even admitted to *that* when he'd arrived.

Still pondering and unsatisfied she transferred

herself to her wheelchair and steered it towards her bedroom, regretting that she had not been just that little bit closer and within earshot earlier.

★ ★ ★

Dusk had fallen when Mark Pemberton led Silvie down the steps into the sunken rose garden. In the fading light the dark red blooms looked almost black and their strong scent clung heavy and sweet on the moist air. Carefully he picked a newly-opened red rose and a scattering of petals fell from the bush. 'The last of the summer roses,' he said as he handed her the flower. 'I don't know its name, but all red roses should be called Silvie.'

'It has a very strong scent,' she felt some response was expected. She didn't feel up to talking and wished she could go and lie down. Her head was spinning. Seldom was she afflicted with headaches and attributed it to the shock she'd had. She placed the rose on the sundial face.

He reached across to take her hand. 'Darling you've said you'll marry me, but you haven't said *when*. Let's make it as soon as possible. I'm glad in a way that you don't want an elaborate wedding because all that arranging takes so long. I'm aware that we have to abide by official rules of procedure with regards to the church ceremony; three weeks I believe is the required notice. If we go to church tomorrow morning — that might count as one week. Three Sundays to call the banns — or whatever they do. We can buy the rings next week. You can give notice at Silvester's, and pay off your

183

landlord. I'd like you to move into Briarwood as soon as you can darling.' He paused long enough to kiss her hand. 'So can we make it three weeks from now my sweet?'

She knew this was the time she should be telling him it was all over and there could be no wedding. She should be leaving first thing in the morning. Instead she was allowing him to go on planning, involving her with his life and future. How to tell him? What reason could she give for changing her mind, for letting him down, for letting them all down, above all Ginny. Certainly *not* the truth. That would be *too* much of a blow for him. He didn't deserve that. One good thing though, the rings had not yet been bought. Her head ached so badly she couldn't hope to think clearly at present. The cool air had not helped. Both her mind and her head were reeling. She leaned against the sundial for support as she said weakly, 'Mark — I'm sorry — I have the most dreadful headache. I'll have to go and lie down.'

At once he was solicitous. 'Darling — I had no idea! You should have mentioned it before. Let's go inside and I'll fetch you an aspirin.' With his arm about her they went back into the house.

'Everyone must have gone to bed,' he observed as they stepped in through the French window. 'Unusual for Father. Although he may be in the library.' He handed her into an armchair and went off to the medicine cabinet in the downstairs cloakroom. Moments later he reappeared with a glass and some aspirin.

She swallowed two of the tablets and sipped the

water. 'I think I'll go to bed now Mark if you don't mind.'

'Of course darling. I'll see you up to your room.'

Outside her bedroom he kissed her lightly and opened the door for her. 'You'll feel better in the morning after a good night's sleep. Goodnight Silvie darling.'

'Goodnight Mark.' Gratefully she escaped into the room. Alone at last!

Gently he closed the door behind her.

Although dark outside now the night was still very warm. After her bath Silvie put on the green satin nightdress and matching kimono bought specially for her weekend stay at Briarwood and lay down on the bed. She had planned to buy her wedding trousseau during the coming week, and had been looking forward to the luxury of spending money on herself without thinking it extravagant. Monetary concerns were at an end — or so she'd thought at the time.

The aspirin and bath had relaxed her. She no longer felt tense and the headache had gone. Now that shock had subsided she felt more able to assess her situation. All the lamenting in the world about her past decision to disallow Adam to speak of his family was futile. She had felt it was right for her at the time. Now there was no alternative but to accept the consequences. Nothing could change the fact that the father of the man she had planned to marry had been her lover and had paid for the privilege.

At this point Mark, in his ignorance, still loved her and expected their marriage to take place. But there could be no wedding because Adam had said so. Her whole life, and Ginny's, would be changed again. Financially they would be back as they were in Queen Street. College fees would be impossible to pay. Continuing with Adam was now out of the question. This then was the practical aspect of their altered position. The other part was worse, much worse. The hardest element was having to tell Ginny that, not only must they leave Briarwood never to return, but also that she would not now be part of Joanne's family after all. Even her close friendship with her beloved friend would be ended. Girls of such an age were sensitive and Joanne Pemberton would turn against the sister of a girl who treated her much-loved brother so unforgivably. She would see it only as a fickle change of mind, just as Mark himself would, for they could never be told the true reason. The dreadful disappointment for Ginny was too unbearable to think about. She groaned and turned on to her side. She knew that she could never return to the life at the Georgian house. She shuddered at the thought. With one hand she had given Ginny the moon. With the other she had to take it back. 'I can't — I can't do that to her,' she muttered, feeling mentally and physically crushed.

Her position on the bed brought her eyes into focus of the door to Adam's dressing room. Almost fascinated her gaze dwelt on the big old-fashioned key that Mark had earlier laughingly tested for her benefit. If only she could speak with Adam to discuss what must be said and done. Those few snatched words at the tennis courts had resolved nothing. More discussion was essential. Would he really tell his son about their past relationship if she refused to call off the wedding? Could things not be resolved in some less destructive way? Was there no other solution to save the situation? She wondered where he was at the present moment. Had he come upstairs to his room yet? Or was he still down in the library where Mark had earlier suggested he might be? The key seemed to beckon her. Her eyes lingered on it fixedly. Slowly she sat up on the bed. Perhaps there was a way . . .

Men, with their open stares, had made her aware of her beauty at a very early age. Only with a cool detachment had she ever appraised it herself. The first time had been when she had decided to use it in the employ of Madam Moss. At that time she had considered it from a purely business aspect. Not until this desperate moment had she realised its possible potential power. It had helped her to acquire the better lifestyle for her mother and Ginny. For Ginny's sake she could use it again — or at least try. Adam was a man and therefore vulnerable because he loved her and needed her. Well — he can still have me at a price — she mused. A price much higher than Madam Moss could ever have asked; for that had been *mere money*.

For a few seconds longer her eyes rested on the key. Then she crossed the room and turned it softly in the lock. Slowly she pushed the door open, then stood momentarily on the threshold of the dressing room to listen before entering. At the far side was the door to his bedroom. Her feet made no sound on the carpet as she crossed the room. Outside the door she listened for the sound of voices which would tell her that he was not alone. All was quiet. A

187

thin ribbon of light showed beneath the door. Softly she knocked and waited, her breath on hold.

Almost immediately the door was opened and Adam stood there, dressed in cream silk pyjamas. Surprise showed on his face as she slipped past him into his bedroom.

'I must speak with you Adam.'

After first glancing to check that she'd closed the connecting door of her bedroom he closed his own. As he turned to her his eyes swept over her satin-clad body. The nightdress clung, emphasising the tempting contours. He swallowed hard as he motioned her to a chair at his bedside before seating himself on the bed facing her. Silently he waited for her to speak.

'Adam — I can't just walk out on Mark and merely say that I've changed my mind. Don't ask me to do that Adam.' The honey tones of her voice were even softer for she spoke in little above a whisper. 'Don't tell him about me — about us. There is so much at stake. The girls too would be devastated now that things have come this far. I promise that I'll make him happy Adam.'

He leaned forward, his elbows resting on his knees. He bent his head and ran his fingers through his thick hair. In a strained voice he answered. 'You don't know what you're asking Silvie. I can't possibly keep quiet and allow this marriage to take place. I just *can't* my darling.'

'Yet you would marry me yourself Adam,' she reminded him softly.

'I know you much better than he does. I understood your reasons which to you seemed the right ones. Mark would never take such a liberal view — believe me. I know for certain that he'd never go through with the marriage if he knew. Not even for such a prize as you Silvie. I promise you that I know his moral principals are too high for that.' He paused briefly before continuing. 'I have to say this my darling to make you understand. He is a far stronger person than either of us where moral standards are concerned. He would never see things your way.'

After a moments reflective pause she replied. 'That's because he's never been in need and wanted something badly enough.'

He raised his head as if considering her words before nodding agreement. 'Marry me Silvie. I can so easily get a divorce from Laura. She doesn't need me or want me. I'd take good care of you and Ginny — you know that.'

'Oh Adam! Now you don't know what you're asking. Just think about the effect on Mark and the girls! Your whole family life would be completely broken up. Joanne and Ginny would practically become enemies, whereas they are so close to each other now. Try to imagine how they would see it and how it would affect them.'

'Silvie we're talking about marriage here — a lifetime! Not just the immediate present for two schoolgirls who'd get over their big disappointment. Mark's whole life is involved!'

Not wanting to be forced into playing her trump card she tried further. 'Ginny is my *world* Adam, she always has been. I am in charge of her young life. She loves Briarwood. She loves Joanne

189

and Mark. Don't force me to take these back from her.'

He gave a deep sigh and his eyes rested on her longingly. 'I'm aware that Ginny comes first in your life Silvie. I would never try to change that. I could buy a country house for the three of us. She could have her very own Briarwood. Joanne could, if she wished, come to live with us too.'

'You are forgetting Mark. What of him Adam?'

'He would have to be told the truth — about us; that I've loved you for much longer than he has. We would explain the same to the girls.'

She shook her head. 'No Adam. I'm sure you would not be so cruel. You haven't thought enough about it.'

They fell into silence. She listened to the bedside clock ticking away the minutes, as if to remind that time was slipping away and pressing for some conclusion — some solution.

He reached out a hand to touch her hair which glistened in the light from the bedside lamp. The hurt he felt was intolerable. Only days ago she had walked out of his life. He'd been forced to accept that he'd never see her again and had entered his own private hell. Now — here she was — in his bedroom, back in his life only to leave it again one way or another unless he could stop her. He reached out his other hand to touch her cheek, then both hands moved down to rest on her shoulders. 'Silvie darling, let's go on as we were,' he pleaded softly. 'If you could only know how much I need you — oh Silvie — Silvie . . .'

'I'm sorry Adam. We would hurt too many

people. And most of all Mark. We couldn't possibly go back to where we left off. Everything has changed. Even if you got a divorce your whole family life would be in ruins and Mark alienated from you. I would not be party to that. It wouldn't work. You must see that Adam. If you will not allow the marriage to go ahead we shall never see each other again.'

'Don't do this to me Silvie — please don't do . . . '

She moved to sit beside him on the bed and put her fingers to his lips to check his words. He felt the soft warmth of her body pressed against him, and smelt the sweet fragrance of her hair against his face.

She leaned closer, her breath on his cheek. He ran his hands over the smooth satin of her clinging gown. 'Oh God Silvie! I can't help myself. I can't exist without you. I can't let you go out of my life again. I can't give you up!' Powerless in the fever of desire which gripped him, obliterating all resistance, he crushed her against him. His hands moved impatiently over her body, his tone urgent and pleading he repeated over and over, 'Don't ever leave me again Silvie. I can't let you go. I can't give you up.'

'Then let Mark marry me. Let me stay here in this house and you won't have to Adam.' She lay back on the bed easing him down with her. Her voice, whisper soft, was close to his ear as she repeated, 'You won't have to Adam. You won't have to I promise.'

★ ★ ★

In his room Mark Pemberton put aside the book on which he'd been unable to fix his whole attention. Restless he got out of bed and put on his dressing gown and slippers. After pacing the room for a few minutes he glanced at the clock on his bedside chest and saw that the hour was still too early for sleep. He opened his door to look across at the thin strip of light visible beneath the door on the opposite side of the corridor. He crossed to knock lightly and called softly, 'Silvie! Are you still awake?' He listened for some response. When none came he turned the handle and opened the door to look into the room. He saw the bed was empty and entered and crossed to the bathroom. With his face close to the door he called again, 'Silvie. It's Mark. How is your head darling?' As he waited for some answer the ready smile on his face gradually faded. He tried the handle and when he found it unlocked he looked in. He turned back to glance around the bedroom as if half expecting her to be playing some game with him, and a smile once again hovered on his lips. For a moment or two he looked nonplussed. Absently his eyes came to rest on the connecting door to his father's dressing room, then passed on. Abruptly he turned to leave the room to go in search of her. The possibility occurred to him that she might have gone to the room of one of the girls. When he turned the corner of the corridor which branched off and led to their bedrooms he saw that both lights were out and the doors ajar. He turned and made his way downstairs where he felt sure he'd now find her.

192

Unaware that she was being sought Silvie re-entered her bedroom. With miraculous unplanned split-second timing she had closed the dressing room door before Mark again looked into the room.

'Ah there you are darling! I've been looking all over the house for you. I'd begun to think that you'd had second thoughts and decamped!' He looked amused now. 'Where were you — under the bed? I looked in the bathroom and downstairs.'

She felt herself trembling slightly at the narrow time margin that had allowed her to enter the room one second before he had — her hand had barely left the doorknob. She was still standing close to it. Hastily she moved away and gathered up her kimono from the bed to cover her crumpled nightgown. 'I — I was at the bookcase along the corridor.' Taken off guard like this she was barely aware of what she said. There had been no time to consider any other possible explanation and she was relieved that he'd mentioned his search before she'd claimed to have been in any of those places.

'Odd! I passed by there. Don't know how I missed you.' He glanced beyond her to the dressing room door and smiled. 'Were you double checking it's still locked!'

She feared that in his present jesting mood he might cross to the door to prove once more to her that it was locked. 'Of course not,' she replied hastily.

He moved towards her. 'So my darling you were looking for a book. That means your head must be better now.' He reached out and pulled her into his arms and kissed her long and hungrily.

When he released her he glanced down at her bare feet. 'You're even more petite without those stilts you call shoes my sweet.'

At this reference to her bare feet alarm gripped her. She had forgotten to put her slippers back on. They were still in Adam's room! At any moment he could walk in to return them to her. Her one desperate thought was to get Mark Pemberton out of the room.

But he was again tilting her face up to him. 'You don't look a day over sixteen without that red stuff on your lips. They'll call me a cradle snatcher.' He embraced her closer and kissed her again.

In panic now she tried to pull away. But he held her fast 'Don't send me away Silvie — please,' he breathed heavily. 'Let me stay for just a while — please my Silvie,' he begged.

She renewed her efforts to free herself from his embrace, her thoughts obsessed only with the fear that Adam would return the slippers. At any moment he might open the unlocked door. 'Let me go please Mark. I do still have a headache — really.'

Instantly he released his hold on her and looked contrite. 'Forgive me Silvie my love. It's just the thought of you being so close by. But before I go will you promise me one thing. That you'll marry me at the first possible time we can arrange it. You didn't answer me properly earlier in the rose garden.'

'Yes — yes I will Mark, of course. I promise.' She spoke quickly and led him by his arm towards the door, her one thought was to get him out of the room. 'We'll go to the church in the morning.' She too wanted the wedding to be arranged and over as soon as possible. Once accomplished Adam could not have second thoughts.

'And will you leave Silvester's and move in here right away? I'll arrange to settle up at Stanford Road. I want you here permanently under this roof as soon as possible.'

'Yes — yes of course,' she cut in on his persistence. 'We'll discuss it tomorrow. Goodnight Mark.'

He moved more willingly now. At the door he turned and to her dismay stopped to embrace her again. 'Goodnight my lovely.' Panic-loaded moments dragged by while he covered her face with kisses before he released her and spoke again. 'We shall go and see the church minister in the morning. At least we've settled that tonight.'

'Yes — yes we'll do that Mark. Goodnight.' With each second of delay in his leaving her fears increased. The biggest obstacle to their marriage had been overcome. It would be the ruination of everything if his father came through the dressing room door carrying her white satin slippers.

At last, to her relief, he said

'Goodnight my sweet.' With a last lingering look at her he left the room.

She closed the door after him and leaned her back against it as she tried to calm the trembling effects of those last dangerous moments. Still reflecting on them she went towards the bathroom. He had come hoping to make love to her. Understandable with the wedding so close. But even without the panic of the forgotten slippers she could not have allowed this for the reason that she was still warm from the bed of his father, whose lips she had sealed by exploiting her beauty, and his feelings for her, in a power game that made him the victim of his own gender.

She had drawn him into a web of ultimate deceit of his own son, using herself as the bait and the prize. For this she despised herself.

Yet what did *that* matter if Ginny could keep her moon.

22

When Silvie came downstairs on Sunday morning Mark Pemberton was seated on a carved oak bench in the hall reading a newspaper. He put the newspaper down on a hall table and came to meet her. 'Good morning fair lady.' He kissed her cheek. 'I trust that your headache has completely gone.'

'Good morning Mark. Yes it's quite cleared now thank you. I'm afraid I overslept. I hope I haven't kept anyone waiting.' Truth was she'd slept little, two hours at most and not until dawn.

'Not at all. We don't stand on ceremony for breakfast because none of us are consistent early morning time keepers. Mother never takes breakfast at all apart from coffee. The girls are out riding. They were up at the crack of dawn. Apparently Ginny looked in on you. Sound asleep she said, and didn't want to wake you.' He gave her his dazzling smile and tucked her arm through his.

'Then you too must have been up at the crack of dawn,' she thought her remark inane, and she hated inanities, but felt the need for something to say in attempt to smother her deep guilt feeling. He seemed so untouched by any sordid element of life and didn't deserve what she was doing to him. But last night she'd made her choice between he and Ginny. She had felt like a tigress defending her cub.

'I was indeed. How could I lie in bed when there was the possibility that you'd be down here on the

197

hall bench waiting for me.'

'Sorry to disappoint you,' she forced a smile in return, at the same time wondering if Adam was down yet.

Laura Pemberton was just leaving the breakfast room as they reached it. After a brief mutual morning greeting she addressed her son, 'Your father is out riding. Said he's calling in on the Major and wouldn't be in for lunch.'

'I can well believe that.' He turned to Silvie. 'The Major's a bit of a talker. Likes company. Father will be there for hours.'

'He won't be in for dinner either. He's going back to the city early for some reason.' Laura Pemberton shot a quick glance of suspicion at Silvie which was lost on her son but not on Silvie.

'Shame. I do think he might have stayed longer under the circumstances! I mean — this being a special family get-together to discuss the wedding plans. I *am* disappointed. Not like him at all!'

His mother gave a shrug. 'As you say — one can't pay a flying visit to the Major.' She moved the chair on towards the drawing room.

'Did the girls say when they'd be back?'

'In about an hour,' she spoke over her shoulder. 'But you know as well as I that when Joanne gets on horseback she forgets time completely. I told your father that you'd want him here to discuss the arrangements but he said he'll go along with any you make.'

Silvie wondered if Adam realised that he was to give her away, since she had no one else to ask, and how he would react to the idea. Yet he really had no choice in the matter: He could hardly refuse!

The wheelchair was now out of sight, but the voice called back. 'We'll discuss it over dinner this evening.'

A strong smell of coffee and bacon came from the kitchen as they seated themselves at the table in the breakfast room. Silvie was relieved to hear that Adam was away from the house and not expected for dinner. It would not have been easy to discuss wedding plans in his presence. She guessed that he was of the same opinion and that it was the reason for his absence.

Dora Glasspool brought breakfast in and was greeted brightly by Mark. 'Morning Dora. I could eat a horse this morning. But for heaven sake don't tell mother I said that!'

Dora smiled at this.

'Good morning Dora,' Silvie said.

'Morning Miss.' Dora threw a quick accusing glance at her then turned to Mark as she continued in a tone of deep concern, 'Your father went off this morning without any breakfast — just a cup of coffee! Has something upset him?' Again she cast a quick glance of suspicion in Silvie's direction.

'Not to worry Dora. He'll eat at Major Ashdown's I dare say.'

'I'm not hungry Dora thank you, just coffee please,' Silvie put in hastily before Dora could place any food before her. 'The girls will use up what you've already prepared when they come back.'

Without saying more Dora returned to the kitchen taking the second breakfast plate with her.

'Are you all right darling? No appetite this

morning!' Mark looked concerned.

'I'm fine. I seldom eat a cooked breakfast.' She could not meet his eyes. To ease the moment she asked, 'I wonder if Dora would like some help in the kitchen. It'll give me something to do while you're eating.'

'Good heavens no! She won't allow anyone in her domain when she's preparing meals. You just sit there looking beautiful. You weren't made for working.'

'Does she look after the housekeeping all by herself?'

'She likes to deal with the domestic running of the household. Resents help. She calls it interference. Mother insists that she has some help of course. This house is far too big for just one person to handle. And Joe Tarrant's sister comes in a couple of times or so a week, not sure how often, to polish and dust and clean — all that sort of thing. You haven't met Joe yet. Saturday's his day off. He lives in the village. Works full time looking after the garden and grounds here. Has extra help when required. We leave it all entirely up to him to organise. Very reliable chap Joe. He'll be out there this morning. You'll meet him. He comes into the kitchen for mid-morning break. A confirmed old bachelor. Well — not that old really. Lives with his widowed sister Mary — the one who comes in to help. Dora's been with us for years. Started here as a girl to help look after the horses. Had an unfortunate accident saving my little sister, who was three at the time, from the hind legs of a rascally racehorse. Can be temperamental creatures racehorses. I was away at school at the time. The stables were out of bounds to her but she managed to wander in there when her nanny was retrieving a ball they'd been playing with from some bushes. Dora happened to be at hand in the stables at the time. Jojo's never been told the full facts of it all though, and was too young to remember. Needless to say the nanny was dismissed.'

'How absolutely awful it must have been for everyone concerned. Poor Dora. Seems to have recovered quite well though fortunately.'

He lowered his tone to reply, although Dora was not within earshot. 'Not one hundred percent I think. But she's harmless. Had nothing to do with horses since. Yet she was as keen as mother before it happened. Extremely accomplished horsewoman. She's very fond of father. I rather think she's always been sweet on him. Always fussing over him when he's at home nowadays. But as I said — she's quite harmless.'

Harmless? What could he know of the dangerous undertow that can be brought to the surface by jealousy.

After breakfast was over Silvie went up to her bedroom to dress for their first visit to the church to arrange for the banns to be called. On waking she had found her slippers placed beside her bed. She had locked the connecting door before going downstairs.

Mark Pemberton had gone in search of his mother and found her, as expected, in the stables. 'We're off to the church now,' he told her. 'I've telephoned the Rectory and made arrangements to speak with the reverend about calling the banns — or what the devil it is we have to do. The girls have just said they want to come with us. I see that they've left you to rub down the horses. Obviously we'll have to attend the church service after we've spoken with the reverend chap. If he can start today it'll mean that the wedding can be in three weeks time!'

Laura Pemberton's hand paused on the horses flank as she looked up at him. 'You're not leaving me much time to arrange everything. Why the hurry? You know what they say — marry in haste — repent at leisure.'

He threw back his head to laugh aloud. 'You're a born cynic Mother and can't be serious. We'll manage to do all that's required since it's not going to be an elaborate affair after all.' As he walked away he called back over his shoulder. 'I'll inform Reverend Bradley that you'll be in church next Sunday morning.'

'You'll do nothing of the kind,' she shouted after him.

He half turned with a laugh and a brief wave. She watched him go, unsure of whether or not she'd been right in not telling him what she'd seen. Yet — what had she seen? Nothing that she could put into words of any significance. He'd have needed to see the scene for himself. The old saying . . . A picture is worth a thousand words — came to her mind. The manner in which Adam had been gripping the girl by the shoulders meant that they'd been more than just mere passing acquaintances at some time. She gave a shrug and resumed work on the horse, her expert hands moving lovingly over its thoroughbred body. The idea of having her son settled and new heirs produced to ensure the continuance of the long established family business was beginning to appeal to her, and she did not want to look too closely for reasons to delay events.

23

The four settled themselves in the front pew of the little old stone church: Ginny, Silvie, Mark and Joanne. At the suggestion of the Reverend David Bradley they had entered by way of the vestry door, having walked with him from the Rectory, and in consequence were a little ahead in time of the rest of the congregation.

Without looking behind them they heard the little church gradually filling until the rustling of clothes and shuffling of feet ceased. The reverend climbed the steps to the pulpit. The two girls had been bowled over by his good looks, and out of his hearing had made this known to Silvie. As Mark Pemberton had remarked earlier — he looked more like an actor than a clergyman.

Reverend David Bradley was in fact the son of a well-known British theatre actor. The manner in which he delivered his sermons indicated that he had a strong leaning towards this talent himself. It showed in his concentrated efforts to captivate his listeners and in his aim to fill the tiny old church to capacity, much as his father wanted a full house at the theatre. Church attendance had increased by a good half in the short time since he'd taken over from his predecessor. Many of the younger unmarried girls of the parish had suddenly become pious. In this, his looks, not his sermons, were the draw card. His hair was almost black, his eyes deep blue, fringed with thick dark lashes, and his handsome features suggested an Irish element in his blood. He possessed an infallible sense of humour which had stood him in good stead while serving as an air-pilot during the war.

This humour prompted his secret thoughts now as he ran his eye over the morning's congregation. Only two pews at the back remained unoccupied and latecomers were still arriving. In a small country village news travels like brush fires. Some had seen the Pemberton car as it passed through Kings Meadow on Saturday afternoon. This in itself was nothing new or unusual. But the girl in the passenger seat was. Word had passed around and they had all come in hopes that she would attend the Sunday service. They had not been disappointed. In his resonant and perfectly modulated tones Reverend Bradley now began to read the banns.

With difficulty he suppressed his amusement as he paused to study the effect of his announcement on the sea of faces below. Had they been donkeys, he thought, their ears would be standing erect at this moment. He knew that their tongues would be eager to react to the news. A few were unable to contain at least some small vocal response and a low murmur mingled in the spice scented air heavy with unvoiced curiosity, followed by a rustling sound as necks craned to get a glimpse of the newcomer amongst them.

He allowed himself the luxury of a quick glance at the girl in the front pew who was the target of so much interest. All eyes were resting on her, hopeful that she would turn her head. He knew that his father's description of her would be, 'She's a knockout.' And he could only agree. He anticipated that for the next three weeks or so the church would be filled to capacity; perhaps even standing room only! Beyond then would depend on whether the young Mrs Pemberton put in regular appearances. The Pembertons, his predecessor had informed him, were distinguished and respected in the village on account of their wealth and social position. Laura Pemberton, he'd been told, had never attended the church services even before her accident. A number of attempts had been made in the past to persuade her to set an example and help boost attendance numbers. On one occasion her response had been a blunt one, 'If you can't draw them in yourself, don't expect me to.' He had called on her at Briarwood himself to no better effect. She had given him a donation though, part of which he had used to get the leak in the vestry roof fixed.

His eyes roved over the varied heads below, one by one, as he spoke. With surprise they came to rest suddenly on a young man seated alone in the back pew. Jimmy Ashdown! The Major's son. What had drawn him in off the street he wondered. Not a belated pious change for sure. This silent opinion was confirmed in the mocking glance raised briefly in his direction before being returned to the flaxen head in the front pew.

'All rise please,' requested the musical voice. 'We will sing hymn number 124.' This his lips knew by heart and left his thoughts free to wonder why Jimmy Ashdown had chosen to attend the service.

Surely not for the same reason as most of the others — for a glimpse of the girl! True he had a reputation of being a womaniser. But this only on the strength of an incident which had involved one of the village girls who had become pregnant. Boredom during a weekend at home had sent him to the local village inn one evening in pursuit of temporary distraction. There he had met the girl. Of the many men whom she had been sighted with on the copse in the past, his name had been the one which had stuck. With high hopes the girl had made no attempt to suppress the gossip and by devious means had made certain that this reached the ears of his father. A rumpus had followed. But not to the girl's hoped for advantage. Later she had married a local boy who, it was eventually concluded, was the father of the child anyway. All this information had been passed on as being local parish history, or more precisely, one of the ingredients concerning the human element of the parish history.

The hymn came to an end. 'Let us all pray,' requested the melodic voice. Reverend Bradley's eyes rested again on the lone occupant in the back pew, whom he'd noted had not joined in the singing.

Nonchalantly Jimmy Ashdown resisted the request and remained seated while the rest of the congregation were on their knees. He returned an expression of amusement at the reverend.

Undaunted David Bradley met the defiant look and waited. The silence was absolute now. Any moment heads would turn towards the back pew where his eyes were focused. His steady blue gaze held as he repeated — 'Let us *all* pray.' He had the advantage. Jimmy Ashdown knew it. Indolently he shrugged and slipped from his seat to a hassock.

As he led the prayers the young reverend wondered why he had bothered to play the game of wills with Jimmy Ashdown since the result was not worthwhile. Whatever reason had drawn him into the church had no religious connections.

The service came to an end. The four in the front pew filed out towards the vestry door. All eyes were intent on them hoping for a backward glance from the girl whose name they now knew from the reading of the banns. The eyes of curiosity included those of Jimmy Ashdown who now stood, broad, lusty and handsome watching her leave.

But Silvie Marsh did not turn her head. So for the present she remained unaware that threads of her recent past followed dangerously close on her heels.

As pre-arranged the four returned to the Rectory with the Reverend Bradley after the service to take morning tea with him. This had been served by his housekeeper.

Right this minute, in the car on the way back to Briarwood, Ginny and Joanne were discussing him between giggles.

'He's not married. He can't be. The housekeeper made the tea and there was no other woman there.' Joanne was saying.

'I wonder if he'd wait for me to grow up.' Ginny laughed delightedly at the idea. 'I shall go to church every Sunday during the hols.'

'Me too, morning and evening!' Joanne vowed, then giggled again. 'Wow he's what I call an eyeful!'

She leaned forward from the back seat to speak. 'What do you think of him Silvie?'

'He has a nice voice.' Truth was his appearance had struck her much the same as it had the girls. He was devastatingly handsome. But most of all it had been his voice that had left an impression on her. She had found it soothing. And she'd needed that.

Mark Pemberton laughed. 'Hey — careful now or I shall have to find another church!'

By the time they arrived at the house Adam had left for the city. He had returned from his ride while they were away.

Silvie felt relief at the news. She could not have faced him easily in the presence of his son. Time was required to adjust to the conditions she had set.

★ ★ ★

During dinner the promised discussion regarding the wedding guests took place. Ginny was presently making a short list on a note pad. Since Silvie was inviting no one, and Laura Pemberton disliked social hobnobbing nowadays, the list consisted of a mere handful of people. Name after name had been mentioned and eliminated.

'They'll probably take offence Mother,' Mark suggested but looked unperturbed. After all Silvie had asked for a quiet wedding.

'To hell with them!' his mother retorted. 'Not obliged to invite anyone at all if we so wish.'

'Well so long as you don't overlook the Major, or you'll find yourself without a bridge partner,' he chuckled.

'Not likely to overlook him. Anyway he's already invited himself as a matter of fact. Telephoned just before you came back from the church.'

'Obviously Father must have told him the news this morning.'

'Apparently not. He didn't call on the Major after all. Must have spent his time wandering in the woods, instead.'

'That's strange! Then how did the Major know?'

'His wayward son evidently. Home for the weekend. Must have heard the news in the village.'

'I saw Jimmy Ashdown in his red sports car,' Joanne announced. 'He pulled in at a field gate just down from the Rectory as we came out on our way to the church. I think he may have stopped there specially when he caught sight of us.' She rolled her eyes appreciatively. 'He's very good looking. Must be my day for meeting handsome men!'

'Takes after his Irish mother for that,' declared Laura Pemberton

Ginny resumed writing. 'I hadn't put Mrs Ashdown on the list. I somehow thought that Major Ashdown wasn't married.'

Mark Pemberton interrupted the movement of the pen by saying, 'No Ginny, she and the Major are divorced. But I suppose we're obliged to invite Jimmy. Can't very well ignore him if his father's coming.'

'Oh I daresay it's safe enough to invite him,' assured his mother. 'He's not likely to be home again for a while. Life's too quiet for him in Kings Meadow.'

'That's a fact. Well let's hope you're right.'

'Now on to something more interesting. When are we going to buy our dresses?' inquired Joanne. 'We haven't got very much time.' Without waiting for a reply she continued. 'I think the best idea would be for me to go back to Stanford Road with Ginny and Silvie for a few days. From there we can easily go into the city to shop.'

'Marvellous idea,' agreed Ginny. 'Don't you think so Silvie?'

'Absolutely,' Silvie agreed. She would be glad to be back amongst her own things for a day or so, having found the sheer size of Briarwood house overwhelming. She supposed that Stanford Road was not a big enough stepping stone from Queen Street for her to adjust easily to such a change.

'It'll be a mad rush but I know we'll manage all right,' Ginny said. 'The summer hols have simply flown! Just think — we have to pack our things next week to go back to the College! And Miss Em's not going to be very pleased when we ask permission for more time off for the wedding the minute we get back to school. She'll probably say 'Goodness me! Why couldn't they have got themselves hitched during the holiday? After all they've known each other for four weeks now. What took him so long!'

The manner and speech of the little principal had been mimicked with such accuracy that Joanne and her brother laughed aloud. Silvie smiled, such humour from Ginny was commonplace to her.

'The improbability of such a statement from the genteel Miss Em reaches dizzy heights.' Mark Pemberton paused briefly before adding, 'True as it may be.'

The girls shrieked with laughter, and Silvie looked amused. Even Laura Pemberton, who was not given to diversion from her sober aspect on life, smiled wryly.

'Now,' Silvie asked, 'is there something I should be doing to help with the arrangements. I really oughtn't to be leaving everything to you Mrs Pemberton.'

'It seems there's very little *to* do. With so few guests we shall hold the reception in the house. I shall arrange the caterers.'

'Very well — if you're sure. We should be leaving or we won't get home this side of midnight. It's a very long journey and I do have to be up early for work in the morning.'

'Come on then girls — get a move on and start packing.' Mark Pemberton took Silvie by the hand as the four left the room. 'Now don't forget — hand in your resignation at Silvester's and arrange to leave Standford Road so that you can move in here next Saturday. This is your home as from now darling. I shall be home every weekend in future.'

She nodded agreement, and wondered how her promise to Adam was going to be kept.

'I'll go and throw a few things in a bag myself,' he continued as they went up the stairs.'

The girls put their packed cases outside their bedroom doors ready for Mark to carry down. 'When we come home from College next you'll actually be living here in this house with me for good Ginny! Sometimes I'm afraid that I'll wake up and find it's only been a dream after all.'

'Me too,' confessed Ginny. 'How unbearable it

would be to wake up and discover that none of this was really happening at all!'

Their voices carried into Silvie's room and as she listened she threw a glance at the connecting door to Adam's dressing room. In reality what they feared could so easily have been a fact yesterday.

★ ★ ★

Ginny eyed the packed suitcases in the hall at Stanford Road. 'I hope they'll all fit into Mark's car!'

'Probably be a bit of a squeeze. Just as well Joanne went back to Briarwood on Wednesday because there wouldn't have been room for her luggage as well. The dress boxes take up rather a lot of space.' It was now Saturday and had been Silvie's last day at Silvester's store. She had one more week to spend in this house. 'Are you sure that you've packed everything you're going to need for the College next week?'

'Yes quite certain. And you must be whacked out, all this on top of working all day today. You'll be able to rest next week. I wish you didn't have to come back to this house at all though.'

'Oh I don't mind. It's a nice house. I've enjoyed living here. It seemed so big after Queen Street.'

'I can't see Joanne or Mark living in the Queen Street house can you? I wonder what they'd say, especially Mark, if they saw it and we told them we once lived there.'

'I honestly can't imagine. The whole house would fit into just part of the front hall at Briarwood.'

Silvie made a last minute check through the house. Ginny followed. 'At least you've got something exciting to look forward to next week Silvie. Buying the rings.'

'Yes — can't have a marriage without those.'

'Are you all right Silv?' Ginny sensed that her sister's thoughts were preoccupied.

'Of course — just a bit tired that's all.' She glanced at the anxious face. 'As you say — I can take things easy next week.' Truth was she couldn't get Saturday night off her mind. That promise she'd made to Adam. At the time she'd not considered just how the promise could be kept. She did not regret it, but the fear that Mark would find out would remain constantly.

'Sit down and rest now Silvie. Everything's done.'

Silvie sank into an armchair and tried to keep her mind on Ginny's chatter.

'Funny idea calling the banns for three weeks in succession. I mean — as if anyone would object to you and Mark marrying! I wonder if anyone has ever stood up in church and made objections.'

'Certain to have at some time or other. The custom must have some basis. Probably to prevent bigamy.'

Ginny laughed. 'I like the Reverend Bradley. I always thought clergyman were old. He's only about Mark's age I should think.'

Silvie glanced around at the furniture. 'We're very lucky not to have to find a buyer for all this. Not that it's worth much. Would have been a problem trying to dispose of it at the very last minute. In Queen Street we could have just given it to the neighbours. Couldn't do that around here! It was a bit of luck the landlord wanting it.'

'Yes. What was it he said about jurisdiction?'

'Gives a landlord more jurisdiction over his own property if he lets a house furnished. By which he means that he can evict tenants if they turn out to be a problem. Tenants are not protected by the Rent Act if a house is furnished.'

'How odd! Well it suits us — his wanting the stuff. And you'll have a bed to sleep in right up until you leave on Saturday.'

'Yes very convenient.'

'Pity we had to give the ornaments and things away though.'

'I agree. But we have to be realistic. Anyway the Salvation Army man was pleased to receive them. They'll raise a small amount of money for their cause, and that's some consolation. Couldn't expect to scatter them about Briarwood.'

'No. I quite liked that blue vase though that I bought Mum last Christmas. But can you imagine Mrs Pemberton's face — a Woolworth vase in the drawing room! If it were a model of a horse she might overlook it — providing it was a thorough-bred.' Ginny giggled. Her humour again came to their aid. It had hurt to part with those things.

A light tap came on the door and a moment later Mark Pemberton walked into the room with his usual bright smile. 'Hello sun and moon.' He bent to kiss Silvie and hugged Ginny's shoulders. 'Has the ravishing redhead said her last farewell to number 32?'

Ginny nodded and her face took on a sad aspect.

'I called on Doctor Meredith this afternoon to say goodbye to him. He was so kind to me when Mum died.'

She crossed the room to stand at the French window. 'Just one last look at the apple tree.' She stood gazing out at the tree. Most of the fruit had been picked. A sudden gust of wind snatched at the leaves and scattered them into the air. She watched them float to the ground. Two apples from those which remained on the tree fell. 'Goodbye tree,' she murmured. 'Already the leaves are beginning to fall.' She turned from the window. But there was no one to hear. They were carrying the cases out to the car.

24

Once again and for the last time the banns were being called. Here in this tiny stone church Silvie Marsh felt an overwhelming sense of peace after the mental turmoil of the past two weeks.

When she and Ginny moved into Briarwood with their few personal belongings she'd felt she was casting off her old world completely. The transition was easy enough. Straight from the poverty of Queen Street the contrast would have been so much greater. Stanford Road had adjusted this. She had cast the future on the waters of deception and everything would have to flow with the tide. There could be no turning back.

The girls had returned to the College. With reluctance Adam had arrived this morning to attend the service with them after pressure from his son. 'Since you're to be part of the ceremony Father you should at least put in an appearance or it'll look odd!' Mark had told him.

Adam had arrived early having started out from the city before dawn. Until they were ready to set off for the church Silvie had not seen him.

Now seated as before in the front pew between father and son she let the rich musical voice of the Reverend David Bradley wash over her: balm to her spirit. The most soothing sound that she'd ever heard. One that could lull her into the sleep that had eluded her since the night she had gone to Adam

217

Pemberton's bed and made her bid to safeguard the future for Ginny.

Here, in this little sanctuary for the last two Sundays she had experienced a special quiescence that was like the soothing of her soul, unmarred by the sounds, an occasional cough, or shuffling feet. After that first Sunday the memory of the musty spice scented atmosphere had lingered long after she had left Kings Meadow. That and the voice was analgesic to her spirit. What was he saying right this minute? Beyond the sound of his voice she could not concentrate, and she felt so sleepy. The Pemberton men moved closer. She felt their bodies hard and strong against her as she struggled to keep her heavy lids from closing. Then she felt her hand being firmly clasped in Mark's. This aroused her momentarily, as it was meant to, and she looked up at the pulpit.

Amusement lurked in the deep blue eyes of David Bradley as he saw her long-lashed lids close again. His gaze moved leisurely on across the sea of faces below. The nave was packed, every seat filled, just as he'd foreseen. A wild crazy thought struck him that if he were to put a sign outside to announce that she was to appear again for evening service there would be a repeat full house. He saw the funny side of it all and would have liked to laugh out loud. Everyone with whom he'd spoken in the village had asked about her. Some had gone out of their way to seek him out to inquire. What did they think he could tell them? Why had they expected him to know more about her than they knew themselves! His eyes came to rest on her again. To his poetic imagination she looked as if she belonged between the pages of a children's picture book. For a moment he allowed his eyes to dwell. He saw the hand which held hers move slightly and she opened her eyes again to look up at him.

Something about her puzzled him, in fact had puzzled him since his first meeting with her. He sensed something was troubling her. But could that be possible — on the threshold of such a marriage! Yet he felt certain that she was not at peace with herself. If it was spiritual help she required — perhaps he could provide that?

His inherent flair for creative drama for his own diversion from the repetitive nature of his work surfaced. He imagined her as the picture book princess in desperate need of spiritual rescue and only *his* words could help her. Closing his book of sermon notes he put it aside. Those biblical readings: those happenings of two thousand years ago had no connection with her life today. She would have heard it before. They'd all heard it — over and over. Why concern themselves with those ancient events. Today and tomorrow mattered now.

With silver-tongued eloquence his heart spoke in terms of the present day. He did not look at her. From his pulpit stage every face became her face, and to her alone he spoke. Suddenly he realised that he had the undivided attention of them all. They were receptive. He had 'communicated' — as his father would say. Often in the past he'd said 'If you can't communicate with your audience you've lost them.'

Apparently in trying to rescue the sleeping

princess in the front pew he had captured the whole congregation with the language of today — straight from his heart.

When he glanced her way again he saw that she was firmly, yet discreetly, wedged between the two men, her head tilted very slightly to one side, and asleep.

When the service had ended Mark Pemberton and Silvie waited in the vestry while Reverend Bradley saw his congregation off at the front of the church. Many had gone round to the side entrance hoping to see her as she left. They had again been disappointed.

Adam had gone, having excused himself and returned to Briarwood alone.

When the Reverend had eventually rejoined them in the vestry he said, 'Sorry to be so long. Record attendance today.'

As they walked to the Rectory by way of the back path he said. 'I believe that some of them are still hanging about outside the church hoping to see you leave. I don't suppose they expected you to leave by this entrance. Dodging the fans my father would call it.'

'Yes it does appear to be a bit like that,' Mark Pemberton agreed.

Silvie smiled apologetically, 'I'm sorry — I must have fallen asleep during your sermon. Not from boredom I promise. Just the soothing atmosphere of the church I believe.'

'Just as well it doesn't have that effect on me. Can you imagine it — half way through the lesson — the sound of snoring from the pulpit!'

They all laughed at this and it eased her embarrassment.

They stayed for an hour. As they were about to leave Silvie handed him a formal invitation to the wedding reception at the house after the ceremony.

'I'd be delighted,' he accepted, then walked with them to the spot where Mark had parked his car in the lane.

★　★　★

On their return to Briarwood Laura Pemberton who was just crossing the hall in her wheelchair announced, 'Someone from the National Press just telephoned to ask if they might send a photographer for some pre-wedding pictures. I knew they would of course the moment the notice went in. They'll be here around three this afternoon.'

Adam Pemberton heard this as he was entering through the French window of the drawing room. His annoyance at the news was obvious as he strode into hall. 'What the hell! You should have refused! Why pander to silly social gossip.'

His wife raised her eyebrows in surprise. 'Such vehemence! I had no idea that you'd object to a little publicity, it's always a good thing in business.'

'Nonsense,' he replied tersely. 'We don't need publicity, as well you know.'

'No need to get into a huff about it Father. I don't mind.' Mark Pemberton looked surprised at his father's over-reaction to the news. 'I have no objection and I don't think Silvie will mind. I don't suppose they'll hang about long. We'll make certain they don't. Although it does seem a bit pointless when they'll be back to take pictures of the wedding.'

They had all moved into the drawing room. Silvie tried to suppress rising panic, 'I'll slip upstairs to change my shoes.'

'We'll go for a stroll around the grounds when you come down darling.' Mark Pemberton seated himself to wait.

His father understood well that Silvie would have qualms about the press photographs and wanted to reassure her that in the unlikely event of a Georgian house client studying the newspaper gossip he could make no mention of recognition without exposing himself. Besides there had been so few, and over such a short time. 'I think I'll go up and change. I'll be leaving before dinner this evening. I have some work to catch up on in the office ready for tomorrow.'

'Must you Father? It's a long way to have come for just a few hours! Sure it won't wait?'

'Positive.' Adam replied as he left the room.

Silvie sat on her bed wondering how she could disguise herself for the photographs. A head scarf perhaps? A topcoat with a high collar? Much too hot for that. Not that she'd mind the discomfort of the heat, but it would look odd on such a warm day. Perhaps she could turn her head at the crucial moment. Dark glasses — a definite must. Luckily she'd bought some for her day at the coast with Adam. They would no doubt ask her to remove them while they took the photos, but she had only to refuse. She'd decided upon the dark glasses and scarf when she heard a quick soft knock on the connecting door. She darted across to lock her door before unlocking the one to Adam's dressing room.

'Listen Silvie,' he quickly tried to quell her fears by giving her the benefit of his own logic. 'It's extremely unlikely that any of Madam Moss's clients would look at the social pages. Even less that they'd ever admit to being on the premises.' His adoring eyes swept over her. Suddenly he snatched her close and kissed her longingly. Then he released her. 'I must go or Laura will get suspicious — both of us being up here at the same time. I'm surprised she hasn't mentioned that day by the tennis courts.'

'She did say something actually. Asked me how well I knew you. I couldn't deny having met you before, because she must have watched us. I told her we'd met through a mutual acquaintance but until that day I did not know that you are Mark's father.'

'Well that's as near the truth as you could put it.' He smiled down at her. 'Best go now darling. Relock the door.'

She did so then went to fetch a scarf and dark glasses ready for the afternoon ordeal. Laura Pemberton had forewarned about the press interest, but to have to face it twice!

For the wedding she would have the veil to screen her face and however odd they thought it she did not intend to lift it.

She prayed that the photographs today would not be clear and that no one who was likely to expose her would see them. But it was too much to hope.

25

Watery-grey eyes peered closer to the newspaper photograph and scarlet-tipped fingers adjusted the spectacles on the wide bridged nose. Aloud Madam Moss addressed the air as she raised her eyes to focus blindly on the gaudy flower in the bay. 'Goot Got! So thet's who he is! Adam Pemberton!' She drew a small lace-edged cambric handkerchief from the sleeve of her blouse and removed her spectacles to polish them. As if doubting her sight first time she replaced them to read again of the forthcoming wedding in the Pemberton family whose ancestors established the famed Whitehorne Importing-Exporting business. She studied the photograph of the man she had known as Rossi only and read again — Adam Pemberton father of the prospective bridegroom.

Although Adam had gone horse riding after lunch that day and had not been at home when the photographers arrived, he had returned just prior to their leaving. Unsuspectingly he had come into view at the side of the house and with ever ready cameras they had snapped him in his riding clothes before he could protest, which he'd promptly done before striding into the house with a wave of dismissal when asked to pose with his son and Silvie.

The photographs had turned out very clear. The day had been breezy and Silvie had used this as an excuse to keep the headscarf on. The photographers had not objected. Even with the scarf and dark glasses she still looked like a film star.

Rachael Moss put aside the newspaper and with the usual effort eased herself from her throne. Ignoring the high-heeled court shoes on the carpet beside the chair she paced the floor in stockinged feet while she continued her soliloquy. 'How ken thet be? Marryink the son! Ken the young vun know? Surely not!'

As she assimilated this unexpected and surprising information her shrewd mind calculated how best to turn it to her own advantage.

The girl, whose photograph she might well have overlooked and passed off as mere coincidental likeness on account of the disguise but for the picture of the man, had apparently used the Georgian house to net herself a rich man and somehow through him, his son! This would make the scandal of the century if exposed! 'How ken it hev come about?' she asked the air before snatching up the paper again to read closely the spelling of the name and that of the country village mentioned.

She crossed to her desk and took up a silver pen to make a note before flicking rapidly through the pages of the telephone directory. With a sudden pounce of her fingers she arrested the flying pages. A vivid nail ran swiftly down the columns then stopped and darted sideways to pinpoint a number. Voicing this aloud she copied it alongside her previous notes. With controlled emotion she paced the floor again while she considered a planned course of action. After a while she returned to the desk and with determined fingers dialled a number.

★ ★ ★

There had been many telephone calls since the wedding announcement, 'Angling for invitations,' claimed Laura Pemberton who had handled the calls with polite but swift expertise. The preparations were now finished and everything organised for the wedding tomorrow morning. All this she had managed over the telephone. The caterers, the flowers, the cars. The arranging had kept her from the stables more than she had liked. Not that this had meant any physical neglect of the horses. A young trainee jockey came from the village every day to exercise them and to give a general hand in the stables. And now she was anxious to get back to her one passion in life.

On her way out the phone rang and she had to turn back when she was half way to the door.

Silvie, with little else to do, was reading in her bedroom. Noting that the ringing tone had gone on a little longer than usual she concluded that Laura Pemberton was outside. She went to answer it herself. Before she reached the upstairs extension the ringing tone ceased. From below she heard the deep voice of Laura Pemberton. 'Madam who? Moss? Silvia Marsh? One moment please — I'll fetch her to the phone.'

With alarm strangling her voice Silvie called down — 'It's all right. I'll take it up here.' Apprehensive she lifted the receiver. This call would not be a congratulatory one. It meant trouble. Yet she'd expected none from this quarter. Rachael Moss was in a too weak position herself; she wouldn't dare!

226

Before speaking into the receiver she called down, 'It's all right I have it.' She waited for the click which would tell her that the phone downstairs had been replaced. It seemed overlong in coming. When it did she spoke.

'Silvie Marsh here.' She held her breath as she waited for the caller to state her business.

'So — you hef done very vell for yourself. Vith my help eh? Rich men. My Rossi's son! I think thet some very funny bisness is goink on, end I suspect thet mother-in-law to be knows nothink about it eh? End vot about the bridegroom-to-be eh? Does he know? I think not or . . . '

With a mixture of panic and anger at the effrontery Silvie interrupted the obvious intent behind the call, 'Why have you contacted me here in this manner! What do you want?'

'Vont my deah? A leetle compensashink for runink off vith vun of my best cli-inks.'

'What are you talking about!'

'Money deah — money!. Shall ve siy £500?'

'Don't be ridiculous! I owe you nothing. Furthermore my private life is none of your concern.' She felt herself trembling with anger at the gall of Rachael Moss. Deep misgivings began to gnaw at her. This gross woman could ruin everything if she chose. With the wedding only one day away there was still time for her to do her worst from spite. Just a few damning words would prevent the wedding from taking place. Yet would she dare when in doing so she would be incriminating herself, with a prison sentence as the possible outcome. Would she, out of spite alone, risk that?

Common sense came to her aid when she considered how much Rachael Moss valued her comfort.

Mechanically she lowered her voice, although she knew there was no one to overhear. 'How dare you telephone me with such demands!'

'I hef told you vy. I don't know vot sort of gime you hef bin playink vith those two men but you vouldink vont anythink to cancel the veddink now vould you? A vord to Mrs P vould ruink it all eh!'

Under surprise attack it was not easy to think or decide how best to handle the situation. Any minute Mark would be arriving with the girls whom he had met off the train in the city. She couldn't afford to risk trouble from Madam Moss who could easily make an anonymous call to tell Laura Pemberton of the past association with Adam. And she would not be hard to convince now that she was aware of some previous link between them. She had saved £200. After tomorrow she would no longer have to concern herself about money. To get Rachael Moss off the line she made a quick decision.

'I shall send you £200. It's all you'll ever get. So don't try to contact me again.' Trembling still she replaced the receiver before anything further could be said. What else could she have done in the time under such pressure? She could not even be certain that Laura Pemberton hadn't listened in out of curiosity.

In order to judge this she hurried downstairs and met her coming from the drawing room. She had as yet not gone to the stables as intended.

'That name,' she stopped the wheelchair in the

centre of the hall. 'It rings a bell. Jewish isn't it? Moss. Rachael Moss. Strange accent. I once knew a Jewish acquaintance who'd fled Russia during the revolution, and she had the same accent. Your dressmaker she said. I hope she's not piqued because she wasn't commissioned to make your wedding gown.'

Silvie relaxed. 'No — no not at all.' But she noted that a puzzled expression remained in Laura Pemberton's eyes. She was spared further questions by the sudden noisy arrival of the girls and Mark, their high voices mingling with his deep one as they came into the house.

They flung down various belongings, including school blazers, onto the marble floor of the hall and swooped across to hug her. As she hugged them back she was still conscious of the watcher in the wheelchair.

Smiling broadly Mark put down the two suitcases he'd carried in and strode across to kiss her. 'Hello darling. You look very calm and collected considering that you've just been practically knocked off your feet by a couple of whirlwinds.'

Calm and collected! How deceptive outward appearances could be at times she thought as the three turned to greet Laura Pemberton.

'Everything under control Mother?' Mark asked brightly.

She made no attempt to answer this. Her moods never did match the natural light ones of her son. Instead she asked, 'When will Peter and Harry be arriving?'

'Should be here very soon. They were about an

hour behind us. They stayed to clear up a few loose ends at the offices. They'll be coming in Peter's car.'

'Will they stay a while on Sunday?' Joanne asked. 'I want Peter to come riding with us in the morning.'

'I daresay he'll go out with you on Sunday morning.' Mark picked up the cases and turned back to Silvie. 'Won't be a tick darling. I'll put these upstairs and change. We'll go for a walk in the garden.'

'Yes all right Mark.' A moment after watching the wheelchair and it's occupant turn to leave the house by the usual route, through the French window of the drawing room, she went upstairs to her bedroom, and with anger behind every stroke of the pen wrote out a cheque for £200 payable to Rachael Moss. Then she sat for a few moments longer staring across at the connecting door to Adam's rooms and wishing he were there to tell about the call. But he had already phoned to say he wouldn't be arriving until morning. He intended to make a pre-dawn start that would ensure his arrival in good time for the ceremony. She had toyed with the idea of phoning him at his flat but decided not to risk making such a call from the house. And no real purpose would have been served. She heard Mark calling her and answered, 'Coming.'

★   ★   ★

While Silvie was changing for dinner Mark Pemberton made one last attempt to persuade his mother to attend the ceremony and again protested

230

strongly when she refused. 'You know very well you could manage it Mother if only you wouldn't be so damned stubbornly independent!'

'I've told you it would take a month of Sundays for me to get in and out of the car with this damned chair. I'd hold up the whole show. I don't intend to make a spectacle of myself for all and sundry in the village to gawp at. You'll manage well enough without me there.' Truth was she hated outsiders to see how incapacitated the accident had left her compared to the active person she had once been. Most of the villagers had at one time or another seen her in her black riding outfit, her dark hair streaming in the wind, never a hat, racing across the countryside in the point to points on her beloved black stallion. Wild and free she'd been in those days: Wild and free!

'Managing without you is not the issue here. As my mother you should be there. It's . . . '

'I don't care what the devil it is,' she interrupted impatiently. 'In any case someone has to be here to supervise the hired caterers. Besides — you won't be in the church above ten minutes. Just long enough for that young clergyman to prompt you into uttering a lot of drivel that you'll have completely forgotten long before you've jumped into bed with the girl.'

He threw up his hands in a resigned gesture, 'What a cynic you are!' He smiled despite his failure to change her mind.

★　★　★

231

Time had hung heavily all week for Silvie. Dora Glasspool was always on the go with some domestic chore or another and rebuffed all offers of help. Laura Pemberton had kept to her own quarters when not either making or answering endless phone calls, or out at the stables. Not that Silvie would have welcomed either of these two as company. Dora's attitude was decidedly cool, and Laura Pemberton's very little better.

Mark's three times daily calls had helped pass some of the hours. And during her walks in the garden she had always stopped to chat to Joe Tarrant in whose company she was more at ease than with the two women in the house. She began to wonder what she would do to fill the long weekdays ahead. Country walks most likely, weather permitting, she decided. But for the present the girls were home and so was Mark, filling the house with sound and movement.

A little over six weeks had passed since her first meeting with Mark Pemberton. During this time he had so often told her that he loved her. Yet not once had he asked her if she loved him. She supposed that he automatically accepted that she did, since she had agreed to his proposal of marriage. She pondered on this now. Was she in love with him? Perhaps a little. He was handsome and certainly pleasant company, seeming not to take life too seriously. Even with the shadow of her past so recently thrown back at her she found herself wondering what sort of lover he would be.

Her thoughts turned to Adam. Was she in love with him? Yes. She had been in love with him from the first meeting at the Georgian house. She'd been attracted to him in the way that young girls often are to older men. There was a certain dependency about him. She wasn't sure if it was physical, or mental. Experienced perhaps was the word.

Now, wearing a dark blue dress ready for dinner she regarded her reflection. Dark blue angel Jack would say. No . . . Dark angel — she corrected her thoughts. Then turned away from the mirror and went downstairs to join the others, which now included Harry Mortimer and Peter Dunning.

★   ★   ★

'Actually the bridegroom is not supposed to see the bride on the evening before the wedding,' Joanne remarked as they were all leaving the dining room.

Ginny supported this. 'That's correct. It's unlucky. Mark will have to disappear for the rest of the evening, or Silvie will have to stay in her bedroom.'

'Well us chaps will spend the rest of the evening in the library,' Mark decided. 'Set your alarms early girls. It'll take you hours to get dressed in those fancy clothes.'

'I have a few last minute things to do anyway.' Silvie turned towards the stairs as she spoke, 'Goodnight Peter, goodnight Harry.'

Both men replied together and their eyes followed her as Mark walked with her to the foot of the stairs. He half turned to call back to them — 'Join you directly boys. You go on in and pour some drinks ready.'

The girls, having said their goodnight's all round, ran on ahead of Silvie up the stairs.

Laura Pemberton came from the dining room and turned her chair in the direction of her rooms. 'Goodnight,' she called to the two men still in the hall.

'Wait Laura,' Harry Mortimer turned to her. 'Come and have a drink with us before you retire.'

'Very well. I'll have one brandy. I have to be up early too.' She liked the company of these two men. She had known them for a very long time. Both genuinely had the interests of the firm at heart, and both were main cogs in the wheels that drove it.

26

Early on Saturday morning Silvie was woken from a half sleep by a tap on her door and the sound of Dora Glasspool's voice calling — 'It's seven o'clock.'

The bedroom drapes were pulled back and from the bed she looked out on a clear blue sky. Dora had stayed overnight on account that there had been extra people for dinner, and for the much better reason of being in the house when Adam arrived. Already she had fussed over him with early breakfast when he arrived at six thirty. 'I'll fetch breakfast up in half an hour,' continued the voice outside the door.

'Thank you Dora — just coffee and toast please.' Silvie had been ordered by the girls to stay in her room until she was ready to leave for the church. She was amused at the way they had taken charge of her.

'We'll be in first thing to help you get ready,' they'd claimed. Probably both still sound asleep, she mused.

Ten minutes later they swooped into the room bright and cheerful, though still in their pyjamas, to check that she was awake. When they saw that she was they ran off again with a promise to be back.

Fifteen minutes later they brought up a tray with her coffee and toast. After depositing it on the bedside table they disappeared again with further promises of return and insisting again that she must not see the bridegroom before she arrived at the church. She wondered how they had come by such information on wedding procedure and decided that they must have made a point of reading up on it somewhere, perhaps a book in the College library?

Constantly during the next two hours they were in and out of her bedroom helping her to get ready. She heard Adam in his dressing room and wanted to tell him of the call from Rachael Moss but would not risk opening the door. Even if the opportunity presented itself when the girls were not present in the room there was a strong possibility that one of the men, or even all three, might be with him checking the last minute details before leaving for the church.

Minutes before they were due to leave the girls ran off to have a last minute peep at the cake in the dining room, and to announce that she was about to come downstairs.

Down in the hall at the base of the staircase Adam Pemberton stood waiting; immaculately dressed, and very handsome, in a light grey suit, white silk shirt and dove grey tie.

As she came down he moved forward, his eyes embracing, possessing, but not estranged from pain and guilt. On the bottom stair she paused, her face nearer the level of his.

'Silvie,' he whispered. The hall was at present empty but for the two of them. A wry smile tugged at his lips as the thought struck him that he was about to give her away in order to keep her. His eyes lingered until the girls appeared, followed by his wife, Dora Glasspool, and the hired catering staff.

Amid exclamations and compliments from the latter Adam gave her his arm.

Envy struck deeply into the mind of Dora Glasspool as her eyes moved from his face and focussed on the silken arm linked with his as he escorted the bride out through the already open door, followed by the two girls in pale blue lace, to the waiting car.

★   ★   ★

The whole village it seemed had turned out for the wedding. As Adam handed her from the car outside the church a unanimous sigh of admiration rose from the crowd. For most it was the first real sight of the new Pemberton to be. Curiosity had brought many there in response to the reports which had been circulating the village about her beauty

'You look a picture my dear,' an old lady in the foreground said.

Silvie turned to smile nervously in acknowledgment. Praise and compliments came spontaneously and ungrudgingly. The feel of Adam's strong arm beneath her hand helped to steady her as she walked.

She had never had this many people all at once peering at her so closely. The press photographers had placed themselves at vantage points. At this stage she pulled her veil down over her face.

They had reached the church doors and entered. Sedately the girls followed. They had no train to support. Silvie had chosen a simple close fitting gown of ivory slipper satin. Her bouquet was made up of cream roses bound with ivory satin and her flaxen hair hung loosely down her back.

The wedding march played them to the altar steps. Here Adam Pemberton hesitated and for a second or two longer than necessary clung tightly to her arm before releasing it and stepping back a pace.

Mark Pemberton turned to look down at her as she took her place beside him. The sheen on her ivory skin was enhanced by the lacy veil through which the pale rose of her lips showed. His eyes lingered for a few more moments, then he turned back to the Reverend David Bradley who had taken the opportune moment to let his own eyes dwell on the bride.

Then came the voice — the sound which helped to calm her doubts and fears . . .

'Dearly beloved we are gathered here in the sight of . . . ' When he came to the words — 'Who gives this woman . . . '

Once again Adam Pemberton hesitated before responding . . . 'I give this woman . . . '

*   *   *

The guests, being few in number, could adequately be accommodated at the dining room table which seated twenty people. These were the Jackson-Brownes who were close friends and regular bridge partners of Laura Pemberton, Adam's second in command Harry Mortimer, Peter Dunning the best man and long time closest friend of Mark and also his deputy at the offices, Joe Tarrant and his sister

Mary, Major Ashdown, his son Jimmy, who had made a point of accepting the invitation even though the prospect of spending the weekend at Kings Meadow with no company was not his idea of a good time, and the Reverend David Bradley.

Having been delayed by photographers and well-wishers Silvie, Mark, Peter Dunning and the girls were last to arrive back at the house.

The guests, some of whom Silvie had not as yet met, were assembled in the hall awaiting the return of the newly weds.

Adam Pemberton presented them now as they came forward to kiss the bride and congratulate the groom.

Major Ashdown bowed stiffly and his bristly moustache touched her cool cheek. He had a deep mistrust of beautiful women. In his experience they spelled trouble. His manner was perhaps a trifle stiffer than usual today. His ruffled feathers had not quite settled since his son had arrived home in the early hours the worse for drink, in which state he'd driven from the city. He had stumbled on the stairs and woken his father who had given him the abrasive side of his tongue. 'You're as tight as a blasted tick!' he'd roared, and would have thrashed him had it not meant telltale bruises next day.

In consequence of his excesses Jimmy Ashdown had been in no fit state to attend the wedding ceremony and was still in bed when his father left for the church. The Major had ordered him to douse himself under a cold shower, take an aspirin, and present himself at Briarwood by the time everyone arrived back from the church.

Right at this moment Jimmy Ashdown was standing in line to greet the bride, his easy good looks belying his true physical state. As she entered the hall his was the first face her eyes had focussed on and she knew that her worst fears had been realised. Mechanically now she accepted the kisses and good wishes of those about her until the dreaded moment arrived.

'Meet my son James,' she heard the Major saying.

She forced a smile. 'Nice to meet you Mr. Ashdown.'

As Jimmy Ashdown bent to kiss the bride his voice gave nothing away to the onlookers as he murmured, 'My pleasure I'm sure.' Then with veiled mockery behind his words he turned to congratulate the man whose bride he'd already sampled in a paid love bed.

Being confronted so unexpectedly by Jimmy Ashdown on the heels of the blackmail call from Rachael Moss almost unnerved her completely. She hadn't liked the way he'd looked at her and certainly would not trust him. Suddenly she had a desperate yearning for the solace of the little stone church where, in its balmy fragrance she could find sanctuary, where the soothing voice like a velvet drug would calm her. Then she saw him. His eyes were on her as though he read her thoughts and knew her craving for the spicy haven in that quiet stone retreat.

He stepped forward and took her by the hand. Then she felt the warm pressure of his lips on her forehead, 'I wish you peace of mind and happiness Mrs Pemberton.' His deep blue eyes held hers for a moment, as if trying to fathom her thoughts. And for some strange reason she dearly wished that she could tell them — as if in the telling her fears might be released and blown away. 'Thank you Reverend,' she said.

As they assembled at the table champagne was opened and poured. Then the catering staff began to serve.

Adam Pemberton did his best to keep his eyes on his liquor and off of Silvie.

Jimmy Ashdown did the reverse. Noting this the Major was pleased on the one hand, but not on the other. Raw with past disappointments and discredits brought about by his son he leaned across and spoke to him in a voice which commanded respect despite its quiet tone. 'Keep your lecherous eyes off young Pemberton's woman or I'll whip the hide off you.' A threat that was to prove prophetic.

★　★　★

The honeymooners had left to spend two weeks in Rome. It was now past midnight. The Jackson-Brownes, the Major and Laura Pemberton were at present in the drawing room playing bridge. The girls had gone off to bed early. Harry Mortimer and Peter Dunning had retired to their respective bedrooms. Tomorrow they were to drop the girls off at the city station for their return to College, and would be leaving by mid morning. The other four guests had left earlier and the caterers long since cleared away and gone.

In the kitchen Dora Glasspool removed her

apron, having just made more coffee for the bridge players and put the final touches to tidying up. She had stayed on to help until late and was to sleep at Briarwood tonight. Knowing that Adam had not yet gone up to bed she went in search of him. During the reception she had noted that he'd been drinking heavily and that he looked unhappy. So well she knew his face, its moods and expressions.

She now made her way to the library where she guessed he would most likely be. A strip of light below the door and the scent of cigar smoke told her as she approached that she had guessed right. She hesitated before knocking softly, then listened for a reply.

'Come in.'

When she opened the door she saw that he was seated at his desk, a whisky bottle and a half full glass in front of him. As she entered he looked up. 'Hello Dora.' His voice sounded thick. He'd drank too much, just as he'd intended.

'I thought you might like some coffee before you go to bed Adam.'

'Good idea Dora. Not too strong though or I shan't get to sleep. Are they still playing?'

'Yes. Will be for another couple of hours most likely.'

'Well don't wait up Dora. You must be whacked. You've had a long and busy day.'

'Oh — I'm all right.' It was nice having him concerned about her. 'Well everything went off well and the weather was lovely. How does it feel having a daughter-in-law?' Knowing something was wrong she watched his face closely. She couldn't help feeling that it was connected with Mark's marriage.

'Not very good Dora.'

Misunderstanding now she put her head to one side, taking the opportunity to let her eyes sweep over him openly, savouring the moments and every inch. He'd looked so handsome today in his grey suit. He had removed his jacket now and it hung over the back of his chair. She longed to touch him, to smooth his silky shirt, to feel the warmth and strength of his masculine body and feel his arms about her. She wished that he desired her and that he'd make love to her on his leather couch in this quiet place.

She said, 'Well it hasn't made you look any older. You never did look your age.'

'How do you know what my age is?'

'Laura told me long ago on one of her birthdays. Said she was four years older than you. So you must now be forty-nine. I'll go and make the coffee.'

'Have some with me Dora. Remember not too strong though or it'll keep me awake. And I must sleep.' He ran his hands through his hair. A habitual gesture that she loved. But she detected an air of desperation in the action this time.

As she went out and closed the door behind her she wondered why he'd been drinking so much and why he looked so desperately unhappy.

Alone again for the moment he realised that he needed company, someone to talk to, to listen to, trivia — anything that would take his mind off Silvie. There was a whole night to get through. And after that — fourteen endless days and nights without seeing her. He had wanted to possess her freely, without constraint or conscience, as it had been before she'd met his son, to whom she now belonged in fact and in law. And he hadn't the moral strength to accept it and walk away. He was too deeply incensed. He was his own prisoner — his own victim.

27

The name had been nagging at the back of her mind ever since the telephone call. It had been submerged beneath the preparations for the wedding reception, and with guests to entertain there had been no time to concentrate — then afterwards the bridge games. All that was yesterday. Today was Sunday. Adam had gone riding with the girls and Peter Dunning. Harry Mortimer, who did not ride, had gone for a walk in the grounds.

At last Laura Pemberton could focus her whole attention on the name. 'Moss? Moss?' As she spoke the name aloud she closed her eyes tightly and bit her lip in a concentrated effort to remember.

'Madam Rachael Moss. Dressmaker.' Yes — dressmaking! But who could possibly have spoken to her about dress making? No one that she could bring to mind. She had no interest in fashions, and her friends knew this. Perhaps Joanne had mentioned someone at College? No — Joanne would never discuss clothes; even her own she chose herself, usually after consulting Mark for his opinion. 'Dressmaking . . . Moss . . . Madame Rachael . . . ?' Again she spoke the words aloud as she taxed her memory deeper.

Recollection clicked and she looked suddenly startled. For a full two minutes she sat frowning — recalling. Then abruptly she turned the chair wheels towards her bedroom where she rummaged through the drawers of a davenport. Moments later she held a scarlet and gold card in her palm. A while back she had removed it from a pocket in Adam's jacket before handing this to Dora for the dry cleaners. Quite absently she had put it away in the drawer at the time, for she had no reason to keep such a card herself, and had put her own connotations on the real nature of Madam Moss's business. She wheeled herself back to the drawing room where she impatiently awaited his return.

Harry Mortimer was the first to appear, followed shortly by the two girls and Peter Dunning.

'Adam is staying out a bit longer,' Peter informed her.

'Is Daddy leaving much later than us Peter?' Joanne asked as she placed her ready packed school case on the hall floor.

'Probably an hour. He has an important call to put through to Ireland. Pre-arranged for 12 o'clock. That's why I'm your chauffeur today.'

Joanne was pleased about this, for she'd had a schoolgirl crush on Peter Dunning for a long time. He was the next best thing to her brother. Perhaps because he and Mark had been such close friends for what seemed like forever to her. Peter had spent so many weekends at Briarwood from way back in their college days before they'd both joined the airforce during the war.

Harry Mortimer came downstairs carrying his overnight case. 'Are we all set?'

Right behind him came Ginny. 'All ready.'

'Me too. We've already said goodbye to Daddy.' Joanne kissed her mother. 'It'll seem ages until we see Mark and Silvie again!'

'Never mind. You'll have your College work to keep you busy. The time will pass quickly enough.' Peter Dunning assured her.

Laura Pemberton was relieved when she heard the car drive off and silence once again reigned in the house. What she had to say to her husband could not bear an audience. She was still in the hall where they had taken their leave of her. She glanced across at the grandfather clock. Any moment now he would appear for he'd want to be in good time to make his arranged phone call. She went into the drawing room to wait.

When he arrived she called him into the room and immediately confronted him with the scarlet and gold card which she held out on display in her open palm. 'Exactly who is this Moss woman?'

Surprise flickered briefly across his face and he wondered how she had come by it. He shrugged and was about to tell her, but some instinct held the words in check. Instead he asked, 'Where did you get that from?' The next instant he felt relieved that he'd acted on intuition.

Without waiting for his reply to her question she continued, 'This Moss woman telephoned Silvia Marsh on Friday claiming to be her dressmaker. I demand to know what the real connection is between them. Why this card is in your possession and the advertiser calling this house asking for her.'

With well-hidden concern he played for time to gain some margin of grace to think. Care was essential in what he now said, since Silvie was involved. 'She is not Silvie Marsh now she is Silvie

Pemberton,' he parried.

'She wasn't on Friday when the call came,' she retorted knowing that he was playing a delay in the answer game. 'Don't try to side step. Who *is* this woman?'

He shrugged. 'As you can see — a dressmaker. Why shouldn't she telephone Silvie? Business cards of that nature are distributed freely in hotels and bars. I can't even remember how I came by it.'

Slowly she shook her head. 'You should know better than to take me for a fool. I know that cards of this nature are handed around among men to advertise whorehouses and that dressmaking is a commonly purported front. That first day the girl came here I was sure by the expression on your faces that you and she had met before. Although you both covered the fact well from Mark.'

'What of it?' he countered, 'I had seen her before. She's not the kind a man would forget.' He went across to stand at the French window, looking out at the garden. He knew that his last remark would cause no jealousy as it might with any other wife. She never had reacted like a proper woman anyway.

'Very well,' she spoke sharply now. 'I shall contact this dressmaker then. If she is genuine, as you imply, she won't put me off with excuses if I say I want some sewing work done.'

He swung round to face her. 'Do that.' Abruptly he dismissed her by striding from the room. He felt confidently sure that Rachael Moss would from necessity have ways of dispensing with such inquiries. Any wife who came into possession of one of her cards was a potential adversary if suspicious.

Helpless to detain him his wife watched him go. But even if her tongue must for the present let the matter of the card drop her shrewd mind did not.

Impatiently she waited for him to make his call to Ireland and leave. Then she immediately dialled the number on the scarlet card. 'Ah — Madam Moss. I believe you have recently done some dressmaking work for an acquaintance of mine and I'm wondering if . . . '

Instinctively cautious Rachael Moss cut her short. 'Ve cennot tike any more verk. Ve hef too much in hend. I em sorry Medem.' She distrusted the call for the obvious reason that it was a lie. Truth was that Sara Hoskins had done no sewing for almost a year now, claiming that her eyes troubled her. For all she knew the caller could be a woman working for the police and carrying out a sneaky inquiry.

'Perhaps later then?' Laura Pemberton persisted

'My regular cli-inktelle keep me busy vith constent orders end my verkroom is so small. I em sorry.'

Before the receiver at the other end could cut her off Laura Pemberton put in quickly, 'Your business cards? Why do you continue to distribute them?'

The scarlet mouth at the other end pursed. So it was one of the cards the woman had come across. Unperturbed she answered, 'It must hev bin around somevhere for a very lonk time. I em sorry. Good efternoon.' She hung up hoping that the reason given had satisfied the caller. If not and she rang again Sara Hoskins would have to get up off her lazy arse and run up whatever was required. Although she strongly suspected the call to be a testing one on

249

account of the lie about recent work having been done.

Unsatisfied Laura Pemberton replaced the receiver on the dead line, her suspicions neither confirmed or refuted. She had the wits to know that had she gone as far as to mention the name of Silvie Marsh it would only have extracted an outraged denial of anything improper.

As she moved away from the telephone and guided the wheels of her chair towards the French window she wondered, with her usual cynicism, what she had hoped to achieve from making such a call. Perhaps she had hoped for a quite different response, such as an invitation to call at a genuine dressmaking establishment! With a mental kick in the pants and a brief sardonic laugh she took her derisive thoughts out to the stables.

28

For Silvie, who had never been further than picnics in the forest and Sunday school outings to the seaside as a child, Rome was another world. The distractions pushed her anxieties to the back of her mind; although her promise to Adam pricked her conscience constantly. Mark was a perfect escort. He spoke Italian fluently. They were booked into a top hotel. The early autumn weather was perfect They had seen the sights and shopped for presents, and now were on their way home.

★　★　★

For two weeks Adam Pemberton had been left wondering about the call from Rachael Moss. From her grasping nature he knew it wouldn't have been a congratulatory one. She hadn't wasted any time! Damn newspapers nosing into peoples lives, making them the object of tittle-tattle, and vulnerable. He silently cursed his wife for making the news public. Why did the damn world have to be notified! He hadn't intended to be at Briarwood when they returned. But that call made it necessary now. Undoubtedly Rachael Moss would have been furious at the loss of both himself and Silvie from her financial grasp. But he could make no move until he'd seen Silvie and established the reason for the call. He hated to think that she'd been harassed or worried by it.

As he drove home to Briarwood he reminisced back on the days when his son was a child, the two of them going on long rambles together in the woods on Saturday afternoons, or horse riding across the two estates. He'd always made a point of being there at weekends to keep Mark company in the absence of a mother who had no time for anything or anyone other than her horses. How could he have possibly dreamed then that they would fall in love with the same girl. Or that he could be capable of deceiving his son so.

He stopped off at an inn to get a drink to steady himself for the meeting to come. When he left the inn half an hour later a fine misty rain was falling steadily.

When he arrived at Briarwood they had already returned. It was just on lunchtime when he entered the house. His son was coming down the stairs.

'Hello Father — glad you could get home for the weekend.'

'Came specially,' at least he could answer truthfully about that, even if the real reason could not be given. 'You look tanned. The weather was obviously good. How was Rome?'

'Wonderful. Sunshine every day and not too hot at this time of year. How's everything at the offices? Peter's been managing all right no doubt.'

'Yes everything's fine.' He turned as his wife wheeled herself from her downstairs quarters towards the drawing room. He went across to her on account of his son's presence and gave her a light peck on her cheek. Appearances must be kept up before the family. If they weren't around he did not bother for he disliked his wife as much as she disliked him.

'Lunch is in fifteen minutes,' she said.

'I'll go up and change.'

'See you at lunch then.' Mark called back as he followed his mother into the drawing room.

Unaware that Adam had arrived Silvie passed his door on the way from the girl's rooms where she had just placed their presents brought back from Rome. For his mother Mark had bought a black silk scarf, patterned with small dove grey horseshoes; dreary to Silvie's mind but would suit the sombre taste of Laura Pemberton. For Adam they had chosen grey leather moccasin slippers. For Dora a blue cardigan which had already been presented to her. Silvie continued on downstairs.

In his dressing room Adam listened at the connecting door then knocked softly. After waiting a few minutes for response he changed from his suit into something more casual and went down to join the others in the dining room, where he endeavoured to behave in the manner expected of a new father-in-law. He greeted Silvie first with a quick but warm kiss on her cheek, aware of his wife's watchful eyes on him, and that her curiosity was still unsatisfied about the call and its connection with the scarlet card. He knew that Silvie would be anxious to speak with him about it.

As usual Mark kept the mood light throughout the meal, the conversation mainly about Rome. Silvie was glad of this to hide her own anxieties.

Because of the rain they were confined to the

253

house. Dora, who as usual had fussed over Adam, was at present in the kitchen washing up the lunch dishes and preparing for the evening meal. She had decided that she would eat in the dining room with them this evening and that she would wear her new blue cardigan. She'd been disappointed to hear that Adam was leaving later to return to the city and wondered why he was not staying the night. The long drive for such a brief stay seemed hardly worth while. But she was glad to have him there even for just a few hours and at least she would have her ride home with him later.

Adam was impatiently waiting for an opportunity to catch Silvie alone. Mark was constantly at her side. The opportune moment suddenly presented itself when Mark announced — 'I think I should check out the car because it's been standing unused for a couple of weeks. Shouldn't take long. I daresay it's perfectly all right.' He was sitting beside Silvie on the window seat in the drawing room, looking out at the drenched flowers and bushes. As he stood up he took her by the hand. 'Come with me darling, the rain's stopped now. You'll need a coat, it's a bit chilly and you'll notice it after Rome.'

'I'll go up and fetch a cardigan. You go on out, I'll follow in a few minutes.'

Adam Pemberton also stood up. 'Yes good idea to check the car. I'll come with you in case you need a hand if the engine doesn't start. I'll just get a jacket.'

His wife glanced up from the book in her lap on the World's Best Thoroughbred Stables, on which, for once, only half her attention had been concentrated. She watched Adam follow them out of the room. From where she sat the base of the stairs was in her line of vision. She saw her son release Silvie's hand and heard his words, 'Come out as soon as you've got a coat.'

'I will. Shan't be long.' She went upstairs.

Adam followed. 'We must talk,' he whispered as she was about to enter her bedroom.

Once inside she opened the connecting door. 'I've been so worried — Rachael M . . . ' she began.

'I know,' he interrupted hastily. 'That phone call.'

She looked surprised. 'Has she contacted you as well?'

'No.' He explained about his wife's suspicions regarding the scarlet card. 'She has no idea what the call was about though. But she's no fool, she suspects the real purpose of the card.'

'Did she say so!'

He saw the concern on her face 'Afraid so. But she can't know for certain. Now tell me what the call was in aid of.'

'Money. She wanted £500 not to tell your wife about us — about me.'

'Grasping bitch!' He frowned in anger. 'What did you say to her?'

'I told her that I didn't have £500 and that I'd send her a cheque for £200. It was all I had.'

'You shouldn't have.'

'I didn't know how to handle the situation Adam. I couldn't be absolutely certain that your wife wouldn't overhear. She answered the call downstairs and I took it up here on the extension. I had to get Rachael Moss off the line quickly.'

'So you've already sent off the cheque?'

'Yes — but I post-dated it by more than a fortnight. She can't cash it until Monday. I wanted to speak with you first. She was so threatening. I couldn't take chances.'

'I'll deal with her. You will telephone your bank first thing on Monday morning to cancel the cheque. You must never give in to such demands. There would be no end to it.'

'But she could have ruined everything Adam. I had no time to consider. By post-dating the cheque I at least was certain she wouldn't be ready with more threats when I got back.'

'Well you've no need to worry any further. Just do as I said about the cheque. Telephone them before the bank opens because she'll be on their doorstep waiting. Didn't you realise that she can't carry out threats like that without exposing what she is herself. I don't think she'd dare risk jail, she's too fond of the comfortable life.'

'I was afraid she might make an anonymous call to your wife.'

'She couldn't do that without naming places. Believe me Silvie darling she can't harm you in anyway. Forget about her and leave it to me to deal with.'

'I'm so relieved Adam.' She felt his dependability as if it were a physical thing as well as mental.

He put out a hand to touch her cheek while his eyes consumed her. His fingers moved slowly down to touch her shoulders and grasp a tendril of her hair.

They heard the sound of a car engine. He let his hand fall away. 'You'd best go down.'

She nodded and as she moved away he closed the door softly behind her and heard her turn the key in the lock.

The focus of Laura Pemberton's eyes on the base of the staircase had not shifted since the two had gone up. She watched now as Silvie came down with a cardigan draped across her shoulder. Then heard the side door, the closest route to the garages, close. She waited for her husband to follow.

The grasped opportunity had been obvious and she knew what his next move would be if her own suspicions were founded. Her curiosity was about to be satisfied.

As she expected he went in the direction of the library. When she heard the faint tinkle of the phone close to where she sat she glanced at it. With just a split second hesitation and a determined set to her thin lips she reached out to lift the receiver to her ear. After a few seconds a voice announced, 'Rachael Moss spikink.'

He came straight to the point. 'Adam Pemberton here. Try any more tricks like that again and I'll see to it that word is passed around every club and hotel in the city. The threat of blackmail can douse a chap's ardour more than a bucket of cold water. Just remember that. And don't bother to try to cash that cheque, it's been cancelled.'

'Vot! But thet's my compensashink. If it hedn't bin for me . . . '

He gave a wry smile as he visualised her throwing up her free hand in protest at having her ill-gotten gains suddenly snatched away at the last moment.

Curtly he cut in, 'Stop whining, you did all right from both of us. I'm warning you — I'll do as I said.'

'Now who is miking threats!' her voice rose plaintively. But tough though she was she found his assertive tone daunting and so made no further protests.

'Fire with fire,' he threatened.

'All right — all right! You vin. But if you siy anythink thet vil . . . '

The phone clicked in her ear as he cut off the line. She knew when she was beaten and when to back down. She had overstepped the line and hadn't reckoned on his intervention. She had seen the strange situation as a golden nest egg, an opportunity never to be repeated, and had been furious at the post-dating of the cheque.

She went to pour herself some wine and her annoyance subsided as it gave way to intense curiosity. An unusual affair altogether. Pondering deeply she returned to her throne in the bay. 'Such goinks on!' she told the gaudy flower on the stand. 'I should like to know vot is really heppinink, end how it all cime about.'

When Adam Pemberton passed through the hall after making the call he glanced into the drawing room as if sensing he was being watched. His wife still held the receiver in her hand purposely to show that she'd listened in on the call. Right this minute admiration mingled with her anger. She had been reminded of those qualities which her father had recognised in him all those years ago when he was twenty years old. That trenchancy — not to be reckoned with. Admiration for the way in which he'd handled the situation, and anger for his having placed them all in it.

He stopped short and entered the room, a look of contempt on his face as he waited for her to speak first.

With a hand shaking with fury she replaced the receiver. 'So — you let your own son marry a whore! How in the name of God did it come about! And why have you allowed it?'

Never before had he heard her speak with such vehemence. Her manner was usually cool and detached. For a few silent moments he just stared at her. He had no defence. A confident manner and well-chosen words could not help him in this as it did in his business dealings. He was unable to deal with his own human failings. With an air of dejection he ran his fingers through his hair as he crossed to the window and stood facing out at the garden. Neither heard Dora Glasspool re-enter the hall through a side door clutching a handful of herbs from the kitchen garden.

He spoke now. 'It just happened. I didn't know until I walked in that first Saturday and saw her here. By then it was too late. They had already planned to marry.'

'You bloody fool putting us in such a position! Making us vulnerable to threats of blackmail — telephone calls from a whoremonger with extortionate demands to keep her mouth shut! Imagine the scandal if the press got wind of it and made it common knowledge!'

'No danger of that. Too fond of her home

comforts. The thought of a prison cell will clamp her lips like a vice.'

Silent for the moment she regarded his back as he stood looking out at the misty rain. Then taunted, 'I don't believe that you stayed silent about the girl for his sake. You did it for your own benefit. Very convenient to have the little trollop under this roof for a handy lay . . . '

Angrily he swung round to face her and cut her words short. 'Hold your filthy tongue. I'll explain nothing to you for you wouldn't begin to understand. Even now your prime concern is the business. Always was and always will be. That and your bloody horses! You've never been a proper mother to Mark or Joanne. Never had the time for either of them. If you tell him now you'll do far more harm than good and ruin his life. Silvie is his wife now and nothing you could do would alter the fact. So let things be and don't interfere.' For a few moments longer he glared at her, every fibre of his body taut and hostile. Then abruptly he strode from the room, fully aware that he had resorted to attack as his form of defence. As he passed through the hall he did not notice Dora Glasspool who had backed into the kitchen, her mind struggling to make sense of what she'd just overheard.

★ ★ ★

In the garage Silvie shivered slightly and drew her cardigan closer around her shoulders. After two weeks of warm Rome weather she found the October day chilly.

'You're cold my sweet. I shouldn't have asked you to come out here just to keep me company.'

'I'm all right Mark. It's interesting to watch. I've never actually seen under a car bonnet before.' Truth was she much preferred to be there than in the house in the company of his untalkative mother, with her suspicious eyes. She wondered what had delayed Adam.

At that moment he entered. 'Any problems?'

Mark was wiping his blackened hands on a cloth. 'No. Everything appears to be in good order. I've just finished checking the spark plugs. I'll go on in and wash my hands. Don't want to spread the oil around. Perhaps you'll put the bonnet down and close up the garage.'

'I'll just get my hair slide that I left in the glove box,' Silvie said in order to delay her exit. 'You go on. I'll be right in.'

Mark smiled at her and nodded, then went out.

The moment they were alone, Adam told her about the eavesdropped call.

'You mean that your wife deliberately listened in while you telephoned!'

'Fraid so.'

She looked stricken. 'She'll be bound to tell Mark!'

He shook his head confidently. 'I don't think she will darling.'

'What would prevent her?'

He wanted to chase the concern from her eyes and give her assurance, but he couldn't be one hundred percent positive himself. 'The scandal and its effect on the reputation of the business. Although

I'm fairly sure she won't say anything about it to Mark, I can't be certain that she won't be abusive to you. Her tongue can be pretty acid on occasions.'

'I don't see how she can just let it pass. Obviously it must have been a shock to her and from what you say I'm in no position to deny that episode in my life — at least not to your wife. I believe that I would deny it all to Mark though if she does tell him, so I hope you really do know her as well as you think you do. What would she gain now anyway by telling him?'

'Exactly. I believe her main concern about you both is that you'll produce a new heir for the old firm, the next Whitehorne. It still trades under the old family name, although I own half share. She has always thought of Mark as a Whitehorne even though he bears my name. If she does confront you just tell her you don't know what she's talking about, then telephone me at the offices. I'll know how to handle it. Trust me.'

She nodded in response her eyes resting on his broad shoulders, and she had a strong urge to feel the security of his arms about her, to rest her head against his chest and feel safe. But they had already been overlong in leaving the garage. One thing she felt compelled to ask him. 'Adam — I want you one day to go to a little back street where I used to live, it's not too far from the city. Only then will you understand the reason why I went to such desperate lengths to get my mother and Ginny away from there. Please — I want you to see for yourself.'

He made a move towards her and to speak, but she quickly turned away to go back to the house.

Deep in thought he closed the garage doors and followed.

★ ★ ★

The afternoon Silvie spent in various parts of the house with Mark. She took him into the girls' rooms to show the presents, now gift-wrapped with paper, they'd bought in Rome.

He smiled approval. 'Come on let's phone them. They'll be expecting us to. We mustn't disappoint them. As it's Saturday we won't be interrupting their school work.'

'Don't let them know about the presents or they won't settle for the rest of the term.'

'If I know my little sister she'll ask us outright what we've brought back for them. But I promise I won't let her wheedle any hint of what it is out of me.' He smiled as he dialled the College number on the telephone beneath the portrait of his ancestor in the upstairs corridor.

She glanced up at the face of his great great grandfather Joseph Whitehorne whose commanding visage, created long ago by the brush strokes of a skilled artist, stared down at her. In her present guilty state of mind she felt the eyes accusing, disapproving, as if his spirit were telling her in no uncertain terms that he considered her unfit to produce descendants bearing Whitehorne blood.

She dragged her eyes away from the portrait as Mark handed the receiver over to her. 'We're through darling.'

The next instant she dismissed the portrait from

her thoughts as she heard the voice of Ginny on the line.

★ ★ ★

After dinner Adam stayed only until his wife had settled down for the evening's bridge games in the drawing room. Her usual partners the Jackson-Brownes and Major Ashdown had arrived ten minutes ago. He knew that until well after midnight she would be fully occupied. So far he had proved to be correct about her. She had made no attempt to confront Silvie, or to tell Mark what she had discovered about his young wife.

If she intended to she would have already done so, and not beaten about the bush either. Adam thought he knew her well enough by now, and what her priorities were.

★ ★ ★

Dora settled herself in the car for the drive to her cottage. Once again she had deliberately left her bicycle behind in the morning, having had advance news that Adam would be home for a few hours. But this evening the pleasure was spoiled for her. Those things which she'd overheard Laura saying to him — about blackmail, trollop, whoremonger and scandal! And his angry response at the time. It had all been circulating around in her mind since. What was it they mustn't tell? Who was the trollop under the roof? Had Laura meant Mark's wife? Adam *had* been looking worried lately, as if

264

he had a lot on his mind.

As he seated himself beside her she asked, 'Why are you driving back to the city tonight? Couldn't you have stayed until tomorrow?'

'No. I have to get back Dora.'

She wanted to ask him about the things she'd overheard. Yet if she did he'd know that she'd listened. Not that she'd meant to intentionally. 'Are you very busy at the office then?'

The question penetrated his preoccupation. 'Yes — yes — always busy Dora.'

'Maybe you'll stay longer next time then. When will you be home again?'

'Probably not for a while. Pressures of work.'

His answer depressed her. Later she lay awake long after she'd gone to bed still puzzling and wondering why things were changing just lately.

★ ★ ★

Silvie was on edge, afraid of the power now in the hands of Laura Pemberton and was not yet prepared with a plan of response if confronted. It was possible, even very likely, that she was awaiting an opportunity to catch her son alone. When the bridge session started she relaxed. At least for the rest of the evening she could feel safe from sudden accusations.

Mark walked her down the steps to the rose garden his arm about her waist possessively. 'I wish you'd change your mind and come back with me to the city next week. My apartment's quite comfortable. The week will seem endless otherwise.'

265

'You have your work to occupy you. I daresay you'll have some catching up to do to make up for your holiday.'

'No more than usual. Peter will have coped perfectly well. So don't try to make me feel better about leaving you behind. I hope the reason why you don't fancy the idea isn't because you think you'd be lonely while I'm at work. You could tour the shops and buy whatever you fancy. I could show you over the offices and introduce you to everyone. I'm wondering whether you might even be bored here on your own all week alone. Mother's no company, especially in the evenings with her endless bridge sessions.'

'I shan't be bored or lonely Mark. I shall love being here. It's so peaceful and quiet. A welcome change. I can go for long walks. Or just sit in the garden and read.'

'And what about rainy days when you can't do either?'

'I like walking in the rain, so long as I'm prepared for it. I shall need to get some rubber boots. I must confess I haven't any.' The mere mention of a visit to his offices made her uneasy since the recent encounter with Jimmy Ashdown. She had paid close attention to the Major's manner towards her when he'd arrived this evening, wondering if his son had told him how and where he had met her previously.

But he had greeted her with his usual stiff old-fashioned courtesy. And taking into account his straight-laced attitude she somehow doubted that Jimmy Ashdown would be willing to admit to his

266

father that he visited such places as the Georgian house.

'Does Major Ashdown's son live at home?' The question had been on her lips since the wedding reception but the right moment to ask had not arisen. It still seemed out of context, but she needed to know.

He looked faintly surprised. 'Jimmy? No he runs some sort of property sales business in the city. He's seldom at home nowadays. I believe he was recently involved in some shady business dealings which came to the notice of his father and he all but cut him off. Major Ashdown is a man of strict principals and integrity.'

'Do you see much of him?'

'Jimmy?'

She nodded trying not to give the impression that the question was of any great importance.

'Very little nowadays. Occasionally come across him when I'm out riding. I go across the Ashdown estate. They use ours. An arrangement we've had for years.'

They had stopped at the sundial. The rose that he'd picked for her five weeks ago still lay there. He lifted the withered remains which had left a brown imprint from the rain.

'Remember this?'

'Yes. I'm afraid I forgot to take it inside.'

'You're forgiven.' He reached across for her hand. 'I remember you had a headache.' He lifted her hand to his lips and kissed it before adding, 'How did I live before you came into my life?'

'You seem to have managed very nicely.' She tried

to make light of his remark. Her conscience bothered her.

'No. I see now that I wasn't really living. Existing perhaps. Waiting for you to come along. If you left me now I'd want to die.'

'Don't say such things Mark. Why would I want to leave you?'

'I'll never give you reason to my sweet.' He moved to her side of the sundial and kissed her before adding. 'And life is just wonderful.'

★ ★ ★

If Laura Pemberton intended to drop the bombshell on her son when he was alone the opportunity never arose. Uncertain of what to expect from her Silvie was in a constant state of anxiety. She longed for the sanctuary of the little stone church with its special soothing atmosphere.

★ ★ ★

Sunday dawned sunny and warm. 'Shall we go to morning service Mark? Perhaps we should.'

'Whatever you say darling. So long as you don't mind being the focus of attention. We'll probably be doing the reverend a favour.' He chuckled. 'I daresay there'll be a good turn out for the service this morning. I guarantee that the whole village will know we're back.'

★ ★ ★

Mark had to leave very early on Monday morning. 'Be certain to wake me so that I can make your breakfast because Dora won't be here at that unearthly hour,' Silvie told him last thing on Sunday night.

'No need my sweet. Coffee's all I shall want. I'll wake you before I leave though. You can always go back to sleep.'

But she had woken when his alarm went off, and had made him a proper breakfast, glad to have the run of the kitchen in the absence of Dora Glasspool. When he'd left she returned to bed, but not to sleep.

As promised he telephoned as soon as he arrived in his own private office, the first of his three calls to her that day, at times they'd pre-arranged to ensure that she was in the house to answer.

The weather was fine again and she spent much of the morning wandering around the estate. At no time did she encounter Laura Pemberton who took her lunch in her own quarters. She saw Dora wheeling the rosewood trolley towards the suite of rooms off the hall. She had expected to be confronted and abused in the absence of Mark. And although not afraid of his mother or her acid tongue she did fear the devastation it could wreak. Why was she staying silent on what must have been a great shock to her, Silvie wondered. Then the thought occurred that perhaps she had waited with the intention of phoning Mark at his office.

But it was obvious that she hadn't yet done so at four o'clock when Mark made his second call.

Silvie sat alone in the breakfast room for dinner, served by Dora in silence.

'Isn't Mrs Pemberton taking dinner this evening Dora?'

'She's dining in her own rooms.' Dora wondered herself why Laura didn't want to join Mark's young wife for meals. Things had changed a lot since the girl had come upon the scene. Even Adam was behaving strangely.

★ ★ ★

By the time Major Ashdown and the Jackson-Brownes arrived for the evening's bridge session Laura Pemberton had still made no reference to the Rachael Moss call. If she had contacted Mark about it since his four o'clock call he would have been in touch again before now. Relieved Silvie went to her room to pass the time reading until he rang again at eight o'clock. It had been a nerve-racking day and she was thankful it was almost over. Although she could not be sure that the threat was over. Only time would tell if Adam had judged his wife correctly, and that the consequences of adverse publicity to the business overruled her duty to her son.

Dora made coffee for the bridge players before she left.

Silvie took the eight o'clock call on the upstairs extension beneath the disapproving gaze of Joseph Whitehorne.

'I miss you my sweet,' Mark was saying. 'I don't know how I'll get through the week.'

'I miss you too Mark.' The big house seemed so empty with them all away. Too quiet, especially upstairs. So many unoccupied rooms of complete silence. The days she could handle, with the diversion of her walks. But the evenings were particularly lonely. She found herself longing for the girls to be home. But half term was still a long while off yet.

He stayed an hour or more on the phone and she wondered at the cost of the calls from such a distance. Feeling too alone she decided to occupy some time in making coffee for the bridge players, and went downstairs. They had just completed a hand and she announced her intentions.

On her way to the kitchen she heard Mrs Jackson-Browne ask the Major, 'How is James getting along? Not bored with quiet country life yet I hope. He's still at home I believe. I saw his car in the village yesterday as I was passing through.'

Silvie listened for the Major's reply. It concerned her if Jimmy Ashdown was still in Kings Meadow. The deep vibrant tones of the Major carried to her ears, 'Yes he's presently at home. Still has his business concerns in the city though. But as far as I can gather he's thinking of selling up and trying his hand in some other field. Dashed if I know what though! He's home for a couple of weeks. I intend to put him to work repairing the fences while he's here. That should keep him occupied and out of mischief for a few days.'

Perturbed at this piece of news Silvie continued into the kitchen. But, she reminded herself, to give her away Jimmy Ashdown would have to point the finger at himself. His father would not treat such a confession lightly. In a state of anxious waiting she

271

retired to her bed long before the bridge players had ended their games for the night.

★ ★ ★

By Wednesday her anxiety relaxed a little. If Laura Pemberton was going to mention the scarlet card and Madam Moss she surely would have done so by now. Also by this time she would have contacted Mark. By his affectionate phone calls it was obvious that he'd not been told. Silvie saw little of her and was left to dine alone, with not even the company of Dora who continued to eat, as usual, in the kitchen. Silvie noticed the strange looks she gave her at times. All attempts to draw her into conversation failed.

But today as she served lunch Dora asked. 'Do you like Adam?'

Taken by surprise at the unexpected question Silvie took a moment to reply. 'Of course Dora. Why wouldn't I? He's Mark's father!'

'I've known him for a very long time.'

It seemed as though Dora was staking some claim on Adam, and Silvie began to suspect that, with her strange reasoning, Dora considered her an inter-loper in the household.

'Yes I know that Dora. Mark has told me that you've been with the family for many years.'

Dora said no more. Yet Silvie sensed that she wanted to and tried to draw more comment from her. But Dora had retreated into her usual silence.

'I'd like to help with the housework Dora.'

'No. Mark would not like that.'

'Well Mark's not here. At least I can do some light dusting and polishing. Or even the cooking or washing the dishes.'

'Mark would be angry if you did.' Dora seemed possessive of her role in the household.

Silvie however was determined. Without asking assistance from Dora she tracked down some dusters and polish and, ignoring her resentful expression, set about self-appointed tasks. Later she informed Dora which rooms had been done.

★   ★   ★

On Monday afternoon Adam telephoned. He chose a time when he knew his wife would be outside

'Hello Silvie. Has she said anything?'

'No. I was afraid she might phone Mark at the office, or his apartment.'

'No — she can't have or he'd have been in to see me by now. Not about you or me, but about his mother. He'd be convinced that she was having some kind of relapse or brainstorm. As I expected, she's decided that the best policy is to say nothing about it. She's not the kind to play cat and mouse. He would never believe her and she knows it. Think no more about it. Before he rang off he added softly, 'I miss you Silvie. I miss you so much.'

★   ★   ★

She looked forward to Mark's calls which he made at the same time each day so that she could take her daily walks knowing he was not trying to contact her while she was away from the house. His evening calls were even more welcome. Although the three bridge partners came each evening to play they could not be considered company. They were always totally engrossed in their play, and silent except when calling bids and short discussions at the end of each game. She had now fallen into the practice of strolling in the grounds during the evenings before the calls from Mark were due. Dora was always gone by seven o'clock.

29

After her usual morning call from Mark she planned a long walk to get away from the house for a spell. Its oppressive lonely silence could not provide the solace which she craved. From her bedroom window she studied the sky. Scattered high clouds seemed no threat and the sun was shining. She considered the need for a top coat and decided against.

In the garden she paused to speak with Joe Tarrant who was clipping a hedge. His down-to-earth friendly manner was welcome after the cold presence of Laura Pemberton and the obstinate muteness of Dora Glasspool.

Ten minutes later she was heading for the path which skirted the property. As yet she had never been as far as the boundaries where the Pemberton estate adjoined the Ashdown's. This she discovered to be much further than she'd expected. But she looked forward to the prospect of a long walk, and having not prepared for any change in the weather she hoped it would hold out fine. A light plane high in the sky seemed to emphasise the still silence which was broken only by the sounds of birds and an occasional lazy drone of a bee. Appreciating the peaceful relaxed atmosphere she inhaled the fragrant air deeply and yielded herself up to the pleasure.

She had kept to the path and by now had covered a fair distance. Deeply engrossed in her own thoughts she had not noticed clouds gathering. She glanced up and tried to gauge whether the sun would re-appear and the day resume its earlier blue brightness, and realised her folly in not having come prepared for the unpredictability of early autumn. Having no wish to return to the house before lunchtime she decided to chance the weather and walk a little further.

Ten minutes later she heard the roll of distant thunder and again glanced up at the darkening sky.

On the point of turning back she became aware of the muffled sound of galloping hooves on soft ground. Glancing back she gave a small gasp of surprise at the sight of Jimmy Ashdown mounted on a Palomino making his way towards her. Uneasy she walked on.

Moments later he reined in the horse and dismounted expertly throwing the reins across its back. With a bold greeting he fell into step beside her. 'Hello there. Saw you from a distance. Couldn't believe my luck. I'm supposed to be repairing fences. What a bore! I've been hoping you'd drop by to pay a visit.'

'Why on earth should I do that!' Her response was cold. She disliked his over-confident manner.

He shrugged. 'A nice neighbourly gesture to an old acquaintance.'

'You are not an acquaintance old or otherwise Mr Ashdown, merely a neighbour. I've met you only once at my wedding reception.' Her coolness was only skin deep, for she was alert to the danger of exposure which he represented.

With a soft laugh he shook his head, undisguised

mockery in his expression. 'You can't seriously expect me to believe there are two ravishingly beautiful lookalikes around and both crossing the path of lucky old me! No — I correct that. I'm not the lucky one, Pemberton has that distinction. How and where on earth did he happen to come across you? Nothing would induce me to believe that he ever entered that iniquitous den of madam what's her name. No — not Mark Pemberton. Any more than I believe he would . . . ' he paused as if he considered it unnecessary to conclude the pointed remark. 'He doesn't know does he.' This was not a question but an obvious assumption. Having grown up alongside Mark Pemberton and being of the same age he was all too aware of his high moral principals. Often during their younger years he had attempted unsuccessfully to enlist his company for a night out on the town. But their ideas of an evening's entertainment differed widely.

Ignoring his inference she hastened her pace.

'Breaking the rules aren't you, marrying a chap like him under false pretences — don't you agree?'

Anger at his blatant and insulting approach rose above her qualms. 'What are you talking about! Either you have taken leave of your senses, or this is some kind of silly joke — or perhaps you're even drunk!' Abruptly she turned to go back along the path.

Unfazed he led the Palomino about face and caught her up again. 'I wish I'd known you were ready to settle for a wedding ring and a country estate. I'd have willingly obliged. Not quite as wealthy as Pemberton but still — '

With a sudden action she swung round and cut his words short with a resounding slap to his face, taking him completely by surprise. As she turned away again he caught her roughly by the arm and with a lusty laugh pulled her round to face him. He released his hold on the horse which dropped its head immediately to crop the lush grass close to the boundary fence. 'Stop play-acting. You must be as damned bored as I am with no young company all week, especially after the wild city life you've led. Come back to my place — there's no one home.'

'I'm not bored,' she cut in, anger driving her once again to retaliate. 'I like the peace and quiet. Now release my arm.' She tried to free herself from his clasp.

'Lonely then?' he eyed her appreciatively.

'Certainly not.' She twisted herself half from his grasp. 'Now take your hands off me!'

Easily he pulled her close to him again, this time in a vice-like grip. Taking a tress of her hair between his fingers he caressed it familiarly as he spoke. 'I don't remember you struggling last time. And I repeat — you're breaking the rules.'

Desperately she struggled to break his hold. 'And so are you — ' she gasped.

'Why not? You're much too beautiful to be squandered on just one lucky devil. It's not fair.' He crushed her closer. He was not wearing a jacket and the sleeves of his shirt were rolled up. She felt his strong muscles straining her against his chest as he cut short any further protest with a hard lingering kiss.

A roll of thunder sounded closer now. Wildly she struggled.

Then it seemed that so many things happened together . . . the noise of pounding hooves . . . the sigh of a whip as it cut the still air . . . and the sound of the lash as it met its target. She felt the broad shoulders of Jimmy Ashdown flinch at the impact. He released her and staggered backwards.

Then she saw the frightening figure of the angry-faced Major astride a big black hunter, starkly etched against the thunderous skyline. The riding crop was once more poised to descend for the second time driven by the weight of blind anger.

With a terrified scream she rushed forward to place herself between father and son. 'No — no Major!' For an aeon it seemed the crop and the man towered, poised against the stormy backdrop, with which man, horse, and whip seemed to blend in angry unison.

Slowly the arm that wielded the crop was lowered. Limply it hung as if its dreadful power had been consumed by its own fury.

Trembling from the shock of the sudden and unexpected violence she was barely aware of her actions or her words. 'It was my fault Major. I knew your son before I was married. I shouldn't have come this far to your . . . ' She stopped abruptly. To her own ears her words sounded like a blend of emotional and hysterical garble.

Breathing hard the Major dismounted, his body still taut with unspent rage.

Heart pounding she held her breath, fearing that Jimmy Ashdown would challenge further violence as hc turned a wild and threatening scowl on his father. Then without a word he reached for the bridle and mounted the Palomino. Swinging it round into a gallop he rode hard across the field towards the Ashdown home.

An angry flush still stained the face of the Major as he turned to her. 'Madam I apologise for the outrageous behaviour of my son. Rest assured that he will not trouble you again for I intend turning him out of the house.'

'Oh no — please Major! Don't do that on my account.' She struggled to control the tremor in her voice but failed. 'I'm all right really. I shall not mention this to anyone — not even Mark. I ask you not to do so either. Please.'

At this request he covered his surprise as he looked down at the flushed appealing face. True to form beautiful women always brought trouble between men one way or another, he thought, and this one beat any he'd ever seen. Still the boy couldn't go around molesting any young woman who took his fancy! Particularly young Pemberton's. Relieved that she was taking such a lenient attitude he nodded assent. Could've made things damned awkward, to say the least.

His deep voice still shook with the aftermath of his physical outburst. 'Very well Mrs Pemberton. As you wish. If you will allow me I'll see you safely back to the house.' He turned the black hunter in readiness.

'There's really no need. Thank you Major. I'll be perfectly all right. I'd rather go alone.'

As she turned to go he touched his forehead in his

habitual semi-salute. 'If you insist Ma'm.' For a moment or two he stood watching her as she started back along the track. Perhaps I was too hard on the boy, he thought, especially in her presence. Still knowing a woman was one thing; damned well molesting her was another matter entirely! Strange though — they'd shown no mutual recognition when introduced at the wedding reception!

Still musing on this he remounted the hunter and set it at a steady canter in the direction taken by his son.

As the sound of hooves receded she hastened her steps. Now half running, half stumbling, she stayed close to the boundary fence. Dry sobs rose in her throat and the sound of the whiplash lingered in her ears. Still fresh before her eyes was the frightening spectacle of the Major astride the big black horse, silhouetted against the thunderclouds. She had been forced to intervene with no time to first consider her words and had committed the folly of revealing too much in order to immobilise the terrible whip before it met its target a second time. There was no detracting her words. Who could say where it might have ended had she not acted so. Damn Jimmy Ashdown! Why had he waylaid her like that! What a reckless irresponsible hothead! What a fool he was not to have first considered the possibility that his father might be within view. As it was the Major must have watched him ride across the field to her.

Breathing hard from haste and exertion over the uneven ground she glanced up at the hovering dark threat suspended just above her. Thunder sounded closer now. The earlier calm from the walk was completely unsalvageable, through no fault of the weather. The hanging threat overhead was as nothing compared with that pending from Jimmy Ashdown. In order to place himself in a better light he'd be obliged to tell his father the whole truth behind her blurted words. How much would he tell? If all — how would his father react? Somehow she felt confident that the Major would keep the knowledge to himself. But with Jimmy Ashdown she felt no such assurance. Now that his pride had been outraged by the lashing he might, out of spite, make certain that word got around about her recent past. With such corroboration any word to Mark from his mother would brook no denial.

At length she reached the house, but still overwrought and trembling was not yet ready to go inside. She craved the quiescent sanctuary of the little stone church where she could leave the outside world behind briefly. She continued on along the path and entered the wooded part at the rear of the estate.

Midway between Briarwood and the church rain began to fall heavily. At a faster pace she kept on along the uneven track. She slipped on the wet earth and twisted her foot as she fell. Painfully she got to her feet and saw that her skirt was soiled from the mud. Lightning lit the dense black clouds followed by a loud burst of thunder very close. Rain fell heavily and large droplets dripped from the trees which overhung the path. Limping she hurried as best she could to cover the short remaining distance. By the time she reached the side door of the church which led into the vestry her thin silk blouse clung wetly, hugging her body and revealing her flesh nakedly through the fine fabric.

Faint with relief she found the door unlocked and entered. Her steps now slower she felt the pain in her foot and ankle. A dry sob rose to her throat as she went through into the nave of the church. In a front pew she sank to her knees on a hassock. Against the musty silence her breath seemed to rasp and echo. She bowed her head on her trembling arms while her racing heartbeats recovered.

★   ★   ★

In this study which overlooked the woods at the back of the Rectory Reverend David Bradley had been reclining in his armchair staring absently out of the window while he pondered his next sermon. His eye had caught a movement among the trees. Suddenly alert he blinked and rose from the chair. Without thought of a topcoat or umbrella he hurried out through the French door. At the end of his garden he paused to look ahead along the path which led to the church and saw it was deserted. Had he fallen asleep and dreamed? he wondered. This was a likely possibility for he'd been unable to banish her from his mind since he'd first seen her.

Compelled to check whether or not she had been fact or fantasy he stood in the vestry moments later looking in through the open doorway into the church. As his eyes rested on the rain-soaked bowed head he knew that this time she was no fantasy.

Uncertain of his approach he hesitated. Then softly he entered the chancel and knelt at the altar while he searched his mind for the right words. Clearly she was distressed.

The slight rustle of his movements startled her and she looked up. Her impulse was to run from the church. She could not face him in her agitated state.

As though he read her thoughts he urged softly, 'Please stay. Perhaps I can help. I want to.'

The velvet voice held her captive. She felt as though she could not move if her life depended on it. As if bonded to the hassock she waited while he came from the altar steps and walked slowly towards her.

When he reached the pew where she knelt he seated himself beside her. In silence he regarded the pale wet hair that clung to her face and fought an urge to gently push it back from her pearly skin. Her eyes were closed now and he saw the rain or tears which glistened on the long lashes. She looked so vulnerable, so young, so lost. He, who had never lacked for words, was suddenly struck dumb. Her white silk blouse and flimsy camisole beneath were saturated and transparently moulded to her body exposing the skin beneath nakedly.

She shifted her position slightly and lowered her arms from their resting place on the wooden rail in front of her. His gaze was involuntarily drawn to the firm contours of her breasts, visibly defined through the transparent wetness. His eyes wanted to linger.

A voice in his subconscious, well rehearsed with ancient words from the Scriptures, rebuked him. With a silent prayer in his head for the return of his senses he abruptly stood up. 'I think perhaps it might be wise for you to come back to the Rectory with me in order to dry off a little or you'll most likely catch a chill.' He stepped out into the aisle and as she rose did not offer a hand to assist. Having disciplined his thoughts he would not risk them out of order again.

Still under the influence of shock she did not speak, but merely obeyed.

They walked the short distance back to the Rectory in silence. The rain had ceased, the sky was now clearer and a breeze had blown up.

He led the way into the garden and towards the French door which was still open as he'd left it. As he stood aside to allow her to precede him into the house he said, 'My housekeeper will no doubt be able to find something for you to wear while your clothes are drying off. Then I shall drive you back to Briarwood. Meanwhile you can telephone the house to let them know where you are, they may be worried about you on account of the storm.'

She began to wish that he'd left her in the little church. Yet at the same time she wanted him to take charge of her. His mere presence soothed and steadied her.

Suddenly she felt totally exhausted and wished only for the oblivion of sleep that had evaded her night after night.

Only when he went into the hall and called his housekeeper, 'Mrs Armstrong — ' did he remember that she was not at home. He slapped his palm to his forehead to indicate his forgetfulness and smiled apologetically. 'I'm afraid I've only just remembered that it's market day and she goes into town to do the shopping on Thursdays. She never gets back until late afternoon. But please come into the living room where there's a fire. At least you can warm yourself and perhaps dry off a little.'

Silently she followed.

'Mrs Armstrong always lights a fire in here every day of the year regardless of weather. We rely on it for hot water. There's a tank behind the fireplace,' he explained. 'Meanwhile I'll fetch a blanket for you and make some tea.' He paused reflectively before adding. 'Unless you'd rather I drove you straight home now?'

For the first time since he'd come across her in the church she spoke. 'No — please — I'd like to stay just for a little while. No one at the house will miss me.' She sank down onto a large sofa in front of the fire. 'It's so peaceful here. It seems to have something of the atmosphere of the church.'

He nodded and smiled. Then went in search of something to cover her with and to put on a kettle. Belatedly he doubted his wisdom in having brought her back to the Rectory in the absence of his housekeeper. But the sight of her had driven all common sense from his mind. Shortly he returned with an eiderdown and a wooden clothes horse. Then immediately left the room again to make tea.

She gave a brief smile despite her present concerns. The blouse and camisole were pure silk bought by Mark when they were in Rome. To dry them before a fire would be sacrilege. She glanced out of the window. The sky was clearing and the breeze quite strong. Her things would dry quickly outside on the washing line. How to get them there?

A light knock came on the door and his voice on the other side.

'I have a towel for your hair. I never thought just now . . .'

'Come in,' she called. She had removed her blouse, camisole and skirt and wrapped the eiderdown around her. 'My things would dry faster outside on the washing line. Would it be too embarrassing for you to hang them up for me.' She held out the flimsy garments, her skirt she had hung over the clotheshorse.

He handed her the towel and without demur took the clothes from her. 'I'll probably be struck off. They'll never believe these belong to Mrs Armstrong.' He smiled and turned towards the door again.

'Who are *they*?' she asked, catching his humour on the surface of her deeper concerns.

He paused in the doorway to answer. 'Anyone who happens to witness me hanging them on the line.'

He hung the silk garments and watched as the breeze caught at the blue ribbons of the camisole sending them flying like streamers. 'I'll never be able to explain this away,' he murmured in amusement as he turned to go back inside.

By the time he had made tea and returned to the room with a tray he saw that she had fallen asleep. Her head was resting against the side wing of the sofa and she had slid sideways. After placing the tray down on a coffee table he crossed the room and stood looking down at her. 'Are you asleep?' he asked softly. She did not stir. He allowed his eyes to feast unhindered but for his conscience. She was so utterly beautiful, like no one he'd ever seen. He put out a hand and gently lifted back the tumbled hair which was now drying back into curl and his fingers brushed her cheek. 'What were you running from today?' he murmured. 'Why did you bring your tears to the church?'

She moved slightly and the eiderdown slipped from her shoulder revealing a white silky breast with a pale pink nipple. The sight held his eyes fascinated. He knew that he should turn away but as if spellbound he could not move. 'Rosebuds and pearls,' he murmured feeling his manhood stir beneath his cassock. He forced himself to walk away towards the door, unsure how best to act in the circumstances. If he dared to try to cover her she might wake and think — oh heaven forbid what she would think! Yet if she awoke to find herself uncovered she would be mortified. Again he realised his mistake in bringing her back to the house with him. It all seemed unthinkable now even if Mrs Armstrong had been present; and a thousand times worse because she was not. Now as he stood with his back to her wondering what he should do she moved again and he swung round mechanically. To his relief he saw that the eiderdown had fallen back into place, leaving only part of her shoulder now uncovered. For what seemed a long while he sat watching her as she slept.

At last, to his relief, she opened her eyes. Instantly he bent over the tray as though he'd just arrived with it. 'Ah now — this should warm you.' As he poured the tea he prayed that it had not cooled enough to betray the lengthy time lapse since he'd made it.

She adjusted the eiderdown about her. 'Oh — I'm sorry. I must have fallen asleep. The warmth of the fire no doubt. I felt so terribly tired.' In the Rectory something of the spicy atmosphere of the church pervaded. Perhaps, she thought, brought back on the cassocks of the many predecessors of David Bradley on their countless journeying back and forth from the little old church. She sipped the tea which had cooled to barely warm. 'I do believe that I could sleep for a week straight off without waking, here in this house.'

'Why this house and not Briarwood?'

'I'm not really sure.' This was true. Whether it was just that special aura or perhaps something to do with his calming presence, she could not be certain. In him she would like to find shelter for her conscience. About him there was a composure which she believed would be unshakeable. Yet at the same time knew that with just a few words about her life she could undermine that composure. She found herself wondering just how much he would understand. Perhaps not even at all. Again she saw that questioning look in his deep blue eyes that she'd seen there before, more revealing than his spoken words.

'Do you want to tell me about it?' He found it an effort to keep his voice steady now, for although she kept the eiderdown close around her body it concealed nothing from his eyes which had seen the exquisite beauty that it screened.

'No — I'm all right really.' She handed her empty

cup to him. 'Thank you. I expect my things have dried off enough now. I should be getting back.'

'Very well. I'll fetch them and drive you home.'

'Thank you. But I really would rather walk. The rain's cleared.'

'As you wish.' He went out to collect the things from the washing line and when he returned left the room again while she dressed.

When she was ready she went into the hall where he was waiting. 'There — Mrs Armstrong will never know I've been here.' She summoned a smile, and dearly wished that she did not have to leave him. 'I'll go back the way I came.'

'Would you like me to walk with you?'

She shook her head. 'No thank you. I'll be fine.'

He went with her to the end of the garden. Before she left him he said, 'If you ever need me you know where I am. Any time. Any time at all.'

Again he regarded her with that questioning look. He has speaking-eyes she thought.

In a lighter tone now he added. 'And next time take a mackintosh.'

'I promise I will.' She returned his smile briefly and moved off along the path.

He watched her until she was out of his sight.

30

Most of this evening she had spent in the drawing room, her attention divided between a book which she'd chosen from the shelves in the library, and watching the bridge players. Any company, silent though it was, was better than no company at times. They had paid little heed to her during the hands, although she'd noticed Mr Jackson-Browne glance her way once or twice. She'd made coffee a couple of times for them. Now in the kitchen she dried the cups and set them back on the tray. She returned to stand briefly in the doorway of the drawing room observing the four players, each presently oblivious of the world beyond the card table.

Unseen, unheard she quietly closed the door on them. At the same time she wondered why she bothered about sound, since it would take the collapse of the house to take their attention from the hand in progress. She recalled Mark once saying, 'They go into a semi-trance when they play.' They were certainly hooked on it, she thought. Always so serious and silent except for the bids and an occasional exchange of reprimands at the end of a game.

Mark had made his evening call earlier than usual for the reason that he had to attend a board meeting which was expected to last until quite late. The time was now nine thirty. As she made her way up the stairs she decided she would spend the rest of the evening writing a letter to the girls after she had bathed.

Later, as she came from the bathroom dressed for bed, she stifled a scream with her hand on seeing Jimmy Ashdown seated in a bedroom chair. She made a dash for the door but found it was now locked. Angrily she swung round to face him and saw the large old-fashioned key dangling from his finger, held up mockingly.

'How dare you come into my room! How did you get into this house? How long have you been here?' Her voice shook with anger at his audacity and with the shock of finding him there.

Nonchalantly he leaned back in the chair grinning. 'One question at a time please! Give a chap a chance. I came by way of a side door and the stairs. I met no one on the way. I've been waiting here patiently for over an hour. I saw Dora leave. She did not see me. I won't bother to answer the first question — you know me. By now you will have heard all about my wicked ways.'

'I don't know you nor do I want to. Now get out!'

He ignored this and pointed to the connecting door to the dressing room. 'Who sleeps on the other side? Your father-in-law? Lucky devil!' He had not paused for her reply, having already looked into the rooms while waiting.

'How dare you,' she repeated, glaring at him. 'Why have you come here?'

'Why do you think m'darling?' He stood up now.

Quite absently, despite her anger she noted the trace of Irish in his public school accent.

She made a dash for the bathroom door with the

intention of locking herself in, but he reached it first and barred her way. She moved back towards the bedroom door again, her anger turning to fear. 'How dare you! How dare you!'

'You're repeating yourself m'darling.' He moved towards her.

'Give me that key,' she demanded.

Smiling he slowly shook his head. Unperturbed he wagged a finger at her. 'Now you know what happened the last time I was caught with you.'

'And you deserved it.' she retorted. 'I thought your father had sent you away.'

He gave a short sharp laugh. 'Oh very delicately put. You mean kicked me out. No. You pleaded my case for me remember?'

'I wish I hadn't!'

'No you don't. You did it to pacify the old trout.' Still smiling he moved closer to her.

She pressed herself against the door. 'If you come another step I'll bang on this door and shout.'

'And how would you explain my presence in your bedroom at this time o'night?'

'Don't you mean how would you explain it! Not that it would be necessary. They all know what you're capable of.'

'Ah — but they don't yet know what you're capable of yourself now do they?'

She ignored this remark as if she'd not heard it. But he knew that she had. 'I warn you — I shall call for help. I'll scream and bring your father and Mr Jackson-Browne up. I shall tell the truth, that I found you in my room.'

'The truth? And how much of the truth would

you tell them m'darling?' He shrugged, 'Anyway those fossilised zombies down there wouldn't hear you.'

He moved closer.

★ ★ ★

She darted away to evade his grasp but he caught her easily against him, his hands roving boldly over her flimsily covered body, and pulling at the ribbons of her nightgown. A serious expression had now wiped the smile from his face. 'You told the old man that it was your fault that day when he caught me kissing you. Well — d'you know something m'darling — it's true. Your bloody fault for being so beautiful. A man commits rape in his mind just looking at you. Even my chaste father in all probability.'

She struggled desperately to free herself, knowing that she was trapped and could do nothing about it.

Suddenly he caught her up in his arms and carried her across the room to the bed where he fell with her. She gasped and scrambled to get up. But he held her firmly down. 'Funny — I don't recall you struggling last time.'

'How would you remember. You've probably spent most of your spare time in places like that,' she said scathingly as she tried to fight him off.

Stung by her remark he stopped molesting her for a moment to retaliate. 'Now get one thing straight about me. I may be considered a black sheep, but once and only once have I set foot in a whorehouse. And that time, by some incredible stroke of luck plus a small fortune, you were the one. I've never lacked willing women. It's getting rid of them I find troublesome.'

Vainly she tried to resist his brute strength. 'Let me go or I'll scream the house down,' she panted.

'And if you do I'll bring it down by just talking,' he threatened, his tone low and urgent and his hands pulling at her nightdress.

'And you'll get ten years for rape,' she gasped

'You'd surely take compassion and admit it was your fault again.'

'Stop being ridiculous and let go of me! I tell you I'll scream and bring your father up. He'll probably shoot you this time!'

'And I'll say you invited me up.'

'And why would I need to do that!'

'Boredom at being left alone all week.'

She strove to keep her wits about her. Suppose she did follow her natural impulse and scream for help? They'd come running up, the two men at least. She didn't care about Jimmy Ashdown now or how harshly his father would deal with him. But, as she'd known from the start, he'd be forced to expose her tainted past in order to save his own skin. In the event of any doubts Laura Pemberton could corroborate his story. Not perhaps in the presence of the Jackson-Brownes but certainly afterwards to the Major. And in consequence the inevitable wrecking of four lives beside her own. It was all too dire to contemplate. There was to be, it seemed, no extrication from the sticky threads of the past which clung more tightly about her.

Desperately she glanced about for some weapon

to use against him physically. Only a small brass clock was available on the bedside chest. She put out her hand to try to grasp it but it was not quite close enough. The only defence she had for use against him was her voice, and that she dare not use. Defeated and exhausted with the struggle against his brute strength she wanted to weep. There seemed no choice but to stay silent and let him have his way and be gone.

When he stood ready to leave he looked down at her with a rueful smile. Had she known his secret thoughts she would have been sure that even the end of a whiplash would not have dragged from him what he knew about her. Even at the Georgian house that evening he'd seen that she didn't belong in such a place, and at the time had judged her reasons to be desperate indeed. Moreover he was the proverbial pot that would not deem to call the kettle black.

When he had left she relocked the door and vowed that it would never again be left unlocked in the absence of Mark or Adam. Jimmy Ashdown would never be given a second opportunity to gain entrance to her room.

Trembling with rage and shame she went into the bathroom to shower and run a bath, too shaken now to write the letters to the girls as she'd intended.

31

In his study the Reverend David Bradley lounged in his armchair gazing out through the French window, idly contemplating the blackberry hedge in need of clipping. His shoe-less feet rested on a small footstool, and his mind had long since wandered from its sermon-seeking course. This was not due to any mental lethargy but to the fact that for more than a week now his mind had been preoccupied with an image which he could not banish from his mind.

Quite suddenly, real or imagined, there she was, passing along the track at the edge of the woods, the morning sunlight reflecting on her pale hair.

Instantly alert he sat forward and his unshod feet blindly contacted the black moccasins on the floor beside the stool. Even as his eyes followed her he doubted them, for she might be just a visual fallacy, an extension of the thoughts and images from which he could not escape. Barely aware of his movements he went out through the French window and followed.

He entered the church as usual through the vestry. In the doorway he stood regarding her bent head resting on her arms in the same front pew as before. It was a scene repeating itself he thought as he moved forward into the chancel and to the altar, wondering how he could help her, for plainly she needed help. After a short silence he spoke. 'Will you come to the altar?'

He knew that she'd look up startled for he'd made no sound on arrival. He did not turn round. Moments later he felt a breath of movement and the subtle fragrance of perfume intermingled with the musty scents and wood polish of the church.

As she knelt beside him he reached for her hands. Their coolness sent a sensation of warmth through his body. Silently he prayed for the mental strength to block out forbidden thoughts and concentrated his mind on the fact that she needed help. He offered up a spontaneous prayer, his mind from practice producing words easily enough.

She found herself wishing that he were a catholic priest so that she could go into the confessional and tell him about her ordeal of the previous night. She felt a need to tell someone. But there was no one she'd dare to tell. She had come to the little church to find brief sanctuary. She had not expected him to see her and follow. Yet she was glad that he had. His golden voice, palliative, soporiferous, seemed to reach into her soul.

A little later as he rose from his knees he released her hands 'I'm always here if you need me,' he reminded.

She stood up, 'Yes I know. Thank you.' She felt less traumatised. Perhaps the drug fix of his voice had calmed her and she wished that she could stay with him a little longer. But how could she explain that to him!

He led the way out and walked with her along the path. When they drew level with the Rectory he continued along the track with her, until she said,

'Don't bother to come any further with me David, I've taken up too much of your time already. Thank you all the same.' She gave a brief smile and walked on.

He stood watching her, the unaccustomed crease in his brow a sign that he was deeply puzzled and concerned.

★   ★   ★

Mark arrived home late on Friday evening. Silvie went out to the garage to meet him. He kissed her. 'Hello my sweet. The week seemed never ending.' With his arm about her they went into the house.

For dinner Laura Pemberton came to the dining table. The uncertainty of what she might say put Silvie on edge all through the meal. But only business talk passed between mother and son.

Later when they were walking in the garden he said, 'Have you been lonely all week Silvie?'

'I've quite enjoyed the solitude. I've found things to do. I often walk to the church and back.' She was careful not to give him extra reason to ask her to go with him when he returned to the city.

'I must teach you to ride. We'll start this weekend.'

'All right,' she agreed.

'But promise you'll think about coming back with me soon to stay the week at my flat darling.'

'I'll think about it Mark — but not just yet. I'd like to settle in here first.'

'Very well my sweet. I shall just have to be content with that. I'm surprised that you don't get just a wee

299

bit lonely though. Mother's no company for you.'

She did not tell him that his mother now took all her meals in her own quarters, for he'd insist on knowing the reason.

That night, as she lay back in the four-poster he traced a finger across her shoulder. 'The days and nights have been long waiting for this moment. My whole world has a different aspect now.'

He watched the long lashes unveil her green eyes as she said, 'Supposing you found out something terrible about me?' The question had been spontaneous and even as she asked it she wondered what compelled her to.

With a hoot of laughter he threw himself backwards on the bed, and as he lay there replied, 'What an absurd question!' And, he thought, not meant for serious response so added, 'I'd put you back in your cardboard box and tie the lid down with ribbons to serve you right for being a naughty doll.' Then he sat up and got into bed beside her. He cupped her breast in his palm and kissed the nipple. Then said softly. 'I couldn't go back to my life as it was before you came into it.' With his lips now close to hers he whispered, 'Silvie — I'd die rather than live without you now.' With this prophesy sealed between his lips and hers he reached out to switch off the bedside lamp.

* * *

During his morning call on Wednesday he explained, 'Darling there's been a sudden change of plan here. Jose Pollinini was to have arrived from

300

Italy for business discussions scheduled for late this afternoon but he's been unavoidably delayed and can't make it until Friday which means that I won't get away early enough to meet the girls from the station as arranged. They want to do some shopping in town before they come home. Can't disappoint them. I'm sure father can be persuaded to collect them.

'I don't know what time Pollinini will arrive now. I'm hoping it'll be early or we shan't be through in time for me to get home for Friday evening. If this turns out to be the case I'll be with you first thing on Saturday morning. I'll drive in the early hours if necessary. Please come back here with me next week my love. *Please?*'

'Very well Mark. Just next week,' she agreed, not really wanting to.

After his call she went for her morning walk. As usual she stopped to speak with Joe Tarrant while he showed the results of his latest planting. Then she continued on to the little stone church where the quiet solitude had now become a necessary part of her existence: her sanctuary. On the Thursday following the one of the thunderstorm when David Bradley had taken her back to the Rectory, she had again passed by on the way to the little church. He had seen her from the window and had come to the end of his garden to call her. She had stopped to speak and he had invited her in and made tea. After that it had become a natural practice for her to take tea with him on Thursdays, mainly in his study where parishioners were received and her visits would not appear out of keeping if one should call while she was there. These special visits to the Rectory took place only on Thursdays when Mrs Armstrong was away shopping at the market town.

★ ★ ★

An unexpected weekend home for the girls was due to the recent death of one of the tutors. Monday had been allocated as a day off as a mark of respect, since it was the day that the funeral was to take place. Boarders who lived not too far distant from the College had taken full advantage of the extra day which gave a long weekend to go home. Silvie was looking forward to having the girls at Briarwood to brighten up the house even for a few hours.

Since the marriage Adam Pemberton had stayed away from the house. Now on account of his son's delayed meeting with Jose Pollinini he was obliged to agree to collect the girls from the station and drive them home to Briarwood.

When they arrived late on Friday evening they greeted Silvie enthusiastically with kisses. Adam did so with his eyes.

'It seems simply ages since we were last home,' Joanne said. 'Miss Em let those who had long distance to travel leave at lunch time and we qualified.'

'It's good to have you both here for a while,' Silvie greeted them, feeling brighter already as she listened to their lively chatter.

'Just wait until you see the blouses we've bought with some money Daddy gave us.' Joanne clutched a brown paper bag ecstatically to her chest.

'They're the latest fashion, tie neck,' Ginny added. 'We're going to wear them at dinner this evening.'

'Which reminds me — come on Ginny, let's go into the kitchen to make sure Dora has kept dinner for us. I'm starving!'

'Dora has,' Silvie called after them. 'We put dinner off until you arrived.' But they had already hurried off to find Dora, food now on top of their priorities list.

Seeing Ginny so settled and happy lifted Silvie's spirits, temporarily casting off the present shadows of uncertainty which dogged her day-to-day existence.

Laura Pemberton came into the hall at that moment. Under her watchful eyes Adam had to postpone the things he wanted to say to Silvie. Then the girls re-emerged and Joanne went to give her mother a fleeting peck on the cheek. 'Hello Mummy. We've bought new blouses!'

Ginny felt obliged to kiss the cold cheek lightly although she did not particularly wish to, and sensed that the gesture was not welcomed. 'Hello Mrs Pemberton.'

Adam had ignored his wife this time, since the girls would not know that he'd not already greeted her. He excused himself and went into the drawing room to pour himself a brandy before going up to bathe and change ready for dinner.

Silvie had gone upstairs and was followed shortly by the girls who, exercising their temporary freedom from the restraints of College rules, whooped excitedly and scaled the stairs two at a time. She went along to their bedrooms to watch them open their gifts from Rome.

When Adam came downstairs he went into the dining room where Dora was about to serve dinner. She had been busy in the kitchen when he'd first arrived. She feasted her eyes on him and wondered what had kept him away from Briarwood so long for he'd not been home for a while now. 'Hello Dora,' he greeted her, 'I daresay you've already been told that Mark won't be here for dinner.'

'Yes. I've made your favourite. Steak and kidney pie. I managed to get some kidneys!' She looked pleased with herself and waited for his appreciative response.

'Clever girl. You've been giving the butcher the glad-eye.'

She laughed in delight. It was nice being called a girl by Adam. 'I think he was giving me the glad-eye.' she said.

Truth was the butcher always looked after her well on account that it was for the Pembertons who had dealt with his family butcher business for years, long before he had taken over from his father.

'Well keep up the good work Dora. Are you going to sit with us for dinner this evening or are you going to shut yourself off in the kitchen?' The more people there were at the table the less tension there would be, generated by his wife's presence.

'Yes. I'll sit at the dining table. You haven't been home for such a long time.'

She hoped he might say why, but all he said was, 'No. I've missed your good home cooking.'

This pleased her. 'Ready to serve in fifteen

304

minutes then. Will you tell the others?'

She returned to the kitchen, her mind already ahead the few hours to the time when he would drive her home. Having had enough notice this time she had especially left her bicycle behind and got a lift in with Joe.

Laura Pemberton was in the drawing room preparing the table for the evenings bridge session. Everything was running late on account of the delayed dinner hour. She had already telephoned her partners to arrange their arrival at a later time.

Adam returned upstairs in the hope of seeing Silvie alone for a few minutes. As he passed he heard the voices of the girls in her room. He waited a while in his dressing room hoping they would leave but they did not. Three minutes before the time set for dinner he could still hear their voices, and went on downstairs.

★   ★   ★

They had just finished dinner when Mark telephoned. Silvie went into the drawing room to answer. 'Pollinini is running late.' His annoyance was obvious by his tone. 'Boat docked later than scheduled. He won't travel by air. Just had a call from his hotel. He wants to postpone the meeting until morning but I've insisted it must be tonight however late.'

'Oh Mark! Have you managed to get dinner somewhere?'

'Not yet darling. I'm just off to join him now for

dinner at his hotel. Then down to business discussions. Probably be well after midnight before we've finished.'

'Don't try to drive through the night Mark or you might fall asleep at the wheel.'

'I'll go back to the flat and snatch a few hours and set the alarm for around three. I'll be home in the morning before you're out of bed.'

'Wake me if I'm still asleep when you arrive.'

'All right my sweet. Goodnight.'

'Goodnight Mark.' As she put down the receiver Laura Pemberton and her bridge partners entered the room. After a brief exchange of greetings with the Jackson-Brownes and the Major she went out closing the door after her.

The girls were at present in the kitchen helping Dora, each with a tea cloth in their hands. Strange, she thought, Dora will accept help from them but not from me.

The offer of help to clear away the dishes was welcome to Dora this evening, although only from the young ones. She couldn't have abided that doll of a girl fussing around her kitchen, quite apart from the fact that Mark would probably be angry if she did.

Silvie went out into the garden. Remembering her promise to Adam she wondered where he was at that moment. At present he was unaware that Mark would not be home until morning for she'd not passed on the latest message to anyone. She sat down on a bench near the lily pond. It was not yet dusk. She heard the girls, now somewhere in the garden, calling her. She called back.

They came running over. 'What time will Mark be here?' Joanne asked.

'I had a call while you were helping Dora. He won't arrive until early in the morning, meeting delayed.'

'Oh.' Joanne looked disappointed. 'Oh well. Can we all go riding in the morning Silvie?'

'I don't see why not. You know of course that I've never been on a horse before.'

'No problem. You've got the three of us to look after you, especially Mark. I wonder if Daddy will come with us. Sometimes he likes to go riding with Major Ashdown.'

'Where is he? Let's ask,' Ginny pulled Joanne by the hand as she spoke. 'Come with us Silvie.'

'He's probably driving Dora home,' replied Joanne as they ran across the lawn towards the house. 'We'd best not go in through the drawing room, they're playing bridge.'

They continued on round to the front and saw Adam in his car about to drive off with Dora.

'Mark can't get home tonight after all Daddy — not until tomorrow morning. Will you come riding with us?'

'What now or in the morning?'

Joanne laughed. 'The morning of course — you know very well what I meant.'

'I think I can manage a ride first thing.' Half his mind was on what his daughter had just said about Mark's delayed arrival. His eyes now turned to Silvie as she arrived on the scene having followed the girls. 'I'll be back shortly,' he said. 'We'll arrange something then.' His eyes still on Silvie he switched on the ignition ready to go.

'Goodnight Dora,' the girls said together.

'Goodnight,' Dora's reply was subdued. Since overhearing what little she had of the hostile exchange between Adam and his wife she had thought a great deal about the words that Laura had used. She was aware of what trollop meant, and whoremonger. But had been unable to figure who was the whoremonger, and whose roof the trollop was under. Briarwood? Which meant the girl was the trollop. Was that what they must not tell Mark! Surely he could never have married a trollop! The words came back again stark and clear now. She had noticed the way Adam's eyes had lingered on the girl. While he'd been away the things she'd overheard hadn't bothered her unduly. But now he was here and Mark not at home her doubts brought twinges of jealousy. But in the car these gradually subsided as she reminded herself that the girl was married to his son. All the same she wished Mark were home. The ride to her cottage this evening was spoiled by her thoughts.

★ ★ ★

The girls had now gone off to bed in order to be up at the crack of dawn for their ride.

Silvie was at present walking in the garden with Adam. The night was clear and moonlit, an Autumn chill in the air. They seated themselves on a bench near the rose garden. He removed his jacket to put it around her shoulders.

'I expect you wonder why I didn't offer to stay

308

behind and confer with Pollinini so that Mark could be here with you tonight,' he was saying. 'The reason is a simple one. We are each good at our own particular role in running the company. For the conferences and discussions with overseas clients he is best equipped, even though he's only been actively involved for about four years, since his war time stint in the forces. I expect he's already mentioned that he served with the RAF during the war after leaving Cambridge. He studied languages. He speaks fluent Italian, French and Spanish. We trade with those countries. Pollinini speaks very little English, and there can be no misunderstandings in our line of business. So you see it had to be Mark.'

'I see. Obviously Pollinini is Italian. But it didn't occur to me that you might have gone in Mark's place. He seldom mentions his work to me. Probably likes to forget it when he's home.'

'Well it's a very old-established concern, the wheels are well oiled, it practically runs itself so we can forget it when we're away from the offices. Sometimes, like tonight, things don't go according to plan where meeting times have been pre-set. Doesn't happen too often though considering.' He slipped his arm around her shoulder and drew her closer. She glanced sideways at him. He would have waited patiently for this opportunity. She gave a small shiver despite the jacket. 'You're cold,' he said. 'Shall we go inside?'

She nodded and with his arm about her waist they walked back to the house and entered by a side door which he locked behind them.

As they went upstairs her conscience weighed heavily when she thought of Mark's blind trust in her . . . in them both.

Later she switched off her bedroom lamp and stood gazing out over the moonlit garden as she waited for him to come through the unlocked door. A promise had been made: More accurately a bargain. Physically not hard to keep, and it had been of her own making, without any coercion from Adam. She had in fact imposed the promise on him by threatening that she would go out of his life altogether if he did not allow the marriage to go through. She had offered herself as a reward to force his compliance, and had made the terms. No blame could be attached to him. He was a man and dictated by his sexual need of her. She was not proud of the method she had used to get her way. Discovery would have a devastating affect on all their lives. She loved Mark. She also loved his father. But she loved Ginny more.

She heard the connecting door open and turned to watch him cross the moonlit room to stand beside her. Taking her gently by the shoulders he whispered in a tone of regret, 'My darling Silvie. I love you so much. I just can't help myself.' He crushed her close to him. She felt the hardness of his desire against her flimsily clad body as he kissed her.

This night, with Adam, or tomorrow with his son she conceived a child. Which of them was the father she would never know.

32

To please Mark she had consented to return with him to the city just this one time. Because the girls were home he especially delayed the departure until after midday luncheon. They would still get to the station in good time for the train that would return them to the College by late afternoon. They were delighted that Silvie was going with them.

Adam had left on Sunday after a long ride with the Major.

'Have you visited our suite of offices yet Silvie?' Joanne asked the dreaded question during the journey.

'Not yet. Plenty of time in the future.'

'I have,' said Ginny. 'Mark took us one day when he collected us from the station.'

'Yes so I did. I had to call back there to clear up some unfinished business. I'd had to dash off to the station or you'd have been waiting on the platform thinking I'd forgotten you.'

'Can you fetch Peter home with you in the next term hols Mark?'

'Well he might have other plans Jojo. But I'll invite him anyway if that's what you want.'

'Has he got a girl friend then?' Joanne sounded as though she hoped not.

'Not sure. He's never mentioned one. But he has a life of his own away from the offices remember.

Now do you both want to come to the flat with me before catching the train?'

'Oh yes,' they answered together, obviously pleased at the idea.

'What will you do all next week Silvie?' Ginny asked.

'I shall look around the shops. So if there's anything special you'd like me to get just let me know. I shall tour the city and visit the art galleries and museums. There — that should take care of my week.' She hoped Mark would accept that her plans would leave no time to visit his offices.

But Joanne was insistent. 'Oh Silvie you must find an hour spare to fit in a quick visit to the office suite. Make the girls Mark employs envious. I expect they're all in love with him.'

Mark laughed aloud at this.

'Do you employ mainly female staff then?' Silvie hadn't considered this possibility.

'A good percentage. Just a couple of chaps beside Peter and Harry.'

She began to relax about the idea of a visit. I've become paranoiac, she thought.

'I forgot to mention that I shall of course be cooking Mark's meals. It'll be a nice change for him, and for me.'

He put out a hand to squeeze hers. 'Sounds delightful, but you're not there to work.'

'I shall enjoy it. Dora won't allow me near the kitchen.'

'I'm glad to hear it.' He laughed before adding, 'Oh — not that I think you can't cook. I remember Stanford Road and know that you can darling.'

By now they had left the countryside behind. It had been a long drive.

* * *

She had been at the flat now for three days. Many hours she'd spent looking round the shops and visiting places of interest. She made lunch for herself and Mark each day and dinner in the evenings. She enjoyed cooking. It seemed so long since she had prepared any meals herself. She had told Mark this when he'd suggested that they eat out to save her the trouble.

Today as he was about to leave after lunch he said, 'Sometime you must let me take you to Mario's where I usually eat. Italian — as you'll have guessed by his name. Serves English food as well though if you prefer. Looks after me well. Not because I'm a regular but because we can converse in his native tongue. He appreciates that.'

'All right,' she agreed smiling. 'Tomorrow we go to Mario's. I know I can't compete with his culinary prowess.'

He laughed aloud. 'Now that's not true!' He picked her up and swung her round holding her close. 'You are not only the best cook in the world, but also the most beautiful.'

* * *

On Thursday morning he telephoned an hour after arriving at his offices to say, 'There's been an unavoidable last minute change of plans darling. An important conference in Manchester has been brought forward ahead of schedule. I shall have to leave tomorrow afternoon. I intend to travel up by train, it's quicker. I don't want to take you with me and leave you in some strange hotel on your own my sweet. Nor do I want to leave you alone in the flat. I'm going to ask Father if he'll drive you home to Briarwood. I know he'll agree. He enjoys being at home when there's company other than Mother. Manchester's a long way, I can't see myself arriving there much before lunchtime on Saturday. I can leave my car at the flat and Father will drop me off at the station. I don't know the return times of the trains. Anyway Mario's is still on for lunch today. Be ready at noon darling. Sorry about the unexpected change. I'm afraid that's typical of how demanding the business can be at times.'

Although Silvie was disappointed for Mark's sake that he had the long and tedious journey ahead of him before he was free to go home to Briarwood, she was, for her own sake, only too thankful to be leaving the fast pace and noise of city life which had strained her taut nerves after the quiet of Kings Meadow. She had missed her visits to the little stone church and Thursday afternoon at the Rectory with David Bradley. She felt as if she had been starved of some drug during the past week, even though her time had been fully occupied. It was only now, when she was about to return, that this strange starved feeling presented itself. She had not mentioned those visits to the church to Mark. He would have been curious as to the reason why she felt the need to go so often. And those long walks around the estate, free from the stares of people, was at least physical freedom, even if her conscience was ever encumbered.

Adam arrived in response to his son's request that he drive Silvie to Briarwood.

First they dropped Mark off at the station and waited with him for his train. 'Take good care of her Father,' he called from the open window as the train chuffed the first few feet of the journey between them.

★ ★ ★

When they arrived at Briarwood it was past the usual hour for dinner. Dora had laid the table for just the two of them having kept their meal hot. She had not been informed until the afternoon that Mark would not be home until next morning and that Adam would be bringing the girl himself. She returned to the kitchen in a sullen mood. Having had no advance warning that he was coming she had not left her bicycle behind, and so would miss out on his driving her home to her cottage later. Her angst was intensified by the thought that he had driven the girl all the way from the city, just the two of them in the intimacy of his car, yet she was to be deprived of just a short ride with him. She was furious with Laura for not letting her know earlier.

Later she cycled home, gradually becoming a vessel of seething envy which continued well into the night, preventing her usual fantasy dreams of sleeping at Briarwood, where around midnight he would come to her room to make love to her.

315

Instead she had been usurped by the girl who would be lying in bed only two rooms away from him. Just the way she herself longed to be.

As she tossed and turned in her bed her envy developed into intense jealousy which her mind, as it now was, could not handle. Those words which she'd overheard between Laura and Adam that day plagued her and took on real meaning. The trollop under the roof, the handy lay, was Mark's wife! From the festering jealousy a deep hatred began to grow for the girl who was where she herself so desperately wanted to be this night, and every night.

★ ★ ★

No bridge session had been arranged for this evening. The Jackson-Brownes had travelled to Surrey to attend the christening of their latest grandchild and would be away overnight. Laura Pemberton had retired to her room, but not yet to bed and was still fully dressed. In the light of what she knew about her husband and her son's wife she would have been less than human had she not been suspicious. Especially since Adam seemed totally incapable of hiding his feelings where the girl was concerned. Mark was blind to it because he had no reason to see it. Her discoveries she had so far kept to herself, knowing that it would be pointless and destructive to do otherwise. The family name would become a laughing stock, with no chance of hushing up the facts in a long drawn out divorce suit which she knew could be the only outcome. Despite not

316

being a dedicated mother she did know her own son's probity, his sensitiveness and his moral standards. These would not withstand the unpalatable truth. Under these circumstances she had conceded that the past must be allowed to die. So long as it remained the past. If it did not — well that was another consideration entirely.

At ten thirty the door of her bedroom opened and in her wheelchair she appeared silhouetted in the doorway, her walking stick in her hand. The upper corridor and the downstairs hall were now in darkness, the lights having been switched off earlier by Adam.

The glow reflected from her bedroom lamp guided the way across the hall to the light switches. When she drew level she raised the stick and flicked the one to light the downstairs hall. Briefly she contemplated the dark upper regions and considered the two-way switch to light the upstairs area. Deciding against, she lowered the stick. She did not want to warn of her approach. She manoeuvred the chair to the base of the staircase, grasped a newel post and with the aid of the stick stood up. She knew that she could, with effort, manage the stairs but it would be a slow progress. Only lack of real necessity kept her from exerting herself nowadays. Shifting her weight to her strongest side she made her way slowly up.

★   ★   ★

At ten thirty the light in Silvie's room had been switched off. The window drapes were pulled back and the room softly lit by a full moon. As he lay with her Adam buried his face in the silky softness of her hair and whispered, 'I can't help myself Silvie my love. It's even harder when Mark hands you to me unwittingly like this. I haven't the moral strength to walk away my darling. You are my whole world.'

Then he felt her voice, soft in his ear. 'Adam — Mark is happy. If I hadn't married him he might not be so. As things are you both have me and I have you both. So nobody is hurt really.'

The shadow of a smile touched his lips as he lifted his head to look at her face. 'There's logic in that somewhere my lovely. Indeed Mark does have you. And for the present so do I. But I can't bear the thought of some day losing you. If ever that does happen I know I should want to die.'

'Oh Adam, don't speak to me of dying!' Her words echoed only in her own ears for the urgent desire of his body was claiming fulfilment.

★ ★ ★

On the stairs her footfalls made no sound against the thick carpet. When she reached the master bedroom she paused briefly before passing on to her husband's room. Here she did not hesitate but turned the knob quietly and entered. The light was switched off and the drapes unpulled. The moonlit room showed an empty undisturbed bed. Her eyes travelled to the wide open door of the dressing room. Her feet and the stick made only silent contact with the carpeted floor as she crossed the small room to stand looking in through the unclosed door of the master bedroom, her eyes confirming the suspicions which had brought her there.

★ ★ ★

When Adam Pemberton returned to his own room he saw that his door was wide open, yet knew for certain that he'd closed it. That door was always kept closed night and day. He switched on the bedside lamp and immediately saw the black silk scarf placed significantly across his bed. It belonged to his wife, he recognised it as one which she often wore, and may well have been wearing that evening, he hadn't noticed. She always dressed in black so everything looked much the same on her. Almost bemused he stared down at the black silk message purposely left to tell him that she'd been in the room. He glanced across at the connecting door, now closed and relocked by Silvie. There had seemed no reason to close it earlier since only the three of them were in the house. The probability of his wife making the supreme effort of climbing the stairs seemed so remote as to be completely out of the question.

Seething he pulled on his dressing robe, snatched up the scarf and went downstairs. The lower hall light she had especially left on. He went straight to the open door of her bedroom where the lamp was still burning. She was seated in the wheelchair facing the door as though expecting him.

With a quick angry movement he flung down the scarf. 'Good God woman what do you think you're up to — spying on me! How long were you in my room?'

'Long enough. And if wanting to know what filthy behaviour is going on under this roof is considered spying then yes — I *was* spying,' she retaliated.

Unflinching he countered, 'You don't give a bloody damn really so how can it matter to you!'

'It would matter to Mark. Unlike you and that young whore his moral outlook is clean and decent, as well you know.'

He ignored the name calling since her opinion was of no concern to him. 'What he doesn't know can't harm him. You're already aware that I was Silvie's lover before she met Mark. I could have prevented the marriage, and he wouldn't have thanked me for it.'

'He wouldn't thank you for laying his wife either,' she spat back at him, then hesitated briefly before adding, 'It explains why you kept your mouth shut about her. After tonight you'll stay away from this house when Mark is not here. If you don't I shall be forced to tell him the truth of what's been going on behind his back.'

His reply to this was not what she wanted, but what she expected. 'I'll do nothing of the sort. I shall come and go as I please. So save your bloody threats.'

Again she was reminded of why he had been her father's choice to succeed him in the business. When he knew his ground, and he thought he knew it now, he would not budge, at least not without a fight. She wondered how he could be so trenchant, so disciplined, in matters of business, even crisis, yet so weak in the flesh. As far as this slip of a girl was concerned his lust ruled his head.

'Then I shall be obliged to tell him,' she warned. But even as she spoke she knew that she was on weaker ground than he.

'Do that,' he flung back defiantly as he turned abruptly and left the room.

★　★　★

Unaware of the drama that had taken place downstairs Silvie bathed and changed her night-clothes before settling back into bed. Mark might well arrive in the very early hours of the morning.

She was still asleep when he came into the house. In the hall he met his father.

'The meeting went well. I'll fill you in later about it. Didn't finish discussions until the early hours. I managed to catch an express back from Manchester. Only stopped at the flat long enough to collect my car, and drove straight here. Is Silvie up yet?'

Adam shook his head and idly watched as his son went upstairs. He had especially stayed in the house to be on hand to protect Silvie against possible verbal abuse from his wife, whose mind he thought he knew well enough. Accurately or otherwise had yet to be determined. He could not be totally certain that he had won the battle and was taking no chances. He felt fairly confident that in her book of priorities the protection of the company name and the avoidance of inevitable scandal would take precedence. She knew as well as he that telling Mark the truth could have only one conclusion. On that one thing they were in positive agreement. Mark's life would be destroyed and the chances of producing an heir from the real Whitehorne blood line perhaps lost forever as far as he was concerned.

Dora heard him go into the breakfast room and took in a laden tray. 'Did I just hear Mark come in?'

'Yes Dora, he went straight upstairs.'

He used to first come into the kitchen for coffee when he arrived, she thought resentfully. And he'd sit and talk while he drank it. Now, since the girl had come on the scene everything was changed and disorganised. She was a disruptive influence. Even Adam had not been out for his usual early morning ride. Well at least she'd had enough warning this time that he was to be home. She had left her bicycle at home and come with Joe in his old Ford. She had the ride with Adam in his car to look forward to at the end of the day. That hadn't changed. She wouldn't let it.

Upstairs Silvie woke as Mark came into the room 'Morning my sweet,' he kissed her.

She sat up. 'You must have been travelling all night! Have you had any sleep at all?'

'Forty winks on the train from Manchester. I believe I did nearly doze off while I was driving. Very little traffic on the roads at that hour though.'

'You must be very tired. Shall I go down and fetch some breakfast up to you.' She made a move but he stopped her.

'Stay in bed my sweet. I'll go down and bring coffee up for both of us. Then I'll have a quick shower. I'm not too tired to make love to you.' He bent to give her a quick kiss, left the room and went down to the kitchen.

'Morning Dora. Any coffee made. I'll take some up for Silvie and myself. I'm not hungry enough yet for breakfast. Perhaps in a couple of hours after a short nap. Been travelling most of the night.'

Dora poured two cups of coffee and set them with a sugar bowl and milk onto a tray then handed this to him. 'Shall I prepare a late breakfast for you around ten o'clock then?'

'Best not Dora. I might still be asleep. If not Silvie and I can find something in the kitchen thanks.'

'No need for that. I'll be in here. I'll make your breakfast when you come down.' Silvie! Silvie! She was sick of hearing the name.

'Thanks then Dora.'

He carried the tray upstairs. While he showered Silvie drank her coffee then lay back waiting for him. At least she always tried to compensate for the terrible deceit which she was committing, by trying to make each time perfect for him.

33

More and more as the days passed Silvie looked forward to the brief suspension of life which she experienced in the timeless, musty atmosphere of the little stone church. Where the euphonious voice seemed to echo for her ears alone, for no one else was ever there during those chosen times. There she listened for the soft rustle of his cassock as he moved.

Reverend Bradley at the French window of his study watched for her each day. She always came along the same track, never looking in the direction of the Rectory. Yet she knew he'd be there. *Always* he watched and waited. *Always* he found her in the same front pew. *Always* he prayed silently with her. But *never* did she tell him what troubled her.

Whether the chosen day for her visits to the Rectory coincided with Mrs Armstrong's day at the market by sheer chance he refused to contemplate. But he was aware that even amiable souls as she did not lack curiosity and a tongue to express it. But since the day of the thunderstorm they had fallen naturally into this habit each Thursday.

At this moment, sheltered from view by a hedge and shrubs, they sat in the garden. This was where they liked to be when weather permitted. Today was a dry and windless Thursday with a slight chill in the air. She drew her coat closer about her and closing her eyes relaxed back against the seat.

A short silence had fallen between them. Suddenly she asked, 'Talk to me David.'

'About what?' he turned in the seat to look at her.

'Anything. Everything.'

'You'll most likely fall asleep.'

'How many times have I done that?'

'I've lost count.' He smiled. 'I've come to the conclusion that my voice has some hypnotic influence on you. A soporific effect perhaps.'

She opened her eyes and regarded him. 'Yes that's true. Spiritual sedation.'

His deep blue eyes rested on her as he wondered — was it enough? He wanted to give more.

34

Early in December Silvie again went to the city with Mark to spend another week at the flat. Although this time mainly for Christmas shopping she also visited a private clinic close to the park. Parcel-laden she caught a taxi back to the flat. Once inside she telephoned Adam on his private line. 'Can you meet me this afternoon in the park near the bird aviary. I have something to tell you.'

'What time darling?'

'When will you be free?'

'For you my love any time. How about two thirty?'

'I'll be there.' She hung up. The time was eleven o'clock. Mark would be in at noon. She set about preparing lunch.

★ ★ ★

Ten minutes before the appointed time Adam arrived at the bird aviary. Silvie arrived five minutes later. He greeted her with a kiss — 'Hello darling.' They seated themselves on a park bench.

'Adam I went to the clinic today I'm going to have a baby.'

Solemnly he took her hands in his and held them tightly as he asked, 'Who is the father, Mark or me?'

'I don't know the answer to that Adam.'

There were few people around. He raised his

hands to cup her face, his thumbs caressing her cheeks. 'I do love you so Silvie.'

He had parked his car close by. He drove her back to Mark's flat and returned to his office. On the way he realised that he hadn't asked her if she had told his son the news yet. The moment he arrived in his private office he telephoned the flat to ask.

'Not yet Adam. I intend to later today before we leave.'

'Well he'll want to tell his mother the news as soon as you get to the house. I'd best come along too. I can't explain here. I have the feeling that I ought to be there. I'll follow in my car.'

As she replaced the receiver she wondered why he felt he should be present when the news was given to his wife. The reason why she had decided to tell Adam first was because Mark, when told, would immediately want to pass the news on to his father. This might have been very awkward for Adam. He would need warning and time to adjust in order to react as would be expected of him.

★　★　★

Her things were packed ready to take out to the car. Mark had just paid the woman who came in each Friday to clean the flat and return his week's laundry. He was about to pick up the cases and her parcels. She chose this moment to tell him the news.

He pulled her close and held her head against his chest. 'Silvie . . . my sweet Silvie. I can't find the right words to tell you how I feel at this moment. I love you so much — it almost hurts; strange but

327

true. I'm glad Father decided to come home for the weekend. He rang me earlier. I wonder how he'll feel being told he's to become a grandfather, you know how young he looks. He wasn't much older than you when I was born. I know Mother will welcome the news of another Whitehorne in the family to inherit the business. She'll never think of our child as a Pemberton. She was practically forced into marriage with Father and I know that she's not been much of a wife to him in the real sense.'

When he released her he picked up the parcels and set the cases by the door ready. 'Let's go my sweet. I don't intend to drive as fast as usual. I hope you feel up to the long ride.'

She nodded and smiled in attempt to lighten her heavy conscience. After all, she thought, he might well be the father of the coming baby. 'I'll be all right. No need to mollycoddle me for ages yet.'

He laughed in the special way that she'd grown so used to and loved about him. She had one last look around for anything forgotten then followed him out to the car.

'Pity Father always wants to leave Briarwood a day before I do,' he said when they were settled in the Jaguar and on the road. 'It would make sense for us to both travel in one car. Quite unnecessary for us to take two cars all that way when we're both going home for the weekend. Just lately he never wants to stay any longer than a day. Beat's me why! Something on his mind I think. Can't be to do with the business. We've no problems. Quite apart from the fact that he never worries about such matters.

He's tough and can handle anything that's thrown at him.'

She could make no reply and her conscience pricked deeper.

Adam, a few miles behind them, was musing on those reasons why he did not stay at Briarwood when Mark was there. The thought of them together in the next room was to him unbearable. Tonight he would stay downstairs in the library. Probably fall asleep on the leather couch after a few brandies. All he knew at present was that it was imperative to be present in order to handle a possible invidious outburst by his wife when she was given the news. There was no telling how she would react now under the circumstances. It would be a testing time. He wished that he had forewarned Silvie about Laura having seen them in bed together. He put on speed to catch up and overtake them in order to reach the house first to be present at the critical time. He pumped his horn as he passed them and gave a brief wave.

★   ★   ★

Again Dora had not been notified until the afternoon that Adam would be home. Having as usual ridden her bicycle to the house she had promptly gone out to let one of the tyres down and hide the pump, regretting that she'd not had the wits to do this last time. Nobody else at Briarwood owned a bicycle so no pump could be produced. She would not be deprived of her ride home in his car *this* time. Tomorrow morning she would get a lift in with Joe and later re-pump the tyre. Knowing that Mark also would be home and she would have no tormenting thoughts of Adam alone up there with the girl tonight she was in light spirits when he arrived.

He found his wife in the drawing room reading an equestrian magazine. He had time to pour himself a brandy and drink it before his son and Silvie arrived. For all their sakes he braced himself to act surprised, knowing this would not be easy.

As he'd expected Mark came straight into the drawing room where he knew he'd find his mother at this hour.

'Some good news for you both. A new addition to the family is expected!' He could barely contain his elation.

Silvie avoided Adam's eyes. And secretly Adam wished that he could be miles away at this moment. But it had to be got through.

Mark Pemberton was surprised when his mother showed no emotion at the news. But then, he thought, she always was a strange woman, at least since her accident. She seemed to live in a world of her own, shutting everything out of her life except the horses and her bridge sessions. Yet he'd expected some reaction even if only for the reason that a future heir for the family business was assured. He looked at his father.

Adam, contrary to his nature, was at a loss for suitable words to acknowledge the announcement.

But his son spoke first to cover the awkward silence. 'It seems that our news has surprised you both speechless.' He gave his easy laugh. 'I'll get a bottle of champagne from the cellar and we'll celebrate properly.' He turned his attention to Silvie. 'You sit down darling. I shan't be a tick.'

He left the room. His mother allowed enough time for him to get clear of the hall before addressing Silvie with words which cut the uneasy air as keen and deadly as bullets. 'Who is the father? My husband or my son?'

Mark Pemberton hadn't got far before he realised that he would need the key to the cellar. Having turned back to fetch it he was close enough to hear the staggering question which stopped him in his tracks. The next few seconds were frozen in silence. It was as if the words did actually carry the power of bullets, striking them all dumb. Suddenly life re-entered his body and in a few strides he was back in the room.

Silvie gasped and swayed on her feet when she saw his anxious expression. Instantly he moved to her side and put his arm about her for support as he guided her to a seat.

Adam was the first to recover and speak. 'You're sick Laura. I shall telephone the doctor to let him know you're having one of your strange turns.' He moved towards the telephone threateningly, thanking God at the same time that he had come home.

Mark's voice cut the ensuing silence, his attention on Silvie. 'I'm so sorry darling. Don't upset yourself unduly. Mother has had strange turns of mind before, although nothing so serious as this. Probably shock. I shouldn't have sprung the news on her like that. You're trembling! Perhaps you should lie down for a while. I'll take you upstairs.' He turned briefly to his father, 'I'll leave Mother to you. We'll get Dora to make some hot sweet tea. I believe it's good for shock.'

Still shaken himself at his wife's blunt question Adam replied, 'I'll ask Dora to make some.'

As Mark was leaving the room with Silvie his mother said contemptuously, 'You're a blind fool. You may have brains but you haven't the wits of your father when he's in a tight spot.' In for a penny, in for a pound, she thought. It had been said, there was no retracting; let come what may.

But her son did not look back. It was as if he hadn't heard.

'This is the bloody limit Laura!' Open animosity showed on Adam's face now as he glared at her across the room. 'What the hell did you hope to gain by that!'

'I didn't do it intentionally. How the devil was I to know that he'd turn back and overhear!'

'You needn't have made things worse with that last viperish insult.'

'Did you expect me to just sit here quietly while you make me out to be mad!'

'Why ask such a vindictive question in the first place!'

'It was and still is a perfectly valid question. I want a family heir, but I want my son to be the father. If the child is yours you and she could go off together any time.'

'And suppose he had believed you. Divorce and no heir at all! That wouldn't suit you either! There's Joanne of course — but too much in the future, and being a girl not the same in your book anyway.'

'He'd soon find someone else if he divorced her,' she retorted, unrepentant now.

'Never! You know very well that he didn't bother much about girls before he met her.'

She made no reply for she knew this was true. Mark was not the gregarious kind and hadn't socialised much. In the past he'd been kept occupied with his studies at Cambridge, then the spell in the air force during the war. Since then he'd been deeply involved learning the business.

'And,' Adam continued, 'he's had no social contact with women at the offices. The rule handed down by your grandfather — family not to mingle with the staff outside business. Or to use his own words, lay off the staff. Well Mark abides to that strictly. Enough female caps are set at him there.'

'He's young yet. He'd meet someone and marry again.'

He shook his head. 'I'm certain he wouldn't. In any event scandal is what would bother you most. And from sheer spitefulness you nearly brought plenty of that down on your own head a moment ago.' As he turned towards the French window to go into the garden he glimpsed by her expression that the truth of his words had struck home.

★ ★ ★

Upstairs Mark helped Silvie off with her top coat. 'The news must have unbalanced her. Obviously didn't know what she was saying. She hasn't been quite the same since her accident. If she shows signs of further disturbance I'll telephone the doctor for advice. Don't concern yourself about it darling. Lie down and rest. I'll bring up some tea, and if you like we can eat up here.'

'Nothing to eat or drink just now Mark. I'm all right really. I'd just like to lie quietly for a while.' She was still trembling from the unexpected confrontation from his mother.

'Very well. I'll come up in about fifteen minutes.' He kissed her lightly on the cheek and left the room.

His blind trust and concern for her cut deep into her conscience. She turned her face into the pillow and wept silently for the things she could not change.

★ ★ ★

On his return downstairs he found that his mother had left the drawing room. Through the window he saw his father in the garden and went out to join him. 'Where's Mother now? Do you think we should have a talk with the doctor?'

Adam shook his head. 'Only a temporary lapse. Best left alone.'

'Damn serious one though! Upsetting for Silvie.'

'I agree. But as far as your mother's concerned I don't think there's cause for further alarm. Obviously the sudden unexpected news. I'm sure she'll be all right now. At least as all right as she'll ever be. I'll keep an eye on her. Seems to be her usual self at the moment.' He reflected sardonically on the threat which she'd flung at him as he'd left the room ten minutes earlier . . . 'If you call the doctor just to save your own face, I'll tell Mark the rest of the story, and not by mischance this time.'

'I don't like leaving Silvie next week in case Mother has another strange mental lapse. But I know it's no use trying to persuade her to come back with me to the flat again just yet. In any case travelling seems to make her nauseous at present. I don't want her upset in any way. Fortunately I don't have any more board meetings mapped out for Friday evenings between now and Christmas so I'll be able to get home. But I do have the Le Havre conference with Leon Chevasseu coming up in the new year.'

'I could go instead,' Adam volunteered, although his words were slowed with doubt.

'Mmm . . . but it's *my* hat isn't it?'

'I used to wear both before you were able to take over.'

'True, but you had Henry Lefebvre to go with you in those days as interpreter. Pity he's no longer with us. As things are you can't even understand Leon's broken English, let alone his French.'

'True. But couldn't he bring an interpreter? He did once before.'

Mark gave a brief laugh. 'Yes I remember. But my French is more reliable than that chap's English was. Peter could of course go but I don't think his French is up to it just yet. He's working on it though. No I'm afraid it has to be me. But I'd be easier in my mind if you could be here on that Friday night. I'll be home by late on the Saturday morning.'

Adam nodded agreement. Then asked the

question which had been uppermost in his thoughts. 'How is Silvie?'

'Tired and I believe exceedingly upset. She wanted to be left alone to rest for a while. I'm to blame I suppose. I did rather spring the news on Mother. But I had no idea that her mind was so vulnerable still. The worst she's been in the past is a bit abstracted. Bound to be pleased when she's settled to the news. I was bowled over myself — you understand.'

Adam nodded. He understood perfectly.

★ ★ ★

Silvie rose shakily from the bed and walked unsteadily to the bathroom as a feeling of nausea swept over her. After vomiting she showered and returned to the bed.

The blunt and unexpected confrontation from Laura Pemberton had taken her by surprise but the worst of her concerns was the fact that Mark had overheard. She was thankful that Adam had been present. Although Mark was protective those accusing words could not be retracted or erased from his memory despite his trust, and could so easily sow the seeds of doubt.

She felt caught inextricably in the web of deceit she had woven.

Mark returned. 'How are you feeling now darling. Would you like me to fetch dinner up here for you?'

'No thank you. I really couldn't eat at present. I'd like some coffee though.'

Dora laid the table in the breakfast room for dinner, since only the two men were to sit down together. Laura Pemberton was to have her meal in her own quarters. She did not trust that her tongue would remain silent if she sat with them. She felt contempt for both. Her husband for his sexual weakness; her son for his blindness. Her urge to tell him the facts was strong. But she'd just had a taste of what the result would be. Quite apart from his believing that some mental relapse was responsible for a wild and mad accusation, no constructive purpose would be achieved. The best that could be hoped for at present was that he would in future be at home whenever his father was.

Dora had seized this opportunity to dine at the table with the two men. She felt happy and content that the girl was not present to take their attention. She noted however that both were unusually quiet and subdued throughout the meal.

Immediately after dinner Mark returned upstairs to Silvie. All the while he was downstairs she had been anxious to know what might be happening. She was relieved when he entered the room smiling. 'How are you feeling now my sweet?'

'Better.'

'Are you ready to eat something now?'

'When Dora's gone I'll go down and make some toast. That's all I can manage for the present.'

'He sat down on the bed and put his arm around her shoulders. 'Well both go down and I'll make the toast.'

337

When Adam returned from driving Dora home he shut himself in the library, smoking cigars, drinking brandy and attempting to read. There he remained until three o'clock in the morning when he awoke with a stiff neck where he had fallen asleep on the leather couch.

Dora arrived early with Joe Tarrant and made breakfast for Adam before he set out on a long ride with the Major.

Silvie breakfasted with Mark, although she ate little. 'We'll go for a walk and take a picnic if you feel up to it darling,' he suggested.

'Yes I'd like that.'

He turned to Dora as she entered to collect the dishes. 'Could you fix up a picnic basket for us Dora?'

She nodded, pleased that the girl would be out of the house when Adam returned. She always felt so dowdy alongside her.

Adam rang to say he was to lunch with Major Ashdown and would be leaving for the city before dinner. Dora took the call since she was the only one in the house at the time. She loved the intimate sound of his voice in her ear. But she was piqued that she would miss out on a ride home in his car at the end of the day. When he had rung off she went out to pump up the specially deflated tyre of her bicycle.

Adam did not want to spend the night at Briarwood while his son was there with Silvie. He felt confident at leaving now. His wife had done her worst. The testing time had past. By the time Mark and Silvie returned he had already left.

After their walk they had returned to drop off the picnic basket and collect the car to go for a drive. They did not encounter his mother for the rest of the weekend. Most of the time she was as usual outside with the horses. She took her meals in her own quarters, and was occupied with the bridge games in the evening.

★   ★   ★

On Sunday morning Silvie asked, 'Why don't you go for a ride Mark? I don't feel up to it today. I can wander around the garden.' She had by now learned to sit a horse. Mark had chosen a particularly placid mare for her.

'No — I shan't go riding without you. Don't you want to attend the morning church service? Do Reverend Bradley a good turn.'

'Not this week.' Truth was that special magic in the church was spoiled when others were there. She now preferred to keep it just for the two of them.

★   ★   ★

Mark left in the very early hours of Monday morning. Before he went he said, 'Promise that you'll call me if you think Mother is not quite herself. It was most likely an isolated lapse so no doubt it won't happen again. But I'd feel easier if I know you'll contact me if there's any problem.'

'Yes — yes of course. But I see so little of her anyway.'

'Don't we all! Still perhaps I ought to ask Dora to stay overnight for a while.'

'There's really no need. You're concerning yourself needlessly. I'll be fine.' She felt deep pangs of guilt that he thought his mother, who had only spoken the truth, was mental. And his over-protectiveness irked her at present since it was not justified. She felt unworthy. When he still looked doubtful she added, 'Don't worry about me — please!'

'It's my place to worry about you.' He held her close, his lips on her hair. 'You're going to have my child. I'm happy beyond words Silvie — my love.'

★   ★   ★

The girls had been writing regularly from the College. One would write for both since they composed the letters between them and each took turns. In reply to the letter which they'd received giving the news of the expected baby Ginny had written . . .

We do not know how to put whoops of joy onto paper. So between the lines read lots and lots of squeals of delight. We are both looking forward to becoming doting aunts and we're absolutely ecstatic! As we can only celebrate the news with lemonade at present we expect to do it properly with champagne when we are home on hols. Please keep on telling us how you spend your days because it's the next best thing to being there for us. We do get homesick at times, especially at weekends. We're kept busy all week with studies. Jojo is getting very proficient at French. Lots of love from both of us. Ginny and Jojo.

At their repeated requests to know how she spent each day she told them, among other things, of her visits to the little stone church, although she did not mention their frequency. She could not explain that special solace that drew her to its fragrant sanctuary, for they would have been curious as to why she felt in need of such a retreat, just as Mark would have. These things about her daily life she could not tell. Nor did she mention the regular Thursday visits to the Rectory, other than the first one on the day of the storm.

Her very existence now seemed woven with small offshoots of deceit, all of which stemmed from the unredeemable past. In this fashion the days passed.

★　★　★

The week before Christmas she again went back with Mark to stay at his flat in the city in order to do some shopping.

Adam phoned to ask her to go to the stores with him to help choose presents for the girls. He took her to a jeweller and she chose identical gold lockets for them. 'Now something for you,' he said. 'I want to buy you pearls.'

The assistant had returned from wrapping the lockets and Silvie could not protest in his presence. She chose a single row of pearls. She could not see its price tag which was turned on its reverse side as were all the others.

'Madam has chosen well,' remarked the assistant who was showing them the usual excess of courtesy reserved for those buying the best. He went on to explain their merits and how perfectly matched they were.

Silvie, who knew nothing about real pearls, and had thought that by choosing a single string she was avoiding extravagance, learned her mistake. But Adam looked satisfied.

When they had left the store she said, 'I hope I didn't choose the most expensive pearls!'

'I wish you had.' he took her arm. 'You were made for pearls. They'll match your teeth.' He smiled own at her. 'Now let's go somewhere for coffee.'

'Don't you have to get back to the office?'

'Not yet awhile. Harry's there. What time do I have to get you back to the flat by?'

'Not until five o'clock when Mark gets in. He knows that we're shopping together for gifts for the girls. We've arranged to shop tomorrow for his presents to them.'

'Well it's only two thirty. Come back to my apartment with me,' he asked softly. 'I need you darling. I'll get you back to the flat before five.'

'All right Adam.' They had little opportunity to be together nowadays. 'We'd best not stop for that coffee then. We'll make some ourselves.'

'You haven't been here for a long time,' he said as

they entered his apartment. 'I hope it brings back pleasant memories.'

'It seems a long time,' she agreed. 'I'll make the coffee.'

Half an hour later he was making passionate love to her where no prying eyes could see them.

★ ★ ★

Next day she went to the shops with Mark to buy their Christmas gifts for the girls. She chose silver-backed hair brush, comb and mirror sets. Then he took her to a furrier. On the way he told her she was to choose a mink coat.

'I can't possibly Mark! The expense! We can find something else less costly.'

'Well the something else will do for your birthday. We'll have to get that today. There'll be no more time for us to shop before Christmas.'

Her twenty-first birthday fell on the 27th of December. 'One present will do for both,' she insisted. 'Especially one so expensive.'

'Do you think I would bypass a birthday so special!' he replied as he led her into the store. Between them they chose a silver-grey mink coat. As she tried it on she saw the clearly printed tag and was staggered. But he was totally unconcerned as he wrote out the cheque.

By chance the furrier was in the same block as the jewellers where she had shopped with Adam. Taking her by surprise Mark guided her inside. 'Now I want you to choose something special. I had in mind a bracelet,' he paused to laugh before adding, 'For *you* of course.'

The same assistant who had served her the day before came forward, and she suspected hid his surprise. She wondered what he might be thinking. Two different men in just two days, each buying her jewellery. She chose a gold bracelet set with rubies and pearls. One again she could not see the price tag without making an obvious display of turning it over.

When they'd left the store she told him that she'd been in there the day before with his father and bought jewellery for the girls. She did not mention the pearls. He would not know that Adam had not chosen them himself at some other time.

'Well I'm sure the jeweller is highly delighted to have a beautiful lady bringing men into his shop two days running to buy her gifts. He'll no doubt be on the lookout for you tomorrow.' He laughed his special laugh and hugged her to his side as they walked.

'I'm wondering what he must be thinking though.' She was as amused as he now.

'The worst I expect,' he teased.

35

Christmas passed, along with Silvie's twenty-first birthday for which Mark had wanted to arrange some special celebration out somewhere. But she had preferred to spend it at Briarwood. With their usual zest the girls had made as much of it as possible. Mark had ordered a cake decorated with twenty one candles.

All that was now in the past. The girls were back at the College. The time of year mid-January, the day Thursday.

For three days the heavy rain had not eased and she had stayed away from the little church. But today the sky was clear and blue with just a scattering of cirrus clouds. Patiently she had waited for this break in the weather and was eager to get away from the house for a while. She put on her mink coat, for the air was crisp and cold.

The scent of pines and the dampened earth smelled fresh and strong. Raindrops still on the trees glistened in the sun and fell like giant tears as she passed beneath them, as if they could foresee what she could not, and wept for her.

★　★　★

There were times in the little church when kneeling beside her David Bradley had the strange feeling that when he opened his eyes he would find that she

345

had disappeared. She seemed so ethereal — as though never quite real — and yet never quite imagined.

As they left the church he noticed that she was trembling slightly. 'Are you cold?'

She shook her head, 'Not cold. My coat is warm.'

They walked in silence to the Rectory. When they reached the garden he said, 'It's too cold to sit out here today. We'd best go inside.'

She nodded agreement, then added, 'In your study David,' — as if she had pre-planned.

They entered through the French window. 'It would be much warmer in the living room.'

'I'd rather stay in here because today I want to tell you about my life.'

He regarded her silently, hardly able to believe that at last he might learn what troubled her: he'd known almost from the beginning that something did. But he'd always been the talker, she the listener. It was her way to be cool and silent. Perhaps that's what made her appear ethereal. He helped her off with her coat and went to hang it on the hallstand. When he returned to the room she was seated in his armchair. He switched on an electric heater and sat down at his desk, at the same time wondering why she chose the study in preference to the warmer living room.

As though reading his thoughts she explained, 'It's not a story for comfort David. It's more a confession really.' She paused. His blue questioning eyes were intent upon her.

She began where she knew she must begin, with Queen Street when Ginny was very young. The day

346

when, as a child herself, she'd bought the green satin bow and vowed, 'Only the best for Ginny.' It was important that he understand the compelling need she'd felt to provide a brighter future for the sister she loved so devotedly. Yet she doubted that he would visualise the despised poverty of Queen Street from words alone.

When she came to speak of the Georgian house she rose from the armchair and went to stand at the French window looking out at the garden. When she again turned to face him she saw that his elbows were now resting on his desk, his hands supporting his bowed head.

She returned to sit in the chair, 'Perhaps I should not go on.'

He raised his head but did not look at her as he stood up and went across to stand at the vacated place at the French window, staring out towards the woods. He lifted his hand briefly in a gesture that spoke more clearly than words. What could she say now that would be more shattering than that already said! Her honey tones could not soften the hard facts. Even as he'd listened he had wanted to implore her to stop. One man possessing her had been hard enough for him to bear. But she had sold herself to another for the price of his silence. Much worse — that man was the father of her husband! And before that — to the Lord knows who! Sold the beautiful body that he lay awake at night thinking about. But all these thoughts were released only in the anguished silence of his heart. Utterly shaken he kept his eyes on the woods beyond the garden, where so many times he had watched for her to pass. Like an elusive and beautiful dream: an Angel amongst the trees, with sunlight on her hair.

He had always hoped that one day she would confide in him. Now he wished that she hadn't. Something had been destroyed in the process . . . illusions.

He felt the light touch of her hand on his arm. 'Look at me David. Don't turn away.'

But his eyes stayed focussed on the woods. He could not bring himself to turn and face her. Afraid to look into her eyes and see that the innocence which he'd found so stirring had never really existed at all.

He felt a slight movement as she turned from him, and heard the catch in her voice.

'I'm sorry David. I shouldn't have burdened you with my conscience.'

As she walked from the room he swung round as though suddenly restored to life by some remote mechanical means. 'Silvie!' He followed her into the hall calling her name again. 'Silvie!'

She did not turn back as she collected her coat from the stand and moved towards the front door. He caught her by the shoulders and turned her round to face him. 'Oh Silvie . . . Silvie!' He took the coat from her and draped it over the banister. 'Don't you know? Don't you see what you're doing to me!' His eyes searched her face and rested on her lips — so close now. 'Oh Silvie . . . Silvie . . . ' he groaned as he drew her close to him and into his arms. 'Haven't you really known all this time how I feel?'

As if by a magnet his lips contacted hers hard and

hungrily. She offered no resistance then surrendered herself to his embrace and his kiss.

When he released her he was breathing hard. His voice unsteady he said, 'So you see I am only a man after all, and not some Deity to whom you can unburden your soul and bring your conscience for absolution. I love you Silvie. Almost from the moment I first saw you. I thought you must have known that.'

'Oh David — of course I've known. I shouldn't have told you those things about myself otherwise. I love you too.'

'But you have a husband Silvie.'

'I love him too. And I love his father. I love you all.'

'You can't love three men Silvie! It's not possible.'

'I *do*. And it *is*.' she replied simply.

Without speaking he looked down at her upturned face. He regarded the innocence, still there in her lovely features just as he'd always seen it. Who was *he* to judge her? *He* who was a sinner himself. Only spiritual love he'd tried to give her. Tried so hard, until he was unable to separate it from the physical. The two had combined and he could not say when the fusion had taken place.

She spoke again now. 'I should not have disillusioned you. You'll stop loving me now. Or you'll love me less.'

'I'll never stop loving you Silvie. I do not love you less. And I've no right to love you at all the way I do.'

Again a silence fell between them. His eyes locked with hers as a struggle took place within him. The

349

man of the cloth wrestled with the man of the flesh and the man of the flesh with the Devil. But the will of nature imposed itself. He crushed her closer and bent his head to kiss her feverishly.

But the Devil was the victor only in a small battle of a war that could not be won.

She clung to him, returning his kisses. Then pulled away breathless. 'I must not separate you from your God. I shall not come again.'

Before he relinquished his hold on her he said, 'I'll never forget you Silvie, and I'll never stop loving you — despite my God.'

She collected her coat from the banister and turned back to the study to leave by the French window. He made no move to follow. For how long he remained there, his bowed head supported on his arm across the banister, he could not have said.

When he returned to his study he stood at the French window staring out at the deserted path in the silent woods.

The stimulation of his ardent kisses still on her lips she walked slowly back to Briarwood. She shivered and realised that she was still carrying her coat. She slipped it on and pulled its warmth closely about her body. She did not regret having told him. But she did regret that in doing so she had hurt him so deeply. And that she could never again find her sanctuary in the little stone church.

36

In his flat Mark Pemberton replaced the phone having just been notified that the cross channel ferry to Cherbourg had been cancelled owing to the extreme weather conditions. Annoyance showed on his face. Already the departure of the ferry had been delayed for two hours, but the gale force winds and storms that lashed the coast had not eased. Almost instantly the telephone rang again. He snatched it up with the hope that it might be more information regarding the crossing which would now have to be put off until morning. But a voice announced, 'Long distance call for Mr Pemberton.'

'Speaking.'

There was a brief pause before the voice resumed. 'Go ahead now caller. You are connected.'

Instantly a voice with a strong French accent came on the line. 'Ah — M'sieur Pemberton. I am Pierre Mousnard, Leon's assistant. I am plissed to find you 'ave not left yet. I telephoned the ferry terminal first because I thought I might catch you zair. I 'ave some very bad news m'sieur. Leon 'as been taken to ze 'ospital wiz a suspected seizure. Zis means we 'ave to cancel ze meeting. Apologies for ze inconvenience to you m'sieur. It is a good thing that you 'ave been delayed by ze bad wezair or I would not 'ave catch you in time wiz ze news. I will keep in touch wiz you M'sieur Pemberton. Shall I call on this number or . . . '

Mark Pemberton answered in French, expressing his regret at the misfortune of Leon Chevasseu and conveying a wish for his speedy recovery. He thanked Pierre Mousnard for the call, gave the Briarwood telephone number and rang off.

He regretted the fruitless delay. The time was now almost six o'clock. At the same time he was relieved that the bad weather had intervened to prevent the channel crossing or he would have been on his way to Cherbourg, resulting in a deplorable waste of time. He telephoned Briarwood to tell Silvie about the cancelled trip and to expect him home after all. As he dialled he brightened at the unexpected prospect of being with her for the night after all. But the line was not connecting. After several attempts he contacted the operator at the exchange and explained the difficulty.

'One moment sir I'll make some inquiries.' After a brief interval her voice returned to the line. 'I'm sorry sir but I can't assist you with your call. The storm has brought down power lines at Kings Meadow.'

As he replaced the receiver lightning lit the room and wind tossed the heavy rain against the window. He gathered up his top coat, brief case and car keys, eager now to be on his way to Briarwood. The sound of the front door as he banged it shut behind him was overplayed by a deep rumble of thunder.

★ ★ ★

In accordance with Mark's request Adam had come home to Briarwood late on Friday.

Silvie had welcomed his company after a long lonely week. This was the first time he'd been home since the day Mark had given his mother the news about the coming baby, and the first weekend that Mark had been absent from the house.

Wet weather had kept Silvie from her usual long daily walks for most of the week. And since she no longer went to the little stone church time had hung heavily.

During the worst of the rain Laura Pemberton had kept to her own quarters and on the few occasions when her path crossed that of Silvie she kept up her stony reserve of silence.

Alone now with Adam Silvie clung to him. 'Oh it's good to see you. Apart from a few words to Dora I haven't spoken to a soul all week. It's been too wet for Joe to work in the garden so I haven't even had my usual daily chats with him.'

Those few daily words to Dora had, as always, brought little response. Silvie was aware that Dora disliked her, and saw too how fond she was of Adam. She wondered if these two facts were in some way connected.

* * *

When Dora had been informed that Adam would be home on Friday but not Mark she decided to forfeit her ride home in the car. 'I'll stay over so that I can make breakfast for Mark when he arrives in the morning,' she'd announced.

Mark had told her the news about the expected baby and had charged her with the responsibility of

353

ensuring that his young wife was provided with a suitable diet for a mother-to-be. Plagued by envy Dora wished that she could include poison on the menu.

★ ★ ★

The connecting door to the dressing room was open. Dressed for bed Silvie heard Adam call her name softly. She went to stand in the doorway to his bedroom. Wearing silk pyjamas he was seated on his bed. He held out his hands to her. She went to him and fell into his arms.

'Oh Silvie! I've missed you so these last weeks.' His kisses were ardent and his impatient hands moved over her lightly clad body as they lay back together.

★ ★ ★

For Mark the drive to Kings Meadow took longer than it would in normal weather conditions. Visibility in some sections of the journey was almost nil. At times the torrential rain was a liquid wall upon the windscreen. He sat forward in his seat in concentrated effort to see the road which at intervals was briefly lit by lightning flashes. Then the rain eased a little. He relaxed. A tender smile rested on his lips as he thought of Silvie snug in bed. Homecoming was so good nowadays. Just thinking about her warmed him. She'd be surprised when he arrived. If she was asleep he would have to rouse her or she might be alarmed if she woke and found an

354

unexpected bedfellow. This thought amused him and he smiled in the darkness. Lately he'd given a lot of thought to the idea of Peter Dunning taking on the responsibility of attending some of the weekend conferences. Knowing every aspect of the business he was equal to the task and genuinely had the interests of the firm at heart. He was the next best thing to family. In fact he was almost family really. Peter was his oldest and closest friend. During their Cambridge days he had spent many weekends at Briarwood. Even back then they'd discussed his entering the business on graduation. They'd each taken the same degrees. In education, intellect and principals they were equal. Yes, most decidedly, he'd allocate some of the foreign meetings to Peter and leave weekends always free to come home to Silvie.

The storm was still at its height as he neared Kings Meadow. When he reached the village he suddenly braked the car and it skidded to a halt as the headlights picked out the thick trunk of a fallen tree which blocked the lane and indicated the spot where the telephone wires dangled loosely. Lightly cursing the delay he turned the car and made a detour down a side lane, thankful of this alternative way round.

Five minutes later as he reached the driveway of Briarwood a hail burst broke in a deafening onslaught, beating viciously on the car roof. Moments later he drove the car into the garages. Since the hour was late he knew that the front door would be bolted for the night. He selected the key to the side entrance closest to the garages. This way was less disturbing and quickest in from the downpour. Lightening lit his way, followed by a loud clap of thunder as he let himself into the house.

A light from an open door downstairs faintly illuminated the hall and dispensed with the need to switch on the lights as he hung his damp top coat on the hall stand and went towards the stairs.

Just as he reached the base his mother appeared in her wheelchair from a far corner of the hall. In the half light total surprise registered on her face.

He continued up the stairs. 'Don't disturb yourself Mother. Meeting was cancelled. Tell you in the morning. Goodnight.'

Gathering her wits she called, her voice mingling with the thunder, 'Mark! — Wait — don't go in Mark — come back . . . ' As she guided the chair towards the stairs, another clap of thunder crashed deafeningly close. Unheard she watched helplessly from below as he took the stairs three at a time. She called again. 'Mark — Wait — don't go in . . . '

On her angular features a spark of motherly concern ignited. But thunder and squall heckled her calls and drowned her pleas. Too late he had already reached the bedroom. The door was closing behind him.

Above the noise of the wild storm they had not heard the car arrive. Nor were they aware of the disabled telephone lines. Mark Pemberton walked into the master bedroom to find it lit only by the reflected light through the open door of his father's dressing room. He saw the four-poster bed undisturbed and empty. He crossed the room to the connecting door before the implications of its being

356

open struck him. From here he could see straight through the wide open door of his father's bedroom.

Time hung suspended as he stood leaning against the door-frame for support and breathing hard with shock and emotion. Stunned, his mind tried to take in what his eyes were refusing to believe.

A mere few seconds grace might have saved the situation had time allowed Silvie to get out of the bed and be seated on it, considering the wild weather, and her condition, for no man would doubt her fear of the noisy electrical storm. But chance was not on the side of sinners tonight. Time had left no margin for pretence and lies.

The sight that met his astounded and disillusioned eyes spoke indisputably for itself as his wife left his father's bed, her nightdress crumpled and unfastened.

An anguished cry came from his soul and hung timeless on the stricken air. '*Oh God no . . . I can't believe it . . . Not my own father . . .* '

A loud clap of thunder drowned his long drawn out groan as blindly he turned away and stumbled from the room and down the stairs.

Unheard or unheeded the distressed voice of Silvie called after him. 'Mark — oh Mark! *Please* come back . . . ' she pleaded

At the base of the staircase he passed his mother who put out a hand to detain him calling his name in attempt to halt his flight.

Unseeing and distraught he passed on by, subconsciously his mind recalling what he'd overheard her say that day when he'd turned back for the cellar key.

'Who is the father . . . the father? My husband or my son?' He did not hear or heed her now as, guiding her wheelchair after him to the side door through which he left the house, she called again and again 'Come back Mark. Don't go. *Please don't go!*'

Only one voice echoed in his mind, over and over. 'Who is the father? My husband or my son . . . ?'

In a rush Adam Pemberton dressed himself, but heedless of the cold and mindful only of the urgency did not stop to put on a jacket. Silvie hurried into her bedroom. 'I'll come with you Adam.'

His voice halted her. 'No Silvie. You must stay here. I'll fetch him back. I'll put things right again.' His tone was hoarse with distress and doubt. This time he had little faith or hope that anything he could do or say would ever put things back as they were. The boundary of no return had been crossed.

Before he'd left she was on her knees beside the four poster. Her cries were silent and deep, yet as fervent as the raging elements outside as she prayed for the safe return of her husband whom she had deceived so unforgivably. Bring him back to me! she pleaded again and again. The wind and rain hurled against the window as though in reproof, unforgiving and relentless, tossing her pleas back into the room.

Curiosity as to why her son had not telephoned prior to his unexpected arrival led Laura Pemberton to the drawing room where she tested and discovered that the line was out of commission. Grave-faced she waited helplessly for whatever was to come.

Adam Pemberton had used the side door, still open, to gain quickest entry to the garages. He heard the car and saw heavy rain spotlighted in the headlamps as it turned a curve in the drive. By the time he got his car out and reached the end of the long driveway there was no sign of lights in the lane. This told him that the car was being driven at a reckless speed for such a night. He lowered the window and listened for the sound of a car engine, but could hear nothing above the heavy rain beating against the roof. Then he drove hard on the accelerator hoping to match the speed of his son's car and prayed that he was taking the same direction.

★ ★ ★

Floundering in a sea of shock and disillusion he felt like a victim of bomb devastation such as he'd witnessed during the war. His life was destroyed just as surely. Not just crushed beneath bricks and mortar but beneath his whole world.

In shock he drove at full speed. Sobs caught in his throat, tears blinded his eyes, and his mother's words, which he'd heard that day and made a pretence of not hearing, rang in his ears, 'You're a blind fool. You haven't the wits of your father, especially when he's in a tight spot.' Words to which he'd attached no real significance and dismissed as merely the ramblings of a brief mental lapse. 'Dear God!', he groaned. 'How could she do this to me!' How long had it been going on! The Silvie that he worshipped no longer existed, and could *never* be resurrected. The disillusionment was unendurable. He could not face a life without her now. All he wanted was to escape from the unbearable hurt. He heard her voice in his mind saying, 'What if you found out something terrible about me?' Then he heard his own laughter at the preposterous idea, sharply and vividly recalled — wild in his ears. Only now did he realise that the question had been a serious one.

With the lovely image of her as she was that night, and his remembered laughter ringing through his distraught mind, he approached the fallen tree across the lane for the second time that night. This time he did not slow the car.

★ ★ ★

At the crossroads Adam Pemberton brought his speeding car to an abrupt halt and it skidded out of control. Desperately he wrestled with the steering wheel until the car recovered from its crazy waltz. As he was deciding whether to take a side lane or the main one, he heard the crash.

With a long drawn out moan he lowered his head onto his arms across the steering wheel: 'Oh God . . . no . . . no . . . no . . . ' With this agonised cry still on his lips he raised his head and turned the car about face and drove off in the direction from which the terrible sound had come.

★ ★ ★

David Bradley too had heard the crash in the lane. He arrived on the scene only seconds before Adam. His own telephone out of commission he drove to fetch the doctor, then on to police headquarters where contact was made for an ambulance.

But even as he did these things he knew, as did Adam, that nothing could be done now to save Mark Pemberton.

He returned to the scene where, in the pouring rain Adam was bent over the body of his son. 'I'll come with you to the hospital,' he offered.

Adam Pemberton shook his head in misery and replied hoarsely, 'It would serve no purpose Reverend. But if you'll go to the house and let them know. Prepare them for the worst. I'll tell them when I get back.'

The ambulance moved off, Adam Pemberton following in his car. The doctor watched until it was out of sight then turned to David Bradley. 'Are you going up to the house Reverend?'

'Yes — I was asked to let them know about the accident.'

'Go easy when you break the news to the lassie. She's four months pregnant. A fragile time. I'll follow shortly.'

★ ★ ★

No lights were visible at the front of the house but a rain-misted glow lit an area somewhere at the side. David Bradley parked his car and made his way in the direction of the light. He found the side door still open.

As he entered Laura Pemberton came from a room at the front of the house where she had waited in darkness at the window for returning headlights along the drive. Her expression was grave, her voice low and lifeless. 'Only bad news would bring you here at this hour and in this weather Reverend. Don't sidestep the facts. Say what you must.'

In the few words necessary he told her. Then he stood silently waiting for her to speak again. When she did not he continued, 'If I may I'll go to . . .'

Before he could finish or move she pointed upwards in the direction of the stairs. 'And don't bother with the velvet gloves — *she's* responsible.'

Troubled he went towards the staircase, then half turned as if to speak again. But she had swung the chair around, and using its mechanical speed across the smooth marble tiles was turning a corner on the far side of the hall.

He raised his eyes to the unlit regions above where a faint glow shone from an open doorway. For a moment longer he stood reflecting on the words he'd just heard. Then continued slowly up.

The door to the master bedroom was open and lit only from a beside lamp which shone through from Adam Pemberton's room. She had not moved from the place where she knelt beside her bed. Her bent head rested on her outstretched arm across the silky coverlet.

'Silvie,' he said gently.

At his light touch on her shoulder and the sound of his voice she raised her head.

A look of bewilderment, then fear, showed on her face. Like Laura Pemberton she knew that he would not be there unless something had happened — something dreadful.

Her lips moved silently as if seeking sound for the unvoiced words which trembled there.

He bent to switch on the bedside lamp and knelt down beside her. She looked no more than a child at present with her tear-ravished face.

'Oh God!' she gasped, 'Mark! Something's happened to Mark!' She gave a small scream of fear. 'Why have you come! Tell me he's all right David. *Please* — tell me he's all right!'

He hesitated — the words stuck in his throat. How could he just spring the dreadful news on her. Yet he couldn't lie and build false hope only to dash it later. He wondered at the meaning of Laura Pemberton's cruel accusation a moment ago. Already he had found it puzzling that the two cars had been heading in the same direction, one almost on the tail of the other at such a late hour and in such weather. And now — finding Silvie alone and in a state of distress — as if awaiting news. How could he tell her of the shattering consequences of whatever had taken place in this house tonight.

With another small scream of fear she leaned against him and buried her face in his chest. His arms closed about her protectively, as if this might shield her from the hurt to come. Still clad only in a flimsy night dress she felt cold to his touch. 'Say something David — please. Where is Mark?'

'At the hospital. There was an accident in the lane. A fallen tree.'

She gasped as if physically struck, even though she had half expected such news. 'No . . . no

. . . no . . . ' The words were low and long drawn out as if this denial might reverse the harsh fate. Everything had happened so fast. She was still reeling from the shock of Mark appearing so unexpectedly. 'Will he be all right? Can you take me to him — please David?'

He didn't know how he could break the truth to her gently as the doctor had warned he must. She hadn't mentioned about the baby that last day in his study two weeks ago. She had kept that from him. 'Silvie the news is bad I'm afraid. Mark did not survive the accident.'

'Oh . . . no . . . no . . . no . . . no . . . It's not possible!'

Gently he rocked her to and fro. He felt the sobs rack her body, the sound drowned by the noise of the heavy rain against the windows.

Like this they waited for — he knew not what. What was done could not be undone. The horror of the night was unredeemable.

★   ★   ★

The thunderstorm had kept Dora awake. But above the noise she had not heard Mark arrive home. Nor had she heard their voices calling him back. It was not until she came from her bedroom to go to the bathroom and noticed Adam's bedroom door open and saw the light from the wide open door of the master bedroom that she suspected something was wrong. She looked into the room and saw Reverend Bradley kneeling beside the bed cradling the girl in his arms.

Alarmed she ran down the stairs and along to the quarters of Laura Pemberton. 'What's happened! Something's wrong! Where's Adam?'

Still in a state of initial shock Laura Pemberton looked at her blankly, having forgotten for the moment that she was staying over for the night. Care had to be taken about what was said to Dora in case she was at hand when reporters came; and come they would like vultures. She kept the explanation as brief and simple as she possibly could. 'There's been a fatal car accident. Mark . . . the weather . . . a tree down.'

Dora's face crumpled as she made shocked responses. 'Oh! Oh!' Then stood as if struck dumb, trembling.

'Go and pour us some brandy.'

Dora nodded absently and as she turned towards the drinks cabinet asked again, 'Where's Adam?'

'At the hospital,' the words were spat out as if in disgust.

★ ★ ★

The sound of the ambulance bell had alerted the villagers and the news of the accident reached the ears of Joe Tarrant and his sister Mary. Joe drove them both to the house immediately. The doctor had arrived just ahead of them and been admitted into the hall by Dora.

'Where's the lassie? I'd best check on her.'

'In her bedroom.' Dora pointed upwards.

Silvie still clung to David Bradley as if some powerful undercurrent was trying to drag her under

365

and he the life line in an alien world. Distractedly, over and over, she murmured, 'I killed him . . . It's my fault he's dead . . . my fault. I can't live with this.'

He had found her dressing robe and placed it around her shoulders to try to stop her shaking. 'Don't say that Silvie. You mustn't think that.' He gently eased her up and seated her on the bed, then moved aside as the doctor entered the room.

'Fetch a glass of water Reverend. I'm going to give her a sedative.'

David Bradley did as he was asked then left the room to wait outside in the corridor, seated on the chair beneath the accusing gaze of Joseph Whitehorne.

Ten minutes later the doctor emerged. 'She's sedated now Reverend. She'll be asleep in a few minutes.' Together they went downstairs. Dora came from the kitchen as though she'd been waiting for them, 'I've just made a pot of tea if you'd both like some before you leave.' Her voice was dulled with shock.

They followed her and joined Joe and Mary, who were seated, pale and subdued, at the kitchen table.

'Where is Laura? I'd best look in on her.'

'In her quarters off the hall Doctor.' Joe answered. 'I've just been along there myself but she doesn't want to talk to anyone.'

'She might want to see *you* Doctor Brodie,' Dora said.

'Well — we'll see. I'll go along to her now before I have the tea.'

He knocked on the partly open door of Laura

Pemberton's bedroom. 'It's James Brodie, Laura.'

The door was opened wider for him to enter. 'You don't need me to tell you how sorry and shocked I am Laura. I know you only want to be left alone and I won't stay if you don't wish it. But I thought a few pills to help you sleep for the next few nights or so . . .'

'No thanks James. I've no use for your pills and potions. Just tell me one thing honestly . . . did my son suffer before . . .'

He shook his head. 'No Laura. You have my word on it. The impact was great and death would have been instantaneous.'

She nodded, satisfied with his assurance. 'Leave me now James. There's nothing more you can do for me. I just want to be alone.'

'Very well. If you need me you know where I am.' He went out closing the door quietly behind him. In this, as with all else, she needed no one. Yet she would find no relief in weeping. Her emotions stayed locked within. She had shed no tears, for she was one of those rare breed of people who never cry; simply because they *cannot*.

Reverend Bradley and the doctor waited for the return of Adam Pemberton from the hospital. It was well after midnight when he came into the house, white and drawn.

With a gesture of his hand he rejected their offered services. He wanted no pills or prayers. If sleepless nights and a guilty conscience were part of his punishment then he accepted it as no more than he deserved.

His tread was heavy as he climbed the stairs. He

first looked in on Silvie, now in a deeply sedated sleep. He idly fingered the small bottle of pills on the bedside table as he stood regarding her face in its temporary state of oblivion. Tomorrow she would wake to a harsh new day, and reality. And he would never have left the cruel night. He sat in his room making decisions for the immediate future. The girls had to be told and brought home from the College. Later he went downstairs. Doctor Brodie and David Bradley were about to leave.

'James — those pills you gave Silvie — when will the effect wear off?'

'About ten o'clock in the morning.'

Adam Pemberton nodded then said, 'Thanks for coming. You too Reverend.'

'I'll look in tomorrow morning,' Doctor Brodie said as he followed David Bradley out.

Joe and Mary were still in the kitchen with Dora who looked at Adam's strained face and said, 'Come and sit with us. I've just made another pot of tea. I was going to bring a cup up to you.'

Adam sat at the table in the place just vacated by the doctor. 'Joe, will you go to the College early in the morning. I'll draw a map route for you. But you'll have to stop on the way to phone the principal. Ask her to break the news as gently as possible, to prepare them before you arrive. Take the Jag. It's more reliable than your old Ford, and there's a fair distance to go. I'll have to stay here to get rid of any reporters that call. Bound to be some. You know how unfeeling reporters can be. I don't want Silvie bothered by them.'

'Of course. I think it might be as well for Mary to

come with me. The girls will need someone to try to comfort them and I can't do that when I'm driving. I think a woman's presence is needed at a time like this.'

'I agree,' said Mary. 'Joanne will take it very hard. She worshipped Mark. I'll sit in the back with them. At least I can be of some small help. A shoulder to cry on.'

Adam nodded agreement on this. 'Best go home now and get some sleep. I'll have a map route ready for when you arrive and money for petrol.'

Joe and his sister left. Adam finished his tea. 'You'd best get some sleep Dora. I shall sit up for a while longer.' He left the room.

Dora watched him go, wishing that she could take away the hurt she saw in his eyes.

In the library he poured himself some brandy. With this as his companion he sat out the rest of the night until five in the morning when he heard Joe's old Ford arrive.

★   ★   ★

Miss Meacher replaced the receiver mechanically, shaking her head in disbelief. She sat for a long while in great shock. She found it difficult to grasp the fact that death in such a manner had come so swiftly and unexpectedly to someone so vitally alive and happy as the tall fair young man so vividly recalled to mind from that summer day at the garden party one year ago. She brushed the tears away. It was some while before she felt in control of herself. Eventually she reached across her desk and

369

turned a small shicld so that it could not fail to be seen by the girls when they came: It bore the inscribed College motto COURAGE IN ADVERSITY.

With a last dab at her eyes she asserted her composure and prepared herself for the impossible task of delivering the dreadful blow gently.

37

The verdict of the Coroner was, 'Accidental death.' Contributing factors were, the extreme weather conditions, the wet road, the fallen tree, and chiefly the speed at which the car had been driven. The possibility that it was other than an accident was never considered.

★ ★ ★

The funeral was over. The express wish that it was to be a private family only service had been made known. The people of the village however surrounded the little churchyard and lined the lanes.

As long-established close friends of the family Peter Dunning and Harry Mortimer, each devastated by the news, had travelled to Kings Meadow and stayed overnight to attend. The grief of Peter must have struck deeper than that of Silvie for he had known his dearest friend for so much longer. But with her grief was the added trauma of profound remorse and blame.

Stricken with grief and shock though he was Peter concentrated his utmost on trying to comfort Joanne who was at present inconsolable.

Laura Pemberton had attended with Major Ashdown and the Jackson-Brownes. They had stayed close to her side to give her support and for once she did not brush aside their assistance with the wheelchair.

Silvie, against the advice of Doctor Brodie attended. A miscarriage had threatened and he warned of the possible outcome. But she agreed to return to her bed immediately after the burial service. Having attended the funeral himself he reminded her to do so as she left the churchyard.

Adam had stayed close to her giving his physical support, along with Ginny who had held on to her throughout the service.

Still frozen in shock, Joanne had clung tightly to Peter. Her mind could not cope with what she felt was a nightmare from which she would surely wake. She was unable to believe that the body of her brother, who had been so vitally alive and happy, was enclosed in the shiny wooden box, cut off from her, and the world, forever. The fact was too big to grasp, for her eyes had not seen the proof. She had not been allowed to see him in death on account of his injuries.

Joe and Mary, who had attended the funeral with Dora and the regular stable hand, left the little churchyard in advance of the others in order to be back at the house before their return.

The Reverend David Bradley conducted the service, his conscience not exempt from guilt. He had coveted the wife of the man whose body he was committing to the earth. He had desperately wanted to make love to her, so was a potential adulterer. Added to this, he knew that the reason for the wrecked body within the casket was not due to any driving error or misjudgement.

His voice had not its usual steady assurance as he delivered the burial rites.

With the exception of David Bradley they were all now back at Briarwood. Silvie had gone straight up to her bed. Major Ashdown and the Jackson-Brownes were assembled in the drawing room with intentions of staying on until late evening to keep Laura Pemberton occupied with a half hearted bridge session in attempt to support her through these first traumatic hours.

Having left Silvie in her bedroom with the girls for company and comfort Adam went down to join Peter and Harry in the library where they stayed in long discussion.

Of necessity life and business had to continue. Peter would take over from Mark. Someone must be found to take over Peter's work. For the present Harry would stand in for Adam as head until his return was possible. This Adam would not be doing until Silvie was in a fitter state to be left.

During those first days when the girls had been brought home from College they had remained constantly with Silvie in her room. Still locked in the relentless embrace of shock they had held hands while, emotionally frozen, they waited. For *what?* Silvie had wondered during those endless hours. Perhaps for stark realisation to strike. Then they would know that it was not after all some dreadful dream from which they would awake. Until the funeral was over emotion had been put on hold it seemed. Nothing could fill those endless days but the silent waiting.

Now that Mark's body had been committed to

the earth in the little churchyard they must each accept that he really was gone.

Quite suddenly Joanne got up from her chair beside the bed and ran off to her own bedroom. At last shock had released its vice-like grip.

Ginny hurried out after her and watched helplessly as the prostrate figure on the bed sobbed out her misery. In desperation she searched along the rows of books in a small bookcase in the room, brushing away her own blinding tears to see more clearly until she found what she was looking for.

★   ★   ★

Adam left the two men in the study and went to check on Silvie. When he reached the top of the stairs he heard the sobs of his daughter. He went along to her room and paused just outside, feeling helpless.

Ginny saw him and came out. 'I'll stay with Jojo Uncle Adam. Silvie's asleep now. I gave her one of the pills Doctor Brodie left. She asked for one. She was asleep before we left her.'

He nodded dumbly and turned to go with the intention of asking Mary to come up — a woman perhaps . . . As he was contemplating this, the door bell rang and Dora answered.

David Bradley stepped into the hall. 'I wondered if I might be of any help — however slight. This is my first free opportunity to call. I've had a fully committed day.' He went towards the stairs and started up.

Adam Pemberton was by now half way down and

stopped. 'Come up Reverend. Kind of you to call.' He turned and accompanied David Bradley to the upstairs corridor. 'Perhaps you could say a few words that may be of some comfort to Joanne. She's taking it very hard. Mark was all to her; father and mother. She idolised him and depended on him so much. I'm afraid my wife and I have not been ideal parents. Over the years the business has consumed so much of my time.' He spread his hands in a helpless gesture and his voice was strained. 'Fortunately she has Ginny.' Unnecessarily he pointed the way to his daughters room, the loud sobs were sufficient guide.

'I'll do all in my power you can depend on it,' David Bradley assured as he went in the direction of the heart-rending sound.

After looking in on Silvie in her brief oblivion Adam returned to the library. Lines of fatigue merged with the grief on his features. During the last week he had slept only in exhausted snatches, brief and unresting.

David Bradley moved towards the young voice raised lachrymosely. 'Put that bible away Ginny! I hate the bible! I hate God! No — I don't believe there *is* a God. If there is he's cruel and I *do* hate him!' The words were punctuated with dry sobs and the overwrought voice trailed off as David Bradley stood in the open doorway.

Ginny looking pale and distressed was about to replace the offending book back on the shelf. She swung round in surprise, 'Oh Reverend Bradley! Thank heaven you're here! Jojo doesn't mean what she said . . . ' tears choked off further words.

He nodded reassuringly as he stepped further into the room. Gently he took the bible from Ginny's hands. 'I sometimes think and feel that way myself Joanne.' He seated himself on a bedroom chair. 'But I don't believe that God does these terrible things. They just happen. And often to the nicest and best people.'

Joanne had fallen silent. Only dry sobs shook her body at intervals as he continued. 'When such terrible things happen I believe it breaks God's heart too. He doesn't *make* them happen. He can't *prevent* them from happening But he *does* give us an inner strength to cope with our grief and adjust to the loss of our loved ones.'

He continued to speak, at times quoting passages from the bible.

After a while she asked brokenly, 'What you said just now — about sometimes thinking that way — not believing there is a God; Do you *really* think that at times Reverend Bradley?'

'*Often* Joanne.' He would never tell her that his doubt was greater than his belief. That he called upon a God automatically in times of stress just as everyone else did. That while his words could comfort or give hope and re-assurance to people, he would continue to speak about a God of whom he was unsure.

To give her some consolation about death itself when she asked him he replied, 'We sleep for one third of our lives. For instance at the age of twelve you had slept for four of those years. A famous writer, I believe it may have been Edgar Alan Poe, once referred to sleep as 'little slices of death'. So death is akin to sleep. We all experience it every night of our lives.'

As he talked on he tried to resurrect her fallen faith. An hour later he knew that he had succeeded. He rose to leave. 'Chin up soldier.' He rested a hand on her head briefly then turned to leave.

'Thank you for coming Reverend Bradley,' Ginny said, looking much less distraught than she had on his arrival.

He smiled. 'Just call me any time you need to talk.'

On his way to the stairs he paused briefly outside Silvie's room before moving on. He felt that he'd done all in his power to reconcile Joanne with her former religious beliefs with which she would recover and adjust more quickly. But he was limited. He had no magic wand. Only words.

Mary met him in the hall. 'There's tea waiting in the pot Reverend. Will you have some?'

'Thank you Mary,' he accepted and followed into the kitchen. He knew that any attempt to offer words of comfort to Laura Pemberton would be futile. She was impervious to such. He had already tried earlier and his approach brushed aside politely as of no consequence. She was as always sufficient unto herself and must be her own salvation.

★　★　★

The cold, now dry February air wrapped itself around him as he left the house and descended the six white steps. He drove to Peartree Lane and stopped at the spot where the fatal tree had fallen.

377

This had now been removed. Only a mass of broken branches in the field, a few scattered twigs still in the lane, and the broken fence, remained as evidence that this was the place where Mark Pemberton had met his end a week ago. Puddles still lay in the fields and water in the ditches. But the clear blue sky seemed to belie that the storm had even been. Since then so much had changed. Yet so much still remained the same. He sat musing as to what was the real truth behind the car crash. Having found Silvie so distressed on his arrival at the house that night, even before he'd broken the news to her, and Adam Pemberton already at the scene of the crash immediately after the accident, he'd thought about it a great deal.

The dreadful event had been accepted by the authorities, without question, as an unfortunate accident. The Coroner had been satisfied of this from the police report given. A missed turning in bad visibility had been assumed. They had not been informed that Mark Pemberton had already been to the house and left again. This information had been kept secret by Adam and his wife. Logical reasoning told him what must be near the real truth behind the accident.

He sighed deeply for the wasted young life, then switched on the car ignition. As he made a U turn in the lane a glint on the road surface caught his eye. Cool clear sunlight reflected on a sliver of uncleared glass from a broken windscreen. The only physical sign here of the tragedy.

★ ★ ★

378

Silvie awoke to the harsh world of self-condemnation and the aftermath of shock. As she slowly opened her eyes she became aware of the two girls seated at her beside. Her gaze, emerging from a sedated sleep, focussed first on the tear-puffed face of Joanne, and she thought, her grief is an innocent grief, a pure grief, not a guilty grief like mine. Further remorse crowded into her already over-burdened conscience. She closed her eyes again as the recurring thoughts of the past week rushed through her mind once more. The urge to confess the truth was almost overwhelming. But the persistent thoughts remained silent. She could not have endured to see the expression on the grief-ravished young face turn to hate by saying aloud the torturing words, 'I killed Mark just as surely as if I'd used a gun or a knife. *I* killed him . . . *I* killed him . . . '

'Silvie,' Ginny's voice drew her attention to her sister. 'Dora and Mary are about to serve dinner in the dining room. You're not well enough to come down. Doctor Brodie said you must stay in bed for a few more days. Shall I bring yours up on a tray?'

'I can't eat anything Ginny.' Silvie answered lifelessly.

'But you must. You must. For the baby,' urged Joanne. 'The baby is the only living link with Mark that we have now.'

Silvie felt the dagger pierce deeper. Even that small consolation she couldn't give with certainty.

'All right Joanne. I'll have something brought up on a tray then,' she conceded.

'Reverend Bradley called and came up to speak

with us. He talked a lot to Joanne. It helped her.'

'Yes — I'm so glad that he came,' agreed Joanne. 'I like him and trust in what he says.'

The girls went downstairs to the dining room and Silvie was left alone with her unendurable thoughts from which there was no escape except in sleep. She wished that she were free to end her own life. But it was not her own to end at will. She had seen what Mark's death had done to his sister. She could *not* do that to Ginny.

Her thoughts dwelt on the two weeks spent in Rome. Mark as usual had been a wonderful escort. He had been an ardent but considerate lover, especially on that first night. She had felt guilty about that. She felt a thousand times more guilty now. She recalled all the little incidents that had made up their two weeks. The hotel had been a top class one where Mark had stayed on his business trips in the past. He had been known there and they, especially herself, had been treated like royalty. A bouquet had been sent to their specially reserved table by the management and the proprietor had come across to drink to their future. A honeymoon suite had been reserved. Mark himself had arranged all those things.

That first evening, just as they had finished dinner, two little girls had come to their table, curtsied and said a few words in their native Italian, which she had not understood. Mark had laughed and translated for her. 'They are asking for your autograph darling. They believe you're some film star but they don't know who.'

Two little books were placed upon the table close

to her and she had asked him to tell them they were mistaken.

This he had done but they only smiled and made another polite request. According to Mark they'd said, 'But she must be senior. She is so beautiful.'

'Just sign your name in the books my sweet,' he had urged smiling. 'Make them happy.'

With a laugh she had duly obliged. Seconds later a man had come across, bowed politely, said a few words, and led the two little girls away.

Mark had explained that the man had apologised for his two daughters and hoped they hadn't made a nuisance of themselves.

These small incidents she might have recalled with great affection in a future that would never now be. A future that she herself had destroyed. Now those sweet recollections brought only pain; a knife twisting in an existing wound. With a dry sob she buried her face in the pillow.

Adam entered with a laden tray. 'Silvie darling — I've brought dinner to you.' He placed the tray on the bedside table and drew this to a more convenient position close to the bed.

Silvie sat up. 'Thank you Adam. Although I'm really not hungry.'

'Must eat Silvie. I'll stay with you.'

'No — please don't Adam. You join the others downstairs.'

'Promise you'll try to eat then.'

'Yes — yes I will.'

She swung herself sideways to sit on the edge of the bed. He clasped her in a tight embrace, kissed the top of her head, and left the room.

* * *

There were twelve seated around the table. The Jackson-Brownes and the Major, Laura Pemberton, Harry Mortimer, and Peter next to Joanne at her request, Ginny, Adam, Joe and Dora and Mary who between them had prepared the meal. After the funeral service Joe, from his own choice, had changed into his gardening clothes on his return that morning and worked for the rest of the day in the garden. He was now changed back into his best clothes for the evening.

* * *

Shortly after dinner was over Harry and Peter prepared to leave for the city. Although tomorrow was Saturday they would need to spend some time at the offices to organise what would be for the time being a heavier work load. Peter would for the present be carrying out his own work and also that which had been consigned to Mark in the past. Harry would be doing his own job and Adam's combined.

'Telephone me sometimes at the College Peter,' Joanne asked as she and Ginny walked with the two men to Peter's car in which they had both arrived.

'Of course. When does Miss Head Mistress allow you to receive calls?' Peter knew that she'd made this request of him because she was going to miss her weekly calls from Mark.

'Evenings after six. Weekends at any time of the day. There's a special telephone in an annex off her main office. As most of the girls have calls we try to stick to a certain time. Mine was on Saturday mornings around nine o'clock.' She sounded tearful again and he guessed that this was the time Mark used to call her. 'Sometimes Friday evening instead,' she added. 'But really any time would probably be all right. Just long enough for you to say hello to me — to us — Ginny will want to speak with you as well.'

He nodded and tapped the top pocket of his jacket where he had placed the slip of paper bearing the College number which she'd given to him earlier.

She hugged him and kissed his cheek.

Adam joined the girls to wave the car off.

* * *

When Mary had helped Dora to wash up and clear away the dinner things she and Joe went home to their cottage. Dora was to stay over for the night. The Jackson-Brownes and Major Ashdown stayed late. Throughout the afternoon and evening during the bridge play they had tried hard to keep their minds on the game and not on the dreadful tragedy that had struck the Pemberton family. These staunch friends of Laura Pemberton were each aware that she was characteristically concealing her emotions and that she would continue to do so.

When they'd left, Adam locked up and Dora went off to her bed.

* * *

383

After a last brandy and a cigar in the library Adam went upstairs. The girls were now in their beds. A light was on in Silvie's room. He looked in and found her still awake. He entered and sat on her bed. She saw how desperately tired and drawn he looked.

'Go to bed Adam. Get some sleep. Don't lie awake blaming yourself. I'm the guilty one, not you Adam — not *you*.'

He grasped her hands. 'Don't Silvie — *please*. We must not hold ourselves responsible for Mark reacting the way he did. He should at least have talked. Divorce would have been the worst outcome. Blaming ourselves will serve no purpose now. We must pick up the pieces and continue for our own sakes, for the sake of the girls, and for the baby.'

He glanced at the bottle of sleeping pills on the bedside table. 'Stop taking those as soon as you can face the nights without them darling.'

'I shall. Why not take one yourself and have a good nights sleep for once.'

He shook his head, then said, 'The girls will be best off back at the College instead of moping here. I'll give them another day or so. The principal said keep them home until the shock had worn off.'

Silvie nodded agreement. He was right. She couldn't think of life beyond the next hour herself. But knew that she must. Without the girls close at hand she couldn't stay at Briarwood.

38

The evening before the girls were to return to the College Silvie told them that she had decided to go back to the city with Adam and would be accompanying them on the drive. Although they were pleased at this they were also concerned.

'Doctor Brodie did say that you were to stay in bed.' Ginny reminded.

'But not forever Ginny. I'm perfectly fit now. I did ask him when he last called. I'll only be sitting, not doing anything strenuous.'

'I must get away from the house for a while,' she'd told Adam when packing a few things in her case ready. 'I'd like to go to Mark's flat to collect his things and bring them back here. You can then dispose of the lease. I shall have to stay in your apartment though. I can't face staying at the flat for long, the memories will be too painful.'

'As you wish darling. I believe that the lease is about due for renewal in any case. Peter might want to take it over since it's closer to the offices than his present flat. I must check first though with Doctor Brodie about you making such a long journey.'

'But I've already asked him,' she protested.

'So you told Ginny. But you didn't say what his answer was.'

He went to make the call on the telephone just outside her bedroom and was told — 'Och the lassie should be fit enough now. Just see that she doesn't stand about too long. And get her to lie down a wee while during the daytime.'

Satisfied he replaced the receiver and returned to her bedroom to repeat the doctors instructions before going to his own room to pack his bag.

★   ★   ★

'We're all off this morning Dora.' Adam told her as she came into the breakfast room.

On his insistence that she must eat before the long journey Silvie had joined him and the girls this morning.

'All!' Dora noted that Silvie was dressed in warm clothes as if going out.

'Yes Dora,' Ginny replied. 'Silvie's coming with us. She'll be staying in the city for the week.'

'I'll telephone in advance as usual when we're coming back Dora,' Adam said. 'You won't know what to do with yourself without all these mouths to feed. You've been kept pretty busy over the last week or so.'

Fuming secretly Dora set the breakfast things on the table without comment and returned to the kitchen. Adam and the girl in the city together! She wanted to stop it happening. She returned to the breakfast room to say — 'Surely she shouldn't travel all that way!' Dora couldn't bring herself to speak Silvie's name.

'I'll be all right Dora.' Silvie had noticed the strange look that Dora had thrown at her despite the words of concern.

After breakfast Adam brought down the bags and

cases which included two empty ones that would be needed to fetch back the things which had belonged to Mark, and carried them out to the car. He informed his wife of Silvie's intentions for the week and she received the news without comment. When he returned upstairs he went through to Silvie's room. 'Wrap up warm darling it's very cold out this morning.'

She nodded and from her wardrobe took out the mink coat. She rubbed her cheek against its softness, silently wept, and murmured, 'Mark . . . Mark . . . Mark . . .'

At the time they were leaving Laura Pemberton was still in her rooms. The girls went along to say their goodbyes. Ginny, uncharacteristically reserved, kissed the unyielding cheek lightly. Joanne, in need of more warmth right then than her mother was capable of giving, put her arms about the stiffly held neck for a moment.

Dora stood in the hallway as they left the house. None of them noticed the look of dismay on her face. She had the wild urge to shout after Adam, to tell him not to take the trollop with him. That temptress with her oil painting face! Even Laura disliked her and hardly ever spoke to her, if at all. The fact that she never came to the dining table nowadays had something to do with the girl. Motionless she stood listening to the sounds of the car die away into the distance, taking Adam and the trollop all those miles together. The thought magnified itself and stoked festering jealousy, blocking out compassion which any normal thinking person might feel at the present time. Dora had no emotion right now other than envy because the girl was with Adam; not only on the long car ride but later in his apartment . . . and for a whole week! Totally consumed by her feelings she made her way dejectedly back to the kitchen. She wanted to stamp out that doll-like face which was taking Adam away from her and Briarwood. All week he had been fussing over her and taking meals up to her room. She seated herself at the table, seeing nothing but the image of the two together. 'I hate her,' she said aloud. Then wept quietly in frustration at her inability to prevent it happening, and for the nights ahead when she knew she would lie awake thinking of them together. It was worse nowadays, knowing *who* he was with during those nights in the city.

★ ★ ★

Adam and the girls insisted that Silvie sit on a bench at the station while they awaited the departure of the train back to the College. 'We'll stand at the window so you can see us.,' Ginny said.

'Remember, you're carrying precious cargo.' A wan smile touched the sad young face of Joanne.

When the guard blew his whistle Silvie stood up to wave with Adam until the train was out of sight. She was reminded sharply of other times when she'd done this same thing with Mark. Cruel memory heaped guilt upon unbearable guilt.

★ ★ ★

In the flat she prepared to pack Mark's belongings to take back to Briarwood.

'Are you certain you don't want me to stay and help darling?'

'Quite certain. I'd rather be alone to sort through the things. I'll be all right Adam.'

'As you wish. I'll just call in at the offices to ensure all is going well. When I get back we'll go out for some lunch.' He kissed the top of her bent head. 'No lifting mind.'

When he'd gone she gave release to emotion as she fingered the things which Mark had last seen and touched on that fateful night before leaving for Kings Meadow. On his desk beside the telephone was silver pencil and a small note pad. On its top page he had written her name several times at various angles, doodles no doubt from times when he'd called her. Tears misted her eyes and the writing blurred and danced. For a while she sat crying unable to continue. He had loved her *then*. But his last thoughts of her must have been of disgust and disappointment. A fallen image with whom he could not face the future. 'Forgive me Mark,' she cried brokenly into the silence of the room. 'Please — please forgive me.'

After a while she rose and placed the notepad and pencil in her handbag. Then resumed her task. On the oak chest of drawers in his bedroom she found a letter of condolence addressed to her from his weekly cleaning lady. The letter, like all the other letters she had received after his death, said the things that she would have expected those who knew him would say. He was, it seemed, the perfect

389

being. And because of her own human imperfections he had ended his life.

Unchecked tears blinded her again. She replaced the letter in its envelope and put this too in her handbag.

Almost everything she was taking back to Briarwood was now packed in the two cases. She fastened the catch of one. Then remembering Adam's order, not to lift anything heavy, left it where it was on the floor.

She stood up now to straighten her aching back. Then she turned her attention to a pile of books which she had earlier placed on the table after sorting them on the floor. She would ask Peter if he'd like to have them. She did not notice an overlooked one still lying on the floor close to the table leg. As she stepped back the heel of her shoe caught the edge of the book, sending her off balance. Her hands clutched out for some hold to steady herself and as she fell backwards grasped a heavy dining chair which toppled. She hit the floor with the weight of the chair across her.

Carefully she moved the chair aside and slowly got to her feet, shaken and unsure what damage if any she had sustained. She felt a pain in her lower back. She sat quite still on a chair for a few minutes while she decided what to do next. Then, having judged it best to call in at the clinic near the park, just to check things out, she put on her coat. Feeling suddenly dizzy she decided to call a taxi, even though it was only a short distance.

Attached to the front of the telephone directory Mark had listed a local taxi company among the emergency numbers. Little had he known at the time that its use one day would be needed urgently by the girl he had loved so much.

She scribbled a hasty note for Adam, then sat down to wait for the taxi cab to arrive and take her to the clinic, where fate or the skill of the doctors would determine whether or not she would lose the child whose father could be the living Pemberton or the dead one.

★   ★   ★

'I regret to have to tell you that your wife lost the baby Mr Pemberton. I'm so sorry,' the nursing sister informed him on his arrival at the clinic. He did, she judged, look old enough to be the father of the patient, but in doubt decided she would rather stand to be corrected rather than offend or embarrass by referring to the young patient as his daughter.

He accepted the mistake absently and took the fur coat which she was handing him. 'We would rather the coat not be left on the premises on account of its value Mr Pemberton. If you will take it away with you for the time being. We shall have to keep Mrs Pemberton in for the next few days until the doctor feels it's safe to discharge her. I'll take you along to see her now.'

In a daze of concern he followed. He arranged for her to be put into a private room where he visited her three times each day. He had, he told her, telephoned the girls to give them the news about the miscarriage.

Day after day, when alone, she had lain with only

the tenuous relief of books as distraction from the prison of her punishing thoughts. This further trauma she bore along with the rest. She could not shut from her mind the fact of the crushing disappointment she had added to Joanne's young shoulders already overburdened by grievous loss. Carelessness, even though accidental, had destroyed what could have been the last physical link with her dead brother whom she had adored from as far back in life as she could remember. Only Silvie herself knew the doubts.

When Adam collected her he drove them straight to Kings Meadow, the packed cases stowed in the car. As he'd predicted Peter did want to take over the lease of the flat along with some of the possessions including the books which had belonged to his sorely missed friend.

When he had telephoned the news of the miscarriage to his wife she had told him bluntly that she had no interest in further news regarding her son's widow. He had not contacted her again. Dora had answered the call and after fetching Laura Pemberton to the phone had stayed to hear the news. After which she went about her business in a lighter frame of mind knowing that Adam was at least not with the girl at nights, when the imaginings were worse.

Several times over the following days Dora telephoned Adam at his office. Professing concern for Silvie presented an opportunity to have his voice in her ear and to claim his attention for a brief few minutes. She always made these calls when Laura Pemberton was not in the house.

Early yesterday Adam had telephoned to say that he and Silvie would arrive at Briarwood around lunchtime next day.

★ ★ ★

They drove in silence for most of the journey. Now and again Adam reached for her hand. His suffering mingled with hers. He too lived with reproach and regret. Had it been possible he would have taken her hurt on board with his own. She was far too young for such trauma.

'I'm so sorry Adam.' Her voice was devoid of life. 'Sorry to have brought more grief into the family, especially to Joanne.'

'You mustn't hold yourself responsible Silvie. Accidents will and *do* happen. I shouldn't have left you at the flat alone.'

'I really needed to be alone at the time Adam.'

★ ★ ★

When they arrived Dora came into the hall. Eyes only for Adam she saw the signs of strain on his face and further blamed Silvie whom she was totally ignoring. 'There's a big fire in the drawing room. I'll make you a nice pot of tea, you look as if you need some.'

'Thanks Dora. We'll come straight down.'

She watched him as he followed with the suitcases up the stairs behind Silvie whose quiet greeting she had not acknowledged.

Muttering she returned to the kitchen; 'We . . .

wc . . . we!' Never just himself any more. He seemed to have taken over complete responsibility for the girl now that Mark was no longer here to do so. The trollop had men at every turn to look out for her. Dora was remembering the Reverend Bradley on the night of the accident.

Ten minutes passed and they had not appeared. The tea would get cold. With this excuse on her tongue she decided to go up and see what was keeping him.

The door to the master bedroom was half open. She had been about to pass on to Adam's room when she heard his voice and glanced in through the doorway. He was seated on the four poster his back towards her. Silvie was lying on the bed.

Jealousy stabbed Dora at this over-familiar attitude as she was about to knock on the door. Her shaking hand was arrested in mid-air when she heard Adam saying . . .

'Perhaps it was for the best darling. We would never have known whether the child was mine or Mark's. Just imagine what that would have been like. Never knowing. I wish it hadn't happened of course, for your sake, but it may have been meant.'

'Oh Adam — how could I have done that to him. It's my fault that he's dead. He killed himself because of me. How can I live with that?'

'Don't go on punishing yourself darling. You mustn't think that way. I'm the one who is to blame, because I couldn't let you go. What a mess I've made of all our lives. It was because I love you so much Silvie. Nothing will ever change that.' His voice sounded weary and he ran his fingers through his hair, 'We can't undo what's already done.'

'You said I shouldn't marry Mark. You were right. I see that now. Things could not have worked out the way I thought they would. I practiced the worst deceit possible. I'm entirely to blame and your wife knows it.'

Hand still raised in mid-air Dora was at present incapable of movement, either to enter the room, or to turn away. She merely stood there open-mouthed with shock.

Then mechanically she forced her slippered feet to step away and carry her towards the stairs. In going she made no more sound on the carpet than she had coming. Her brief but fatal presence outside the room went undiscovered. Like a sleepwalker she returned to the kitchen where she sat morose and brooding until the tea in the pot grew cold. Resentment and jealousy enveloped her in a chrysalis until she became a vessel of virulent hate for the girl who had taken over the lives of the Pemberton men, and had just claimed it was her fault that Mark had died — even though everyone said it had been an accident! Wallowing in ebullient hate she became obsessed with thoughts of revenge against the girl who had Adam in her evil clutches.

She recalled the night of the wedding when she had sat late into the night with Adam in the library. He had been depressed and unhappy even then. And there were those times when he was at Briarwood and Mark absent. Those Friday nights — up there in his room — so close — with only the connecting door between them. Intense envy racked her mind as it lingered on vivid imaginings.

In the past she had been forced to accept that he would at times date smart women. But she'd always imagined they would be his own age. This girl was young enough to be his daughter, in fact *was* his daughter in law!

The limited resources of her tormented mind premeditated on destruction of the beauty she could fight in no other way.

Suddenly she was aroused from plotting black mischief by his voice as he appeared in the doorway to ask with forced brightness. 'What about this tea then Dora.'

Slow to relinquish her dark thoughts she turned a vague expression on him 'Oh! I thought you were coming down for it. It's got cold. I'll make a fresh pot.'

'I'll wait and take it up. Silvie's resting. I'm just going into the library to phone the office. I'll be back directly.' As he went into the hall he heard the French door of the drawing room close as his wife came in from outside. She had not been in the house on their arrival. He did not stop or look back to greet her.

Moments later Laura Pemberton wheeled her chair into the hall and steered it to the kitchen. 'Have they arrived yet Dora?'

Dora had made no move yet from the kitchen table. Although still engrossed with her own plotting she noticed a distinct challenge in the tone of voice. 'Yes. Adam's in the library. The girl's upstairs.'

'Go up and tell her I want to speak to her down here immediately.'

By the manner of the order Dora sensed trouble

396

and hurried off. As she entered the bedroom she flashed a look of hate at Silvie who was lying on the bed, eyes closed, and still fully dressed except for top coat and shoes.

'Laura wants to see you downstairs immediately,' she snapped and left the room.

Silvie opened her eyes in surprise at the unexpected voice in the room. 'Oh! Very well. I'll come down.'

Still feeling weak and tired she slowly sat up on the bed. She swung her legs to the floor and put on her shoes.

When she reached the hall Dora, who was waiting, said tersely, 'In the drawing room.' Then, ears alert hovered to listen.

Laura Pemberton came straight to the point the moment Silvie entered the room. 'I shall expect you and your sister out of this house by the end of the month. You have no legal hold here. The property would have become Mark's only in the event of my death. No part of the business was registered in his name, or shares. All that he would have inherited. And for his death I hold you directly responsible!'

Silvie stood pale and silent during this hostile speech. Now she replied quietly. 'As you wish.' She had no redress against the order. And the accusation was justified. She turned abruptly and returned to her bedroom where she sat shaking slightly and upset. Not on her own account, but for the devastating effect it would have on Ginny to be told they must leave the house — on both the girls. What explanation could she give them as to why Ginny was now obliged to leave her friend and the house she loved so much. What possible reason to justify the cruel separation of the girls in such a manner and at such a crucial time.

When Adam came up with the tray ten minutes later she told him what had occurred. In anger he turned to go downstairs but she detained him. 'No Adam. Please don't bother. It could make things worse. I shall . . . '

He listened no further but continued on out. She followed and stood at the top of the stairs helpless to prevent him as he hurried on down.

Purposeful strides took him into the drawing room where in fury he faced his wife. 'What's the bloody idea? You can't turn Silvie out of the house! What could you possibly gain from it?'

She returned his glare contentiously. 'The right to choose who lives under this roof.'

'As Mark's widow she has rights too! She has no other home. Or means. Mark wasn't even insured!'

'Understandably. He didn't expect to die so young. As to the money aspect,' her tone became scornful, 'that's what she married him for in the first place. Well she was mistaken, he had none of his own yet. As for a roof — I'm sure you'll oblige again. Failing that she can go back to whoring!'

'You vindictive bitch!,' he spat out the words, then turned on his heel and left the room.

Unobserved Dora Glasspool stepped back out of sight into a doorway off the hall.

Adam returned to Silvie. 'Unfortunately her name only is on the deeds of this property. Which leaves me in no position to oppose her or make demands. It's true that Mark had no money of his own yet. He

398

would have inherited everything at her death. He never bothered unduly what he spent. He always drew from the firms account without ever having to consult her or justify. I've always done likewise. She's never stinted or questioned how the money was spent. Although I do have my own personal bank account and a half share in the company made over to me by her father when I married her.'

'I'm concerned only about the girls Adam. It will be cruel to separate them just when Joanne needs Ginny to help her recover from losing Mark.'

'There'll be no reason to separate them Silvie. I'll buy a house in the country. They can still keep the horses. We'll tell them that you no longer want to stay here now that Mark . . . ' He did not finish the painful words. 'They'll understand.'

'I can't allow you to leave your home on account of me Adam. You have every right to stay here. It's only Ginny and me that she wants gone, you're still married to her.'

'Don't remind me! In any case it wouldn't be very pleasant for you living here now. We've got to start picking up the pieces of our lives and a complete break from this house and it's associated memories would help us to do that. I think the sooner we make the break the better. As things are I shan't like leaving you here in the house with her all week. She can be bloody nasty. It would be best for you to come back to stay at the flat with me and we'll go house hunting from there.'

'Later Adam. I'll stay here for the time she's allowed. Don't be concerned about me. In any case I'll need time to pack my things and Ginny's.'

'As you wish darling. But I'll start house hunting immediately. I know a good chap in the rural property market. I'll make inquiries as soon as I get back to the city. Meanwhile we have my apartment.'

Silvie looked doubtful. 'What makes you think that Joanne will be willing to leave Briarwood to live elsewhere?'

'I'm pretty certain of it. So long as she has Ginny, the horses and enough country space to ride in. There's little else to hold her here.' He smiled reassuringly. 'I'm sure everything will work out fine. At least there's Dora here to look out for you until you're stronger. Would you feel easier if I asked her to stay overnights for a while until you're ready to leave?'

'No — don't do that Adam.' He must be quite unaware of the cold shoulder Dora always presented to her, she thought, and yet it had been so obvious just recently. 'I'd prefer to manage myself.' She poured the tea and he seated himself beside her on the bed.

'Anything you say Silvie. Nevertheless I'd feel easier knowing that she's keeping half an eye on you for me while I'm not here.'

★   ★   ★

Outside in the driveway Adam kissed her on the cheek then got into his car. 'I'll telephone you every day darling and I'll be back on Friday evening. Meanwhile take care and call me immediately if you need anything.'

'I will. Goodbye Adam.'

'Not goodbye — *please*. Au revoir. Don't walk too far if you go out.' He drew her hand to his lips briefly and with a wave drove off. Silvie waited until the car was out of sight then went back into the house by the side entrance.

Watching enviously from an upstairs window Dora was thinking that she'd gladly die tomorrow if that look on Adam's face could have been for her today. Her eyes followed Silvie until she could no longer see her. Then she resumed dusting while forming mad plans to a conclusion.

39

Silvie had just got into the bath when she heard the telephone ringing. Painfully she was reminded of the morning calls from Mark which he used to make at this time of day. Only when the ringing persisted unanswered did she realise that no one beside herself was in the house. It would be pointless to get out of the water she decided, for she couldn't possibly make it to the phone before it stopped ringing. Whoever it was would call again. She lay back in the bath as the last of the rings reverberated shrilly through the house. She guessed that the caller was probably Adam who had already started house hunting. Despite her having asked him not to he had instructed Dora to fetch meals up and generally look after her. Already breakfast had been brought up to her room. She reflected on the undercurrent of strangeness about Dora Glasspool beneath the superficial concern since Adam had left two days ago. When she'd brought the breakfast tray in today she'd said, 'It's very cold out this morning. I should stay up here if I were you.' Could it be that she was merely carrying out orders from dog-like devotion to Adam? The cold hostility in her manner, and lack of warmth in her tone, remained despite the spoken concern.

Ten minutes later as Silvie came from the bathroom she was suddenly startled by Dora's voice just outside the bedroom door, and again that strange tone. 'You haven't gone out have you dear.'

Recovering from her surprise Silvie was almost overcome by a wild fit of hysterical laughter with a pressing urge to answer yes to the absurd question as she knew Ginny would have done. Instead she composed herself and called back. 'No Dora.'

'Good. Rest until lunch time. I'll call you.'

'Yes — yes I will. Don't disturb me until then.' Even as she spoke the words she wondered what possessed her to lie about her intentions. Dora was not her jailer! Perhaps it had been that peculiar tone of voice, or even the mad question. Wondering if it was herself who was going to pieces she asserted her wits.

Nevertheless, ten minutes later she found herself leaving the house by a side door like a thief in the night, and doubts as to whether *she* was the one cracking up returned briefly.

Once outside she felt easier and her head cleared of vague fancies. Drawing her mink coat closely about her against the cold breeze she walked slowly in the direction of the little churchyard.

★ ★ ★

Adam Pemberton reached out for the receiver almost before the first ringing tone had ended. Always now he anticipated a call from Silvie. But it was the voice of Miss Meacher on the line. 'Don't be alarmed at this unexpected call Mr Pemberton. But we have a very severe outbreak of influenza at the College. A number of extreme cases are in sickbay which is now full to capacity. I regret to say that Joanne is one of these. As we wish to exercise the utmost caution with regards to the spread of the outbreak we are arranging, where possible, for the girls not affected to spend a few days away from here. Virginia is amongst these. Needless to say she did not want to leave Joanne but has been assured that it's for the best. We have excellent doctors in attendance and on call so there is no need to concern yourself unduly. Rest assured Joanne will be well taken care of and I shall keep you informed. By the way I did telephone the house first but received no answer. I should otherwise not have troubled you at your office. Perhaps you will arrange to have Virginia collected from the train. She is catching the 9.15 and will as usual be driven to the station at this end. I apologise for the short notice but the outbreak came so suddenly and the sooner those not affected get away the better.'

'I see. Yes of course. Will you tell her to get off at the city station as usual. I'll be there to collect her and take her home myself.' Hearing Ginny referred to as Virginia sounded strange to his ears. He'd never known her name was other than Ginny. He thanked the Principal then replaced the receiver and glanced at his watch. At the same time he wondered why no one had answered the telephone at the house. About to call to find out he changed his mind. Instead he sent for Harry Mortimer. 'Emergency cropped up Harry. Have to leave the ship in your hands for a bit.' He explained the situation and then indicated a batch of papers on his desk. 'A few orders outstanding, otherwise everything up to date. Not sure when I'll be back. I'll be in touch.'

★ ★ ★

Walking along the familiar path Silvie felt the physical freedom she badly needed after being confined to the bedroom for too long. She had not come this way since the day in David Bradley's study. It would be her first visit to the grave of Mark since the funeral.

As she passed the back of the Rectory she paused transiently to glance in the direction of the study then continued on.

★ ★ ★

From habit now the Reverend David Bradley stood at the French window looking out towards the woods. Five long weeks had passed since she'd been with him in this room. With a nightmare in between. He knew that sooner or later she would come to the little churchyard.

For long spells he had neglected his church obligations to stand at the window watching and waiting. Suddenly there she was. Unlike all those past times she paused, almost imperceptibly. He saw her draw her coat closer around her as the cool March breeze caught at her and fanned her hair into rays of sunlight amongst the trees. But for his heartbeats he stood motionless, watching until she disappeared from his view.

He released his breath and opened the French

door to follow, just as he'd done so many times in the past.

* * *

Silvie knelt on the grass beside the grave and rested her head against the marble headstone. She couldn't bear to read the inscription because of the deep guilt she felt. Tearful words tumbled almost soundlessly from her lips. 'Forgive me Mark. I'm so sorry. I was not worthy of your love. Or of your death.'

* * *

He came slowly closer then stopped. She sensed him there and raised her head.

Neither spoke as he moved forward to stand beside the place where she knelt.

The breeze tossed her hair against her cheeks, and tears emphasised the green innocence of her eyes, despite the ravages they'd known. At last she spoke, her voice still so soft, unchanged by trauma, 'David. I'm glad you came. There is one more thing I have to tell you.'

'I know Silvie.' He drew her to her feet and led her to a seat in the shelter of the wall of the old stone church.

* * *

Seated beside Adam Pemberton on the drive to Kings Meadow Ginny said, 'I do feel absolutely awful about leaving poor Jojo Uncle Adam. I'll miss

406

her terribly. I've never been at Briarwood without her before. Although of course it will be lovely to see Silvie.'

'Well getting away from the College is the main thing for the present Ginny. No reason that you shouldn't enjoy the break. Joanne would want you to.'

They rode in silence for a long while then he spoke again, 'How would you feel about leaving Briarwood. I'm looking around for a country property for the four of us to move to. Just Silvie, Joanne, yourself and me. I haven't mentioned the idea to Joanne yet. Silvie and I only decided recently that it would be best for all of us. We'll take the horses of course. Silvie would be better away from the memories here of Mark. Perhaps Joanne may feel the same way about that.'

In surprise Ginny listened. Truth was she liked the idea. As much as she loved Briarwood she always felt distinctly uncomfortable with Joanne's mother, whom she'd noticed seemed not to like Silvie. 'I think I'd like that. Although I do love Briarwood of course.'

'Well Briarwood is a little over-large anyway. But I'll get a decent-sized property I promise you. One with plenty of acreage.'

'I'd love any place where all of us are. So whatever you and Silvie decide I'll be happy.'

'Good, that's settled then. I'm sure Joanne will be willing. I shall have to stop off at the next telephone box to call the house and let them know to expect us. I didn't have time before I left the office. I was rather held up and wouldn't have made it on time to meet your train. I could have got my secretary to make the call but without a long and involved explanation Silvie would've wondered why only you and not Joanne were coming and she might have worried.'

From her bag Ginny took a diary and for the next few minutes was occupied with making an entry in it. Suddenly she looked up. 'I say — why don't we just surprise Silvie. I mean don't let's telephone in advance. Dora won't mind. It's still very early and there'll be heaps of time for her to arrange the meals to include us.'

He noticed that she hadn't mentioned his wife. Not even earlier when he'd spoken of plans to move away from Briarwood. 'Don't you think I should let my wife know?'

By his tone she detected a lack of seriousness in the question. 'I don't think she'll care one way or another, whether we're coming or not. I hope I haven't offended you in saying so. Of course she'll be concerned about Jojo when she hears.' She felt certain that he'd not take umbrage at the voiced opinion. Unavoidably she'd noticed that he and his wife had little to say to each other.

In reply he patted her hand lightly. 'Very well we'll surprise Silvie. But only *surprise* mind. Mustn't suddenly jump out at her from some dark corner.' He glanced sideways at her and smiled. She had noticed the soft concern in his tone as he spoke of her sister.

She leaned forward in her seat slightly so that she could study his face. But she could not see the expression in his eyes now for they were intent upon

408

the road ahead. 'Uncle Adam,' she ventured tentatively. 'Do you love Silvie?'

Showing surprise at the unexpected question he cast a quick glance at her again. Then returned his eyes to the highway before making a reply. 'Of course I do. Don't we all?'

'What I mean is, are you *in love* with her, in the same way that Mark was?'

Further surprised he hesitated briefly before replying, 'What makes you ask that Ginny?'

'The way you look at her. The same way that he did.' And she thought secretly, the way Jack Thorndyke always looked at her. Then she added. 'I've never had the opportunity to speak with you alone before or I might have asked long ago. You see I've often wondered. I hope you don't mind my asking such a personal question?'

He did not reply immediately. He was pondering on how best to. If they all moved into a new house together the question could not be evaded indefinitely. Nor would he lie about such a serious matter.

'Are you in love with her?' she prompted, her tone suggesting that she already knew what his answer would be.

'Yes Ginny. I love Silvie in the way that Mark loved her. Now that he's no longer here to take care of her I shall do so. I'll take care of you both.'

She leaned back in her seat again. He glanced at her face and saw her expression showed no surprise at his answer, which he felt sure, she would treat with the same discretion as her past curiosity. His daughter could have no such inkling. Her tendency favoured bluntness, no shilly-shallying and she would have asked outright. With Laura and himself for parents this aspect of her nature did not surprise him.

They rode the last lap of the journey in silence, during which Ginny wrote more in her diary for the day. 'I was right. Uncle Adam *is* in love with Silvie. I've just asked him.' This, she felt sure, would be the most important thing she would learn that day; even more so than the proposed move from Briarwood, already entered on record. Only news and events of paramount importance or significance in her life were ever recorded in the diary. It was also the last entry she ever made.

★　★　★

From the screen of a large shrub Dora Glasspool watched as Joe Tarrant worked the motor mower to the far side of the lawns, away from the potting sheds where the gardening tools and equipment were stored. Impatiently she had waited, biding her time unseen, until his gardening tasks had taken him out of view of the shed where she knew she'd find what she wanted. But she needed time to search. Three trips into the garden she'd made so far this morning. Each time Joe had been within sight of the shed. It had been during one of these absences that the call from Miss Meacher had gone unanswered.

When the right moment arrived she scuttled across to the shed unseen. Wild-eyed and muttering she searched the many shelves and rummaged amongst the variety of garden aids. Above the sound

410

of the mower she did not hear the car arrive. Nor was she aware that its occupants had entered the house. With a sudden exclamation of success she swooped and snatched up a ball of strong black twine, invisible in its darkness, which Joe used for weaving amongst the currant bushes to discourage the birds when the fruit was in season. She concealed the twine in her pocket along with the scissors she'd placed there earlier.

She tilted her head to listen. As the sound of the mower became louder she darted over to a small dusty window to peer out. Joe was not in sight. She attempted to judge his position, then waited for the sound to recede. Impatient she darted out and ran back into the house by the side door through which she'd left. Breathless and wild-eyed she came into the hall and glanced at the grandfather clock. With relief she saw that ten minutes were still wanting till lunchtime when Laura would be in from the stables.

Feverishly she mounted the stairs. At the top she paused to listen to the sound of a toilet cistern flushing. Unaware that her intended victim had left the house she looked satisfied and backed down two stairs. Then she crouched to secure one end of the twine to the banister at ankle height at one side just above a deep turn of carving so that it could not slip down. She stretched the twine across to meet the opposite post at the same point and cut it off from the ball. She tied it securely then returned the ball to her apron pocket along with the scissors. With her fingers she tested the trip wire and found it taut and totally invisible against the dark polished wood and deep rich colour of the carpet.

411

As she ran downstairs she heard the French door of the drawing room open and close. A moment later Laura Pemberton came into view and guided her chair towards the cloakroom.

'Lunch is not quite ready.' Dora's voice sounded breathless and Laura Pemberton threw a cursory glance at her. At this same time the sound of the French door in the drawing room opened and closed again. Dora about to go into the kitchen froze waiting. She knew it could not be Joe for he always came in through the back door to eat in the kitchen. As Silvie came into view Dora stared dumbfounded.

Then as if some mechanical clockwork on their bodies had run down the three in the hall stopped their movements abruptly at the sound of a door above opening suddenly.

They looked towards the top of the stairs as Ginny appeared and called, 'I'm home Silvie! I saw you from the window . . .'

For a transient moment Silvie's eyes lit up with surprise.

Then, for those who watched, the world stood still for a second, and an *eternity*, as Ginny's voice died away and she became airborne.

Immediately behind her Adam had appeared. He watched helplessly as she plunged headlong the length of the staircase.

Then as if the mechanical clockwork had been suddenly restarted those down in the hall came to life again.

With a small scream of horror Silvie rushed forward as her young sister's body hit the merciless marble floor of the hall, and lay white and motionless. The bright hair was spread out vividly around her head which rested at an unnatural angle.

With an exclamation Adam Pemberton made a precipitant descent of the stairs and was on his knees beside the still figure before Silvie reached the spot. Instantly he got to his feet to telephone for an ambulance, but saw that his wife was already dialling. He knelt again and felt Ginny's pulse. His face turned ashen.

Silvie was now bending over her young sister and moaning in horror and disbelief.

Adam cradled Silvie in his arms, her head against his chest.

No one paid any attention to Dora's incoherent whimpering. 'I thought she was in her room! I didn't know she'd gone out.' And even in this profound moment, brought about by her mad handiwork, the sight of Silvie in Adam's embrace rekindled her hate. After all her careful planning the girl was still there to take him away forever. Listless she went into the kitchen, still muttering to herself, unheeded, for no ears were listening at present. 'It was meant to be her — meant to be her.'

While Silvie in her mental agony wished fervently to heaven that it had been.

From the shelter of Adam's arms she said brokenly, 'This is my punishment. It's *too* high a price to pay. Oh Adam — I can't live without her!'

'Hush darling.' He had no other words for the present.

He heard the ambulance at the front of the house and saw that his wife was opening the door in readiness.

A black depression settled on Dora Glasspool as she sat hunched in a kitchen chair. This was *not* how she had meant it to be. *Not* how she had planned. By now she should have gone up to cut the twine from the posts before Laura came in for lunch — before anyone found the girl. But it was the *wrong* girl. And the twine was still there because everything had gone wrong. From the dark depths of impaired reasoning the instinct of self-preservation emerged. Alert now she sat waiting to seize the first chance to go up and remove the telltale twine.

★ ★ ★

Above the sound of the mower Joe Tarrant heard the ambulance bell. Alarmed he switched off the motor. By the time he arrived at the front door of the house the ambulance was moving off along the driveway. The front door was open. He went in and saw Laura Pemberton still in the hall. In a few words she explained what had happened.

'Dear God in heaven!' He was deeply shaken. 'From top to bottom?' He sucked in his breath as his eyes rested briefly on the marble floor. 'I didn't know the lass was home.'

'I didn't know either. It was unexpected. Adam brought her. Apparently no one was in the house to answer the phone when the call came from the College to tell us they have an influenza outbreak there. Dora must have been outside when it rang.'

414

Repeating what Adam had told her while they had awaited the arrival of the ambulance she explained why Ginny was there and not Joanne.

'Close the front door and come into the drawing room. I'll pour us a brandy and get Dora to make some tea. And I'll telephone the infirmary shortly for news. But I saw Adam's face. I don't hold much hope.'

Joe shook his head in dumb shock. Then said, 'Poor lass. As it turned out she'd have been better off taking her chances with the flu.' He looked upwards to the top of the stairs before following her into the room. 'How did it happen? Did she miss her footing?'

Without waiting for her reply he turned back towards the stairs. 'I'll just go up and take a look to see if there's a loose rod.'

Hearing his voice so close Dora came rushing in panic from the kitchen and saw him ascending the stairs. She made a pathetic attempt to get him to turn back. 'Wait Joe! Have a cup of tea first!'

But Joe carried on up. 'I want to make certain about the rods — just in case.'

Like a frightened child she stood at the bottom of the staircase watching while he checked the rods and inspected the carpet for loose threads. He had been working in the bright light of outdoors all morning and his eyes were not adjusted to the comparatively darker interior at the top of the stairs. He did not notice the now separated ends of the deadly twine.

When Laura Pemberton saw that Joe had not followed behind her she turned the chair back into the hall. She saw the terrified expression on the face of Dora.

Joe came down the stairs. 'Nothing loose. Lass must have missed her footing. Shocking business!' Again he slowly shook his head.

Laura Pemberton again turned her chair into the drawing room, 'Make us some tea Dora and fetch it in here.'

Grave-faced Joe followed her into the room. 'Lass looked bad then did she?'

She nodded. 'I don't see how anyone could survive such a fall. Ambulance got here fast though.'

'Got away fast too. Before I could get across the garden.'

She went to the drinks cabinet and poured brandy into two glasses.

'Just a small tot for me then Laura. I'll drive to the infirmary in the Jag to bring Adam and young Mrs Pemberton back. They won't have any transport seeing as they went in the ambulance. They won't want to ride home in a taxi at a time like this.'

She nodded. 'When I telephone for news in a few minutes I'll leave word that you'll be there.'

When Dora Glasspool brought in the tray with tea Laura Pemberton noted her beaten dog expression. 'You'd better have a tot of brandy too. You look like death yourself. Pour the tea and then sit down. Joe's going to the infirmary shortly.'

But Dora did not want to sit down with them. She wanted to be alone to lick her wounds. And there was the twine to remove — the evidence — before it was discovered. She was still badly shaken at the close shave a few minutes ago. She poured the tea and muttered some unintelligible excuse to leave the room. In the kitchen she waited for an opportunity to remove the twine. It could not be risked while Joe was in the house.

In silence the two in the drawing room waited out the minutes. Then Laura Pemberton made the call to the infirmary.

After an interval while the news was relayed to her she gave the message that Joe would be arriving with the car. She replaced the receiver, shocked despite her prediction to expect the worst. 'My God! The child is dead!'

'Oh dear Lord!' Joe Tarrant paced the room in shock-driven movement.

Laura Pemberton poured herself another brandy, and thought, this house has seemed cursed since the older Marsh girl first entered it.

Joe stopped pacing. 'I'll get the car out and go to collect them. The sister — poor lass — will take it hard. I could see how fond she was of the youngster. Dreadful waste of a young life.' He strode out through the hall and the side door to the garages.

The moment he'd left Dora came from the kitchen to collect the tray. On the way out she closed the drawing room door behind her. This was rarely done and only then during evening bridge sessions in colder weather. Laura Pemberton liked to keep the doors open wide for easy passage of her wheelchair. But Dora's distracted mind was too obsessed with removing the twine from the posts, and totally beyond the sphere of rational thinking.

After hastily depositing the tray in the kitchen she

scuttled up the stairs, taking the scissors from her pocket on the way. Detaching the twine from around the posts took longer than she had expected. Being so fine and dark made it difficult to locate. Finally she succeeded and put the length of twine and the scissors into the pocket of her apron where the rest of the ball was still hidden.

As she turned to go back down she made a low sound of fright as she saw Laura Pemberton in her wheelchair in the middle of the hall watching her. Slowly, fear in her eyes and movement, she continued on down the stairs. 'I was just checking . . . in case.'

The wheelchair glided across the smooth floor to the base of the stairs and as Dora passed Laura Pemberton shot out a hand and snatched at the apron, yanking it off viciously and breaking the strings. From its pocket she withdrew the scissors and twine to which the recently cut length clung, barely visible off the roll.

'My God! What have you done!' Shock and disbelief registered together on her face.

Muttering incoherently Dora Glasspool hurried off into the kitchen. Laura Pemberton followed her in. Dora turned to her wild-eyed and agitated. 'I didn't mean it to be the *young* one! It was meant to be *her*.' Plaintively her voice rose to an hysterical pitch. 'I didn't know she'd gone out. I thought she was up in her room. I didn't see the others come home.'

'Stop gibbering you mad fool! Don't you realise what you've done! Oh Christ I can't believe this is happening!' Uncharacteristically Laura Pemberton felt out of control. This bombshell turned what was thought to have been an accident into deliberate and premeditated murder. 'In God's name why?'

'She was going to take Adam away from here. I heard you tell her to leave. He was going with her. And *she* killed Mark. I heard her say so.' From the chaos of her mind more words tumbled. From the confusion Laura Pemberton grasped the gist as Dora became hysterical between laughter and tears as she continued to madly justify her mistake in causing the wrong death.

'For Christ's sake pull yourself together you raving lunatic!' Laura Pemberton strove to compose herself as she guided her chair back to the drawing room and towards the telephone. As she began to dial the three numbers she could hear Dora Glasspool whimpering and gibbering. Her trembling fingers stopped short of the third nine as thoughts of the consequences seeped into her mind. She replaced the receiver slowly. Murder on top of Mark's suicide! Even though that had been recorded as accidental death she, along with Adam and the girl, knew otherwise. Scandal! The press! Never would they live it down. Reporting the truth and having Dora Glasspool, who must be completely insane, arrested would not bring back the child.

She poured herself another brandy to abate the inner trembling which seized her. For the next few minutes she sat in deep contemplation, at times arguing with herself about the course she wanted to take. It was not the right one and she knew it. Yet what point was there in pursuing justice through the punishment of Dora Glasspool. According to events her place was in a mental institution. Yet she had come partly to that state through saving the life of Joanne ten years ago. Some degree of responsibility for her, other than that already assumed, must rest with the Pemberton family.

How was it that none of them had been aware of the deterioration of Dora's mind? She had seemed contented enough and capable of carrying out the work she did. The fact that she'd had a crush on Adam for years had been obvious. But that was all any of them had thought it to be — just a crush — not a mad passion which would evoke jealousy and finally murder.

Having come to a decision she sipped her brandy while she waited for the return of Joe.

Meanwhile she called Dora into the room and instructed her to return the ball of twine to the place where she'd found it and come straight back.

★   ★   ★

At the Infirmary Silvie looked down upon the scattering of freckles on the beloved face.

She wanted to run — run — run — until she met oblivion. Run from the cruel reality that she could not face. 'You must be mistaken, Ginny can't be dead,' she had said to the nursing sister in charge who had had the unenviable task of breaking the news, which Adam had already known, and Silvie had been unwilling to believe during the nightmare journey in the ambulance.

'It's true my dear,' the sister had replied.

Silvie felt her world disintegrate about her. She

wished herself in a vortex, to be carried away into non-existence, for she could not stay in this bleak empty space that no longer held Ginny. Frozen in shock and disbelief she allowed Adam to guide her away.

Joe Tarrant arrived and wordlessly led them out to where he had parked the car. No one spoke on the journey back to Briarwood. Joe drove. Adam sat with Silvie in the back seat, his arms about her protectively. Words had no place or meaning in the presence of such profound grief and loss.

When they arrived at the house Adam supported Silvie up to her room then went to telephone Doctor Brodie.

Awaiting the return of Joe Tarrant Laura Pemberton called to him from the French window as he crossed the garden after garaging the car. 'Poor lass. Terrible shock for her,' he said as he came into the house.

'Joe I want you to take Dora home. She's gone all to pieces about the accident. It's completely unbalanced her and she's rambling a lot of nonsense. I want her to stay home for a few days until she recovers. Will you ask Mary if she can come and take over meanwhile. It may be for some time. If she can't I'll have to hire some stranger. I'd rather it was Mary, she knows the ways of the household here.'

'Yes she'll come and help out I know. Only too willing. Send Dora out as soon as you like. I'll see her settled indoors and then bring Mary back with me.'

Laura Pemberton went into the kitchen where

Dora was still seated at the table and now whimpering softly. 'Now listen to me Dora,' she said firmly, 'Joe is going to drive you home. You are to stay there until I say you can come back. You must keep your mouth shut. Is that clear? You must say nothing about the accident to anyone. Do you understand?'

Blankly Dora stared back. Laura Pemberton leaned forward in the wheelchair and thumped the hunched shoulders. 'Do you understand what I'm saying you fool? You'll hang if you tell anyone!' Fear sparked in the blank expression as Dora nodded.

'Now go and put your coat on and get out of my bloody sight!'

★ ★ ★

In the master bedroom Silvie stood at the window gazing out over the garden. She was recalling the day when she had first come to Briarwood. Her eyes sought out the direction of the tennis courts hidden from her view by trees. She should have listened to Adam that day and walked out of the lives of the Pemberton's for all their sakes. If she'd done so both Mark and Ginny would be alive now.

Her eyes followed a solitary snowflake as it fluttered on the air, drifted across the window, and came to rest on the sill where it disintegrated to extinction. She wished fervently that she could do likewise.

She had a clear view of the rose garden where a scattering of fine snow fell and melted on the bare branches; This garden that would never again know the presence of Mark and Ginny. A vast empty void stretched before her and she could not bear to think of time which now held only a deserted future. She looked upon Ginny's death as a punishment, retribution for her sins, and she wondered at the strange fate that had brought her to Briarwood today to die — the flu outbreak that she had been sent home to avoid.

She recalled what Ginny had said one day at Stanford Road when telling how much she loved Briarwood. 'I'll live there until I die.' It had been innocently prophetic.

Doctor Brodie had called and left sleeping pills. This was all he could do to help her. He had seen that shock and grief had frozen all emotion into a vacuum, on hold in a deadlock, for release at some later time. 'Be brave lassie,' he had told her.

★   ★   ★

Once again it fell upon Miss Meacher to break the devastating news to Joanne Pemberton. This time Peter Dunning travelled to the College to be at her side and give what comfort he could. Since the death of Mark he had telephoned her regularly and sent a letter or two in attempt to be a substitute, however tenuous or inadequate, for the brother she had adored and was missing so intensely. But this time there could be no such surrogate link to cushion the impact of losing the friend who had helped sustain her.

On seeing him she had broken into a fit of hysterical sobbing. He had held her tightly until it had burned itself out from exhaustion. But it was decided that she could not be brought from her sick bed to attend the funeral.

★　★　★

Adam attended the inquest alone. Once again death by misadventure was recorded. Three reliable people had witnessed the fall, and the court accepted unequivocally that the child had missed her footing and stumbled without gaining a hold to save herself.

While he was gone Silvie wrote two letters. These she concealed for the present in the drawer of a small antique writing desk in her bedroom. Rarely had Adam left her side. Sometimes he had coaxed her into taking a walk in the garden with him. Once she had allowed him to take her for a drive in the quiet countryside. But mostly she had kept to her room. Mary Tarrant came up at regular intervals to see if she needed anything.

Only at nights could Silvie find any release in her emotions. Every night she went to Adam's bed where they made love while she clung to him and wept. Sometimes he wept with her.

This time she had not taken the sleeping pills which Doctor Brodie had left for her. In addition to these she still had more than half of the bottle he had previously prescribed after the death of Mark. Both bottles were in the bathroom — waiting.

Although still numb from shock she attempted to show Adam as much love as she could for what she intended to be their last days together.

40

At last the funeral was over. All the waiting had come to an end. Ginny was buried in the churchyard next to the grave of Mark. No preparations had been made for mourners outside the family other than Peter Dunning who had promised Joanne he would attend. Harry Mortimer had respected Silvie's wishes of no mourners and had sent her a letter of condolence instead.

Laura Pemberton had not attended. With the dreadful knowledge of the truth behind the fall she could not have watched the casket containing the child lowered into the ground and kept her silence.

Reverend David Bradley had taken the service mechanically, at times barely in charge of his own voice, knowing what ravages of grief the woman he loved was suffering, only a few feet away, yet beyond the reach of mere words.

When the news of Ginny's death had first reached him he had telephoned the house to ask if he might call. But Adam, who had answered, told him that Silvie was in deep shock and for the present it was best that she saw no one.

During the burial service she had leaned on Adam heavily for physical support.

Joe Tarrant had attended. Mary had stayed back at the house to prepare for their return.

★ ★ ★

For a week Silvie had lived in a twilight world, empty and unreal. Now the waiting for escape was ended.

Adam had remained with her constantly. 'Together with Joanne we'll start a new chapter Silvie.' He had told her of a house he was going to inspect. She was thankful that he hadn't actually bought a property yet. Her conscience weighed heavily at what she was about to do to him.

Late that night she reached for the bottles which held the sleeping pills and filled a glass with water. A few minutes later she went into Adam's room and kissed him. 'Goodnight Adam. I'm very tired tonight.' She left him and went to her own bed, and at his request she left the connecting door open.

He lay in his bed staring up at the ceiling as he contemplated the future for himself, Silvie, and Joanne. He wanted to interweave the broken threads of their ravished lives into some pattern of continued existence. He knew it would take time. A *long* time.

★   ★   ★

The bottles in Silvie's bathroom were empty. Beside these lay two letters. One addressed to Adam, the other to David Bradley.

Not until late the next morning did Adam discover what she had done. Earlier he had looked in through the open door and thought her still sleeping. Only later when he saw that she had not stirred did he call her name and go to her bedside.

41

Slowly from habit the black Humber moved along Queen Street. No small children played outside today. An old woman, huddled against the cold March wind with eyes downcast walked stiffly along the narrow pavement. As the car drew level she glanced up briefly to call, 'Hullo Jack. Cold ain't it.'

Jack wound down the window. 'Hello Flo.' His greeting was cordial but his heartiness had left him nowadays. 'Yes bloody freezing! Probably get some snow.'

The woman turned to call after him, 'Shame about Ginny Marsh wasn't it!'

Jack frowned. Had he heard right? Did she say Ginny Marsh? He stopped the car and put his head out of the window to call after her. But once again her head was bent against the biting wind as she continued along the street. The Humber moved on.

Only three boys were in the street today. They stood on the corner, hands deep in the pockets of thin jackets inadequate against the weather.

''Ello Jack,' they chorused through lips stiff from the cold, and their half closed eyes lit up briefly in anticipation. But Jack appeared not to hear them. He went straight into number five without even glancing their way. The old Jack they'd known had gone, changed suddenly way back last summer. Although he still doled out the tanners, sometimes a bob each, he never issued his old warnings about touching his car. It was as if he didn't care much any more. What if he ceased to care altogether! — well they didn't like to think about that. Despite this change in Jack he never forgot about them. But the time might come. They'd noticed too that the Humber was not quite so shiny nowadays. But even without the reminder they still respected the old rules.

Before Jack was barely inside the door, still open even today, he spoke. 'What's this about Ginny Marsh Ma? Flo Wilson's just said something but I didn't catch . . . '

'Hello Jack luv. Sit down and I'll get you a nice hot cuppa tea.' She went through to the back room calling over her shoulder as she went. 'When did you get back from Ostend then?'

'Late yesterday.'

'Well you won't have seen the papers then luv.' She re-entered the room. 'I've put the kettle on to boil. Ginny had an accident and died. I'm not sure if the funeral was yesterday or whether it's today. I haven't even been able to send a sympathy card to Silvie because I don't know where she lives. I believe it's a long way away, out in the country somewhere.'

'What! Ginny dead! Are you sure Ma?' Jack looked shaken as he lowered himself onto the old sofa.

'Quite sure son. Mrs Barnes said it mentioned Silvie and that she had been recently widowed. Poor girl! Doesn't bear thinking about. Mrs Barnes left the newspaper with me so that you could read about it when you came back. I told her you was away. As you've been gone nearly two months luv you won't even have heard about the accident that killed her young husband. About a month ago now I believe. I suppose I could've got Mrs Barnes to write to you at the hotel address on the postcards you sent me, but I don't like people to know I can't write. I must try to get a sympathy card sent though if you can find out the address Jack. *Poor* Silvie! You know how she doted on young Ginny, even when she was only a child herself. My mother used to say beautiful women always seem to be ill-fated. Perhaps she was right.'

Jack's ears had been deaf to most of what his mother had said. He'd been reading the newspaper account of the accident, and now looked up dazed. Such a simple accident! A fall down the stairs! 'Where did you hear about the funeral Ma?'

'Mrs Barnes came and told me. She must have read it somewhere. I believe it may have been held yesterday though. Not too certain. Ask her when you pass. Do you know the place mentioned? A country mansion according to the paper Mrs Barnes said.'

Jack nodded and glanced at his watch. It was still fairly early morning. He had arrived home from Ostend late yesterday and having not seen his mother for a much longer spell than usual had come early to check all was well.

'The kettle'll be ready.' She went through into the back room again.

He stood up now and called to her, 'I won't stop for the tea after all Ma. I must go and see Silvie. I don't think she has any relatives. It might help her to see someone who knew Ginny so well. I'll come

429

and see you again tomorrow.' He put some money on the table.

'But y'tea luv! It's so cold out today! You need something warm inside you.'

'Not now Ma. Tomorrow. And for Christ's sake close this bloody front door. The place is like an ice box! You'll catch pneumonia.'

'All right then. Ta-ta luv.'

As Jack emerged from the house the three boys took frost-nipped hands from their pockets hopefully and watched, lips too stiff now to call, as he got into his car and switched on the engine. Disappointment showed on their faces as it made a U turn in the street and moved off.

In the driving mirror Jack caught sight of the three dejected figures, shoulders hunched, moving away from the corner.

'What the bloody hell's the matter with me lately,' he muttered as he stopped the car and pumped the horn.

As if puppets on a string the boys came to life when he put his hand out of the window and beckoned. They had reached him before he'd got the coins from his pocket. He handed them each a half crown piece. 'Poor little sods. You look shrammed,' he said as blue hands darted from pockets and pinched faces lit up at the unexpected size of the handout. Through chattering teeth they thanked him, and one remarked. 'I saw some finger marks on yer car Jack but none of us did it.' His stiff lips were barely able to form the words.

'Go on with you then. Buy your stick-jaw and get

off indoors in the warm. Too bloody cold outside today.'

'Fanks a lot Jack.'

'Ta Jack.'

'Fanks Jack,' they chorused again looking a lot brighter despite the bitter wind as they scuttled off to the corner shop.

Jack drove on, not stopping to find out from Mrs Barnes the exact day or time of the funeral after all. Even if it had been yesterday he still would go and see Silvie and visit the grave. If it was today — he might well still be in time to attend.

Out on the main road he headed the car in the direction of Kings Meadow, topping the speed limit all the way. 'If a bloody copper stops me he'll either take a quick bribe or a punch on the bleedin' jaw,' he muttered. 'Nothing and nobody is going to hold me up.'

He was glad that he already knew where the place was. He even knew where the house was. This would not be the first time he'd driven to Kings Meadow. Curiosity had taken him there just after the wedding which he'd read about in the paper. But he'd not been able to see the house from the road. Having made that previous trip would save delay on the way to ask directions as he'd done last time. Except to refuel the car he drove non-stop.

When he reached the village of Kings Meadow he stopped at the tiny stone church and parked his car in the lane. He walked around to the side and into the little churchyard.

Instantly he saw the newly covered grave, topped with a mass of bright flowers. Only then did he realise that he had not stopped to get flowers himself. He'd been too shocked and hell bent on getting here. Slowly he walked across to the graveside and stood looking down. Then he bent to read some of the cards attached to the wreaths, to convince himself that there had been no mistake. He stared down at the newly placed earth. Tears sprung to his eyes and a lump to his throat as he thought of the bright-haired Ginny that he knew, so full of life, now lying beneath the mound.

After a while he moved away and went to sit on a bench against the church wall. He could still barely believe this could really have happened. He sat thinking of the past, back to when Ginny and Silvie had lived in Queen Street.

A movement caught his eye and he looked up as David Bradley came from the side door of the church a few yards from where he sat. 'Good morning. I see that I've arrived too late for the funeral of Ginny.'

David Bradley stopped and looked at Jack blankly for a moment or two, his thoughts elsewhere. While waiting for some response Jack continued. 'I'm an old friend of Silvie and Ginny. Known them both since they were born. Lived in the same street.' He held out his hand. 'Jack Thorndyke.'

'David Bradley.' Having surfaced from his preoccupation he shook the proffered hand. 'Funeral was yesterday morning.'

'I only heard the dreadful news this morning. Been out of the country for a few weeks. I know Silvie must be devastated. She lived for Ginny.'

David Bradley nodded agreement. Nobody knew

better than himself the extremes to which Silvie had gone for her young sister. 'I hadn't seen Silvie all week until yesterday at the funeral. I intend to go to the house later to see if I can be of any comfort.' He regarded the man who claimed to have known Silvie for so long. 'Have you come far?'

Jack told him the distance.

'Would you care to come back to the Rectory with me for a drink of some kind? I'm on my way.'

'Thank you. I'm much obliged. It's a bit nippy today.'

As they walked Jack cast a quick glance at David Bradley. He was the youngest-looking clergyman that he'd ever seen. Certainly the best looking. Didn't somehow look like a man of the cloth. 'I didn't even know about Silvie's husband until today. Incredible bad luck — two accidents so close together! How long ago did . . . ?

'Five weeks.' David Bradley wondered why Silvie hadn't mentioned Jack Thorndyke that day when she'd spoken of her past and talked of Queen Street.

They entered the Rectory through the French window into the study. 'How about some Irish tea?'

'Just the thing. Thanks.' Jack wondered what clerical title to use. He was about to ask when Mrs Armstrong looked into the room and asked, 'Shall I make a pot of tea Reverend?'

'Please Emily. I have a visitor.'

While they waited for the tea David Bradley poured whisky into two glasses and told what he could of the two accidents.

Jack wondered at his tone and expression as he spoke of Silvie.

In his dressing room Adam Pemberton put on his jacket. He had bathed and had breakfast long ago but Silvie hadn't yet stirred. He glanced at his watch, then went into her room and across to the bed. 'Silvie darling.' He touched her arm which was lying outside the covers. It felt cold to his touch. 'Silvie!' He grasped her shoulder and gently shook her. 'Silvie — wake up darling!' When she did not stir he gently tapped her cheeks. 'Silvie — wake up.' His first thought was that she was still under the influence of the nightly sleeping pill. He shook her, more roughly this time. It was at this point the thought struck him of what she might have done. With a strangled cry he felt her wrist. There was a pulse but it was weak. He dashed into her bathroom and saw the two empty bottles, evidence beyond doubt, and two letters lying along side. He snatched these up barely glancing at the names they bore and absently put them into his jacket pocket.

He dashed to the telephone in the upstairs corridor and rang Doctor Brodie, and then for an ambulance. He returned to Silvie and lifted her onto her feet, at the same time slapping her lightly on her cheeks. 'Silvie! Oh God Silvie! Wake up! What have you done!' With a sob he swung her up into his arms and carried her downstairs to the drawing room, at the same time calling, 'Mary — come and give me a hand. Silvie's taken too many sleeping pills. We must keep her moving.'

'Oh my godfathers!' Mary ran from the kitchen to assist.

Between them, they attempted to keep Silvie on her feet, constantly calling her name and shaking her to try to revive her. But she was too far gone to hear their pleas.

★　★　★

In the Rectory as they sipped their Irish tea and talked, the emergency bell of an ambulance sounded harsh and close. David Bradley paused mid-sentence to listen. 'It's going through the lane.' The sound receded and suddenly cut off. His expression showed alarm. 'It's stopped. Not too far away. Can only be the Pemberton's house. Must be Laura.' He thought her the most vulnerable health wise. Probably this recent shock on top of the other one.

'Are you sure it's Silvie's place?'

'Certain. The Ashdown's are further away, and there aren't any properties between here and Briarwood.' He was stroking his chin as though trying to make a decision. 'I'll phone the house to inquire. But best hang on a few minutes. There's obviously a crisis. Don't want to hinder.' Despite his assumption that it must be Laura Pemberton he looked anxious as they waited.

Jack noted the expression and felt uneasy. Restless he stood up and paced the room.

They heard the ambulance bell start up again. David Bradley took up the receiver and dialled. Jack watched intently and saw a change come over the handsome features as someone answered the call. Ashen-faced David Bradley slowly replaced the receiver. 'Silvie!' The name escaped his lips in a sob.

'She's overdosed on sleeping pills. The Infirmary — I must go to her.'

'Christ!' With this quick exclamation Jack dashed to the door. 'My car's in the lane. We'll go together.'

'I'll direct you.' David Bradley got into the car beside Jack. But for his occasional directions they drove tense and silent on the wake of the diminishing sound of the speeding ambulance bell.

* * *

The three men paced the room where they had been taken to await news. The sister in charge entered. 'I'm so very sorry gentlemen. The doctors could not save her.' She paused in the moments of stunned silence while they each stared at her blankly. Then she continued. 'If you would like to see her now I'll take you along.'

In silent shock and disbelief they mechanically followed.

Adam Pemberton blamed himself for not being more vigilant. Yet at the same time knew there were limitations. Silvie had administered the pills in the privacy of her bathroom. How could he have known she would take her own life!

* * *

As they came out of the main door of the Infirmary Joe Tarrant wordlessly indicated the Jaguar. It was apparent that he'd already inquired and been given the news.

'Do you mind if I ride back with you,' David

Bradley asked Adam listlessly. 'It'll save Jack a journey back to Kings Meadow.' The question really required no answer. Before getting into the car he turned to Jack and held out his hand. 'I'm glad you called Jack. Perhaps you'll drop in again some time.'

Jack returned the handshake. 'I might do that.' Yet he didn't really believe he ever would. He watched the Jaguar move off with Joe at the wheel.

Adam Pemberton sat in the back with David Bradley. No one spoke on the journey, not even Joe.

Visibly upset Adam felt in his pocket for a handkerchief and his hand contacted the two letters he'd found with the empty pill bottles in Silvie's bathroom. In the crisis he'd thought no more about them. He drew them out and after glancing at them absently he wordlessly handed across the one addressed to David Bradley. The other he returned to his pocket.

In silence David Bradley accepted the letter and after a quick glance at his name on the envelope put it in his pocket for later. There was no hurry now and having guessed that Silvie had written it would rather be alone when he read it.

When Joe dropped him off at the Rectory he did not go in. Instead he went round to the side and through the garden to walk along the path that Silvie used to take to get to the church. He walked and walked, hardly aware that he did so. Torturing thoughts echoed through his mind; all pointless now, yet he could not stop them. If only he'd had a chance to speak with her after Ginny's death. Could he have found the right words to make her see the future without her sister differently? He who was supposed to be adept at finding the right ones to comfort, as balm for the grieving. He had failed her. Yet he *had* tried to see her and been told that she was too distraught to see anyone at all. He had tried several times during the week that followed. What measures could he have taken without violating her right to be left alone with her grief!

His subconscious mind urged him to walk, walk, walk: walk away from the knowledge that she was dead and that he would never again see her passing along the track at the edge of the wood, or speak with her in the garden, or pray with her in the little church. Never again would he hear her soft voice, or look upon her lovely face. The thought that she no longer existed on earth in the flesh seemed more than he could bear.

But there was no way off the bleak and deserted world except by the route she had taken; self-annihilation.

* * *

Much later, he had lost track of time, he seated himself on a stile and read the letter she had left for him.

Later still, fatigued, he returned to the Rectory. He had missed evensong service — but what the hell — nobody ever attended that anyway.

When they arrived back at Briarwood Adam left Joe to garage the car, and walked into the house like a man dazed or blind. The whole direction of his life had changed. He could not face going to the room now so empty of her presence. Nor could he bear the thought of sleeping in his own room — not now. He went into the library, poured himself some brandy, lay down on the leather couch and wondered how he would get through the night, and all the other nights. He couldn't face the hours and days that stretched ahead without her. He sat up, shoulders hunched, his head resting in his hands while sobs racked his body.

Like this Mary Tarrant found him when she brought his evening meal in to him on a tray and tried to coax him into eating.

When she left him she was dabbing at her eyes with her apron.

42

Shocked villagers lined the lane and surrounded the small churchyard. Others packed into the church, since no one had said it was a private family service.

The story of the triple Pemberton tragedies, such as they knew of it, was destined to be handed down for many years to come. Nothing like it had ever happened before in this quiet backwater.

Solemn-faced three men stood close to the graveside.

One who had loved her with an obsessive passion, to whom she had given herself countless times because he had been powerless to resist and release her, even for the sake of his own son.

One who would have renounced his God, and gladly relinquished his soul to the Devil for her love. But he had kisses to remember.

And one who stood a little apart from the others. He who had loved her longest of all; who had no kisses or fulfilment to remember. But he had many more memories, for his eyes had known her for twenty years. The card on a heart of red roses beside the grave read . . . Goodbye my Angel . . . Jack.

Unequal to the ordeal of conducting the burial service himself on account of his emotional involvement and distress Reverend David Bradley had called upon the church minister of the next parish to officiate.

Laura Pemberton did not attend. She could feel no grief for the girl whom she considered had destroyed the foundations of her family and brought adverse attention to its name. Joe and Mary Tarrant, the Jackson-Brownes, the Major and Jimmy Ashdown had attended.

Dora Glasspool, already a recluse in her own cottage, had been given the news by Joe. Her strange reaction had surprised him. No sympathetic comment. In fact she had appeared to look brighter and merely said, 'Really!' He had come to the conclusion that her mind was in a worse state than Laura suspected.

The news had in fact pleased Dora and after Joe had left she set about the business of cleaning and polishing in her little cottage, smiling and humming, with one thought uppermost in her mind now. Temptation had been removed from Briarwood and Adam would not now be moving away from his home.

Joanne not yet fully recovered from her illness, and still in shock over the news of Ginny's death, remained at the College on the advice of the doctor in charge.

Peter Dunning had once again travelled to the College to break the latest crushing news. Already twice afflicted with shock and grief this third blow proved too much for her young mind and the doctor had found it necessary to sedate her to stem her hysteria.

★ ★ ★

The burial service was over. David Bradley returned to the now deserted church where, in the enveloping silence, he felt closer to Silvie. But he knew that with time her warm presence would become more elusive. Each passing day would take her further away from him.

* * *

Having rejected the ride back to Briarwood in the funeral car Adam Pemberton took the path home the back way through the woods. He walked slowly engrossed in his own grief. At the graveside he had wondered vaguely what connection Jack had with Silvie. Those words on the heart of red roses . . . identical to his own.

But where was the point in wondering now. Nothing mattered any more.

* * *

In the shadow of the church wall Jack Thorndyke seated himself on the bench. He had waited, alone and silent, for the mourners and villagers to leave. How long he'd sat there he would not have known, for his world had become a timeless vacuum. Now all was quiet and deserted. His thoughts reflected on the past when they had all lived in Queen Street, Silvie, Ginny and himself. In *his* world when she had seemed so close, and all his hopes had not yet died. He brought to mind his last living sight of her on that day when he had called at Stanford Road and she had told him she was to be married. He had gone there to ask her again himself.

So clearly he could see the image of her now as they sat beneath the apple tree, the late afternoon sun filtering through the leaves onto her pale gold hair. That unforgettable day when he knew that finally all hope for him was dead.

At length he rose from the seat, tears still wet on his face. At the gate he paused for a last backward glance at the grave before passing on out of the churchyard taking his memories with him.

Moments later the black Humber, no longer immaculate and shiny, moved slowly away.

★　★　★

On his arrival back at the house Adam Pemberton went straight into the library and seated himself at his desk. From a drawer he took an army service revolver, a souvenir from the recent war, loaded on the night after Silvie's death when he'd promised himself he would not live a second longer than was absolutely necessary.

During the week, locked in the library in his own private hell, he had written several letters which he'd enclosed in a large envelope addressed to Major Ashdown with instructions for their delivery. This was now placed prominently on his desk.

For a few moments he contemplated the heavy cold metal in his hands. As he raised the revolver to his temple his finger already on the trigger the telephone on his desk rang. The sudden shrill sound, so close, startled him and he stared at it blankly. Without lowering the gun he reached out to lift the receiver and ask lifelessly, 'Who is it?'

Then he heard the voice of his daughter answer tearfully, 'Oh Daddy! Thank heaven you're back! I've been trying for twenty minutes to get you. Obviously there was no one in the house to answer. Please come to the College and collect me and take me back to your apartment. I really must get away from here for a while or I think I'll go mad. I can't face coming home just yet — not now — now that — .' Her voice petered off brokenly before she continued, 'Oh Daddy — I really can't bear any more. I know mother wasn't fond of Silvie — not the way you and I were. You're all I have left now — besides Peter. Miss Meacher says it's all right for me to have a break. The doctor here suggested it might be best. But only on condition that somebody comes here to collect me. Please come Daddy, or if you can't then send Peter. But I'd rather it was you this time because I know you'll be feeling as unhappy as I am about it all. Come as soon as you can.' She paused briefly before continuing, 'Are you still there Daddy? Say something — *please.*'

As her tearful voice in his ear pleaded to the silence he gradually lowered the gun. With some shock he realised that he hadn't given any thought to the consequences that his suicide would have on his own daughter, other than financial, and for that he had provided in his will which he had changed and drawn up only days ago. Somehow he had subconsciously believed that she did not need him. The thought struck him violently that his life did not belong to himself alone. He was not free to end it of his own volition.

His eyes rested on the wedding photograph of Mark and Silvie. He had let his son down. Betrayed him beyond all measure of forgiveness. He had been about to let his daughter down also. Living on would be his punishment.

'Daddy are you still there?' Joanne's young voice rose as though her nerves were at breaking point. 'Speak to me! *Say* you'll come!'

He struggled to cast off the black depression that had settled on him, and emotion strangled his words, 'Yes — yes Joanne I will come for you — right away. Be ready.'

He heard her give a cry of relief and a moment later the voice of Miss Meacher came on the line to say a few words, which he barely took in. Mechanically he responded. Then came silence as the receiver was replaced at the other end.

How strange, he thought absently, to have been carrying on a conversation, although it had hardly been that, with a loaded gun in his hand and half way to his own death.

He unloaded the revolver and placed it back in the drawer. He picked up the envelope addressed to the Major and carried it into the drawing room where a big fire was burning, and threw it deep into the flames. He waited until it was eaten up to an unrecognisable charred mass.

Then slowly he made his way upstairs to pack his clothes.

43

The last Sunday in July and the College garden party had come around once again, and for Joanne Pemberton the final time. Dispiritedly she employed herself with the refreshments which she would shortly be handing around to unseen faces about her. Daily she willed the time to pass and leave a gap between her present heartache and whatever the future had in store. Very soon now her father would arrive to collect her.

She glanced up and her eyes met those of Miss Meacher who had been regarding her and thinking — I'm glad she's being sent abroad to recuperate. She's been like a lost soul since the tragedies, her old vivacity completely extinguished — not surprising.

With this brief eye contact alike thoughts were exchanged as they each recalled this time one year ago. Then the little principal paused in the shadow of an old oak tree. For the moment secluded and alone she gazed across to the high metal entrance gates. She caught her breath as she fancied that she saw a beautiful girl in a summer blue dress, and a picture hat the colour of her pale hair, walk into the garden and into the life of the tall, fair handsome young man. Both so vitally alive.

Then — for a transient moment — a light shadow seemed to hover overhead. She raised her eyes and watched a delicate white cloud drift high across the clear summer sky, followed closely by another, and then both merge together and disappear into the blueness.

Shadows of the past, she murmured, as she discreetly dabbed at the corners of her eyes before continuing on her way.

★　★　★

There were times when, standing at the French window of his study gazing out towards the woods David Bradley fancied he saw her passing along the track. Just as he'd seen her so many times in the past. A shaft of sunlight amongst the trees would evolve to become her moon colour hair. Sometimes it seemed to him that she turned to glance his way and raise a hand to beckon. Then he would hear her soft voice, no more than a summer breeze whispering. It was here that he saw her most.

Sometimes from the pulpit in the little stone church he would look down at the front pew and remember her as he'd seen her that day of the third reading of the banns when she had fallen asleep between the two Pemberton men during his first unpremeditated sermon.

There were the times too when he would recall that day of the thunderstorm when she had arrived after being caught in the heavy rain, her wet silk blouse clinging transparently to her body as she knelt there, in that same front pew: Never quite real. Never quite imagined. Always ethereal.

And there were times when he would recall the memory of her that day in his study when she had

447

told him those things about herself and her life. It was then that he relived those warm sweet kisses that had set his manhood aflame.

There were times when he would walk along the track to the spot where he had left her the day when she had first visited the grave of her husband. He had walked back with her as far as the garden of Briarwood, all the while thinking of his futile love for her. Even when time had permitted he could never have asked her to marry him because she would have always been anchored to her conscience over the death of her young husband. Nor could she without callousness have discarded Adam Pemberton's love, since it had brought about the death of his son. Yes — he remembered thinking those things.

She had said 'Goodbye David,' that day, and he had watched her walk away for the last time, her hair blowing in the breeze.

Strangely too, at times, he wondered whether she had ever really existed at all outside his own imagination.

It was then that he would wander into the little churchyard to read the inscription on the headstone, press his face against the cold marble, and know that she had.

APPENDIX SCARLET ANGEL

AUGUST 1949 JOANNE

Arrangements had been made for Joanne Pemberton to travel to America where she would stay with a cousin of her mother who had married a U.S.A. naval officer during the war. There she would be met when the liner docked. A change of scene had been considered as the best way to help her to recuperate from the ravages of her young life. She would finish her studies at a private college in New York.

There she would stay for the next three years if she settled in well. Her return was to be left to her own inclination.

From MISS MEACHER'S COLLEGE that last day Adam had collected her and taken her, at her own request, to his city apartment to await her departure from England in two weeks time.

Her mother had contacted the cousin and explained the situation within two weeks after the death of Ginny and only days after that of Silvie.

A passage was booked on the ocean liner the *QUEEN MARY*.

Because of painful memories associated with Briarwood at present Joanne had returned for only a few hours to collect the things she would be taking with her on the journey, and to say goodbye to her mother, to Joe and Mary Tarrant, to Major Ashdown and the Jackson-Brownes and the Reverend David Bradley.

During the two weeks in the city Peter Dunning had endeavoured to keep her company as often as possible by taking her to museums, art galleries, and the theatre, in attempt to draw her out from the silent depression into which she had withdrawn.

★ ★ ★

On the Southampton dockside Adam Pemberton and Peter Dunning blew kisses to the slight figure at the ships rail. The strip of water widened as the great liner put distance between them until Joanne became a mere dot amongst the crowd.

They had no qualms regarding her welfare on the journey. A stewardess had been appointed to supervise her until the ship docked in New York where she would be met by her hosts.

Both men felt an acute sense of loss as they moved away from the dockside towards the boat train which would return them to the city.

★ ★ ★

Here on this same dockside Peter Dunning met her on her return more than three years later.

During that time many letters and photographs had passed between them. Regularly he had written with news of the business and his work in which he had completely immersed himself and become joint head of the company with Adam.

Often he had stayed weekends at Briarwood to

report to Laura Pemberton on matters relating to the business, for Adam seldom went there now.

★ ★ ★

In her letters Joanne had kept him up to date about her life in America where, away from painful associations, she had settled remarkably well.

★ ★ ★

Adam too had kept up a steady flow of letters to her and from these she gathered that he led a quiet and solitary life when away from the offices.

Truth was he led no social life at all. His mourning for Silvie was deep and permanent, lasting until his death which had come swift and unexpected. The kind of end for which he had constantly prayed — one that would leave no stigma on his daughter: a sudden and massive coronary while at the offices. This occurred only a matter of weeks before Joanne was due to return home from America.

★ ★ ★

Among some personal possessions that had belonged to Ginny, and been kept by Joanne, were several diaries. For a very long time she had stored these locked away in a small attaché case, unread.

One rainy day in America she had taken them out. The reading had been painful just as she expected it would be, and was the reason why she had put this off for so long. She had known that the days at Briarwood would be part of those long dead pages which, when read, sparked the past back to life.

The last entry, made on the day of Ginny's death, intrigued her. Words written in clear round handwriting which told her that her father had been in love with Silvie.

Straight away she had written to her mother to ask if this had been true.

At first she received only unsatisfactory and evasive replies to the question. 'Let things be Joanne. Don't disturb the dead.'

But Joanne could not let it be. 'They will *never* be dead to me Mother. *Never*. I must know. *Please*. Now that Daddy's gone you are the only one who can tell me the truth.'

In three subsequent letters she had persisted for some definite answer.

At last it had come. 'Very well if you insist. Yes.'

From that time on her curiosity about the past grew into an obsession. Step by step she was to embark on a retrospective journey that would lead her to the whole profound story.

But all this was in the future and would take time.

1952 PETER AND JOANNE

On the dockside at Southampton Peter Dunning waited.

Joanne, aged eighteen, now tall and to his eyes quite beautiful, came down the gangplank straight into his waiting arms.

'Welcome home Joanne. I've waited a long time for this day.'

She had sent him photographs at various stages of her growing up. He was in love with her long before she ever returned in the flesh.

And *she* had always been in love with *him*.

He drove her to Kings Meadow where he had arranged to spend his well-earned holiday from the office. He wanted to be at hand in case the homecoming to Briarwood proved distressing for her. But he knew she would want to be alone with her memories for a while.

When they arrived late afternoon he went into the library to leave her to re-unite with her mother.

Right now Joanne was asking the long awaited questions. 'Mother I know there must be a great deal more that you can tell me about Silvie and my father. I have a right to be told — to know. It really is very important to me.'

'Leave it be Joanne. Let the past stay buried with them.'

'You already know my answer to that Mother.' Joanne slowly shook her head. 'Don't you understand *yet*? I loved them all so much. They will never be dead to me — *never*. I want to know the truth about Silvie, my father, and Mark.'

Laura Pemberton regarded the determined yet haunted expression on the face of her daughter. Perhaps she did have the right to know that the love she had felt for the girl who had married her brother, and the grief at her death, was not justified.

'The truth is ugly and sordid. It will hurt. And

you've already had more than your share of that.'

'The hurt has toughened me Mother.'

'Very well — if you insist. Remember I did warn you.'

She told all she knew of Silvie and her deceit of Mark. She kept nothing back. She added nothing. She told of the insane jealousy of Dora Glasspool and the tragic consequences that had cost Ginny her life.

Alone she had carried the burden of this knowledge on her shoulders for more than three and a half years. Only under pressure did she disclose it now.

* * *

By the time she had finished Joanne was ashen-faced with horror. 'My God! Why did you let Dora go unpunished! No — don't bother to tell me. I already know the answer to that. Scandal! That would have been your prime concern.'

'Unpunished! Unpunished!' The voice usually so matter of fact rose to an angry pitch, indicative of the strain that concealment had imposed on her. 'Go to her cottage and see for yourself whether or not she has gone unpunished — if you dare! She has been her own jury and punishment.'

'But you should have informed the police Mother! You should not have concealed deliberate murder! Ginny was my best friend. I loved her like a sister.'

'Would it have brought the child back? Or altered the circumstances? I admit that I did consider the scandal and adverse publicity. In a family such as

454

ours it sticks. Nothing would have been achieved or changed if I had handed Dora over to the authorities.'

Stricken and appalled, and for the moment stunned to brief silence as this new-found knowledge sank in Joanne rose from the chesterfield and went to stand at the window looking out over the garden. Suddenly she swung round to face her mother again. 'My God Dora must have been totally insane! I always thought her a bit peculiar — but not to such an extent! Why on earth did you employ her? You must have known she was not quite right in the head!'

'Oh yes she was — to begin with. I kept her on here for reasons which you've never been told. But as you've forced my hand today you may as well know the whole sorry story. When you were three years old she saved you from the hind legs of one of the racehorses. In doing so she was kicked herself. Your nurse had taken her eyes off of you while she recovered your ball from the shrubs. During that time you wandered off and into the stables. Dora happened to be on hand. She spent a long time in hospital. When she came out . . . ' Laura Pemberton shrugged, 'what could I do but keep her employed. Not with the horses as before. She never regained interest in horses, but she certainly could cope with the position of housekeeper here.' She regarded the distress on the face of Joanne, sighed deeply and shook her head. 'I did warn you. Just try to remember this . . . what's done can't be undone or changed no matter what. All this should have been left undisturbed with the past.'

'Oh no — you're wrong. I'm glad you told me.' Joanne turned away again to gaze out at the garden. 'Did you know that Dora Glasspool felt like *that* about Daddy? Did *he* know?'

Again her mother shrugged. 'How could anyone know what was in Dora's mind. She always used to fuss over him whenever he was home — cook special things for him that she never bothered to when he wasn't here. Obviously I had no idea that she harboured some secret passion for him, and *he* certainly wasn't aware of it. I suspected she'd always had a crush on him — no more than that.

'I sent her home the moment I discovered what she'd done that day Ginny died. I never let her return. Joe and Mary call on her regularly and report to me on her condition. They arrange for groceries to be delivered to her cottage and the account sent to me. I pay her a weekly pension. Apparently she never leaves the cottage. Call on her and satisfy yourself that punishment by the law would have made little difference to her. The most accursed day for this family was the one on which your brother met Silvia Marsh.'

'I know you never liked Silvie. I saw it even then. You never once called her by her proper name, and even now that she's dead you still don't.'

'Do you really expect me to have liked her? A whore!'

'How do you know that's true Mother? I find it so hard to believe.'

'Well there is a way for you to find out, if you still insist on digging further into the dirt. Just find an individual by the name of Rachael Moss who kept a high class brothel — if there can *be* such a thing!'

Joanne half turned from the window to say, 'Harrowing as it's been I'm glad you told me Mother. Now I must be alone for a while.' Feeling the need to be mobile she went out through the French window into the garden. The early evening of late August was still warm from the daytime sun. As she crossed the lawns vivid memories returned of that first day when Mark had brought Silvie to Briarwood. Tears sprang to her eyes as she called up images of that hot summer day. Of her father walking across the grass with Silvie towards the tennis courts. Her eyes travelled in that direction as if half expecting to see their ghosts. She fancied she could hear the old swing squeaking and above its sound the voice of Ginny calling across the garden. At the far side of the lawn it still stood, rusting and neglected from disuse and the weather. As her eyes rested on it now she heard clearly the sound of her brother's happy laughter as he pushed the swing and Ginny higher. She saw the flames of bright red hair ignited by the sun flying in the breeze. And above all — above all — so clearly — her brother's words . . . 'It's quite all right you slave drivers. I suppose I owe you something. If it weren't for you two I would never have met Silvie in the first place would I.' Again the sound of his laughter drifted across to her ears.

With a sob she turned away. It had been a mistake to return and resurrect old ghosts.

She blinked to stem the tears, and after composing herself returned to the drawing room.

Her mother was still there but now had a glass of brandy in her hand.

'Mother I must leave. I could never come back here to live. There are too many painful associations and too much heartbreak. Although happy memories will always remain with me.'

At this point Peter Dunning appeared in the doorway, 'I saw you in the garden from the window.' He noted the stricken look on her tanned face and went straight to her side.

'Peter I'm leaving. Please take me to your flat, or your home. Anywhere — anywhere — but I must leave this house.'

'I'll take you wherever you wish. I'll telephone my home and arrange to take you there.' He turned to Laura Pemberton for approval. She nodded agreement and said, 'It'll be for the best.'

'I'll be in touch and I'll come as usual to keep you up to date with matters at the offices Laura,' he said as they left Briarwood.

Joanne seated beside him in the car said, 'Dear thoughtful Peter. How like Mark you are. I do love you.'

★   ★   ★

Six months later Peter Dunning and Joanne were married. She was just eighteen and a half years old and he thirty-one. The simple wedding ceremony took place in a small registry office near his home in Surrey. No press announcement was made since any resultant newspaper reportage would have garnished the covering story by dragging up the tragic family history.

As a wedding gift to them Laura Pemberton bought a house which they had chosen midway between the city offices and Peter Dunning's family home.

★   ★   ★

Joanne became obsessed with an urge to uncover as much of Silvie's past as was possible. To this end she explored every track. All the letters which Silvie had sent to them at the College, giving news of her days, had been kept by Ginny and subsequently locked away in the case with the diaries by Joanne. She read again of those visits to the little stone church and remembered the Reverend David Bradley.

★   ★   ★

She called the Rectory and discovered he was no longer residing there and was told where she would find him. He too had left Kings Meadow where memories were too poignant. Nowadays he administered his oratory gifts to a much larger parish.

JOANNE AND DAVID BRADLEY

Although immersed in his work David Bradley was still often tempted to join his father in the London theatres, to find distraction and try to fill the empty void that Silvie had left in his existence.

Joanne's earnest sincerity to know more about Silvie's days and those visits to the church, and her admission that she knew of the lover relationship between her father and Silvie surprised him. In the circumstances he told the truth of his own feelings for Silvie and of the part he and the little stone church had played in her troubled life.

He told of the day when, soaked from the rain she had first come there alone, and of the resultant visit to the Rectory in the absence of Mrs Armstrong, which had become the first of the many subsequent Thursday visits.

He made no mention of the day when Silvie had confessed to him about her past at the Georgian house.

JOANNE AND JACK THORNDYKE

In Ginny's diary for the year in which her mother had died she had recorded the telephone number of Jack Thorndyke in the entry made for that day. Joanne had telephoned him and when she explained who she was and the reason for her call Jack invited her to his home in Baron Wood.

From Jack she learned of his enduring love for Silvie, and about the life of Queen Street. At her request he explained exactly where it was and drew a rough map to guide her.

To Jack she was a welcome companion with whom for a few hours he could share his deepest feelings. Like David Bradley, out of loyalty to Silvie's memory, he made no mention of her brief spell at the Georgian house.

1955 JOANNE AND PETER

Two years after Joanne's marriage her mother died of a massive stroke. Lack of daily physical movement after a particularly active life coupled with the anxiety of a guilty conscience may have accelerated her demise.

In compliance with her written request, lodged with the family solicitor, her body was cremated and her ashes scattered to the four winds on the Briarwood estate.

Sorting through the personal belongings in her mother's rooms she came across the scarlet and gold card which for some reason had never been destroyed.

Reading the name on the card Joanne recalled it as the one mentioned by her mother that day in the drawing room when she had demanded to know the truth about her father and Silvie.

She and Peter had returned to Briarwood for the specific purpose of sorting what furniture and effects they would keep and have transported to their own home. The rest would be auctioned with the house.

There also was the sale of the racehorses which her mother had been breeding. This presented no problem since the two daily stable hands knew much about the racing world and had contacts with potential buyers.

JOANNE AND JIMMY ASHDOWN

Briarwood they decided to put up for auction. To this end Joanne called on Jimmy Ashdown, still in the real estate business. He would, she felt, be familiar with its assets and full potential and know how to best represent its sale. His office was in the city. She walked in and introduced herself. He looked surprised for he had not seen her since before she had gone to America and in the interval she had grown up. He took her out to lunch over which they discussed the business of selling Briarwood. When they had concluded arrangements for this they talked of life in general.

Then they touched upon the past and she told him that she wanted to write about the family tragedies and of Silvie's life. 'Since I have gathered so much of the story I'm determined to go on,' she told him.

'You seem very keen and determined. I don't know what you have discovered so far. I can give you another small link in the chain if you like. It will put me in a very bad light,' he shrugged, 'if it's the truth you're after . . . '

This he gave without diluting, or making excuses in his own favour.

For her benefit he recalled the day of the sudden thunderstorm when he had waylaid Silvie and got a whiplashing from his father. He even told her of the night when he had walked unseen into Briarwood and up to her bedroom where he had lain in wait for the purpose of molesting her again, and of the consequent rape with the threat of blackmail relating to something which he knew of her past. But, he truthfully concluded, a threat he never would have carried out. He told of his remorse when he heard of her death.

'It seems to me,' she remarked when he had finished, 'that Silvie was too beautiful for her own good and everyone else's.'

'Especially for everyone else's,' he agreed then added, 'As for myself I've sobered up since the days of my extended youth.'

JOANNE AND MADAME MOSS

Joanne made a preliminary telephone call to the Madam Moss and explained who she was and the object of her call.

Always inquisitive Rachael Moss invited her to visit.

Joanne went to the address printed on the card and was invited into the private room of Rachael Moss where, seated in her usual place on the throne-chair, she told of the short while that Silvie had worked at the Georgian house.

'She vos too sensitif for the verkink here. Too refined. She vos not here lonk. A few veeks only. So I hev very little I ken tell you.'

'I only wanted to confirm that she really was here at one time. Did she meet my father here — his name was — '

'Yes — I know who . . . end yes — she did meet him heah — he vos a regular cli-ink. But he took her

avay.' Madam Moss told of the financial arrangement which the man she had then known as Rossi
had made to cover the expenses of her losses from
other potential clients. She told all of what little she
really knew of the lovely girl who had stayed such a
short time in her employ.

'I em gled thet you cime before I leef this house in
two veeks time. I em retiring. I hef bought a house
in Brighton.'

A tap came on the door and a voice called, 'It's
me Momma.'

'Vot do you vont Sempson?'

'It's about the packing Momma . . . '

'Come in then.' When he entered she said, 'This
yunk lidy is vonting to know about the girl ve called
Evette.'

Sampson's face lit up and he immediately told of
the trick that he'd once played just to hold and kiss
her in the Rose room.

'You ver a naughty boy,' said his mother amused.

He chuckled.

Joanne shuddered inwardly just looking at
him, having instantly recognised his mental
shortcomings.

JOANNE AND QUEEN STREET

Following the noted directions given by Jack
Thorndyke, Joanne one day drove to Queen Street
and parked her car on the corner. As she regarded
it's shabby narrow confines she was totally unable
to picture either Ginny or Silvie against this

464

impoverished backdrop. Then she understood completely why Silvie had been so desperate to escape. But if only she had married Jack . . . the story would be different.

Feeling sick at heart and suddenly very lonely she left the scene behind her and made her way home to her two-year-old son Mark Peter whom she had left for the day in the capable hands of his doting Grandmother Dunning. One day he would take over at the helm of the still thriving export and import company, which at the present time was in the competent hands of his parents, now the joint owners and partners.

JOANNE AND THE
LITTLE STONE CHURCH

On the day of the auction she went to Briarwood with Peter.

On arrival she found Jimmy Ashdown and the auctioneer already there but she did not stay to witness the sale.

Before the bidding commenced amongst the many potential buyers she made her way alone along the track so often taken by Silvie to the little old stone church. She entered but found that she was unable to face the images and ghosts of her brother and Silvie at the altar on their wedding day, or the vivid recollection of the shiny casket that had held the body of her brother.

She went out and found the seat against the wall. From here she could see the graves which held the people she had loved. She was thinking . . . Perhaps they are together somewhere in another dimension of spiritual existence. But for her they would live on in the book she would write. She had discovered that time does not heal. It is merely palliative. The past would ever mingle with the present.

But she had much to look forward to in the future, with Peter and their son.

We do hope that you have enjoyed reading
this large print book.

Did you know that all of our titles
are available for purchase?

We publish a wide range of high quality
large print books including:
Romances, Mysteries, Classics
General Fiction
Non Fiction and Westerns

Special interest titles available in
large print are:
The Little Oxford Dictionary
Music Book
Song Book
Hymn Book
Service Book

Also available from us courtesy of Oxford
University Press:
Young Readers' Dictionary
(large print edition)
Young Readers' Thesaurus
(large print edition)

For further information or a free
brochure, please contact us at:
Ulverscroft Large Print Books Ltd.,
The Green, Bradgate Road, Anstey,
Leicester, LE7 7FU, England.
Tel: (00 44) 0116 236 4325
Fax: (00 44) 0116 234 0205

DEAD FISH

Ruth Carrington

Dr Geoffrey Quinn arrives home to find his children missing, the charred remains of his wife's body in the boiler and Chief Superintendent Manning waiting to arrest him for her murder. Alison Hope, attractive and determined, is briefed to defend him. Quinn claims he is innocent, but Alison is not so sure. The background becomes increasingly murky as she penetrates a wealthy and ruthless circle who cannot risk their secrets — sexual perversion, drugs, blackmail, illegal arms dealing and major fraud — coming to light. Can Alison unravel the mystery in time to save Quinn?

MY FATHER'S HOUSE

Kathleen Conlon

'Your father has another woman'. Nine-year-old Anna Blake is only mildly surprised when a schoolfriend lets drop this piece of information. And when her father finally leaves home to live with Olivia in Hampstead, that place becomes, for Anna, the epitome of sinful glamour. But Hampstead, though welcoming, is not home. So Anna, now in her teens, sets out to find a place where she can really belong. At first she thinks love may be the answer, and certainly Jonathon — and Raymond — and Jake, have a devastating effect on her life. But can anyone really supply what she needs?

GHOSTLY MURDERS

P. C. Doherty

When Chaucer's Canterbury pilgrims pass a deserted village, the sight of its decaying church provokes the poor Priest to tears. When they take shelter, he tells a tale of ancient evil, greed, devilish murder and chilling hauntings . . . There was once a young man, Philip Trumpington, who was appointed parish priest of a pleasant village with an old church, built many centuries earlier. However, Philip soon discovers that the church and presbytery are haunted. A great and ancient evil pervades, which must be brought into the light, resolved and reparation made. But the price is great . . .

BLOODTIDE

Bill Knox

When the Fishery Protection cruiser MARLIN was ordered to the Port Ard area off the north-west Scottish coast, Chief Officer Webb Carrick soon discovered that an old shipmate of Captain Shannon had been killed in a strange accident before they arrived. A drowned frogman, a reticent Russian officer and a dare-devil young fisherman were only a few of the ingredients to come together as Carrick tried to discover the truth. The key to it all was as deadly as it was unexpected.

WISE VIRGIN

Manda Mcgrath

Sisters Jean and Ailsa Leslie live on a small farm in the Scottish Grampians. Andrew Esplin, the local blacksmith, keeps a brotherly eye on the girls, loving Ailsa, the younger sister, from afar. Ailsa is in love with Stewart Morrison, who is working in Greenock. Jean is engaged to Alan Drummond, who has gone to Australia, intending to send for her when his prospects are good. But Jean shocks everyone when she elopes with Dunton from the big house . . .